Praise for *The Heir*

"Burrowes debuts with a luminous and graceful erotic Regency… a refreshing and captivating love story that will have readers eagerly awaiting the planned sequels."
—*Publishers Weekly*, starred review

"The heroine of Grace Burrowes's erotically charged romance is a woman of such mystery that both the hero and the reader become obsessed with her."
—*USA Today*

"A witty, sensual, Regency romance featuring complex characters who ring true to the time period, leaving readers saying huzzah!"
—*Booklist*

"Burrowes's enchanting romance charms from the beginning… tenderness and sensuality, lighthearted verbal battles, and tense moments combine to delight."
—*RT Book Reviews*

"With tons of intrigue, searing seduction, and wonderful humor, Grace Burrowes's first book is a… must read for fans of Georgette Heyer and Regency romances."
—*Night Owl Romance*, Top Pick

"A scorching, romantic novel; it is both hot and sweet, and it is sure to touch readers' hearts."

"An irresistible love story... Ms. Burrowes's smooth writing style engages all the senses."

—*The Long and the Short of It Reviews*

"A blooming author who promises to become a household name... the lovemaking is highly passionate and fiery, and utterly enthralling."

—*Romance Fiction on Suite101*

"A sweet, sexy, tender romance between two characters so vibrant they seem to leap off the page. Burrowes's fresh, gorgeous writing held me riveted from start to finish."

—Meredith Duran, author of *Wicked Becomes You*

"Fascinating, mysterious, and engaging... The book was researched well to bring out the Regency flavors that make reading this genre so much fun."

—*History Undressed*

"A realistic and touching (and not to mention scorching hot) romance... Burrowes has created the perfect mix of love story, mystery, and intrigue."

—*Read All Over Reviews*

"An incredible book... there's nothing like a good romance with heat that sizzles."

—*Yankee Romance Reviewers*

"An intelligent, witty, and intriguing, passion-filled romance."

—*Rundpinne*

"An amazingly touching and genuine Regency romance."

—*Bookaholics*

THE Soldier

GRACE BURROWES

sourcebooks
casablanca

Published by Sourcebooks Casablanca, an imprint of Sourcebooks, Inc.
P.O. Box 4410, Naperville, Illinois 60567-4410
(630) 961-3900
FAX: (630) 961-2168
www.sourcebooks.com

Printed and bound in the United States of America
QW 10 9 8 7 6 5 4 3 2 1

The Soldier is dedicated to my oldest brother, John,
who is a soldier in the best sense of the word,
and to all those soldiers in uniform and otherwise
who find the road to peace an uphill battle.
Your sacrifice is not in vain.

One

"WHY IS *THAT* SITTING ON MY FOUNTAIN?"

Devlin St. Just, the Earl of Rosecroft, directed his question to the wilted specimen who passed for his land steward. "And why, in the blazing middle of July, is my fountain inoperable?"

"I'm afraid, my lord, the fountain hasn't worked in several years," Holderman replied, answering the simpler question first. "And as for the other, well, I gather it conveyed with the estate."

"*That*"—the earl jerked his chin—"cannot convey. It is not a fixture nor livestock."

"In the legal sense, perhaps not," Holderman prevaricated, clearing his throat delicately. He'd given the word a little emphasis: lee-gal, and his employer shot him a scowl.

"What?" the earl pressed, and Holderman began to wish he'd heeded his sister's advice and stayed pleasantly bored summering on their uncle's estate closer to York. The earl was not an easy person to work for—well over six feet of former cavalry officer, firstborn of a powerful duke, and possessed of both arrogance and temper in abundance.

The man was a Black Irish terror, no matter he paid well and worked harder than any title Holderman had run across. Devlin St. Just, newly created first Earl of Rosecroft, was a flat, screaming terror. Gossip, even in York, was that the French had run for the hills when St. Just had led the charge.

"Well, you see, my lord…" Holderman swallowed and stole a glance at the fountain. He was the land steward for pity's sake, and explaining the situation should not be left to him.

"Holderman," the earl began in those low tones that presaged a volcanic display, "slavery and trade therein were outlawed almost a decade ago here in merry old England. Moreover, I have no less than *nine* younger siblings, and I can tell you *that* is a child, not chattel per se, and thus cannot convey. Make it go away."

"I am afraid I cannot quite manage just precisely what you ask." Holderman cleared his throat again.

"Holderman," the earl replied with terrifying pleasantness, "the thing cannot weigh but three stone. You pick it up and tell it to run along. Tell it to go 'round the kitchen and filch a meat pie, but make it go away."

"Well, my lord, as to that…"

"Holderman." The earl crossed his arms over his muscled chest and speared the land steward with a look that had no doubt quelled insurrection in junior officers, younger siblings, miscreant horses, and drunken peers, regardless of rank. "Make. It. Go. Away."

Holderman, in a complete abdication of courage, merely shook his head and stared at the ground.

"Fine." The earl sighed. "I shall do it myself, as it

appears I have to do every other benighted task worth mentioning on this miserable excuse for a parody of an estate. You, off!" He stabbed a finger in the general direction of the distant hills and bellowed at the child as he advanced on the fountain.

The child stood up on the rim of the dry fountain—which still left the earl a towering advantage of height—pointed a much smaller finger in the same direction and bellowed right back, "You, off!"

⁂

The earl stopped, his scowl shifting to a thoughtful frown.

"Holderman." He spoke without turning. "The child is too thin, dirty, and ill-mannered. Whose brat is this?"

"Well, my lord, in a manner of speaking, the child is, well… Yours."

"The child is not in any *manner of speaking* mine."

"The responsibility for the child, I should say."

"And how do you reach such a conclusion?" the earl asked, rubbing his chin and eyeing the child.

"That is the former earl's progeny, as best anyone can figure," Holderman said. "Because the Crown has seen fit to give you Rosecroft, then its dependents must fall to your care, as well."

"Sound reasoning," the earl allowed, considering the child.

But, dear God, St. Just thought on a spike of exasperation, it needed only this. The former title holder was dead and had left no legitimate issue. As the Rosecroft estate was neglected and in debt, the

Crown had not looked favorably on taking possession of it through escheat proceedings. An earldom had been produced from thin air, as a minor title *would not do* for the firstborn of a duke, and the estate had been foisted off on a man who wanted nothing to do with titles, responsibilities, or indebtedness of any kind, much less—merciful God!—*dependents*.

"Listen, child." The earl sat on the rim of the fountain and prepared to treat with the natives. "You are a problem, though I've no doubt you regard me in the same light. I propose we call a truce and see about the immediate necessities."

"I won't go," the child replied. "You can't make me."

Stubborn, the earl thought, keeping his approval to himself. "I won't go, either, but may I suggest, if you're preparing to lay siege, you might want to store up some tucker first."

The child scowled and blinked up at him.

"Eat," the earl clarified. It had been quite a while since he'd had to converse with someone this small. "Armies, as the saying goes, march on their bellies not on their feet. You need to eat."

His opponent appeared to consider the point. "I'm hungry."

"When was the last time you ate?" The child might be as old as seven, but it would be a thin, puny seven if that. Six seemed more likely, and five was a definite possibility.

"I forget," the child replied. "Not today." As the sun was lowering against the green Yorkshire hills, the situation required an immediate remedy.

"Well, come along then." St. Just held out a hand.

"We will feed you and then see what's to be done with you."

The child stared at his hand, frowned, and looked up at his face, then back down at his hand. The earl merely kept his hand outstretched, his expression calm.

"Meat pies," he mused aloud. "Cheese toast, cold cider, apple tarts, strawberry cobbler, sausage and eggs, treacle pudding, clean sheets smelling of sunshine and lavender, beeswax candles…" He felt a tentative touch of little fingers against his palm, so he closed his hand around those fingers and let his voice lead the child along. "Berry tarts, scones in the morning, ham, bacon, nice hot tea with plenty of cream and sugar, kippers, beefsteak, buttered rolls and muffins…"

"Muffins?" the child piped up wistfully. St. Just almost smiled at the angelic expression on the urchin's face. Great blue eyes peered out of a smudged, beguiling little puss, a mop of wheat blond curls completing a childish image of innocence.

"Muffins." The earl reiterated as they gained the side terrace of the manor and passed indoors. "With butter and jam, if you prefer. Or chocolate, or juice squeezed from oranges."

"Oranges?"

"Had them all the time in Spain."

"You were in Spain?" the child asked, eyes round. "Did you fight old Boney?"

"I was in Spain," the earl said, his tone grave, "and Portugal, and France, and I fought old Boney. Nasty business, not at all as pleasant as the thought of tea cakes or clean linen or even some decent bread and butter."

"Bread and butter is good. I'm the Earl of Helmsley."

The Earl of Rosecroft stopped and frowned. "Better you than me. I'm Rosecroft, of all the simple things to name an earldom."

"This estate is Rosecroft, and it belongs to the Earl of Helmsley."

Would that it still did, St. Just fumed silently. Had no one told the child of Helmsley's death?

"We are in the midst of a truce," the earl reminded his companion. "A gentleman does not bring up conflicted matters during a truce."

"I'm still the Earl of Helmsley. Can we have supper anyway?"

"We can." The earl nodded his agreement and began towing the child up the stairs. "But one must be decently turned out for dinner, and you, my friend, are sadly lacking in both wardrobe and proper hygiene."

The child looked down at scruffy britches, a tattered shirt, and very dirty brown toes. "I'm decent."

"But when opposing generals show one another hospitality the night before a great battle, they do not merely present themselves as decent."

"They don't?" The child peered around at the private suite the earl had appropriated. The rooms were spacious and full of interesting things no doubt begging to be touched.

"'Yon Cassius has a lean and hungry look,'" the earl quoted. "Have a seat." He half lifted, half led the child to a settee, though even on that modest piece of the furniture, those dirty little toes swung several inches above the carpet. St. Just began to divest himself of his garments, having long since learned to make do without a valet, batman, or other sycophant.

"Well, get busy," the earl said when he was in the process of shucking his breeches. "A gentleman doesn't go down to dine unless he's properly bathed, and you, I fear, will take a deal of bathing."

"I am not a gentleman," the child said, the truculence back in full force. The earl glanced down at his own naked chest and recalled that grown men were not necessarily an easy thing for not-so-grown men to compare themselves to. He shrugged into a dressing gown and tossed his shirt to the child. "For your modesty. Now let's be about it, shall we? The sooner we're clean, the sooner we eat."

He eyed the child's hair and suspected getting clean might involve a quantity of shampoo, but merely held out his hand again. "Come along, child."

"I am *not* a gentleman," the child said again, scooting back against the sofa.

"We can remedy that," the earl said with what he hoped was a reassuring tone. "A little scrubbing, some decent attire, small refinements of speech." He slipped the child's shirt off in a single motion. "If I can master it in not quite thirty-two years, there is certainly hope for you."

"I am not a gentleman," the child ground out, standing on the sofa cushions and swatting at the earl's hands, "and I do not want to *be* a gentleman."

"Then you can be a pirate," the earl reasoned. "But if you are eating my food, you shall do so with clean fingers." He made a deft grab for the scruffy britches, yanking them down over narrow hips and bony knees with a swift jerk.

The child stood up on the sofa, naked and indignant. "*I am not a gentleman. I do not want to be a gentleman!*"

"Jesus, God, and the Apostles!" The earl swiftly wrapped the child in his shirt and stood panting in shock. "You are a benighted damned female!"

"Do I still have to take a bath?"

❧

"What is a benighted damned female?"

They were dining in the breakfast parlor because the earl refused to put his staff to the trouble of a formal evening meal for one person, and the breakfast parlor was closer to the kitchen. "You will forget I said that," the earl instructed. "Elbows off the table, and what is your name?"

"Brat," the child replied, elbows slipping out of sight. "My mama used to call me Winnie, but everybody else calls me brat." The earl raised an eyebrow, and his dinner guest dropped her gaze. They called her worse than that, but he knew she wasn't about to share it with him—yet.

"I will call you Miss Winnie. Where is your mama?"

"In heaven. May I have some more peas?"

"You are an unnatural child," St. Just said as he spooned more buttered peas onto her plate. "Children abhor vegetables."

"I like what comes out of the garden." Winnie tucked into her peas as she spoke. The earl suspected, watching her consume her food with single-minded focus, she liked what came out of the garden because she could help herself to it all summer long.

"Then you will like apple tarts."

"Do you like them?" Winnie didn't take her eyes off her peas as she asked.

"No talking with your mouth full. I am very fond of apple tarts, particularly when made with lots of butter, cinnamon, and a brandy glaze. For pity's sake, child, nobody is going to steal your peas."

"Not if I eat them first." Winnie tipped her plate to scrape the butter sauce onto her spoon.

"None of that." The earl put the plate back down on the table. "You need to leave room for your apple tart." He signaled a footman. "Miss Winnie will be having some very weak tea with her apple tart."

"Of course, my lord." The man bowed and began collecting plates, stoically ignoring the look of longing with which Winnie watched his departure.

"So tell me, Miss Winnie, did you enjoy the lavender bubbles?"

"They smelled like lavender but they weren't lavender colored." Winnie eyed the basket of rolls and the butter, the only food remaining on the table.

"You wanted purple bubbles in your bath?" St. Just almost smiled. "Fine earl you'll make."

Winnie's chin came up. "I am Helmsley. My mama said so."

"You can be Helmsley all you like, as long as you take your baths, say your prayers, and behave yourself. Who looks after you?"

A sly look came across the little girl's features, or it would have been sly were it not such an obvious prelude to dissembling.

"A lady. She lives in a house down by the river." The Ouse flowed past the western boundary of the property, so the earl concluded that like all good lies, this little tale was somewhat grounded in truth.

"Is she a nice lady?" the earl asked, wondering when the damned apple tarts would be arriving.

"She's old, but she bakes pies and cakes and they smell ever so lovely, especially in winter. She has two cats, and they are hugely fat from eating cheese."

The earl stifled another smile. "And what are their names? Scylla and Charybdis?"

"Io and Ganymede."

The earl's eyebrows rose, as most children would not know the names of Jupiter's moons. "Are they friendly?" he asked, getting ready to ring for his damned tart if need be.

"Very." Winnie nodded vigorously. "At least to me. They don't like everybody, but I share my cheese with them, so we get along *famously*."

"And what is the name of this lovely old dear who lets you cozen her cats and steal her pies?"

"Miss Emmaline Farnum," the child informed him, her air serious. "I call her Miss Emmie. She is my best friend."

"How sweet." The earl drummed his fingers on the table, but it occurred to him that since arriving at Rosecroft more than a week ago, he'd not seen one other child. In all likelihood, Winnie had no playmates her own age. Then, too, children could be cruel, particularly to an orphaned by-blow of a penniless and unpopular earl.

"My lord, I beg your pardon!"

The door to the little dining parlor banged open, the apologetic footman rushing in behind a young woman St. Just had not seen before. She was trussed up in a shapeless black bombazine dress covering her from ankles to wrist to neck, an equally hideous black bonnet on her head.

"That is not my tart," the earl observed to no one in particular.

"Bronwyn!" The woman leapt across the room and wrapped her arms around Winnie, the bonnet tumbling off in her haste. "Oh, Winnie, you naughty, naughty child, I've been searching all over for you."

"Hullo, Miss Emmie." Winnie beamed a grin, hugging the lady back. "Rosecroft says we're going to have apple tarts."

"Madam?" The earl rose and bowed. "Rosecroft, at your service."

"My lord." She bobbed a nervous curtsy then swiveled back to the child. "Winnie, are you all right?"

"I had to take a bath." Winnie frowned at the memory. "But I ate and ate and ate. I am not a gentleman, though."

"You took a bath?" Miss Farnum's eyes went round. "My lord? Did I hear her aright?"

"With lavender bubbles," the earl replied gravely. "And you would be?"

"Miss Emmaline Farnum," she said, eyes narrowing. "Just how did you get her to take a bath?"

The earl narrowed his eyes, as well. "Perhaps that is a discussion we adults might reserve for later. And as I wouldn't want to be guilty of breaking my word to a child, may I invite you to join us for apple tarts, Miss Farnum?"

The footman withdrew at the earl's lifted eyebrow while the child's gaze bounced back and forth between the adults. Winnie sat, all innocence in an old nightshirt somebody had dragged out of a trunk. Her golden curls gleamed, and on her feet were wool socks many sizes too big.

"Apple tarts sound delicious," Miss Farnum said. The earl graciously seated her, taking the opportunity to notice that the lady—for all her egregious taste in attire—bore the scent of lemons and meadow mint, a tart, pleasing combination that went well with the summer evening. His gaze happened to stray to her neck as he pushed her chair in, and the smooth expanse of female skin suggested she wasn't as mature as he'd first surmised.

"Miss Winnie was just telling me about your cats," the earl began, continuing his assessment of his latest guest. She was a dressmaker's disaster, but then, what else would one expect in the wilds of Yorkshire? Fading black was seldom a good color for blondes, and she was no exception. "Your cats have interesting names."

"Gany and Io?" Miss Farnum replied, removing her gloves. At the earl's discreet signal, the gloves were whisked away, but not before he noticed the tear on the right fourth finger. "They were from a litter of four, the other two were named Europa and Callisto."

"Somebody enjoyed either stargazing or my-thology," the earl said as the tarts were brought in. He would have to settle for one, he supposed, as the third tart would go to his uninvited guest. "Winnie, may I cut yours for you?"

The question hung in the air just as Winnie reached for her tart with her fingers.

"Bronwyn?" Miss Farnum's voice was perfectly

polite. "His lordship has offered to cut up that delicious tart for you."

The child sighed mightily but nodded. "Yes, please." She watched, eyes near crossed with anticipation, as the earl cut hers into small pieces, then slid the plate to her.

"Thank you."

"Go ahead. Mind you don't choke, lest I have to turn you upside down and whack at you to save your scrawny neck."

Miss Farnum looked like she'd take great exception to his comment, but when Winnie only picked up her fork and began taking dainty bites, the lady held her peace.

"I take it you are a neighbor, Miss Farnum?"

"I am," she said, regarding her tart rather than her host.

"Shall I cut yours, too, madam?" The earl lifted an eyebrow when she blinked at him. Rustics were an odd lot, and women left to rusticate too long were the oddest of all. She wasn't old by any means, but her expressions and mannerisms were old. Careful, as if she expected to be unpleasantly surprised at any moment.

"Thank you no, my lord." Her frown was aimed directly at him now. "I am your neighbor to the immediate north, or I am if you now own Rosecroft?"

"I do," he said, knowing full well the gossip mills in rural settings were never idle. "As the place has been neglected in recent years, I expect I will be spending a fair amount of time here, at least in the foreseeable future." There was no part of him, however, seeking to spend the winter in Yorkshire.

Picturesque, idyllic, dress it up a thousand different ways, the dales were miserably cold and prone to heavy snows, and there was an appalling paucity of company. Even York itself offered far less than London in the way of society and entertainment.

"Will you rebuild the greenhouses?" Miss Farnum asked, spearing a bite of tart.

"I honestly don't know. Winnie, you have a serviette for that purpose." Winnie paused in the act of wiping her mouth on her sleeve, then picked up the linen on her lap as if noticing it for the first time.

"Heavenly days," Miss Farnum expostulated on a soft breath. Her eyes were closed, and her mouth was moving in a slow caress over the bite of apple tart. "Where on earth did you find your chef? This is the best dessert I can ever recall having."

"Better than your gran's plum cake?" Winnie asked between bites.

"Better. I must winkle the recipe out of your cook, my lord."

"I can write it down for you," the earl said, polishing off his own serving. "It's not very complicated, provided you get the crust right."

"You expect me to believe you know the recipe for this apple tart?" She aimed her smile at him, and he had to push the last bite of tart down his throat with a concerted swallow. Despite the awful black clothing, despite her hair being scraped back into a nondescript bun, despite the complete lack of anything approaching feminine adornment, that smile *charmed*. It made him aware her mouth was generous and her lips were full. Her eyes, he noticed, were a soft gray blue, and her features were actually pretty.

Not classically pretty—her nose was by no means small, but rather would be accurately described as giving her face character. Her chin was cast in the same, probably Teutonic, mold, and her jaw followed suit. But graced with that smile, the whole was pleasing, winsome, and utterly, arrestingly feminine.

"Start with a clean, cored apple," the earl recited, "and one quarter of a piecrust, preferably made with butter, not lard, and white flour twice sifted, a dash each of cinnamon, nutmeg, clove, and salt added to the flour. Shall I go on?"

"You know a recipe," Miss Farnum said, her smile softening into a muted glow. "I own I am impressed."

"I can count to ten, as well, provided I am not interrupted. Winnie," he waited until the child raised her eyes to his, "you need not sit here and listen to me boast of my culinary and arithmetic talents. Would you like to go up to bed?"

Winnie's gaze locked on his. "I can sleep here?"

"You are more than welcome to sleep here. You are Helmsley, after all."

"Where? The stables are hot, up in the haylofts, anyway. Down by the river in the trees, it's cooler, but the cows like to go down there, and my feet would get dirty."

"Child, you will sleep in a bed, with clean sheets, pillows, and a nice cup of peppermint tea to aid your digestion." Ye gods, had no one taken any interest in this girl?

"Will I have to take another bath?" Winnie

searched his gaze, and the earl knew she was alert for warning of when he would start lying to her.

"Not until you are dirty again, though it being summer, one can find oneself in need of frequent ablutions."

Winnie's expression was wary. "What are blutions?"

"Bubbles." The earl signaled a footman. "If you would fetch the tweeny who was so helpful at bath time, she can escort Miss Winnie up to the bed. Now attend me, Winnie. When you want to leave the table, you inquire of your host, 'May I please be excused?'"

"Are you my host?"

"I have that great honor."

"May I please be excused?"

"Well done. You may, but don't forget to wish Miss Farnum good night before you go. I gather she was concerned about you."

"G'night, Miss Emmie." Winnie hopped down from her chair, scampered over to the lady, and gave her a tight hug around the neck. "G'night, Rosecroft!" She inflicted the same affection on St. Just, grabbed the footman's hand, and pattered out, leaving the earl an unobstructed field upon which to upbraid Miss Farnum.

"Miss Farnum, shall we adjourn to the library for a cup of tea, or perhaps you'd prefer a cordial?"

"The apple tart was quite sweet enough," she replied, seeming to realize the child's absence meant matters were no longer going to be so neighborly. "If you could just answer a few questions for me, then I will be going, though I'll collect Winnie in the morning, shall we say, and my thanks for the very delicious…"

The earl stood beside her chair, waiting for her to rise, and as her voice trailed off, he offered his arm.

"I must insist on just a little more of your time." He picked up her hand and placed it on his arm. "You are my first visitor here, you see, and I wasn't aware the custom in Yorkshire was to burst in upon a neighbor at table, without explanation or invitation, and disturb his meal."

As they made a leisurely progress through the once-gracious manor, Emmie Farnum reminded herself that, drunk and mean, the late Earl of Helmsley hadn't been able to make her back down. Sober and chillingly polite, the Earl of Rosecroft wasn't going to be any greater challenge. Life's circumstances had made her a good judge of character, particularly a good judge of male character, as it was invariably a shallow, trifling subject. In less than ten minutes in the earl's company, she'd come to understand he was a very deceptive man.

Not willfully dishonest, perhaps, but deceptive.

He looked for all the world like an elegant aristocrat come to idle the summer heat away in the country. A touch of lace at his collar and throat, a little green stone winking through the folds of his neckcloth, a gleaming signet ring on his left hand, and even in waistcoat and shirtsleeves, he projected wealth, breeding, and indolence.

His speech was *expensively* proper, the tone never wavering from a fine politesse that bespoke the best schools, the best connections, the best breeding. He wielded his words like little daggers though, pinning his opponent one dart at a time to the target of his choosing.

His body deceived, as well, so nicely adorned in attire, tailor-made for him from his gleaming boots to his neckcloth, to everything so pleasantly coordinated between.

And he was handsome, with sable hair tousled and left a little too long, deep green eyes, arresting height, and military bearing. His face might be considered too strong by some standards—he would never be called a pretty man—but it had a certain masculine appeal, the nose slightly hooked, the chin a trifle arrogant, and the eyebrows just a touch dramatic. No honest female would find him unattractive of face or form.

Beneath the well-tailored clothes, great masses of muscle bunched and smoothed with his every move. The hands holding Emmie's chair for her were lean, brown, and elegant, but also callused, and she'd no doubt they could snap her neck as easily as they cut up Winnie's apple tart. He was clothed as a gentleman, spoke as a gentleman, and had the manner of a gentleman, but Emmie was not deceived.

The Earl of Rosecroft was a barbarian.

But then, there was the most puzzling deception of all: He was a barbarian, but barbarians did not notice when small children grew tired, they did not think to cut up a little girl's tart for her, they did not coax and charm and guide when they could pillage, plunder, and destroy.

So he was an intelligent, shrewd barbarian.

Emmie let him seat her on a green brocade sofa in

the paneled library. "My lord, if you would permit me to ask just one or two questions?"

"I will not," he replied, seating himself—without her permission, barbarian-fashion—in a wing chair opposite the sofa. "I will ask the questions, as you are under my roof and without my invitation."

"I apologize for interrupting your meal," Emmie said, trying for humility, "but I was concerned for the child."

"So I gather. Tea, Miss Farnum?" He excused the footman when the elegant service was sitting on the low table between them.

"Tea would be lovely," she said automatically, resenting the delay in his inquisition. "Shall I pour?"

"No need. I will pour for you so I might pour for myself, as I abhor a cup of tea prepared not as I prefer. Worse than no tea at all."

"I see. Well then, cream and two sugars in mine, if you please." He passed her the tea cup, his fingers brushing hers as she accepted it, and Emmie felt a low current of awareness spark up from her hand.

"Thank you, my lord," she managed. Barbarians, she knew, had that ability to seem exciting. It was a deplorable truth, one she had learned early on.

The earl prepared his own tea and took a cautious sip. "What is your relationship to the child?"

"One might say I am her cousin, of sorts, though it isn't common knowledge, and I would prefer to keep it that way."

"You don't want the world associating you with the earl's bastard?" her host asked, stirring his tea slowly.

Emmie met his gaze. "More to the point, Bronwyn

does not realize we are related, and I would prefer to be the one to tell her."

"How does that come about?" The earl regarded her over the rim of his teacup even as he sipped.

"My aunt was kind enough to provide a home for me when my mother died," Emmie said, lips pursed, as the recitation was not one she embarked on willingly. "Thus I joined her household in the village before Bronwyn was born. When the old earl got wind of that, he eventually sent me off to school in Scotland."

"So your aunt brought you here, and you were then sent off to school by the beneficent old earl."

"I was, and thereafter, my aunt became the young earl's mistress. I suspect his grandfather sent me off to spare me that fate."

"And Winnie is the late earl's by-blow? Your aunt must have been quite youthful."

"She was ten years older than Helmsley but said, since his mama died when he was young, she suited him."

"Did you know the late earl?"

"I knew him. When the old earl grew ill about three years ago, I was retrieved from where I was a governess in Scotland, with the plan being that I could help care for him. When his lordship saw I was subjected to unwanted attentions, he established me on a separate property."

"In what capacity?" The earl topped off her teacup, a peculiarly civilized gesture, considering he was leaving her no privacy whatsoever.

"I support myself," Emmie replied, unable to keep a touch of pride from her voice. "I have since returned to Yorkshire. On the old earl's advice, I never rejoined my aunt's household in the village, hence Winnie doesn't understand we are cousins. I'm not sure it ever registered with Helmsley, either."

"Did it register with Helmsley he had a daughter?"

"Barely." Emmie spat the word. "My aunt did well enough with Winnie, though she was careful not to impose the child on her father very often. Helmsley was prone to... poor choices in his companions. One in particular could not be trusted around children, and so Winnie was an awkward addition to her father's household after my aunt's death."

"And now she's been appended to your household?"

"She is... she finally is." For the second time that evening, Emmie smiled at him, but she teared up, as well, ducking her face to hide her mortification.

"Women," the earl muttered. He extracted his handkerchief and passed it to her.

"I beg your pardon." Emmie tried to smile and failed, but took his handkerchief. "It was difficult, watching her grow from toddler to child and seeing she'd had no one to love her since my aunt died."

"One must concede, you seem to care for the child." The earl regarded her with a frown. "But one must also inquire into what manner of influence you are on her. You aren't supporting yourself as your aunt did, are you?"

"I most assuredly am *not* supporting myself as you so rudely imply." She rose to her feet and tried to stuff his damp hankie back into his hand. "I work for honest coin and will not tolerate your insults."

"Keep it." He smiled at her slightly while his fingers

curled her hand around his handkerchief. "I have plenty to spare. And please accept my apologies, Miss Farnum, as your character is of interest to me."

"Why ever is it any of your business how I earn my keep?" She resumed her seat but concentrated on folding his handkerchief into halves and quarters and eighths in her lap rather than meet that piercing green stare of his again.

"I am interested in your character because you are a friend of Miss Winnie's, and she has become my concern."

"About Bronwyn"—Emmie rose again and paced away from him—"we must reach some kind of understanding."

"We must?"

"She is my family," Emmie pointed out, then more softly, "my only family. Surely you can understand she should be with me?"

"So why wasn't she?" One of his dark eyebrows quirked where he sat sipping his tea. Emmie had the thought that if he'd had a tail, he'd be flicking it in a lazy, feline rhythm.

"Why wasn't she what?" Emmie stopped her pacing and busied herself straightening up a shelf of books.

"Why wasn't she with you? When I plucked her off that fountain, she was filthy, tired, and hadn't eaten all day."

"I couldn't catch her." Emmie frowned at the books.

"I beg your pardon?" The earl's voice came from her elbow, but she was damned if she'd flinch.

"I said, I could not catch her." Emmie did peek then and realized the earl wasn't just tall, he was also a big man. Bigger than he looked from across a room, the scoundrel.

"And I could not run her off," the earl mused. "It might comfort you to know, Miss Farnum, I am the oldest of ten and not unused to youngsters."

"You do seem to get on well with her, but I have an advantage, my lord. One you will never be able to compete with."

"An advantage?"

"Yes." Emmie said, feeling a little sorry for him, because he really would not be able to argue the point much further. "I am a female, you see. A girl. Well, a grown woman, but I was a girl, as Bronwyn is."

"You are a female?" The earl looked her up and down, and Emmie felt herself blushing. It was a thorough and thoroughly dispassionate perusal. "Why so you are, but how does this make yours the better guidance?"

"There are certain things, my lord…" Emmie felt her blush deepening but refused to capitulate to embarrassment. "Things a lady knows a gentleman will not, things somebody must pass along to a little girl in due course if she's to manage in this life."

"Things." The earl's brow knit. "Things like childbirth, perhaps?"

Emmie swallowed, resenting his bluntness even while she admired him for it. "Well, yes. I doubt you've given birth, my lord."

"Have you?" he countered, peering down at her.

"That is not the point."

"So no advantage to you there, particularly as I have attended a birth or two in my time, and I doubt you've managed that either."

"Why on *earth* would…?" Emmie's mouth snapped shut before she could ask the obvious, rude, burning question.

"I was a soldier," he said gently. "And war is very hard on soldiers, but even harder on women and children, Miss Farnum. A woman giving birth in a war zone is generally willing to accept the assistance of whomever is to hand, regardless of standing, gender, or even what uniform he wears."

"So you've a little experience, but you aren't going to tell me you're familiar with the details of a lady's bodily… well, that is to say. Well."

"Her menses?" The earl looked amused again. "You might have some greater degree of familiarity than I. I will grant that much, but as a man with five sisters, I am far more knowledgeable and sympathetic regarding female lunation than I had ever aspired to be. And surely, these matters you raise—childbirth and courses—they are a ways off for Miss Winnie?"

"Bronwyn," Emmie muttered. Standing so close to him, she could catch the earl's scent, and it managed to combine both elegance and barbarism. It was spicy rather than floral, but also fresh, like meadows and breezes and cold, fast-running streams.

"She *answers* to Winnie," he said, "and she got away from you."

"She did." Emmie's shoulders slumped as some of the fight went out of her. "She does. I've lost her for hours at a time, at least in the summer, and nobody has any real notion where she gets off to. It wasn't so bad when my aunt first died, but it has gotten worse the older Bronwyn gets. I was terrified…"

"Yes?" The green eyes steadily holding hers bore no judgment, just a patient regard with a teasing hint of compassion.

"I was terrified Helmsley would take her south, or worse, let that cretin Stull get hold of her; but Helmsley was her father, so I'd no right to do anything for her nor to have any say in how she goes on."

"And had your aunt lived, the law would have given Helmsley no claim on the child, nor any obligation to her either."

"Oh, *the law*." Emmie waved a dismissive hand. "The law tells us the better course would have been to allow the child to starve while her dear papa gambled away the estate. Do not quote the law to me, my lord, for it only points out what is legal and what is right do not often coincide where the fate of children is concerned."

"Legalities aside then, I am in a better position to assist the child than you are. Just as the old earl gave you an education to allow you to make your way as a governess, I can provide every material advantage for Winnie, too. If it comes to that, I can prevail upon the Moreland resources for the child, as well."

"But I am her cousin," Emmie said, feeling tears well again. "I am her cousin and her only relation."

"Not so, though the reverse might be true. The child's Aunt Anna is now married to my brother, which makes me an uncle-in-law or some such, and I am one of ten, recall. Through her aunt's marriage, Winnie has a great deal of family."

"But they don't know her," Emmie quietly wailed. "I am Winnie's family. *I am*."

"Shall we compromise?" he asked, drawing Emmie's arm through his and escorting her to the sofa. "It seems to me we are considering mutually exclusive outcomes, with either you or myself having Winnie's exclusive company. Why can't she have us both?"

"You could visit," Emmie said, warming to the idea. Maybe, she allowed, he was an enlightened barbarian, though his arguments for leaving Winnie in his care were sound. "Or perhaps Winnie might spend time here, as she considers this her home."

"I do not *visit* my responsibilities, Miss Farnum," the earl replied, resuming his seat across from her. "Not when they require regular feeding and bathing and instruction in basic table manners that should have been mastered long ago."

"So how do we compromise?" Emmie ignored the implied criticism by sheer will. "If Winnie lives here with you, how is that a compromise?"

"Simple." The earl smiled at her, a buccaneer's smile if ever she saw one. "You live here, too. You've said you have experience as a governess; the child needs a governess. You care for her and hold yourself out as entitled to assist with her upbringing. It seems a perfectly feasible solution to me. You remain as her governess until such time as I find a replacement, one who merits your approval and mine."

"Feasible." Emmie felt her mouth and eyebrows working in a disjointed symphony of expressions, none of which were intended to convey good cheer. "You want me to be a governess to Bronwyn?" She rose, and the earl watched her but remained seated.

"There's a difficulty." She hoped her relief did not show on her face.

"Only one?"

"It is formidable." Emmie eyed *him* up and down. "I am qualified to supervise a child of Bronwyn's age, but I have always been more a friend to her than an authority figure. I am not sure she will listen to me, else I would not find myself fretting so often over her whereabouts."

"Having not had a papa to speak of and having lost her mother, the child has likely become too self-reliant, something that can only be curbed, not entirely eradicated. And while the child may not listen to you, I have every confidence she will listen to me."

"*Every* confidence?" Emmie arched an eyebrow and met his gaze squarely.

"I got her into the house." The earl started counting off on his fingers. "I inculcated basic table manners, I engaged her in civil discussion when she was intent only on repelling boarders, and"—he arched an eyebrow right back at her—"I got her into the bathtub, where she was soaped and scrubbed into something resembling a lovely little girl."

"You did." Emmie scowled in thought. "May I inquire how?"

"Nelson at Trafalgar. One can only demonstrate sea battles under appropriate circumstances."

"*You* gave her a bath?" Emmie's eyes went wide.

"Soap and water are not complicated, but the tweeny is hardly likely to comprehend naval strategy. I'll provide the child the right bath toys, and my direct involvement shouldn't be necessary from this point out. You do, I assume, have a grasp of naval history?"

"Naval history?" Emmie all but gasped in dismay.

"Well, no matter. I can teach you a few major battles, and any self-respecting child will take it from there. So are we agreed?"

"On what?" Emmie felt bewildered and over-whelmed, perhaps as if a cavalry regiment had just appeared, charging over the nearest hill, and her all unsuspecting in their path.

"You will be her temporary governess until we find somebody we both approve to serve in that capacity. I shall compensate you, of course."

"I will not take money for looking after family."

"And how will you support yourself if you do not take money for services rendered?"

"That's the other reason I cannot agree to this scheme." Emmie all but snapped her fingers, so great was her relief. "I cannot let my customers down. If I stop providing goods for any length of time, they'll take their business elsewhere, and I'll get a reputation for being unreliable. It won't serve, your lordship. You'll have to think of some other compromise."

"What is your business that your customers would be so fickle?"

Emmie smiled with pride. "I am a baker, my lord. I make all manner of goods... breads and sweets especially."

"I see. There is no impediment, then."

"Of course there is." Emmie gave him a version of the local art-thee-daft look. "I cannot abandon my business, my lord, else I will have no income when we find a permanent governess for Bronwyn."

"You don't abandon your business," the earl

informed her. "You merely see to it here. The kitchens are extensive, there is help on hand, and you were obviously prepared to look after your cousin and your commercial obligations at the same time, so you should be able to do it easily at Rosecroft."

"You would have me turn Rosecroft into a bakery?" Emmie all but squeaked. "This is an old and lovely manor, my lord, not some…"

"Yes?"

"My customers would not be comfortable coming here to pick up their orders. Helmsley was not on good terms with most of his neighbors, and you are a stranger."

"Then we'll have your goods delivered. Really, Miss Farnum, the measures are temporary, and I should hope the good folk hereabouts would understand Winnie has lost both father and mother. As her family, we must put her welfare before somebody's tea cakes and crumpets."

She met his gaze and sighed a sigh of defeat, because he was, damn and blast him, right. Nobody's tea cakes, crumpets, or even daily bread could be as important as Bronwyn's future. And he was also right that Bronwyn did so have family—powerful, wealthy family—who could offer her much more than a cousin eking out a living baking pies in Yorkshire.

"I'll want your apple tart recipe," she said, chin up. If she was to allow this man to take from her the child she loved most in the world, then she was owed that much compensation at least.

The earl's lips quirked. "Dear lady, why wouldn't I give out such a thing to everybody at whose table

I might someday sit? I've never understood the business of hoarding recipes. Now, how quickly can we arrange for you to start?"

He was gracious in victory. She had to give him that. He'd also gotten Bronwyn into the tub, and he had the best apple tart recipe she had ever tasted. The picture wasn't entirely bleak. Moreover, the Rosecroft kitchens might need a thorough scrubbing, but as he led her on a brief tour, she saw the ovens were huge, the counter space endless, and the appointments surprisingly modern and well kept.

"My inventory will have to be moved, and I will need storage for it, as well."

"Details, and ones I'm sure you'll manage easily." The earl put her hand on his arm as they left the kitchen. "As we've lost the light, Miss Farnum, I must conclude the hour has grown late. Will you allow me to call the carriage for you?"

"I am not but a half mile up the lane. It will not serve to bother the stables for so paltry a journey. I walked here; I'll enjoy the walk home."

"As you wish." He led her through the house to the front door, where her frayed gloves and ugly bonnet were waiting on a table. "Shall I carry it for you?" He held the bonnet up by its ribbons, her gloves folded in the crown. "It's not as if you need to protect your complexion at this hour."

"I can carry it." She grabbed for the bonnet, but his blasted eyebrow was arching again.

"I do not comprehend yet all the local nuances of manners and etiquette, Miss Farnum, but I am not about to let a young lady walk home alone in the dark." He angled his free elbow out to her and gestured toward the door held open by the footman.

Barbarian. She wanted to stomp her foot hard— on his—and march off into the darkness. She'd capitulated—albeit grudgingly and perhaps only temporarily—to his idea of sharing responsibility for Bronwyn. She'd put up with his sniping and probing and serving her tea. She'd agreed to move her business activities to his kitchens, but she would not be bullied.

"I know the way, my lord," she said, glaring at him. "There is no need for this display."

"You are going to be responsible for Winnie's first efforts to acquire a sense of decorum and reserve, Miss Farnum." He picked up her hand and deposited it back on her forearm, then led her down the steps. "You must begin as you intend to go on and set a sincere example for the child. She'll spot fraud at fifty paces, and even my authority won't be able to salvage your efforts then. A lady graciously accepts appropriate escort."

"Is this how you trained recruits when you were soldiering?" She stomped along beside him, ignoring the beauty of the full moon and the fragrances of the summer night. "You box them in, reason with them, tease, argue, taunt, and twist until you get what you want?"

"You are upset. If I have given offense, I apologize." His voice was even, not the snippy, non-apology of a man humoring a woman's snit. She hauled him through the darkness for another twenty yards or so before she stopped and heaved a sigh.

"I am sorry," Emmie said, dropping his arm. "I suppose I am jealous."

He made no move to recapture her hand but put his own on the small of her back and guided her steps forward again. "You are jealous of what?"

"Of your ease with Bronwyn. Of the wealth allowing you to provide so easily for her. Of your connections, enabling you to present her a much better future than I could. Of your ability to wave a hand and order all as you wish it."

"Are we being pursued by bandits, Miss Farnum?" the earl asked, his voice a velvety baritone in the soft, summery darkness.

"We are not."

"Then perhaps we could proceed at less than forced march? It is a beautiful night, the air is lovely, and I've always found darkness soothing when I took the time to appreciate it."

"And from what would the Earl of Rosecroft need soothing?" She nearly snorted at the very notion.

"I've felt how you feel," he said simply. "As if another had all I needed and lacked, and he didn't even appreciate what he had."

"You?" She expostulated in disbelief but walked more slowly and made no objection to his hand lightly touching her back. "What could you possibly want for? You're the firstborn of a duke, titled, wealthy; you've survived battles, and you can charm little girls. How could you long for more than that?"

"My brother will succeed Moreland, if the duke ever condescends to expire. This harum-scarum earldom is a sop thrown to my younger brother's conscience, and his wife's, I suppose. He and my father had considerable influence with the Regent, and Westhaven's wife may well be carrying the Moreland heir. Anna made the suggestion to see Rosecroft passed along to me, and Westhaven would not rest until that plan had been fulfilled."

"How can that be?" Emmie watched their moon shadows float along the ground as they walked. "A duke cannot choose which of his offspring inherits his title."

"He cannot. According to the Moreland letters patent, it goes to the oldest legitimate son surviving at the time of the duke's death."

"Well, you aren't going to die soon, are you?" She glanced over at his obviously robust frame, puzzled and concerned for some reason to think of him expiring of a pernicious illness.

"No, Miss Farnum, the impediment is not death, but rather the circumstances of my birth." There was a slight, half-beat pause in the darkness, a hitch in her gait he would not have seen.

"Oh."

"Oh, indeed. I have a sister similarly situated, though Maggie and I do not share even the same mother. The duke was a busy fellow in his youth."

"Busy and selfish. What is it with men that they must strut and carry on, heedless of the consequences to any save themselves?"

"What is it with women," he replied, humor lacing his tone, "that they must indulge our selfish impulses without regard to the consequences even to themselves?"

"Point taken." For a barbarian, he reasoned quickly and well, and he was a pleasant enough escort. His scent blended with the night fragrances, and it occurred to her he'd already admitted to being comfortable with darkness.

And in his eyes, in odd moments, she'd seen hints of darkness. He referred casually to serving King and Country, and he admitted now to being a ducal bastard. Well, what would that matter? By local standards, he would be much in demand socially, and the squire's daughters would toss themselves at him just as they did at Helmsley once long ago—poor things.

She was so lost in her thoughts she stumbled over a gnarled old tree root and would have gone down but for the earl's arm around her waist.

"Steady on." He eased her up to find her balance but hesitated before dropping his arm. In that instant, Emmie gained a small insight into why women behaved as foolishly as her mother and aunt and countless others had done.

"My thanks," she said, walking more slowly yet. The heat and strength of him had felt good, reassuring in some inconvenient way. For twenty-five years, Emmaline Farnum had negotiated life without much in the way of male protection or affection, and she'd been at a loss to understand what, *exactly*, men offered that would make a woman suffer their company, much less their authority.

And she still didn't know, exactly, what that something was, but the earl had it in abundance. The sooner they found Bronwyn a real governess, the better for them all.

"Why do you still wear black?" the earl asked as he ambled along beside her. "Your aunt died several years ago, and one doesn't observe full mourning for years for an aunt."

"One doesn't have to, but my aunt was like a mother to me, so I dyed my most presentable wardrobe black and haven't had the coin to replace it since—nor much need to. Then, too, wearing black made me less conspicuous to Helmsley and his cronies."

"You did not respect my predecessor. I suppose you don't respect many men, given your aunt raised you alone."

Another pause, but again his hand was lightly at her back, steadying her.

"My mother told me my father tried hard, but he became restless, and she could not find it in her heart to force him to stay."

"She did not care for him?"

"She did. I never want to fathom a love like that, a love that puts a loved one aside and says it's for the best."

"Did she know she carried his child when she wished him on his way?"

"No." Emmie sighed, feeling his hand at her back as she did. "She was not... she did not have clear indications of her predicament, early on, and by the time she was convinced the unthinkable had happened, her fellow had shipped out for India."

"Be very, very glad she didn't follow the drum," the earl said, something in his voice taking on the darkness. "It is no life whatsoever for a woman."

"Particularly not when the man ends up dying in battle, and there you are—no man, no means, no home and hearth to retreat to, and babies clinging to your skirts."

"This is an abiding theme with you, isn't it?" The earl's voice was merely curious now, but he was identifying a pattern accurately.

"I have avoided the Rosecroft grounds as much as possible," Emmie said, her steps dragging. "Helmsley was an eloquent reminder of how dishonorable a titled, supposed gentleman can be."

"He was a thoroughly disagreeable cad," the earl agreed. "A more disgusting excuse for a man, much less a gentleman, I have yet to meet, unless it was that porcine embarrassment colluding with him, the Baron Stull."

"So you met Helmsley?"

"I killed him," the earl said easily, taking her hand in his. "Watch your step. We've reached a rough patch."

Two

EMMIE STUMBLED AGAIN, MORE HEAVILY, BUT HE caught her this time, as well. His left hand went around her left wrist; his right arm secured her to his chest by virtue of a snug hold about her waist. They stood for a long moment in an off-balance version of a promenade, while Emmie used the earl's height and strength to regain her balance.

"Well, good," Emmie said with a certain relish. "The man was in want of killing." Next to her, she heard and felt the earl exhale, a deep, slow breath, sending air fanning past her cheek. She had the sense he'd been holding it a long time. Weeks, maybe, months—his whole life.

"He was, at that," the earl replied. "Shall we proceed?" His voice gave nothing away, though Emmie thought he'd call his earlier words back if he could. Not because he regretted taking the man's life, but because announcing such a thing while escorting a young lady home through darkness wasn't at all the done thing.

Even a barbarian would know that.

"He made a few tries at me," Emmie said. She kept hold of the earl's hand as she walked along, then adjusted her grip as they negotiated more roots, so her fingers laced through his. "It was Helmsley's attentions the old earl sought to preserve me from."

"Did Helmsley ever… achieve his ends?" Rosecroft asked, the same foreboding in his voice.

"I am a baseborn girl, my lord. What difference would it have made if he had? He threw more than a good scare into me, and the lesson served me well when I went into service. Beastly nuisance of a man. I am glad you killed him. Glad and relieved. The old earl, much as he loved his grandson, would have applauded you for protecting his granddaughters."

It was safe, somehow, to speak so openly with him in the darkness, even though holding hands with him this way was also *not* safe. Not safe, nor smart, not what a prudent woman would do. A prudent woman wouldn't take such pleasure from it nor speculate about what other behaviors Lord Rosecroft might engage in on a dark and breezy night.

Emmie turned the topic to the details of moving her bakery to Rosecroft, then prattled on about the neighbors surrounding the property and the various tradesmen and farmers in the area. She cast around for topics that were pleasant, soothing, and even humorous rather than make her escort dwell on a past better left in silence. And she did not drop his hand until they approached a stately two-story house, the structure more grand than a tenant farmer's cottage, but certainly not a manor in itself.

"The old earl put you here?" Rosecroft asked as he led her up wide porch stairs.

"He did. He purchased it as a sort of dower house."

It was a pleasant place, or so Emmie told herself. Flowers abounded, a small barn with adjacent paddocks stood back from the house, and large trees afforded a shifting mosaic of moon shadows. In sunlight, it was cheery, airy, and gracious.

"This is a lot of property for one person to maintain," the earl said as Emmie settled on the porch swing. He set her bonnet on the steps and turned to look at the moonlit landscape. "You have a nice view to the river, though."

"I do, and I love my trees. The shade is lovely, and in winter they provide protection from both wind and snow."

"I missed the greenness of England terribly when I was on the Peninsula," her companion mused. "Missed it like some men missed their sweethearts."

"We English are basically homebodies, I think." Emmie set the swing to rocking gently with her toe. "We wander hither and yon for King and Country, but we come home and are glad to be here."

"I will take that as my cue to wander home," the earl said, holding out her bonnet.

"Thank you for your escort, my lord." She rose from the swing and retrieved her bonnet. "I will see you on Monday."

"Until then." He took her hand in his and bowed over it, a courtly gesture one might show a lady but not the daughter of a mere soldier, earning her living in some Yorkshire backwater.

"You can find your way in the dark?" she asked then realized the question was silly. What if he said no? Would she escort him back to the manor?

"I'll manage." His teeth flashed in that buccaneer's smile, and he waited as an escort should until she was safely inside her house. Before she lit a single candle, she turned and peered through her parlor window, watching him disappear into the shadows, his stride brisk, his sense of direction unerring.

When she said her prayers that night, Emmie dutifully thanked the Almighty for the good turn that had finally befallen little Bronwyn. If Emmie could just loosen her grasp of the child, the earl would provide for Winnie, provide generously, and not in any absentminded way, either. He would personally notice what she needed and provide it. The adjustment to not caring directly for Bronwyn, to not worrying about her, would take time, but Emmie vowed she would make it. If she loved that child and wanted what was right for her, she absolutely would.

But before she bid her Creator good night, Emmie also asked for more than the usual measure of fortitude to see her through the coming days, and not just with respect to letting go of Winnie. With the earl's competence, air of command, and masculine appeal—there, she thought, that term would suffice—Rosecroft was going to be a temptation. Fortunately for her, he was also possessed of pride, arrogance, and a lofty title. If all went well, he would notice Bronwyn and ignore Bronwyn's cousin.

The fortitude was necessary, however, to assist Bronwyn's cousin in ignoring—or at least pretending to ignore—the earl.

As that gentleman strode toward his new home, he considered the developments of his day and let his pace slow to a more thoughtful amble. The fountain would need to be repaired, as first impressions were important, and a drive ending in a broken fountain would hardly serve. The stables were adequate but in need of a thorough scrubbing. The previous owner's neglect meant none of the pastures had been harvested of hay for several years, though. There was an abundant if overripe crop to be cut in the next few weeks, and that was a good thing—provided he could find the labor—for Yorkshire winters were nothing to be trifled with.

He planned and organized his way right back to his own doorstep but hesitated before going inside. The night was lovely, and though the hour was late, he paused at the front terrace.

The porch needed a swing. If there was going to be a child on the premises, that was a high priority. Thinking of Winnie, he went inside, trying to recall where he'd had her quartered. The nursery and children's rooms would have been on the third floor, but something in him had rebelled at isolating the child from others when she'd been ostracized her whole life.

As there were no sentries to see to the matter, he made a circuit of the interior, knowing it was foolish. In summer, an estate like this would hardly secure its windows and doors, the breezes being welcome, and the likelihood of mischief none at all. Still, he prowled his darkened house before going upstairs then patrolled that floor in its entirety before checking on Winnie.

She looked tiny in her bed; and in sleep, her mouth worked as if she'd been a thumb sucker in infancy.

The earl had seen new recruits with the same characteristic ten years her senior. He traced a finger along her downy cheek, and she quieted, so he withdrew.

Leaving him to face the rest of his night alone.

When morning came, he was surprised to realize he'd slept through the night. It was a rare, though no longer unheard of, occurrence. He took the good nights when they came and endured the bad as best he could. In London, he'd gotten into the habit of riding with his brothers before breakfast, and it still seemed like a worthy start to the day.

"Good morning, my lord." Steen, the butler, bowed, bearing a week-old edition of *The Times* bound for the iron. "Will you and Mr. Holderman be taking tea in the library after your ride?"

"We will, but as Miss Winnie has joined the household, we're going to have to put together something in the way of breakfasts."

"I will inform the kitchen, my lord. And will you be passing along some breakfast menus for Cook?"

"After my ride." Ye gods and little fishes, could his staff not even produce a breakfast without being told to toast both sides of the bread?

"Spare me from menus," he muttered, frowning as he approached the stables. He clattered out of the yard shortly thereafter, desperately grateful to be mounted and moving. He had let the horses rest and settle in for a few days after their two hundred-mile journey north from Surrey, then put them to light work in the riding ring last week. This week, it was time to graduate to hacking out, taking the horses cross-country, over hill and dale, stream and log.

"You're trying to convince me you're a city boy, aren't you?" The earl patted Red's muscular neck. The gelding had done well enough in his earliest training, but the open countryside was another matter altogether, as Red reminded him when a rabbit shot across the path. A prop, a halfhearted rear, and some dancing around, and Red was eventually convinced it might have been only a rabbit, not a tiger. The entire ride progressed along the same lines, until the earl realized he was circling back toward the manor along the route he'd taken with Miss Farnum the previous night. He brought Red back down to the walk and changed directions, heading for her house instead.

By day, particularly in the fresh light of early morning, her property was as pleasant and peaceful as he'd imagined it by moonlight. Following his nose, he rode up to the back of the house, not surprised to find several fragrant pies cooling on the porch rail.

He'd slipped Red's bridle off and set him to grazing Miss Farnum's backyard when a cheerful voice called to him from the porch.

"Good morning, Lord Rosecroft." Miss Farnum called, smiling at him broadly. She put two more pies on the rail and waited while he approached the porch. She wasn't in black, but wore what looked like an old cotton walking dress with a full-length apron belted around her waist—apparently not part of her "most presentable" wardrobe. The apron nipped in and revealed what his hands had told him last night: She was curved in all the right places, both curved in and curved out. He resisted the urge to dwell on that pleasant revelation.

"Good morning, Miss Farnum." He bowed, finding himself tempted to return the smile. Well, a good night's sleep was sure to improve a man's spirits. "I trust you slept well?"

"I did not." She shook her head, her smile still in place. "It's a baking day, and in summer one likes to get that done as early as possible. As late as I ran yesterday, I decided to simply get to work when I got home last night. I am almost done with my day's work."

"You slept not at all? My apologies. Had I known how limited your time was last evening, I would not have detained you."

"You would, too," she contradicted him pleasantly. "But you are here now, so you can give me your opinion. I am of the mind that you excel at rendering opinions."

The earl felt the corners of his mouth twitching. "I will make allowances for such a remark because you are overly tired and a mere female."

"You noticed. I'm impressed. Have a seat." She gestured to a wrought iron table painted white, surrounded with padded wicker chairs, while the earl admitted to himself that, indeed, he *had* noticed, and was continuing to notice. "May I offer you some cider? I keep it in the spring house so it should be cold."

"Cider would be appreciated," he replied, wondering at her working at her ovens through the night and now greeting the day with such obvious joy. She banged through a swinging door, leaving him swamped by a cloud of delicious kitcheny scents and contemplating the profusion of flowers growing in her backyard.

She swung back through the door, a tray in her hands. "Prepare to opine." She sat down in one of the wicker chairs, propped her elbows on the table, and rested her cheeks on her fists.

"Regarding?" The earl lifted an eyebrow, noticing Miss Farnum had a little smudge of flour on her jaw.

"My experiments." She nodded at the tray and the three separate plates thereon. "Tell me which you prefer and why."

"You will not join me?" the earl asked, eyeing what looked like three identically delicious flaky pastries.

"I believe I will." She deftly cut all three in half, put three halves on one plate and the other three halves on a second plate. "Baking is hungry work." She picked up a pastry without further ado and bit into it, cocking her head and frowning in thought.

"Well, go *on*," she urged, "or my opinion will carry the day. The dough is adequately turned, I suppose."

Seeing she had not provided utensils, the earl slid off his riding gloves and picked up a pastry. He bit into it, realizing he was hungry. "Tea in the library" after his ride would have included scones, butter, and jam. The same scones, butter, and jam he'd had every morning since arriving to Rosecroft.

"You put ham and cheese in a pastry? It's good."

"What would make it better? Ham, eggs, and cheese tend to become soggy and are boring."

"Not to an empty stomach, it isn't." The earl demolished his first half in two more bites. "Maybe a bit more butter inside?"

"I butter the dough so heavily it practically moos, but it needs something."

The earl frowned. "Leeks? Garlic for breakfast might be a bit much, but even celery would give it texture. Bacon would add both variety and substance."

"I will try that," she said, smiling at him. "Onions, at least. Bacon lacks subtlety, unless I used it very sparingly. Thank you. Try the next one." The next one had some sort of sweet, soft cheese inside, a rich, heavy filling that made a half portion adequate.

"I'd add a little lemon zest. It will lighten the flavor considerably, make it more a breakfast food than a dessert."

"Oh, I like that." Miss Farnum nodded enthusiastically. "Have you lemons in your orangery?"

"I don't know." The earl eyed the remaining bite. "If there were lemons in there three years ago, there should be some salvageable stock now."

"One hopes; try the last one." Miss Farnum's eyes were alight with anticipation, and the earl couldn't help but draw the moment out with a slow sip of his cider.

"You're stalling." She smacked her hands down on the table and took his cider away. "Get busy, my lord, or I'll hold your drink hostage."

"Nasty tactics," he said, picking up the last half pastry. He bit into it to find it was flavored with cinnamon, raisins, honey, and nuts, all layered within the pastry as the dough had been folded onto itself.

"It reminds me of an Eastern dessert, baklava. I like it and think it would go particularly well with hot tea on a cold morning."

"But?" she pressed, sliding his cider across the table toward him.

"But nothing. I like it."

"You like it. You say that about as enthusiastically as I might say I like bread that's only one day old. What would make it better?" She was going to pester him on this, he saw. She took her little experiments seriously.

"It's bland. Just sweet, with the spices you expect in sweet things. Cinnamon, I suppose, and a dash of clove, but not much. Mincemeat would be more interesting, pear butter with brandied pecans."

"Make it something definite, not just a breakfast sweet. I will work on these, but you confirm my suspicion they are not ready for public consumption. My thanks."

"You are eying my cider." The earl gestured at the mug sitting between them. "Help yourself."

"I will," she said, bringing his mug to her lips. "I would have to make another trip down to the spring house to fetch more." She'd drained the mug, he saw, feeling just the least bit thirsty now that she had.

"You would have done well as an officer's wife," he heard himself comment. "They were remarkable women, most of them. Far more stoic than the men and just as brave."

"I swipe your cider, and you are willing to offer me my colors?" Miss Farnum smiled then hid a delicate yawn behind her hand.

"Those ladies did not stand on ceremony. They were practical, resilient, good-humored, and resourceful. You put me in mind of them." They were also women who understood the place killing had in the greater scheme of life, and Emmie Farnum, smiling and yawning in the soft summer air, shared that wisdom, too.

She nodded at Red. "Was that one of your mounts?"

"He was too young to have served. I own a stud farm in Surrey, and he is one of three whose training I did not want to see lapse over the summer. His name is Ethelred. Shall I introduce you?"

"I'd be delighted." She rose without assistance. "It isn't every morning a lady finds two such handsome fellows on her back porch."

"He will be happy to opine regarding your grass, I'm sure," the earl said, walking down the steps beside her. "I think he believes it to be too long and in need of his attentions." Red looked up as they approached but continued chewing.

"Is he a bit thin?" she asked, holding out a hand for Red to sniff.

"He is. He's three and a half. He'll continue to grow for at least another year, and he's in a weedy stage. Then, too, they all dropped weight on the journey north." As he had himself.

"Well, aren't you handsome?" She addressed the horse, the minx. "I am pleased to make your acquaintance, Mr...?" She arched an eyebrow at the earl.

"Ethelred," the earl reminded her, "or Red, which he seems to like better." Red was making sheep's eyes at Miss Farnum, sniffing at her hand then wiggling his lips against her palm. "Shameless beggar." The earl scratched at Red's ears. "He must like the sugary scent of you." Without thinking, Rosecroft grasped her hand and sniffed at her palm. "Sweet," he remarked, "and a little spicy."

She shot him a quizzical look. "Perhaps I will experiment with making treats for your steed."

"And wouldn't you love that?" the earl asked his horse. Red went back to grazing, seeing the introductions were not going to afford any more attention. "Do you ride, Miss Farnum?"

"I was taught," she said, eyes still on Red. "It has been years."

"Would you perhaps like to ride, then? The countryside here is nothing if not beautiful, and I'm going to have to find some quiet mounts for Miss Winnie."

She smiled at him wistfully. "Maybe someday. Winnie loves animals, you know. They've been her chief companions for the past two years."

"Then we will keep her well supplied. I've an affinity for them myself, horses in particular. Actually, I am intruding on your morning in hopes you can advise me on a matter related to Winnie." Well, he amended silently, tangentially related to Winnie.

"Oh?" She stifled another little yawn, and the earl recalled she'd been up all night.

"Come." He put a hand on the small of her back and steered her toward the porch. "You are tired, and I should not keep you. I wanted only to inquire regarding Winnie's preferences at breakfast. I need to review the menus now that breakfast will be a necessity, and I thought as you—"

"You aren't having a proper *breakfast*?" Miss Farnum turned to stare at him. "For shame, my lord. You wouldn't expect Ethelred to go to work without his breakfast, would you? My lands, what must you be thinking? Come along *this instant*." She bustled up the steps and banged through her back door again, leaving the earl to follow in her wake. He found himself in a hallway leading to a large, tidy kitchen as Miss Farnum went to a desk—who put a desk in a kitchen?—and withdrew a piece of paper and a short pencil.

"Breakfast is the best meal of the day," she informed the earl as she sat at the desk. "Show me a man who doesn't appreciate his breakfast, and I'll show you a man who couldn't possibly be English. Now…" She fell silent as she scratched away. "There."

She brandished the paper at him, and he took it.

"Winnie loves her muffins." Miss Farnum nodded for emphasis. "But she needs the variety of fresh fruits and the substance of some butter and cheese to start her day. She is not particularly fond of meat, but one needn't belabor that point."

"Not at breakfast," the earl agreed. "My thanks, Miss Farnum. I'll take my leave of you and recommend you seek your bed."

"I will dream of the perfect pastry."

"Until Monday, then." The earl couldn't help but smile at her, so pleased did she seem with the prospect of her dreams. He bridled his horse, mounted up, and rode on home, oblivious to the pair of blue-gray eyes watching him canter off into the shade of the trees.

Rather than take herself immediately off to bed, Emmie wrote out instructions for Anna Mae Summers, the assistant who would show up in an hour so, then paused to consider her previous visitor.

As she shucked down to her skin then washed, Emmie reflected that the earl had a disarming willingness to speak plainly, to put his questions, desires, and aims into simple speech: What does Winnie like for breakfast? Did Helmsley ever succeed in his attempts to bother her? Help yourself to my cider.

He was like no kind of aristocrat she'd ever seen, much less dealt with. The great families around York might occasionally patronize her bakery, for a wedding cake, perhaps, or for particular confections. But even their footmen sent to collect the goods didn't *see* her, and she'd always preferred it that way.

The earl saw her, and worse, she liked that he did.

Giving herself a mental lecture about bad judgments and the whims of the aristocracy, Emmie took herself off to bed. She tossed and turned for a long time before falling asleep, thinking of just how to perfect her latest experiments. Her cogitation might have been more productive, however, were she not constantly distracted by the memory of the earl's aquiline nose tickling her palm as he sniffed at the sweetness and spice he found there.

The woods were lovely, cool and quiet, and a much-needed change of pace from Holderman's bowing, scraping, and throat clearing. The man had little clue how to get the fountain re-piped and had only mumbled into his tea about getting a haying crew together before the crop got any older. The only thing for it, St. Just decided, was to go for a ride lest he strangle his steward over luncheon. So he'd saddled up and headed for a part of his property he'd yet to explore, only to find the steadiest of his mounts was tensing beneath him, ears pricking forward.

Knowing better than to ignore the horse's reaction, the earl cautiously urged the animal to a halt. This was his third and final ride of the day, the one he saved for last, because the horse—Caesar—was such a pleasure to spend time with. Something large was moving just a few yards away. Not a wild dog, or Caesar would have been alarmed, not just alert. Something big enough to startle a horse, though.

Rosecroft's mouth went dry, then his heart sped up, for there, through a leafy curtain, was Emmaline Farnum, naked as the day she was born, floating serenely on her back. Her hair was still bound, but the rest of her was as God made her—and God had done a magnificent job. Her breasts were full, with small pink, puckered nipples, her waist nipped in sweetly, her legs were long and muscular, and there at the juncture of her legs…

The earl was a gentleman, raised with sisters and cousins and enough females that he comprehended why the fairer gender was deserving of respect. He told himself to leave, he even cued the horse to step back, but he must have also cued the animal to remain at the halt, because five minutes later, he was still staring.

She'd gotten out of the water and was kneeling on a towel, letting the long, wet ropes of her hair down from her bun. Even wet, her hair was golden, falling in abundance to her hips. She raised her hands to work up a lather in her hair, the action causing her breasts to hike and shift gently. He surveyed the line of her back, graceful and strong but mouthwateringly feminine, too. Sitting on his horse, he had the urge to bite her nape, to steady her hips with his hands, bend her over, and show her what pleasures could make a lazy summer afternoon perfect. When it was time to rinse, he was almost relieved to see her slip back into the water, her rounded derriere flashing in the sunlight as she dove under.

With a distinct sense of disorientation, the earl found the fortitude to nudge his mount quietly back up the path, but he was in such a condition that the walk was the only feasible gait.

And he was smiling like the lunatic he feared he was becoming, more pleased and relieved with his body's reaction than he could have admitted to another living soul. A half hour later, he and Caesar ambled into the stable yard, the echo of that smile still in his mind.

"Same drill tomorrow, Stevens." The earl handed off the reins.

"Tomorrow's the Sabbath," Stevens reminded him, clearly bewildered.

"Sabbath." The earl frowned. "My apologies. Monday, I suppose. We'll have crews on the grounds to work on various projects then, as well. When the roof and the haying are done, the stables are due for some attention."

"Aye, milord." Stevens sounded less than enthusiastic about a schedule put forth by a man who could forget the day of the week.

Well, thought the earl, suppressing a grin, when a man experienced his first conscious trouser salute in more than two years, the day of the week faded in significance by comparison.

"My lord." Steen bowed to him at the front door.

"You have a visitor in the library. He, um…" Steen found something worth examining on the earl's sweaty riding gloves. "He arrived with luggage, my lord."

"Did he leave a card?" Luggage?

"He said he was family." Steen's entire bald head suffused with pink.

"Ah." For Steen to have asked exactly how this fellow was family would have been rude, of course, and one couldn't *be* rude to the earl's family. "I will see him; send along some refreshment—lemonade, sandwiches, a sweet or two."

His father, having suffered a heart seizure just weeks previously, would not have journeyed north. His brother Gayle, having just married, would not have journeyed two feet from his bride, left to his own devices. It had to be his youngest brother, Valentine.

"So, Val," the earl strode into the library then stopped dead. "*Amery?*" The man before him was not tall, green-eyed with wavy dark hair, as each of the surviving Windham sons were. He was tall, blond, blue-eyed, and the most poker-faced individual St. Just had ever met, for all that his features had the austere beauty of a disappointed angel. "To what, in all of God's creation, do I owe the honor of a visit from my niece's stepfather?"

"Pleased to see you, as well, St. Just." Viscount Amery put down the book he'd been perusing and turned his gaze on his host. "Or should I say, Rosecroft?"

"You should not." The earl frowned, advancing into the room. "What have I done to be graced with your presence?" He didn't mean to sound so unwelcoming, but he was surprised. No cavalry officer liked surprises.

"I am here at the request of the Duchess of Moreland and at the request of my viscountess, both of whom are fretting over you—and with some grounds, I'd say."

"Good of them, though I am well enough."

"You are thinner, you appear fatigued to me, and your fences, St. Just, are sagging."

"Ever the charmer, eh, Amery?" The earl arched an eyebrow, and Amery arched his in response. Douglas Allen was the most unflappable, steady, serious person St. Just had encountered. The man had had the balls to stop a wedding between St. Just's brother Gayle Windham, the Earl of Westhaven, and Douglas's present wife, Guinevere, mother to Rose, the only Moreland grandchild. The wedding had badly needed to be stopped in the opinion of all save the Duke of Moreland, whose conniving had brought it about in the first place.

"I do try." Douglas picked his book back up and put it in its proper place on the library shelves. "Rose is with your parents, and Welbourne is between planting and harvest, as most of the country is, so my lady could spare me. She suggested Rosecroft might be a bit of a challenge after three years in Helmsley's care. I see she did not exaggerate."

"She did not," the earl said, grateful for plain speaking. He was also grateful when a knock on the door, heralding the tray of refreshments, gave him a moment to collect his thoughts and get him and his guest seated.

"So how bad is it?" Douglas asked as he took a long swallow of cold lemonade.

"Bad enough." The earl passed Douglas a sandwich. "The fences are indicative of the situation as a whole: sagging but still functional."

"You've established priorities?"

"Haying, the roof on the manor, the stables, the tenant farms, a dock on the Ouse."

"What of your home farm?" Douglas reached for his lemonade and paused. "Assuming you have a home farm?"

"I do. For some reason, my steward hasn't seen fit to tour it with me."

"Best remedy that." Douglas met his eyes. "You don't want to be buying your eggs and cheese when you've all this land. What of a home wood?"

"There is plenty of wood on the property, but again, it isn't something my steward has put on our agenda."

"This far north, you'll need as much firewood as you can harvest without depleting your wood. If you see to it now, the deadfall you cut will be seasoned by the new year."

"Good point. But before we descend further into the catalog of my oversights and my steward's short-comings, how fares your wife and your stepdaughter? And you have your heir now, if I remember aright."

Relief flashed briefly in his guest's eyes, as if Douglas hadn't been sure his host was to be trusted to manage the burden of interfamilial civilities.

"My wife thrives," Douglas replied, "as does our son, though he keeps his mother up at all hours with demands for sustenance and comfort."

St. Just grinned. "Typical male, or so Her Grace would say."

"And so his mother says."

St. Just chewed his own sandwich, thinking the chicken could have done with some seasoning and the bread with some mustard, or butter, or even pot cheese, but it was filling, and the journey had no doubt left his guest hungry.

"Your niece has specifically told me to warn you she will hop on her pony and come introduce herself should you fail to remedy the oversight in the near future." Douglas eyed the tray as if considering a second sandwich.

"My apologies to Miss Rose. I assume her Uncle Valentine calls upon her regularly?"

"As does her Uncle Gayle, with her newly acquired Aunt Anna, but you are her father's oldest brother, and she wants to meet *you*."

"I am her father's illegitimate half brother. She can have a happy and meaningful life without making my acquaintance, though for the record, it isn't that I haven't wanted to meet her."

"She's a little girl, St. Just," Douglas said gently. "Little children forgive anything, even things they should not. You put this off much longer, and you will hurt her feelings, and as the current holder in her eyes of the title Papa, I cannot allow that."

"You came all this way to scold me for not meeting my niece?"

"In part." Douglas nodded, apparently finding that a more than adequate justification for a two-hundred-mile journey in high summer. "But also because the ladies were concerned. Moreover, it is beastly hot in the south, and I have never seen this part of the world."

"You would have me think you're rambling the countryside for your own pleasure?" The earl stood, cocking an eyebrow.

Douglas stood, as well. "It pleases your family to be concerned for you, but your brothers could not come north. No matter whether you are a half brother, one-eighth brother, or less, you are a brother to them. I would not whine too loudly, were I you."

The earl had the grace to keep silent, knowing Douglas had arrived to his title after the death of his older brother, then lost his younger brother shortly thereafter under miserable circumstances.

"Point taken. Well, I am glad you are here, despite appearances to the contrary. Let's get you settled in upstairs, and perhaps you'd like a bath before supper?"

"A bath." The viscount closed his eyes. "Please God, a bath."

"We've bathing chambers upstairs," the earl assured him as they gained the front hallway. "The water is piped from the roof cistern and one of the few luxuries to be had here. Did you come by horseback or by coach?"

"Horseback. My great and good friend, Sir Regis, is enjoying the hospitality of your stables as we speak."

"Your room will be in here." St. Just opened a door and led Douglas into a sunny, pleasant back bedroom. A soft leather satchel and a pair of saddlebags sat on the bed, the water pitcher was full, and the windows had been left open to admit a soft breeze.

"Lovely, and that bed looks like it will serve for a much-needed nap while my bathwater is heating."

"I'll leave you to it, then." The earl glanced around

the room, hoping it was adequately prepared. "We keep country hours here, and it will be just the three of us at dinner."

It wasn't until Douglas was soaking in a lavender scented bath that it occurred to him to wonder just who the *three of us* at dinner might be.

⤲

Leaving his guest, the earl struggled with a sudden, irrational temper. He liked Amery as well as he liked any man of his acquaintance, save his brothers, of course, but he did *not* like having the peace and privacy of his new home destroyed. He did *not* like unannounced visits from distant relations by marriage. He did *not* like having his routine upended; he did *not* like…

He wasn't in the kitchen, where he'd intended to go. He'd been so lost in controlling a seething, disproportionate irritability, he'd taken himself to the stables, where all three geldings, along with Amery's bay, were lounging in their stalls to avoid the worst heat of the day. He stepped into Caesar's stall and rested his head against the horse's muscular neck.

"Steady on," he reminded himself, taking a deep breath. God above, if his men could only see him now. Raging over nothing and going two years without so much as thinking of bedding a woman. The malaise in him included his poor sleeping, too, he supposed. In active service, he'd slept in trees, on church benches, and frequently on his horse. Now he couldn't find sleep in a damned canopied featherbed. And when he did sleep, the nightmares came.

But it was getting better, he assured himself,

stroking the gelding's neck. The rages weren't so frequent, and they were more swiftly over. There was an occasional decent night's rest, and just this afternoon, at the pond…

It was definitely getting better. He never expected to be quite the man he was, or the man he'd thought he'd been, but Fairly, who served more or less as the family physician, had been right: He wasn't going mad. He was recovering slowly from years of serving his nation.

On that reassuring thought, he turned his steps to the kitchen, there to inform Cook they would be three for dinner for the foreseeable future.

Three

"Of course I can't make you go to services." Douglas glared at his host over what passed for Sunday breakfast. "But you are a grown man who should at least be on nodding terms with his Creator, for pity's sake."

The earl marshaled his patience while he subdued a stale scone with more butter, then forced himself to consider Douglas's "advice."

"You will tell Her Grace I am not going to services. Not very sporting of you, Amery."

"I will not tell your mother you are acting like a petulant eight-year-old boy," Douglas shot back. "But can't you consider this in the way of reconnaissance? Your neighbors won't call on you until you make the first move, so services are a simple way to get the lay of the land."

"I'll go, but I will be damned if I'm dragging Winnie along with us, so don't even try. She has the lay of the land, thank you very much."

"I would not dream of imposing on Miss Winnie's time." Douglas sat back, but then his eyes narrowed.

"You don't want to bring Winnie along because you don't know if the good folk of Rosecroft will accept her."

The earl dragged a hand over his face. "In deference to the Lord's Day, Amery, and your august presence, I have not yet ridden on this fine summer morning. You try my patience with your insights, well intended though they are. Perhaps you could wait until I've graced the back of at least one horse before you start peering into my soul?"

"My apologies." Douglas poured them both another cup of tea. "I do not mean to pry, but rather to commend your caution. For the first five years of her life, Rose had not one playmate. She was not taken to services, she did not attend family functions, she existed only in the confines of the Oak Hall estate and within the ambit of her mother's love. Winnie hasn't even had that much. You are right not to let the world get an open shot at her just yet."

"The world will never get an open shot at Winnie, if it's left to me."

"Nor at Rose. When do we depart for church?"

St. Just glanced at the wall clock. "About thirty minutes, which gives us time to finish dressing and tack up."

"I'll see you in the stables, then." Douglas withdrew, leaving the earl to frown at his tea.

A raging cockstand yesterday, church today, the earl thought with a pained grin. Somehow both were related to fixing what was wrong with him, but he'd be damned if he could figure out how.

∽❦∾

"I am off to compose an epistle to my wife," Douglas announced as the horses were led back to their stalls two hours later. "Also one to my daughter. Might I enclose something from you, as well?"

"Don't seal your missive." St. Just sighed, knowing Douglas would wear him down. "I'll dash something off tonight for my niece." The words "my niece" felt odd on his tongue. Not bad, just odd. "But how does one write to a little girl?"

"One writes clearly and sincerely. She'll never enjoy correspondence if you don't make it an honest exchange, and I can assure you, you will receive a reply."

"I have never aspired to correspond with the ladies," the earl said as they wound through the neglected gardens. "My sisters received some efforts from me, but Bart was a better correspondent."

"According to your brothers, you have all but given up doing anything with the ladies." Douglas paused to sniff at a lone rose. "I could do something with these gardens, if you like. Rose and I share an interest in ornamental horticulture. Miss Winnie might like to join me, as poking at the dirt has ever fascinated most children."

"As the tweeny no doubt believes in the requirement to rest on the Sabbath, you are welcome to entertain Winnie any way you like. She wanders though, so keep a close eye on her."

"I have been trained by the best." Douglas's eyes warmed with humor. "But it is a nice day to wander."

"I'm going to wander off to that stone wall behind the stables and see what progress I can make. I'll see you at tea."

Behind the stables, the earl—stripped to his waist and wrestling with sizeable rocks—was pleased Amery hadn't wanted to join him. While it had been a pleasure to ride back from church with the man, and church had been a worthwhile sortie—despite the number of young ladies he'd seen casting him looks there—that much socializing created a need for solitude. Then, too, Douglas had the habit of somehow being a very quiet, undemanding guest, and yet hard as hell on the nerves anyway.

The earl had just heaved a rock to waist height, intending to position it at the top of the wall, when Miss Farnum came striding into sight around the end of the barn wall.

"My lands!"

So unexpected was the sight of the lady in a soft green walking dress, he barely managed to put the rock on the wall and not on his booted foot. Her hair was neatly gathered at her nape, and she looked in every way tidily turned out, but rough leather work gloves graced her hands.

"You're not going to help me with this wall, are you?" The earl reached for his shirt, but slowly, knowing it was naughty of him in the extreme. He took his time deciding where the armholes went and figuring out just how a man managed to don such a piece of attire, all the while watching from the corner of his eye while Miss Farnum gazed at him wide-eyed.

"Ye gods. You need more meat on such a gloriously healthy frame, my lord."

"I need more meat?" No coy pretenses from Miss Farnum. She stared at him shamelessly as he shrugged into his shirt, leaving it unbuttoned in deference to the… heat.

"You most assuredly do need a bit more flesh. Perhaps I can remedy the situation while I am in your kitchen."

"Sit with me?" The earl gestured to the stone wall, knowing it was a graceless offer. Ladies did not sit on rocks with half-naked, sweaty men, title be damned. Miss Farnum, however, plopped down on the wide, flat surface of the wall the earl had finished putting to rights.

"Have you and Cook parlayed regarding your shared territory?" the earl asked, noting again the work gloves on Miss Farnum's hands. They were so incongruous with the graceful, smiling rest of her, but they somehow made her look… dear.

"Cook is not pleased with the state of your household, my lord. You lack a housekeeper, and so Cook is constantly having to intervene with the maids, and with Steen, and among other domestics outside the kitchen."

"Would she rather be a housekeeper? Or something like it?" He appropriated the place beside her, sitting closely enough that their thighs touched. His entire attention wanted to focus on the sensation of her leg brushing against his, while she seemed unaware of the contact.

Miss Farnum frowned. "Cook might be receptive to such a notion. A cook is an authority only in the kitchen itself, whereas the housekeeper's authority is much broader. She would probably consider it a promotion."

"Were I at all impressed with her culinary efforts,

I would hesitate to propose any changes, but as a cook, she is pedestrian at best." He picked up a skin of water and frowned at it. "I am compelled by manners to offer you a drink, but I have only the one skin."

"A drink?" she asked, her gaze raking his face and no doubt taking in the results of his exertions. And as she watched, St. Just tilted his head back and held the skin out at arm's length, aiming a cool, clear stream of water directly into his open mouth.

"I've never seen such a thing! Did you come across this while on the Peninsula?"

"I did. Would you like to try it?" Oh, yes, he was feeling naughty indeed, and worse still, he was enjoying himself.

She looked intrigued but dubious. "What if I miss?"

"I'll do the aiming. Open your mouth."

"This isn't dignified," she muttered but obediently tilted her head back and opened her mouth. He held the skin out to arm's length again and shot a stream of water directly on target.

"My goodness!" Miss Farnum laughed, looking pleased with herself and just, perhaps, with him. "I've done something new today. My thanks, my lord."

"You are welcome." He casually took another drink, trying to blot from his mind the picture of Emmaline Farnum, mouth open, eyes laughing as she gazed at him expectantly. Other very erotic contexts in which she might have assumed that same pose had come instantly into his mind's eye, and his system had begun to hum with the possibilities. Emmie Farnum, naked and laughing up at him; Emmie peeking at him as her mouth…

And why did his imagination choose *now* of all times to recover its prurient inclinations?

"What brings you to my stables on this lovely Sunday afternoon?" the earl asked, inhaling a pleasant nose full of roses and well-scrubbed female.

"Not a what." Miss Farnum shifted on her rock. "A who. If I'm to be here tomorrow morning, then it made sense to bring Herodotus over. My baking days are Monday, Wednesday, and Thursday, and I deliver on Tuesday and Friday."

"You have that much custom?" the earl asked, hopping off his rock and turning to squint at the line of the stone wall. "Does this look level to you?"

Miss Farnum obliged the second question by hopping down from her seat, as well, and standing directly in front of him, her back to him so she could survey the same portion of wall.

"You mean the part you've done out from the building?"

"From there"—he raised an arm over her shoulder— "to there." He moved his arm so his linen-clad bicep nearly brushed her ear, and angled his neck so his mouth was less than an inch from her skin.

"It's level in relation to the ground," she decided. "Which means it slopes away from the building as the land does, which is what you want it to do."

"It does," the earl said, frowning. She was tall for a female, but the top of her head would still fit nicely under his chin were she to turn around and wrap her arms around his waist.

"It will be very handsome when you have it repaired." She did turn then but stepped away, as well, flashing that warmhearted smile at him. "Herodotus will be pleased you take the appearance of his quarters so seriously."

The earl found himself smiling back, if for no other reason than the slight throbbing in his groin. "You'll introduce me to this fine specimen?"

"Come along." She gestured with a gloved hand, then seemed to notice for the first time her hand wasn't bare. "My lord, the next time a woman comes calling wearing work gloves, will you bring her attention to the matter before she embarrasses herself?"

Except Miss Farnum wasn't embarrassed; she was amused as she pulled off the gloves and preceded him into the stables.

"This fine gentleman is my partner, Herodotus. Herodotus, may I make known to you the Earl of Rosecroft?" Long fuzzy ears, long yellow teeth, long whiskers, and a long, slow perusal met the earl's gaze.

"Herodotus, my pleasure."

"You aren't going to laugh at my mule? He's a very good mule, a gift from the old earl when I moved to the cottage."

St. Just reached out a hand toward the animal. "Mules are hardier than horses, footwise, but they also survive on the worst rations and can make do with far less water. They are canny about danger and brave when it comes to a fight. Pound for pound, most are stronger than horses and have greater endurance, though most are not quite as fleet. I am pleased to make Herodotus's acquaintance. He will give my juvenile miscreants someone to look up to."

"These are your stock?" Miss Farnum asked,

moving to stand by Wulf's stall. The gelding roused himself from his doze along the back wall and came to investigate. She waited patiently for the initial sniffing-over to be completed then found a spot under the horse's chin that wanted scratching. "Oh, you are a love, aren't you? And so handsome, and such eyes you have. Won't you tell me your name?"

The horse was making the kind of faces the earl might have made were Miss Farnum to be running her hands over him with such enthusiasm.

"That shameless tramp is Beowulf," the earl informed her. "His cohorts in crime are Ethelred, whom you've met, and Caesar, who bestirred himself to take me to services today. Which reminds me, why weren't you there this morning?"

She moved to Red's stall and obliged the horse with an ear-scratching in silence. Her companion waited, content to enjoy the sight of his horses flirting with her. She fit in here, somehow, fit in in a way the earl wasn't sure he himself did.

"I do not attend. I never have, down here. In Scotland, it was a different matter, of course. I am on good terms with Mr. Bothwell, as he is a very amiable gentleman, but I never got in the habit, even when my aunt was alive."

The earl came to stand beside her but faced out, hooking his elbows on the top of Red's open half door. "You mean you are not welcome?"

"I don't know, and it hasn't been important to find out. I am content the good folk hereabouts will buy my breads and pies. Asking them to sit in church with me could jeopardize my livelihood."

"Why should they hold you in such low esteem? You cannot help your familial circumstances any more than I can help mine."

"My aunt might have been tolerated for the sake of the old earl and his countess, but her dealings with Helmsley were not kept private, so I am tarred with the same brush. You should know this before you put Winnie in my care even temporarily."

He settled his hand on her shoulder and turned her to face him, then waited until she met his gaze. This topic had routed his wayward inclinations quite thoroughly.

"I do not give that"—he snapped his fingers in her face—"for the opinion of the dames and squires who show up at church merely to be seen. Winnie cares for you; that is all that matters for the present."

"I see."

Catching himself and realizing his temper was threatening to flare again, the earl retreated a step. "I do not mean to state my position with such emphasis," he said, busying his fingers closing the buttons of his shirt. "I am intolerant of intolerance, if that makes sense."

Her gaze was glued to his chest as he took the narrow strip of flesh from her view. He'd been arguably indecent to allow her to see even that much, but she wasn't turning up missish on him, thank the gods.

"I'd guess your men listened when you gave an order."

"All good soldiers obey orders. I was not as good at command as my brother, but I became adequate." He turned away to stuff his shirt into his waistband, though he knew that presented her with damp material covering his sweaty back.

"I did not know you served with a sibling," she said, moving to give some attention to Caesar. "Was that better or worse?"

"Excellent question," the earl replied, watching as Caesar fell under her spell. "It was better while Bart was alive, and worse—much worse—when he died. After we broke the sieges he'd seek me out, and to see him—just to see him—steadied me." He fell silent, wondering when the conversation had gotten so... pointless. Cuidad Rodrigo had been years ago and as recent as his last nightmare, but it was not a fit topic of conversation with a lady.

"You have not forgotten those sieges and it shows," his companion said. "In your eyes there are shadows. But that is a price soldiers pay, is it not? And for that price, you have the knowledge all the squires and dames in their tidy little churches can continue to exercise their ignorance and pettiness in safety."

He paced off, turning his back to her. She had a way of exposing wounds with her gentle tone and soft words, wounds he didn't realize were still so close to the surface.

"I am sorry." She took his hand in her own and squeezed his fingers. "I did not mean to make your sacrifice sound meaningless, but I comprehend it can feel unappreciated." He glanced down at their joined hands then raised her bare knuckles to his lips and kissed her hand before replacing it on his arm.

"You are a dangerous woman, Miss Farnum. I have wondered for two years why I continue to be so easily provoked at odd moments. Why the sight of a mother shaming a boy for wetting his trousers, or the image of a former soldier without his legs turned beggar should send me into a towering rage. I think you have just provided part of the explanation."

"Those things should make us angry, but there must be a balance, I think, such that the sight of a child like Winnie, safe and happy on her own turf, can restore a little of your peace, as well."

"You echo the sentiments of the only physician with whom I've broached the matter," the earl said, leading the lady from the stables toward a particularly grand oak. "He said one doesn't cure eight years of war with a few months of peace, not for a nation and not for a soldier."

"Would that countries had physicians. I take it you enjoy Bronwyn? She hasn't become a nuisance and worn her welcome thin?"

"I enjoy her," the earl said, more than willing to let the topic shift now. "I've always been the son of a duke, so a certain amount of social deference has always been my experience. Having this silly little earldom conferred upon me has meant that, instead of most people toadying to me, now everybody does. I do not enjoy it, and little Winnie is a refreshing change."

"But you enjoyed having rank in the military."

"I did not particularly." He was certain of this much. "If I wanted to be of sufficient consequence to be stationed more or less in my brother's vicinity, then I needed a commission."

"And that's why you went, isn't it?" Miss Farnum's smile was sad as a little grumble of thunder sounded off in the distance. "You didn't go out of a burning desire to defeat the Corsican, you went to protect your brother, and you were successful in protecting him from every hazard save himself."

"Just so, Miss Farnum." He glanced at the sky then bowed slightly. Unease was sweeping up from his innards, though whether it was due to the approaching storm or the lady's keen insight, he could not say. "If you will excuse me, Lord Amery will be wondering at my whereabouts. My thanks for your company, and I will expect to see you tomorrow at some point."

❧

"I want to write to Rose." Winnie announced her intention as she bounced into the library near midnight, pleased to find the earl was up, too, and sitting at the desk in his shirtsleeves.

"Good evening, Miss Winnie." St. Just took off a pair of gold-rimmed spectacles and eyed her balefully. "Has no one told you to knock?"

"It's late," Winnie pointed out, her nightdress flapping in the breeze coming in through the window. "The house is dark, and I did not think anybody was in here."

"So you've come to find writing implements?" He frowned, glancing at the clock.

"I was going to go see the horses first. The front door creaks, and the kitchen door is usually locked, but if I leave these doors unlocked, I can get back in."

"Your talent for reconnaissance is impressive. Well, come here."

"Am I to get a lecture?" Winnie cautiously approached the big desk, only to find herself scooped up and deposited in the earl's lap.

"I am supposed to write to Rose, too," he said, "but I didn't know what to say. Have you any suggestions?"

Winnie settled on his knees, deciding she liked this perspective. In all her varied life, she'd never sat in the lap of an adult male whom she actually liked, and she rather thought there were things to recommend about it. She felt safe, for one thing. Safe and protected, and better, she felt powerful, just like when she was up on old Roddy's back. The earl smelled good, for another, like meadows and flowers and security. And he was warm and comfortable, at least compared to a tree limb.

"So what would you like to write?" he prompted, setting paper, pen, and ink before her. He reached his long arms around her to do this, and Winnie noticed he'd turned his sleeves back, leaving his forearms revealed for her inspection.

"Your arms are hairy. We should write, Dear Rose."

"Is this your letter or mine?" the earl asked, glancing at his forearms.

"Mine. Dear Rose. My name is Winnie, and I live at Rosecroft. Your papa is visiting, but I would like to borrow him while he is here."

"Slow down," the earl growled, setting pen to paper. "You want to borrow Douglas?"

"Your papa is nice," Winnie went on. "I would give him back when he leaves. I did not ask him, because he is *your* papa. I do not have a pony, but if I did, I would let you make him a knight. Sincerely, Bronwyn Farnum."

The earl finished writing, sanded the page, and sat back to arrange Winnie crosswise on his lap, which let her see his face.

"You are jealous of my niece?" he asked, frowning.

"She has a papa, a mama, and an uncle. I have Miss Emmie, who is my friend, but that's all. I like Lord Amery because he listens and climbs trees, but I only want to borrow him."

"You want to borrow him for what?" the earl pressed, shifting her again but keeping an arm around her as he did.

"To be my papa," Winnie said, trying to keep the exasperation from her voice. "He is not Rose's real papa, so I thought she might not mind if he wasn't mine either."

"I see." The earl's frown was becoming thoughtful, but Winnie didn't think he was seeing much at all. The earl was not the quickest fellow to her mind, but he had horses, and he was bringing Miss Emmie to the manor. And he had not ever, ever lied—yet.

A large male hand began to make slow circles on her back, and Winnie felt her eyes wanting to close. "I will send your letter, Winnie, but you must help me write mine." Winnie sighed, leaned against the earl's chest, and let her lashes flutter down.

"I'll help," she said. "Lord Amery says Rose likes stories about her real papa. He was Lord Victor. I don't know any."

"My letter might go something like this," the earl began, his voice a soothing rumble in the ear Winnie lay against his chest. "Dear Rose, Your papa has come to visit, and we are very glad to see him. By we, I include in my household Miss Bronwyn Farnum, a very pretty and intelligent little girl who is kind to animals and nimble at climbing trees. Your papa told me she reminds him of you, but I saw Winnie first, and he cannot have her. She is mine now, though while your papa is here, Winnie will be all that is polite and friendly to him. I hope Sir George is doing well and not eating too much summer grass, and I hope your brother and mother are thriving. You must look after them until I can visit this fall. Uncle Devlin."

"Devlin?" Winnie murmured through a sleepy smile.

"My mama named me Devlin. Like Miss Farnum is Emmaline."

"And I am Bronwyn, at least to Miss Emmie." Winnie nodded, eyes closing again. "I don't suck my thumb anymore." She yawned and felt her seat rising as the earl came to his feet. "Should I get down?" she asked, blinking.

"Hush. I'm just moving to a rocking chair, and you are just going to sleep."

⟡

St. Just rocked slowly, thinking of all the nights when he'd been unable to sleep or afraid to sleep. Winnie was soon snoring softly, her mouth slightly open, her features angelic in repose. As he carried her through the house, he wondered what would keep a little girl up until midnight and what she would have done if he weren't still at his desk.

Probably fallen asleep in the hayloft, he mused as he tucked her in.

He made his way to the library, lit an extra candle, penned a slightly different note to his niece, then found his bed. For the second time in less than a week, the earl of Rosecroft slept peacefully through the night.

And for the first time in two years, he awoke with a cockstand he could hang a bridle on. Seeing the sun had yet to rise, he rolled to his back, savoring the fullness in his groin. This wasn't just a morning salute, he concluded, as fragments of a dream drifted through his awareness. A pond and Miss Emmaline Farnum, naked and sleek as an otter, then Miss Farnum, mouth open, still naked…

He pushed the sheets aside and began to stroke himself lazily, content to enjoy the simple fact of arousal, not even intending any pleasure beyond that. But his body, too long indifferent to any source of erotic inspiration, had found its rhythm, and so he continued, letting the arousal build and build as he thought of Emmaline Farnum's nape, of the soft swell of her breasts, the lovely pink delicacy of her nipples, wet and ruched as she lifted her hands to her hair.

His breathing deepened, and he recalled the wet nest of her pubic hair, slightly darker than the mane she tucked into such a deceptively demur bun. Pleasure bore down on him as his mind's eye flashed on her buttocks slipping beneath the water in a perfect, sweet pair of curves.

On a soft groan, he came, a lovely, voluptuous experience of intense satisfaction that left him relaxed, pleased, and so profoundly relieved he felt his throat constricting with gratitude. Some losses were so personal they could not be discussed, but they could be contemplated at grim and miserable length while a man tried to tell himself they didn't matter.

Whatever else had been taken from him, it seemed the simple sexual pleasure of being male was no longer on that list. Joy welled up to join with relief, and the earl prayed the day would become unbearably hot, just so he could again picture Emmaline Farnum at her bath.

He got up to wash, dress, and start his day wondering if Emmie was already pothering about in his kitchen.

How did he reconcile that cheerful, brisk woman with the wood nymph to whom he owed such a glorious sunrise? The same woman, he realized as he dragged a brush through his hair, who would be sleeping under his roof that very night?

Ah, well, he concluded as he descended the steps in charity with the world, there were worse problems than how to behave around a luscious woman.

❦

By ten o'clock in the morning, St. Just was convinced every problem imaginable had chosen that day to visit itself upon him. Douglas had brought up the idea that Winnie needed an adult escort into town if she wasn't to be tempted to wander there on her own. Caesar looked to be starting on an abscess, making the earl regret his impromptu steeplechase home from church the previous day. His work crews had appeared, but Holderman for some reason was nowhere to be found, and breakfast had been again nothing but the damnable scones and butter.

He was mad enough to spit nails when Emmaline Farnum appeared at the large house cistern, a tray of mugs and a plate of cookies in her hands.

"I do not mean to disturb you." She smiled at him as he scowled in her direction. "The heat is building quickly today, and I thought lemonade would not go amiss."

"Lemonade." As if lemonade would locate his steward. He reached for a mug then gestured for his two assistants to do the same. "We can enjoy the drink while puzzling out the whereabouts of both Timmens, who was to repair the fountain, and Holderman, my steward, using the term loosely."

"Holderman's gone back to his uncle," Mortimer, the older of the earl's assistants, volunteered. "Or summat like."

"He's scarpered." The other fellow grinned. "My sister's husband's brother works for old Holderman, and the nepphie's dog lazy, by him."

The earl's temper threatened to seize the day, and he shifted his gaze to the blue heavens. "It appears I am without a steward, without a mechanic, and without the means to replace either."

"You are not without resources," Miss Farnum said, collecting empty mugs. "Perhaps you'd walk me back to the kitchens while the gentlemen enjoy a few minutes in the shade, my lord?"

He had the presence of mind not to explode when his laborers were within earshot, but once they'd rounded the corner of the house, he stopped and glared at Miss Farnum.

"Are you humoring me, madam?"

"Good heavens." She tossed a glance up at him. "Why would I bother to do that?"

"Because," he ground out, forced to move his feet because she was moving hers, "I am almost angry enough to fire the lot of them, pack up my horses, and ride back down to London."

"If you think that's what you should do, no one can stop you. I can, however, offer you something to eat before you go."

"What?" He blinked, feeling like a bear who'd just realized he was charging in the wrong direction. "Food?"

"If you wouldn't mind?" Miss Farnum, carrying the tray, gestured with her chin toward the kitchen door. She stepped back so he could hold it for her before following her into the cool interior of the big kitchen.

"Hello, Rosecroft." Winnie, wearing a heavily floured pinafore, beamed at him from where she stood on a chair at the big wooden worktable. "I'm rolling the pie dough."

"And doing an excellent job," Miss Farnum piped up before turning her gaze on the earl. "Sit you down, milord, and we'll plot your campaign."

"You *are* humoring me." But his disgust was laced with reluctant humor.

"I am feeding you," she corrected him, setting a plate down before him with two fat pastries on it and more cookies. "Eat, and all will look better. Cider or lemonade?"

"Either." He bit into a pastry only to find it was filled with ham, eggs, a little bacon, and some seasonings that made it a considerable improvement over its previous incarnation—and worlds beyond a mean old scone.

"Better?" Miss Farnum asked, plunking down a tankard of lemonade before him.

"Much," he said around a mouthful of culinary heaven. "The pastries, that is. They are much improved."

"You will be, too." She flashed him a grin. "Not so much flour, wee Winnie, and don't forget a dash of cinnamon, cloves, nutmeg, and allspice."

"You are making apple tarts?" The earl's nose fairly twitched with anticipation.

"We are," Winnie said, "but you get dessert only if you eat your vegetables."

"I will eat my vegetables. I'd also best be on my way back to the ongoing debacle that is my fountain."

"Why not send Stevens off to collect Timmens from his fishing instead, as it appears you won't need Stevens in the stables for the present?" Miss Farnum suggested from where she was watching Winnie roll out dough. "And as for Holderman's disappearance, good riddance, I'd say. My guess is you could call upon Lord Amery to serve at least temporarily and see a great deal more accomplished."

"I cannot impose on a guest, Miss Farnum."

"Why can't you?" The voice was masculine and slightly amused. Douglas sauntered in, hands in his pockets, cuffs turned back. "I was prepared to ride out with you this morning but found you were not at the stables and not expected to ride before luncheon."

"Caesar's lame, and I cannot impose on you to serve as my land steward in Holderman's absence."

"Is the man ill?" Douglas reached for a cinnamon

cookie, closed his eyes, and sniffed at it before taking a bite. "Wonderful." He gestured with the remaining cookie. "My compliments."

"I'm making the pie dough." Winnie waved her rolling pin for emphasis.

"Miss Winnie, good morning." Douglas bent down and planted a loud smacker on her cheek. "You are going to abandon me for the charms of pie dough?"

"Only for today."

"I am desolated, but I can be revived by ample doses of cinnamon cookie. St. Just, how can I be of service?"

The earl blew out a breath and scrubbed the back of his neck with one hand. "The steward has departed for the comforts of his uncle's estate, and I have two crews, one of which is idling by the cistern; the other is supposedly mending wall, but I can't be sure of that, and the roofing fellows are supposed to be on grounds this morning, as well. Then, too, you reminded me I've yet to inspect my own home farm, and while I've ridden some of the paths in the wood, I can't say I've taken note of the deadfall... for starters."

Douglas looked like he was concentrating on something in the distance for a mere instant, then nodded his head.

"I can toddle by the stonemasons," he suggested, "then saddle up Regis and nip past the home farm, perhaps take a peek at the wood on the way. But what about the haying?"

"Damned haying." The earl closed his eyes in exasperation. "I don't know what kind of storage we have on the property, and I haven't seen a team of anything big enough to pull a hay wagon."

Miss Farnum glanced from the earl to the viscount. "The hay barn stands empty between the home farm and pastures, and Mr. Mortimer can bring a wagon and team tomorrow if you ask him. He might be able to scare up two, in fact, and some more crew, because his wife's people have their own small holding just up the river."

"Mortimer's the one with the nose?" the earl asked, snagging two more cookies.

"The one with the smile. Where shall I serve lunch, and did you expect the men to bring their own?"

"I did, or I told Holderman those were my terms. You can bring it…" He glanced up at the clock and saw the morning was half gone. "I'll come back to the house."

"And I can do likewise," Douglas chimed in. "Winnie, I will pine for the sight of you until then."

"'Bye, Lord Amery." She waved a floured paw but didn't look up from her dough.

"He will pine," the earl growled at Douglas's retreating back. "Winnie, you must learn to make a fellow work for your attention."

"I must?" Winnie did look up and blinked at him in disarming confusion. "But I like Lord Amery."

"I know." The earl made one last foray at the cookies. "And you want to borrow him for your temporary papa, you little traitor. I should have you court-martialed for treason."

"Treason?"

"High treason." The earl nodded then dipped his head to blow a rude noise against her neck. "Until luncheon."

Emmie watched him disappear, letting the back

door bang loudly in his wake, while Winnie's squeals of delighted indignation faded to a huge, bashful smile.

"So, Bronwyn, what shall we feed your admirers for lunch on this glorious summer day?"

"They like sweet things," Winnie observed, frowning at her pie dough. "Especially the earl. He ate a *lot* of cookies, Miss Emmie."

"He did, but he is a big, strong, hungry fellow, and this is his kitchen. He does like sweets, however, on that you are absolutely correct."

He liked sweetness, and if Winnie's conquest of him was any indication, he liked innocence, as well—two qualities Emmaline Farnum had not called her own for a good long, lonely, miserable while.

She cast her mind back to the previous day, to the sight of the earl half naked, sweating, his muscles bulging with exertion as he hefted rocks Emmie could never have budged. She ought to have been scandalized, but she'd been… fascinated. And then he'd asked her about his wall, standing so close to her she could feel the heat of him, feel his breath on her neck as he'd spoken virtually in her ear.

Indecent thoughts. A man who liked sweetness and innocence would be appalled to know how Emmie was recalling him, how she'd wanted him to turn his head just a fraction and put his mouth on her flesh. Emmie ought to be appalled herself.

She really ought to be.

Four

THE EARL GLANCED AROUND HIS DINNER TABLE AND felt a soothing sense of sweetness. The day had started well, then veered temporarily toward frustration, but soon righted itself. He was in good company, had consumed a wonderful meal, and felt a pleasant sense of accomplishment.

"If you gentlemen want to linger over your port, I can absent myself," Emmie volunteered. "The day has been very, very long, and my bed is calling me."

"You are adequately settled in?" the earl asked, rising as she gained her feet.

"I am. So I will bid you both a good night."

Douglas rose, as well, and wished her good night, but sat back down and nodded when the earl gestured with the decanter.

"She is such a lovely woman," Douglas observed. "I think the child owes much to her care."

"I don't know how much care she was able to take of Winnie." The earl frowned as he poured their drinks. "She is lovely. She does a better job with my apple tart recipe than I do, and I can promise you, Douglas, it won't be just stale scones for breakfast tomorrow."

They got out the cribbage board and whiled away another hour until they'd both won two games. As they ambled up the stairs, thunder rumbled in the distance and Douglas turned to survey his host.

"Will you be able to sleep?"

"Are you offering to read me a bedtime story, Amery?"

Douglas eyed him dispassionately. "I hired a fellow for my stables who served under you on the Peninsula. I have to warn him any time I plan to discharge a firearm, and thunderstorms unnerved him completely for the first six months of his employ. He hid in the wine cellars to get away from them. Flat reduced him to tears."

"They don't reduce me to tears. Let me light your candles." He preceded Douglas into his bedroom and lit a candle on each side of the bed, only to find Douglas regarding him solemnly as he moved around the room.

"I would, you know."

The earl paused by the door. "You would what?"

"I'd read you a bedtime story, beat you at cribbage, get you drunk. I'd do anything I could to make it better."

"There's nothing to do," the earl said, shaking his head. "But thank you for the sentiment."

"You're wrong."

"About?"

"There are things to do, and you are doing them. Now get to bed." Douglas's words were gentle. "You have more dragons to slay tomorrow, and you really must not compound your woes with avoidable exhaustion."

"Good night, Douglas." The earl blew him a kiss and left without a sound, but stood for a long moment in the corridor. Thunder did not reduce him to tears, but neither did it ease his slumbers. The storm was moving closer, lumbering across the hills at its own ponderous pace, but not yet upon them.

A belt of Dutch courage might see him more quickly asleep. He headed back downstairs to the library by the light of his single candle and found the brandy decanter on the sideboard. He had knocked back a tot of what really should have been sipped and was contemplating pouring another, when the library door opened slowly, and Miss Emmaline Farnum peered around the frame.

"I could not tell if there was a light in here or not," she said. "Will I disturb you if I get a book?"

"You will not." Of course he was lying. She eased around the door, closing it behind her, and glided in, carrying a single candle. The breeze from the windows winked it out, but not before the earl saw she was barefoot and clad only in a nightgown and wrapper.

"You are having trouble sleeping?" he asked, drawing the windows closed and offering her his candle to relight her own.

"I am. I am not used to having to be up or asleep or anything at a particular hour, as long as my baking is done."

"You and Winnie seem to run on your own clocks," the earl remarked, leaning a hip on his desk and watching her peering at book titles.

"I suppose we do have that in common, though I tried to always know where Winnie was, at least approximately. This summer..." She frowned at a book.

The earl shoved away from his desk. "This summer, Winnie has gotten more and more daring and more and more mobile. Douglas told me she's made a pest of herself in the livery and frequents the back porch of a certain old gentleman who gives her peppermints and has a dog."

"Grandpapa Hirschmann? He's not always sober, but probably harmless, as is his dog."

"I am imbibing as we speak." The earl gestured with his empty snifter. "Care to join me?"

"A lady does not drink strong spirits," she recited, taking out a book and opening it to the first page.

"A lady has the option of sleeping in as late as she pleases," the earl rejoined, watching her. "Miss Emmaline Farnum does not." He poured her a half finger into his glass and brought it to her, holding it up to her mouth. "Sip slowly."

"Your hands are cold." She frowned, wrapping her hand over his and bringing the glass to her lips. A clap of thunder close by had her pausing, listening, then sipping carefully.

"It warms the insides," the earl said, watching her with a slight smile.

"Oh, my lands." Emmie's gaze lifted to his. "It most assuredly does. The scent is lovely, the feel of the glass in the hand pleasurable, and the heat wonderful, but the actual flavor is rather... different."

"Its appeal grows, but I'd still caution you to sip slowly. Shall we sit?"

She looked torn, but then the thunder sounded again, causing the earl to hunch his shoulders in a brief involuntary bracing. After the artillery bombardments came the cavalry charges into the enemy's waiting lines of infantry…

"I will finish my drink," she said, taking a seat on the sofa. He pulled up a wing chair, and from the look on her face, surprised his guest by lifting his stocking feet to the coffee table.

He met her eyes with a challenging smile. "We men like to stomp around in our boots almost as much as we like to take our damned boots off at day's end."

"We women are of like mind." She wiggled the bare toes of one foot at him, smiling in the dim light. "But you do not enjoy storms, I think, whereas I do."

"I do not, but it's getting better. Slowly."

"Congratulate yourself on your good timing," she said, passing her brandy under her nose. "If you'd cut hay today, this storm would have been a nuisance. Now we'll probably have a few fair days, and your hay can be cut and stowed safely."

"Good point." The earl crossed his feet, wondering if this was what Amery and his wife discussed at the end of the day. "If the weather does remain fair, I would like to take Winnie with me into town soon."

Emmie nodded but pulled her feet up under her, making herself look smaller and even a little defensive.

"Miss Farnum, nobody will treat her badly in my company."

"They would not dare," she agreed, but her tone was off. A little flippant or bitter.

"But?" He sipped his drink and tried not to focus on the way candlelight glinted off her hair, which was swept back into a soft, disheveled bun at her nape.

"Winnie will parade around town with you," she said, an edge to her voice, "and have a grand time as long as you are at her side. Emboldened by your escort and her happy experiences, she will wander there again on her own, and sooner or later, somebody will treat her like the pariah she is."

"Go on." He was a bastard, but he hadn't considered this.

"I wonder, when I watch you and Lord Amery cosseting and fussing over Winnie, if I don't do her a disservice by allowing such attentions. She is desperate for your regard and affection, your time, and yet she cannot grow to depend on it. Still, her instincts are right: She is deserving of just such care, and had her father been a decent man, she would have had at least some of that from him."

"But?" The earl watched the emotions play across the lady's face and saw there was much she wasn't saying.

"But she cannot grow to rely on such from others," Emmie said, setting her drink down with a definite clink. "Sooner or later, you will return to London or take a wife, and Winnie will be sent off, to school, to a poor relation, to somewhere. Her future is not that of the legitimate daughter of an earl, and she must learn to rely on herself."

"As you have?" He watched as she rose and started pacing the room. She crossed her arms and hunched her shoulders, her expression troubled.

"Of course as I have." She nodded then startled as

thunder rumbled even closer. "Winnie deserves the hugs and cuddles and compliments and guidance you give her, but what she deserves and what life will hand her are two different things. She needs to know not every friendly gentleman who offers her a buss on the cheek can be trusted to respect her."

The first few drops of rain spattered the window, and the earl rose, securing the French doors and moving the candelabra to the mantel. Lightning flashed, two heartbeats went by, then thunder rumbled again.

"Miss Farnum." He waited until she'd turned to face him at the end of the space in which she paced, then held out her drink to her. "It warms and it steadies the nerves."

He let her approach him and didn't speak again until she was taking a sip of her drink, almost finishing it.

"Let us discuss these points you raise, as I think you are largely in a state over nothing." He paused as a great boom of thunder sounded, the breeze became a whistling wind, and rain began to pelt the windows in angry, slapping sheets. The candles flickered and went out, and in the dark, his companion gave a small, startled, "Yeep."

"I've dropped my drink," she said, a barely noticeable quaver in her voice. "My apologies, my lord. If you'll just…"

"Hold still." He hadn't meant to be giving a command, exactly. "If you move, you might step on the glass, and it will slice your foot open." He hoisted her easily against his chest, one arm under her knees, the other around her shoulders. "Arms around my neck," he growled, but rather than taking her to the door, he moved across the room to sit in a large, over-stuffed wing chair.

"You can put me down," she said, and in his arms, her spine was stiff, her body rigid.

"Soon," he replied, arranging her legs over the arm of the chair. "This will do for now."

"It will *not* do," she protested, but she put her arms around his neck, and St. Just would have sworn he felt her nose graze his collarbone.

As the rain pounded against the windows and the wind rattled the panes, the earl settled them in the chair. His hand moved in slow sweeps along her back, and his chin rested against her temple. He was stealing comfort from her under the guise of protecting her feet; he knew it; she likely knew it, as well.

"It occurs to me," he said as if she weren't ensconced in his very lap, "you labor under a misapprehension with regard to my role in Winnie's life." He tucked her a little more securely against him and heard her sigh.

"What is your role in Winnie's life?" She wasn't fighting him, but neither was she comfortable cuddled up in the chair with him. Well, she shouldn't be, but he wasn't about to turn her loose quite yet.

"I hold myself responsible for orphaning her," he said. "I must be as a parent to her and provide for her in every way a parent would. I owe her this, and to be honest, it... absolves me, somehow, to do it for her."

"You would take her from Rosecroft?" Her voice was careful, but a load of emotion was being kept in check.

"Sooner or later, children leave home, Emmaline

Farnum. I did not expect to spend my life under my father's roof. Winnie already has the beginnings of a lady's education. You forget her Aunt Anna will be a duchess. Winnie will be handsomely dowered, she'll make a come-out, she will have every advantage a young lady of good family deserves. It's no less than was done for my sister Maggie, who is my father's by-blow. The duchess insisted on it."

"You would do this for Winnie?" Emmie asked, and in his arms, the earl felt a tremor pass through her.

"Of course." She went silent but shuddered again. When it happened a third time, he realized the woman he was holding was near tears, and he forgot all about thunder, artillery, and infantry.

"Miss Farnum?" She burrowed into his chest. "Emmaline?" The crying was still not audible, but her body gave off heat, and when he bent his face to her, his nose grazed her damp cheek. "Hush, now." He gathered her into his embrace and stroked her hair back from her face in a long, slow caress. "You mustn't take on. Winnie won't go anywhere for many years, and you will always be dear to her."

He pattered on, no longer aware of the storm outside, so wrapped up was he with this much more personal upheaval. Her words came back to him, the words about Winnie's deserving and not having a papa's affections, Winnie's not being able to trust a gentleman's advances, Winnie's being sent away.

Winnie, indeed.

He let her cry, and soothed and comforted as best he could, but eventually she quieted.

"I am mortified," she whispered, her face pressed

to his chest. "You will think me an unfit influence on Bronwyn."

"I think you very brave," he said, his nose brushing her forehead. "Very resourceful but also a little tired of being such a good girl and more than a little lonely."

She said nothing for a moment but stopped her nascent struggle to get off his lap.

"You forgot, a lot embarrassed," she said at length. "I get like this—" She stopped abruptly, and he felt heat suffuse her face where her cheek lay against his throat.

"You get like this when your menses approach. I have five sisters, if you will recall." He tried without much success to keep the humor from his voice.

"And do they fall weeping into the lap of the first gentleman to show them simple decency?" Emmie asked sternly.

"If he were the first gentleman in years of managing on their own, then yes, I think they would be moved to tears." He rose in a smooth, unhurried lift and shifted them to the couch.

"My lands, you are strong."

"An officer should be fit," he said, letting her scramble off his lap, but only to tuck her in beside him, under his arm. "But if you think this loss of composure is daunting, you should be among recruits when a battle joins. The body, when in extreme situations, has no care for dignity."

"What do you mean?" She stirred but eventually got settled against his side.

"To be blunt, the stomach heaves, the bowels let go, the bladder, too. And here these young fellows are, worried about dignity when the French are charging in full cry."

"War flatters no one."

"Not often, anyway," the earl agreed, unable to resist the lure of her hair. He brought his hand up and pressed her head to his shoulder, then sifted his fingers through the soft, silky abundance. "Why is your hair not yet braided?"

"I do it last thing. My schedule yet called for drinks with the earl, creation of a dreadful stain on his carpet, and a fit of the weeps like nothing I can recall."

"You are entitled to cry. Sit forward, and I'll see to your hair."

His hands were gently taking down her bun, then finger combing through her long blond hair before she could protest. "One braid or two?"

"One." Which disappointed him, as two would take a few moments longer.

"Will you be able to sleep now?" he asked as he began to plait her hair.

"The storm is moving on. What of you?"

"I don't need much sleep." His answer was a dodge; he took his time with her hair. He hadn't looked for this interlude with her tonight, but after that exchange with Douglas, it eased him to know he could provide comfort to another.

And it angered him such a decent woman was so in need of simple affection.

"I cannot think of you as Miss Farnum," he said as he worked his way down her plait. "May I call you Miss Emmie as Winnie does?"

"You liken your status to that of a little girl?" Some

of the starch had come back into her voice, and the earl knew she was rebuilding her defenses.

"Emmie." He wrapped his arms around her from behind and pulled her against his chest, his cheek resting against hers. "There is no loss of dignity in what has gone between us here. I will keep your confidences, as you will keep mine."

"And what confidences of yours have passed to me?"

"You knew I was unnerved by the thunder. Douglas knew it, too, and offered to read me a bedtime story. You let me hold you."

"I should not have." She sighed, but for just the smallest increment of time, she let her cheek rest against his, as well, and he felt her accept the reality of what he'd said: Maybe not in equal increments, maybe not to the same degree, but the comfort had been shared, and that was simply good.

"I will light you up to your room." He sat back and let his arms slide from her waist. "But let me find your brandy glass before you leave this couch."

She waited while he lit candles, set her glass on the sideboard, then tugged her to her feet. He didn't drop her hand and didn't wrap it over his forearm. He kept his fingers laced with hers until they were outside her bedroom door.

"Shall I light your candles?" he asked, not moving to open the door.

"Not necessary. Until tomorrow, my lord."

He snorted involuntarily at that salvo.

"What?" She stood her ground.

"My name is Devlin." He resisted the urge to invite—or order—her to use his name. He just informed her of it, then lifted his hand to cradle her cheek before leaning in and kissing her forehead. He paused, so his breath fanned across her skin for a moment before he pressed his lips to the spot between and above her eyebrows.

For the sake of his own dignity, he needed to stop there. He brought his free hand up so her face was framed in his palms and told himself to step back. The sweet, female scent of her beguiled his wits; the feel of her skin so soft and warm against his callused palms stole his common sense. He angled his head and pressed his lips to her cheek, knowing that did he touch his mouth to hers, there would be no rescuing this moment. A carnal motive he could not have aspired to only days ago was threatening to trample honor, and some emotional need he could not even properly name was going to create disaster where a simple, good night kiss was intended.

By force of will, he managed to drop his hands. "Sweet dreams, Emmie Farnum."

She nodded and slipped into her room, closing the door silently behind her.

Her dreams were so sweet, she awoke again in tears and wondered how the earl's well-intended kindness could feel so devastatingly painful.

❧

"Vicar." The earl joined his guest in the spacious parlor that looked out over terraced gardens and a bright, sunny morning. "You are a man of your word."

"I am a man who needs some time away from my desk," Hadrian Bothwell replied, smiling genially as he turned from the window. Clergy were supposed to be charming up to a point, but Bothwell surpassed that point. He was also tall, blond, blue-eyed, younger, and altogether better looking than any vicar St. Just could recall from his youth.

"Mondays, I let myself go completely to pot." Bothwell's smile became a grin. "I make it a point to don neither jacket nor cravat. Tuesdays, I toddle around but avoid the church work."

"It never occurred to me the Sabbath is not a day of rest for a man of God. May I ring for some tea or perhaps some cider or lemonade?"

"Lemonade would be a guilty pleasure. Is your orangery producing, or did you import?"

"Despite inadequate care, the orangery is making an effort." The earl signaled the footman and rejoined his guest. "Shall we be seated?"

"You've such lovely views here. There's a great deal of chatter at the pub regarding the possibility you could revive the old earl's flowers."

"You mean trade in flowers commercially?" The earl waited for his guest to take a wing chair. "That had not crossed my mind. I'm more inclined toward the breeding and training of riding stock."

"So my brother informed me," Bothwell said, taking a seat. "The old earl was much loved, and his gardens were a source of local pride."

"Your brother." The earl frowned in concentration, trying to think of what title went with the Bothwell family name. "Viscount Landover?"

"The very one. I comfort myself that while I'm in Yorkshire, he's doomed to Cumbria."

"Pretty over there, though. At least in summer."

"Which, if you're lucky, lasts six entire weeks. I see you have made the acquaintance of the misses Farnum." Out across the gardens, Emmie was leading Winnie along by the hand, a bucket of gardening tools in her other hand.

"As Miss Bronwyn dwells here, I could not avoid Miss Farnum's company."

"Bronwyn is an exceptionally bright little girl," the vicar said. "And considering Miss Farnum's circumstances, she has done what she could for Bronwyn."

"Her circumstances?" The earl felt his temper stirring to life but kept his expression bland.

"Miss Farnum did not dwell at Rosecroft," the vicar pointed out, "but Miss Bronwyn did. No young lady with any care for her own safety would frequent the late Lord Helmsley's household, so Miss Farnum's access to the child was limited. Then, too, Miss Farnum has her own concerns."

The earl counted slowly to twenty while the refreshments were brought, then speared the vicar with a glower.

"Are you trying to politely remind me Miss Farnum's origins are humble?" the earl inquired, handing his guest a cold glass of lemonade.

The vicar met his gaze, stalled by sipping his drink, then studied it.

"Emmaline Farnum's position in this community is precarious. I do not like it, but the damage was done before I arrived. It is a sad fact that association with her will not inure to Miss Bronwyn's benefit, though your own influence will weigh considerably despite that."

"Miss Farnum is judged for her lack of standing?"

The vicar nodded as he set his drink down. "For her lack of standing, as you put it, and for her financial independence, for her good looks, and her smile, and her unwillingness to bow her head in shame. For her excellent baking, her education, her having traveled beyond this benighted valley. If it's a good quality, a strength, then someone will condemn her for it."

"You sound sympathetic to the lady."

"I offered for her," the vicar said, a soft note of chagrin in his voice. "She turned me down so gently, I almost didn't know I was being rejected."

"Let me guess." The earl's lips pursed. "She pointed out a vicar's wife must be above reproach, pretensions to gentry, at least, but in truth, Miss Farnum wasn't going to make any move that took her farther from Miss Winnie's ambit or limited her own independence."

Bothwell's eyebrows shot up, and then he nodded. "I hadn't put my finger on it, but she was certainly not listing the reasons that really motivated her. Unfortunately, my respect for the woman is undiminished."

"You think being a vicar's wife such an improvement over her current circumstances?"

"I think being this vicar's wife could be," Bothwell retorted. The earl was forced to acknowledge Bothwell was attractive, well built, and possessed of a pleasant demeanor. Like many men of the church, the man was also nobody's fool when it came to dealing with people. "I work for the church to appease my late father's sense a man should not simply be idle in this life, my lord, but I am at least comfortably well off and not that hard to look on."

"Not that modest, you mean." The earl had to smile. "If it's any comfort to you, Miss Farnum has agreed to serve as a temporary governess to Winnie here at Rosecroft. That puts both ladies under my protection, and I will not countenance disrespect to either one of them."

"Thought that might be your inclination."

The earl's smile turned sardonic. "As your brother no doubt informed you, the circumstances of my own birth left something to be desired."

"My brother, the esteemed viscount, was a six months' wonder." The vicar grinned as he picked up his drink again. "And that type of miracle occurs with alarming frequency among the good flock at St. Michael's."

"You don't preach temperance? Self-restraint, abstinence?"

"I preach tolerance," the vicar shot back, "and looking to one's own house before judging another, and loving one's neighbor as one's self."

"And as long as you're unmarried you can preach any blessed thing you want, and at least the females in the district will be raptly attentive."

The vicar's smile dimmed. "Now that is an unarguable fact. I did not appreciate until my wife died just how vulnerable a vicar is to the schemes of a potential mother-in-law."

"My condolences, Bothwell." The earl watched as Bothwell took a hefty swallow of his drink. The man looked entirely too young to have buried a wife.

"It has been a few years." Bothwell shrugged. "The first year is the hardest, and the congregation has been considerate. I'd forgotten you lost a brother in the war."

The earl smiled at him in understanding. "Would that I could forget."

"Well." Bothwell glanced away, out the window. "Now that you've heard my confession, I'll move along, and maybe some great inspiration for the week's sermon will come to me while I'm walking home."

"You don't ride?" A younger son of a viscount had no excuse for not riding.

"When I came to Rosecroft village four years ago," Bothwell said, getting to his feet, "the fellow who held the living previously had died. The congregation had fitted him out with a nice sturdy driving horse, as the old boy was too stiff to sit a horse. It would insult my parishioners were I to trot around on some piece of bloodstock, but it offends my sensibilities to stare at that... plough horse's fundament whenever I want to make a call."

The earl rose, as well. "I am burdened with more horses than I have time to exercise, so perhaps you'd join me on the occasional hack?"

"I would love to." The vicar closed his eyes as he spoke, as if uttering a prayer, and the earl perceived the situation was dire.

"Come along," he said, leading Bothwell toward the door. "My breeches will be loose on you, but my boots will likely fit."

❧

"Hello, ladies." Hadrian Bothwell smiled as Emmie

and Winnie approached the stable and Stevens led the horses away. "Is that libation you bear?"

"It's lemonade," Winnie said, "and we brought some cheese breads, too."

"Cheese breads?" The vicar struck his chest with a dramatic fist. "Oh, let me die in this state of bliss, to know cheese breads are in my immediate future." Emmie set her tray down on a shaded bench and smiled at the vicar.

"Hello, Miss Emmie." Bothwell smiled back at her, and to the earl's watchful eye, there was just a bit too much longing and wistfulness in that smile. When the vicar brushed a kiss on the lady's cheek, St. Just would have rolled his eyes, except Winnie was watching him too closely. Winnie rolled her eyes though, and that restored his humor.

"Hullo, Miss Winnie." The earl swung her up onto his shoulders. "You are the lookout, so spy me some of these cheese breads."

"Over there." Winnie pointed. "On the bench near the lemonade."

The earl ambled over and bent at the knees to retrieve one.

"Hold my gloves." He held both hands up for Winnie to whisk off his gloves. "On second thought, you need to eat, too. I can barely tell you're up there. Toss the gloves to the bench."

She complied and accepted a small, golden brown roll. As she munched, crumbs fell to the earl's hair.

"These are good," the earl pronounced, taking a bite of his own cheese bread. "Aren't you going to have one, Miss Farnum?"

"I believe I will," Emmie replied, avoiding his eyes. "Vicar?"

"But of course."

"Lock your elbows, Winnie." St. Just hefted her up and over his head, then set her on the ground.

"You have crumbs in your hair," Winnie said around a mouthful of bread.

"I am starting the latest rage in bird feeders. May I have some lemonade, Miss Farnum?"

"You may, but bend down."

He complied, bending his head so she could swat at his hair. Except she didn't swat; she winnowed her fingers through his hair and sifted slowly, repeating the maneuver several times. The earl was left staring at her décolletage and inhaling the fresh, flowery scent wafting from her cleavage.

"Now you are disheveled but no longer attractive to wildlife."

"Pity," he murmured as he accepted a glass. "Vicar, are you drinking?"

"I am, and eating. Shall we sit?" He gestured to the little grouping under the shade a few yards from the barn and seated himself with enough room on either side of his bench for a young lady to join him.

Clever bastard.

"You haven't made cheese breads for a long time, Emmie," Bothwell said. "I was missing them."

"I'm glad you like them. May I send some along home with you?"

"I would be eternally indebted and the envy of all who call on me for the next two days." The small talk went on for a few more minutes as the cheese breads and lemonade disappeared, but then Bothwell rose on a contented sigh. "Rosecroft, thanks for a great gallop."

"Are you busy tomorrow afternoon? I'm working them almost every day, but when they're not in company, they spend half the ride dodging rabbits and outrunning their own shadows."

"Ah, youth. I will present myself in riding attire tomorrow at two of the clock, weather permitting. Ladies, good day, and Emmie, you know I would love to see you any Sunday you take a notion to join us."

"Thank you, Hadrian." Her smile was gracious, but the earl, watching her closely, saw a hint of something—regret, sorrow, sadness?—in her eyes. "Bronwyn, shall we take the tray and mugs back to the kitchen?"

"Leave it," the earl ordered, watching the vicar disappear into the woods. "I take it the vicarage is somewhere in the vicinity of your cottage?"

"Just the other side of the hill. Two vicars ago, we had a fellow here with ten children, and the little place by the church was just too modest. The old earl had the present manse built, and the house by the church is now the parish hall."

"And Bothwell is your nearest neighbor." *Lovely*.

"You are my nearest neighbor, my lord. Winnie, would you mind taking these gloves into the tack room, and I thought you were going to offer the carrots to the horses?"

"If Stevens says the horses are cool enough," the earl added then turned his gaze back to Emmie. "Shall we get it over with?"

"I beg your pardon?" She kept her eyes on Winnie's retreating form.

"Isn't this where you apologize for your lamentable lapse of composure last night and I assure you it is already forgotten?"

"Is it?" She sounded hopeful. "Forgotten, I mean?"

"It is not." He grinned unrepentantly. "The feel of a lovely woman in my arms has become too rare a treat to banish from memory. Even your hair smells luscious."

Emmie frowned. "Why?"

"Because you use scented soap, I suppose." His tone was admirably solemn.

"No." Emmie shook her head and raised a serious gaze to his. "Why has the company of a pretty woman become rare? You're handsome, wealthy, titled, well connected, and without significant faults. You even have a recipe for apple tarts and are patient with children. Why aren't you surrounded with pretty women?"

"It's complicated, Emmie." He realized too late he'd used her given name but wasn't about to apologize for it. "When you are the son of duke, you are a target for any ambitious woman. My brother's last mistress went so far as to conceive a child with somebody who resembled him in hopes she would find herself with a ring on her finger." And he ought to be apologizing for such a disclosure to a lady of Emmie's gentility, except she looked intrigued more than shocked.

"My lands! Whatever became of such a creature?"

"With my brother's prompting, the child's father married her, and they are in anticipation of a happy event on the lovely little estate Westhaven deeded them as a wedding present. My point is that the women trying to spend time with me wanted something I was not prepared to give."

"And what of other women?" Emmie asked, a blush suffusing her face. "The women like my aunt and my mother?"

"Coin I have to give, but the interest in such an arrangement was lacking on my part." It was on the tip of his tongue to say what popped into his mind: *I've seen too much of rape.*

But Emmie's gaze was downcast, and he couldn't say those words to her. She was too good, too honest, and too innocent for him to burden her with such violent confidences, though he stored the thought away for his own consideration later.

"Come." He rose and angled his arm out. "Let's retrieve the prodigy and repair to the manor. If we put her in a tub full of lavender bubbles now, she might be clean enough to join us by supper time."

"I'm not as fragile as you think," Emmie said as they strolled along. He gazed over at her curiously, but kept walking. "I'm not as fragile, or as virtuous, or as… You could have told me, whatever you just didn't say. You could have told me."

He stopped but kept his eyes on the wood some distance from them. It was almost as if she considered his reticence not a courtesy but a rejection, and that he could not abide.

"Women can be victimized in ways men cannot be, as you are no doubt aware. When the victimizing is blatantly violent, it can raise the question why any woman would ever have anything to do with any man."

"What do you mean?"

"Ah, Emmie…" He dropped her arm and paced off a few feet. "After a siege, the generals would let the troops storm a city. Those fellows whom you've seen parade about so smartly in their regimentals become animals, murdering, looting, and worse, until strong measures are taken to curb their behaviors. It's tactical, as each city so abused is an inspiration for the next one to capitulate without resistance."

"So even a man's base urges become a weapon for the Crown. His own commanders set him up to lose his dignity, his humanity."

"War sets him up."

"Were you one of those so used?"

"I was not." He shook his head and risked a glance at her over his shoulder. "I was one of the stern measures applied to bring back order when the looting, pillaging, and rapine were done, but that could be as much as several days after breaching the walls."

Emmie's fingers threaded through his, and he felt her head on his shoulder. "So after turning a place into hell on earth, the generals expected you to restore it to civilization."

St. Just merely nodded, his throat constricting as memories threatened to rise up.

"But nobody has been sent along to retrieve you from hell yet, have they?" Emmie asked, and she sounded angry, indignant on his behalf. She slipped her hand over his arm, and in silence, accompanied him back to the manor house. Their proximity was completely proper, their appearance that of a couple at peace with each other, but neither could speak a single, civil word.

Five

"I HAVE NO EXCUSE FOR MY EARLIER COMMENTS," THE earl said when he met Emmie in the front parlor before dinner several hours later. "Please accept my thanks for your understanding, so I can try to gather my dignity before Amery comes down and starts sniffing about. Would you like some sherry? You may consider it medicinal."

"Sherry appeals." Emmie nodded, but she noticed, as well, the strain around the earl's eyes. "Are you all right?"

"I am not," he said, frowning. "Or not as all right as I'd wish to be, as you've just seen. I march around here, giving orders and accomplishing my list of tasks, but it's as if I'm standing on a trapdoor, and without warning, I land in a heap at my own feet." He looked nonplussed at his own honesty. "You did ask, and I've the sense you wanted to know."

"I did and I did. I wish I could catch you."

The words were out, and she regretted them until she saw the earl looking at her over his drink with such an expression of… disbelief, or relief. Appreciation, even.

"You are wonderfully kind, Emmie Farnum." His eyes smiled at her while his mouth remained solemn. "And it is good... no, it is essential to know there are such people in the world. In my world. Your sherry."

When he handed her the drink, his fingers lingered over hers, and Emmie let herself enjoy it. She was relieved, of course, to think she wasn't the only person who occasionally got upset or overwhelmed or flustered. But she was also still angry at the violence done to a good man in the name of King and Country. He looked so strong and fit and competent, but he'd been, again, deceptive. He was a wounded barbarian. A kind, shrewd, handsome, wounded barbarian.

The conversation at dinner moved along as Emmie mostly watched, with the earl and his guest discussing the estate business, mutual acquaintances, and even horses they both knew.

Emmie let them prattle on, the long day and the excellent meal catching up with her. Getting up very early to bake and pack her goods for delivery, then spending the days trying to keep up with Winnie, and her nights not exactly sleeping soundly, was taking a toll.

"She's asleep on her feet," Emmie heard, only to turn her head to find the earl smiling at her.

"I beg your pardon, gentlemen." She offered a tired smile. "I was woolgathering."

"Come along." The earl rose and offered his arm. "The company here is obviously too dull compared to the dreams that beckon. I'll escort you above stairs while Douglas removes to the library and finds us the playing cards."

Dinner had been pushed back in deference to the haying, and the sun had long since set. Emmie barely stifled a yawn as she was towed along on the earl's arm.

"I cannot allow you to burn the candle at both ends, Emmaline," St. Just scolded. "Either we find you some assistance in the kitchen, or we get you some more rest. You look exhausted, and Douglas agrees, so it's a bona fide fact. I'm going to take Winnie out with me tomorrow morning, and you're going to sleep in."

"Sleep in," Emmie said, the way some women might have said "a dozen new bonnets" or "chocolate" or "twenty thousand a year."

"It isn't a baking day tomorrow," the earl went on. "Winnie has acquainted me with every detail of her schedule, and baking isn't on for tomorrow. So you will rest?"

"I will sleep in," Emmie said as they reached her room and pushed her door open. He preceded her into the darkened chamber and lit several candles while she watched.

"You will go directly to bed," he admonished. "No languishing in the arms of Mr. Darcy or whatever it is you read to soothe you into slumber." She listened to him lecturing as she drifted around the room in slow, random motion.

"Emmie?" He set the candles down and frowned at her. "What is amiss?"

"Nothing." But her voice quavered just the least little bit as she sat on her bed. "I'm just tired. My thanks for a pleasant evening."

He went to the bed and paused, frowning down at her mightily. He let out a gusty exhalation, then drew her to feet and wrapped his arms around her. "We will both be relieved when your damned menses have arrived."

For an instant, she was stiff and resisting against him, but then she drew in a shuddery breath, nodded silently, and laid her cheek on his chest. He held her, stroking her hair with one hand, keeping her anchored to him with the other, and the warmth and solid strength of him left her feeling more tired but in some fashion relieved, as well. Winnie would thrive in his care. Thrive in ways Emmie could never have afforded.

"There is no crime, Emmie, in seeking a little comfort betimes. Being grown up doesn't mean we can't need the occasional embrace or hand to hold."

She nodded again and let her arms steal around his waist. Slowly, she gave in to what he offered, letting him support more and more of her weight. His hand drifted from her hair to her back, and when he swept his palm over her shoulder blades in a slow, circular caress, she sighed and rubbed her cheek against him.

She could have stood there all night, so peaceful and right did it feel to be in his arms. His scent was enveloping her, his body warming hers.

"Thank you," she said, mustering a smile when he stepped back. "And good night, good knight." He must have comprehended her play on words, because he returned her smile, kissed her forehead and her cheek, and withdrew.

She treasured the moments when they touched, because as he intended, she was comforted. But he'd held her close enough she knew he was being merely kind. His heart did not race as hers did; his body did not stir in low places as hers did; his thoughts did not tumble along paths no decent person visited outside of marriage.

And all too soon, this kind, lovely man was going to take Winnie away from her, so what in God's name was she doing, spinning fantasies about him, when she should be steeling herself for the pain he would bring her?

❧

Emmie awoke to a particular, pungent scent. One she associated with Winnie's increasingly rare and unpleasant accidents.

"I hate him." Winnie glowered from beside Emmie's bed. "He's mean and he can just go back to London and Lord Amery can stay here and run Rosecroft."

"Good morning, Bronwyn." Having slept heavily and long, Emmie had needs of her own to attend to. "Would you excuse me while I ring for a bath?" The bell pull was behind the privacy screen, so Emmie heeded nature's call while summoning the requisite reinforcements.

"You should hate him, too," Winnie stormed on. "He is taking over Rosecroft and you have to bake when he says and you have to look after me and sleep here when it isn't even where you live."

Emmie sighed, her sense of well-being quickly evaporating. "You need to get out of those clothes, Winnie, and I am happy to be here if it means I can keep a better eye on you. And he does not tell me when to bake."

Winnie turned around so Emmie could undo the bows of her pinafore, but every muscle and sinew in the child's posture bespoke truculence. Winnie in a temper was not a good thing, as the child had been known to disappear for hours when severely out of charity with her life.

"So what has the earl done to earn your wrath, Bronwyn?"

"That awful old Lady Tosten, with the..." Winnie humped her hands way out over her flat little chest. "She found us in the pub and would not stop yammering, even though I was sitting right there. She did not say hello to me, she did not ask me for a curtsey, she did not even smile at me, because she was too busy trying to hog the earl. She didn't even say hello to Lord Amery until he butted into the conversation, so I butted in, too."

Emmie hid a spike of her own temper, wondering if the earl's plan had been to sneak the child into town while she herself slept. Maybe he wasn't that devious, but cunning was stock in trade for any self-respecting barbarian.

And, my lands, his idea of a good night kiss...

"What did you say?" Emmie asked as she carefully lifted Winnie's sodden clothes over her head.

"I said I had to pee," Winnie said, bristling with righteous indignation, "and that was the *truth*, but that silly Miss Tosten acted like I'd asked for a licorice. I told her I was supposed to stay with the earl, as that was a rule of engagement, but she looked at Rosecroft like *he* was a big licorice. Lord Amery got us out of there, but it was awful, and now they're going to come calling. I hate him, and I hate those women, and I don't want them here. I wish Lord Amery was my papa."

"If they do come to call, they will call upon the earl, Bronwyn. They aren't coming to see you."

"Why not?" Winnie shot back. "The earl told Mr. Danner at the livery if the King had written my papa's something-or-other differently, then I would be Helmsley, like my mama said. He told Mr. Danner I need a pony, and I am under his protection. Then he ignored me when that old biddy came flapping up to him. And I was sitting *right there*."

"So you were rude to get his attention," Emmie summed up. "And he probably did not appreciate your embarrassing him like that."

"He should have been embarrassed!" Winnie railed. "Lady Tosten was pushing her..."—she waved her hands over her chest again—"right up against his arm, and she's old, and fat, and disgusting. And I didn't... didn't..." Winnie's voice hitched, and she heaved herself against Emmie's legs. "I didn't... get... my... licorice!" The last word was drawn out on a hooting wail of rage and misery and indignation.

Emmie wrapped her in a towel and scooped her up, knowing that a bout of crying would have to be endured before the situation could be addressed any further. A quiet knock on the door heralded the arrival of breakfast, she hoped, so she went to the door with the child still sniffling on her shoulder.

"I beg your pardon." The earl stood in the hallway. "I was hoping you would be awake and would know where Winnie had gotten off to."

"She hates you," Emmie said pleasantly, turning to kiss the child's crown. "I am not particularly in charity with you either."

"Nor I with her, but now I know she is safe, I will contain further expressions of displeasure until another time." He strode off, but not before Emmie had gotten another whiff of eau de accident from his person. She frowned at the child whose nose was buried so innocently against her neck but held her questions until Winnie had soaked herself clean and shared some of Emmie's breakfast.

"I still hate him," Winnie decided while contemplating a section of orange. "If I apologize, do you think I can have a licorice?"

"For being rude? You should apologize whether you get the licorice or not."

"I wasn't just rude," Winnie said, suddenly glum.

"What did you do?" Emmie slipped an arm around the child's waist and hugged her.

"When we got home, but before we got off, I peed on his saddle, but I got him, too," Winnie said, hiding her face. "I could have held it, but I was too mad to talk to him, so I peed."

Emmie was holding the child, so she dared not laugh, even silently, but the urge was there. The urge to commend Winnie for being herself, for seeing the Tosten females for the prowling nuisances they were, for spiking the great cavalry officer's guns with the few weapons available to a child.

But she loved Winnie, so she did not laugh.

❦

"I see you ogling Douglas," the earl growled from behind where Emmie sat weeding a bed of daisies.

"He is married," Emmie said, "though his dear Guinevere is not on hand to do the honors, so I find myself willing to appreciate certain of his attributes in her place."

"He's honorable, Emmie." The earl was watching Douglas and Winnie as they tacked across the yard toward the stables, and there was a note in his voice, a warning maybe.

"As am I." Emmie rose to her feet. "The man is attractive, charming, and kind to Winnie. I like him, and I hope he likes me, as it appears he makes a superb friend. Is there more that needs to be said?"

When he met her gaze again, the earl's expression bore a hint of humor. "Not on that subject, unless it's to offer an apology."

"Accepted." Emmie nodded but didn't trust his mood. Did he think she would dally with Lord Amery? Because she'd tolerated a kiss that came so close to improper it was almost worse than improper? But no—he was apparently not regarding it as such—a mere kiss to the forehead *and* the cheek—which rather dauntingly confirmed her sense that whatever the attraction she felt for the earl, he was oblivious to it and indifferent to her as a woman.

"Will you walk with me?" the earl asked, his gaze measuring.

"Are we going to parse your visit to town this morning?" *Or perhaps a certain kiss?*

"We are, or make a start on it."

Emmie glanced around and saw the bench under

Winnie's favorite climbing tree. "Come along." She took him by the hand as Winnie might have, and tugged him over to the shade. "State your piece."

She arranged her skirts, and when he would have paced before her, captured his hand again and indicated his piece would be said from the place beside her. "I will not watch you march around while you hold forth. Save your energy for your horses."

"You were right." He leaned back beside her and stretched out his booted feet before him. "Winnie was not quite ready for a trip to town, though I think some good was accomplished, despite an ignominious retreat."

"She has very quickly become possessive of you."

"Possessive of me or of her licorice?"

"You." Emmie smoothed her skirts again, trying not to wonder when and how she'd become so familiar with a peer of the realm. Maybe letting him kiss her had something to do with it. "You ran into Lady Tosten and Miss Tosten, and Lady Tosten has nothing better to do than lord her rank over the other women in the neighborhood, and of course, she must be the first to make your acquaintance. Winnie, on some level, divined a rival and was not pleased with your abandonment."

"I was not supposed to greet acquaintances? Winnie will have to get over that."

"She will, though Winnie has done a lot of getting over in her short life. When she was four, she got over my aunt's death, and she started wandering the property. We thought she was done with nappies and accidents and so forth by then, but she lost a lot of ground in this regard. Then she got over the old earl's death, and he doted on her, as did his countess. Then she got over the countess falling so ill. Then she got over her aunts disappearing without a word. Now, just when I thought she was beginning to find her balance, she's to get over her papa being dead and her home falling into the hands of a stranger. Her first question to Lord Amery was whether he was going to go away, and he had to tell her that yes, he was going to go away, like her mama and papa, the earl, the countess, her aunts, and in time, myself."

The man beside her was quiet for a long time, staring down his long legs at his boots, his brow knit in thought.

"I am coming to see," he said, "our Winnie has been at war."

"How do you mean?" Emmie replied, feeling the stillness in him from deep concentration.

"The hell of the Peninsular campaigns," the earl informed his boots, "was that Spain itself became the battleground—the old walled towns and cities, the hills and plains."

Emmie waited while he gathered his thoughts.

"There were French sympathizers at every turn, of course, as a Frenchman held the throne. They were not above using children as spies, decoys, messengers, what have you. But any child—any child of any age— was subject to the impact of the violence. Orphans were everywhere, begging, scavenging, being taken in by this relative only to have to flee to that relative when the next town fell. They became old, canny, and heartbreakingly self-sufficient and necessarily without conscience in their efforts to survive."

His eyes were so bleak, Emmie could only guess at the horrors he was recalling.

"Winnie has a conscience."

"She does." The earl turned his gaze to hers with visible effort. "Thanks to you, she does. But it's not quite as well developed as her instinct for self-preservation."

"Or her temper." Emmie decided to meet honesty with honesty. "When Winnie feels threatened or ridiculed or upset, her first impulse is anger, and it's a towering, unreasonable, often violent rage, much like a child several years her junior. I hadn't seen her in a truly mean temper for a few months, but I gather she put on a display for you."

The earl smiled. "She was brilliant. She kept her powder dry, so to speak, then ambushed me and scampered off while I was still agog with indignation."

"You can't let her get away with it." Emmie made the observation reluctantly. "She must be punished somehow. She cannot be rude to her elders, much less to her betters."

The earl shook his head. "The Tostens aren't better than her. On that, I would like to argue, but I cannot. Winnie accurately surmised I'd fallen into the cross hairs of a scheming old biddy, the likes of whom I left London to avoid."

Emmie lifted a sardonic eyebrow. "Well, brace yourself. You are now accepting callers, I gather, and you will have no peace short of winter setting in."

"Christ." The earl sat forward, rested his forearms on his thighs, and bowed his head. "I am a soldier, Emmie, or perhaps a horseman, a landowner. Her

Grace made sure I knew how to dance, which fork to use, and how to dress, but… Christ."

But, Emmie surmised with sudden insight, he felt like an imposter in the drawing room, among the dames and squires. Well, God knew she'd felt like an imposter often enough, so she told him what she frequently told herself.

"You have a certain lot in life, my lord. Some of it you chose, some you did not, and much of it you did not realize you were choosing. Still, it is your lot in life, and you must make the best of it. A man in your position receives callers and returns the calls. He entertains and is agreeable to his neighbors. He marries and secures the succession. He tends his land and comports himself like a gentleman under all circumstances."

While I will bake bread, Emmie silently concluded, precisely one property and an entire universe distant from you.

"I comprehend duty." The earl sat up and frowned at her. "But only in a rational context. A soldier obeys orders because an army falters without discipline and lays itself open to slaughter. A gentleman protects the weak, as they cannot protect themselves. He tends the land because we must eat, and so forth. But what in God's name is the purpose of sipping tea and discussing the weather with strangers when there is work to be done?"

He was genuinely bewildered, Emmie saw, puzzled. But then it occurred to her he'd probably gone from university to the battlefield and stayed there until there were no more battles to fight.

"Aren't you ever lonely?"

"Of course I'm lonely. Every soldier makes the acquaintance of loneliness." He was back to scowling at his riding boots.

"And what do you do when you're lonely?"

"There isn't anything to do. I work, go for a ride, write a letter. It passes."

"No," Emmie said, "it does not. These people who waste your time over tea and small talk, maybe they are what you should be doing."

"Hardly." He rose. "They are not potential friends, Emmie. I'm not sure what they're about, but I comprehend friendship. My brothers are my friends, and I would die for them cheerfully. Lady Tosten is not a friend and never will be."

"She will not." Emmie rose, as well. "And I likely misspoke. She will not be your friend, but perhaps she will be your mother-in-law?"

"Not you, too." The earl braced his hands on his lower back and dropped his head back to look straight up. "Douglas told me I am now to be auctioned off to the most comely heifer in the valley, but the prospect hardly appeals."

"It doesn't speak to that certain form of loneliness single men are prone to?" Emmie asked, smiling.

"Actually, no, Emmie." He speared her with a particularly fierce look. "The prospect of taking some grasping female to my bed so she can dutifully submit to my pawing has no appeal whatsoever. Ah, I've made you blush. I account the conversation a success."

"You are being naughty." Despite her serene tone, his comment disturbed her. It was too blunt, too personal, and too much what she wanted to hear.

"I am being honest." He slipped his fingers through hers and tugged her toward the house. "A soldier does obey orders, and I did that for very long and unpleasant years. It is going to take me some time to accustom myself to following a different set of orders, when I cannot comprehend the purpose behind them."

"You are like Winnie," Emmie said, shifting so they walked arm in arm. "Very wary, and self-reliant, and prone to seeing enemies where they may not lurk."

"Perhaps I am, but I am not a child, and I have not suffered as many losses as she has. How do you propose I punish her?"

"Winnie adores you, but her adoration must be tempered with respect. I'm sure you'll puzzle it out, just as you puzzle out your horses."

"You are no help." He dropped her arm and bowed, the corners of his mouth tipping up as he straightened. "I am going to join my opponent in the stable, but I look forward to seeing you at luncheon, by which time I might have a treaty negotiated that allows for both social calls and possessive children."

"Good luck, my lord. Remember that respect is essential."

❧

"You tossed me into the horse trough!" Winnie bellowed.

"You got me wet." The earl towered over her. "So I got you wet." But then he grinned. "And it's a hot day, and you look happy in there."

She grinned back and splashed him. "I'm nice and cool," she cooed, "and you are all hot and miserable,

and besides, you won't fit in the horse trough, so there!"
She splashed him again, provoking him to whip off his
shirt, splash her back, then advance on her, growling
and threatening while she shrieked her delight.

Douglas emerged from the barn, his frown clearing
at the display of negotiations before him.

"So we are back in charity with one another?" he
asked as Winnie stood up and pulled her pinny over
her head.

"We are wet," Winnie retorted, "because he dunked
me, because I... Well, I am wet." Her pinafore hit the
grass with a sodden plop, and she grinned at both men
in her short dress. "But I am nice and cool."

"So you are," Douglas said, "and you've very
considerately seen to the comfort of the earl, as well.
I, however, am going to repair to the house for
luncheon and hope there is something left for the two
of you, as you must now change before you can come
to table."

"Here." The earl lifted Winnie out and wrapped his
shirt around her. "You are turning blue, and while the
color goes with your eyes, Miss Emmie will tear a strip
off me if you catch a cold."

He carried her back up to the house, strolling along
beside Douglas. It should not have mattered that he
was in charity with a stubborn little girl. It should not
have mattered that she felt so good perched on his hip,
smiling from ear to ear. It should not have mattered that
a six-year-old female had grown possessive of him.

Like holding Emmie Farnum's hand or offering her
a hug for simple comfort—or risking the unnameable
with a good night kiss threatening to stray from its

bounds—those were things that should have been insignificant, beneath his notice. But with those things in place, the prospect of dealing with his neighbors' social calls was not quite as daunting.

∽⊱

St. Just had one lovely day when it seemed like peace and plenty were in his grasp. One day of working his own land, mingling with his laborers, becoming familiar with the broad speech and circumspect manner of his tenants.

From dawn until late afternoon, St. Just worked, raking and binding hay in the broiling sun, using his body until a pleasant state of exhaustion could claim him. When the hay crop was in, he spent the evening hacking both Wulf and Red, as Caesar had yet to work through his abscess.

And then he had bathed and fallen asleep, the boneless, dreamless sleep of a man who has labored hard and well. When he rose the next morning, however, it was to realize haying had wearied muscles unused to the task, and even in Yorkshire, the summer sun meant business.

He'd gone to bed feeling a little younger than his thirty-two years; he rose feeling decades older. When he creaked down to the breakfast parlor, he found Douglas in the same condition.

Douglas passed him the teapot. "I will not visit you again in the summer, St. Just. It gives me delusions of youth."

"Which fade by morning," the earl agreed. "I feel like I took a hard fall from a fast horse and was left to bake in the hills of sunny Spain for a few days thereafter."

"Good morning, gentlemen." Emmie sailed in, all smiles. "Oh, my goodness." She looked from one bleary-eyed fellow to the other. "Did we overdo yesterday?"

"We did," Douglas said. "Though we both know better."

"I have a salve that might help with the aches. And you look like you were in the sun, my lords. It will help that, too."

"I thought I was permanently immune to sunburn after being in Spain." The earl sighed as he poured her tea. "Too soon old, too late wise."

"But it brings out the green of your eyes very becomingly. And now your hay barn is full, and you've impressed Mr. Mortimer to no end."

Douglas rose carefully. "I am off to sum up the week's adventures for my viscountess and my daughter. I will pass along your compliments, St. Just."

When Douglas had departed, his pace a little less brisk than usual, the earl sat back and treated himself to the pleasure of watching Emmie Farnum demolish her breakfast. She wasn't dainty, not in her dimensions and not in the gusto with which she went about life. She laughed, she cried, she ate, she raged, all with an energy a more proper lady would not have displayed.

And before he could stop his naughty mind from thinking it, he wondered if she loved as passionately as she did everything else.

"More tea?" he asked when she was between slices of toast.

"An orange, I think." She took the orange he selected from his hand without any hint of awareness their fingers had touched. She was like that, willing to touch, to hold hands even, as if it were perfectly normal to do so. He found it a surprising and likeable quality, but lowering, too.

She never gave off those little signals that suggested it meant anything to her—no swiftly indrawn breath, no dropping of the eyes, no becoming blush. It might as well be Winnie's hand she held.

"What will you and Winnie get up to today?" he asked, forcing his gaze up to meet hers.

"Winnie is composing a letter in reply to her new friend, Rose. I gather they are exchanging more than just letters, as Winnie asked for drawing paper. I have not been consulted regarding the particulars."

"Have we toys on hand?" He watched her fingers tearing the skin off the orange. Strong, competent fingers that had winnowed so gently through his hair.

"We have toys. There are many of Anna and Morgan's old toys, and even some that belonged to Winnie's papa. She likes those especially."

"You must tell me if she needs anything." The earl rose, but stiffly, lest he continue to ogle her at her breakfast.

Emmie frowned in sympathy. "You are not doing very well, are you?"

"I'll locate some horse liniment and keep moving. I will not, however, touch a damned hay rake until Judgment Day."

"Oh, for shame, Devlin St. Just," she scolded softly, rising and taking his hand to examine the blisters on his palm. "Come along, and no whining. I promise not to hurt you."

Six

WELL, DAMN. ST. JUST LET EMMIE LEAD HIM BY THE wrist upstairs into the bedroom she was using. She closed the door behind them without a thought, and it occurred to him in London, were he to be found being private with a lady in her bedroom, that lady would be his wife, or his intended, will she, nil she.

God bless Yorkshire, he silently concluded as Emmie rummaged in her wardrobe, for Emmie Farnum deserved better than the likes of him. She emerged with a silver tin and waved it at him.

"Shirt off," she ordered, crossing her arms and waiting.

When he lifted an eyebrow, she just waved the tin again. "I've seen you without, my lord," she reminded him, "and I am hardly a blushing debutante. You cannot put this on your own back, and Lord Amery is nowhere to be found, though you should send him to me when we're done here."

Slowly, he unbuttoned both waistcoat and shirt and shrugged out of them, all the while trying not to feel her gorgeous blue eyes taking the measure of him as he shed half his clothes.

"My lands." Emmie drew in a breath. "I am going to scold Mortimer within an inch of his life. You are as red as an apple."

"So be careful with me," he said, prepared for something that both stank and stung to be applied to his skin.

"You should have been more careful with your-self," Emmie scolded, moving around to the back of him. He heard her open the tin, then felt the softest dab of something cool right between his shoulder blades. Her fingers feathered over him as gently as a breeze, spreading the salve, and leaving a tingling relief wherever she touched. Delicate scents of rosemary and lavender wafted to him as Emmie worked down his back then over his shoulders and down his arms.

"Am I hurting you?"

Killing me.

"Not at all," he managed. But the blood pooling in his groin argued that a woman's bare hands were gliding over him, touching him with gentle concern, in places he hadn't been touched in so terribly long.

"Turn around, my lord. Sit on the bed and close your eyes. Don't open them until I tell you, because you will be most uncomfortable if this gets into them."

He did as bid, glad for the chance to sit and disguise the evidence of his unruly imagination. Her fingers moved over his throat, her touch both soothing and arousing.

"You should keep your shirt off as much as possible today," she said, moving her hands down over his collarbones. "My heavens you've a powerful lot of muscle for an idle lord." She might have been commenting on Mortimer's team, so dispassionate was her tone, but her fingers were gliding over his chest, and he had to open his eyes.

She was leaning close, studying him as she spread more salve on his sunburned skin. Through the rosemary and lavender came the flowery scent of her, and he inhaled deeply.

"Are you all right?" Her thumb brushed innocently over his nipple, and he had all he could do not to shoot off the bed. Instead, he snatched the tin from her, set it on the night table, and closed his eyes again.

"Is it stinging? It isn't supposed to, but you are well and truly sunburned," she said, concern in every word.

"Emmie…" He opened his eyes and found her peering down at him. He dared not stand lest the havoc in his breeches become apparent. She laid a hand on his bare shoulder, her fingers cool and gentle.

"Being in the sun too long…" she began, but then he did stand and swooped his mouth down to cover hers. She gave a startled little "mmm" but did not resist.

Stop, stop, stop, stop… His common sense was trying to signal his body, but two years of abstinence had sent self-control from the stables at an exuberant dead run. This was Emmie, he tried to remind himself, a woman under his protection, a woman in his employ…

A woman in his arms, who was arching into him with the sweetest sense of yearning to her. She made little noises, like she was tasting something delicious as her arms stole around his waist and her body pressed against his. God above, she was lush. He anchored her to him, heedless that his erection was evident against her stomach. If she comprehended what it was, she certainly wasn't put off by it.

He heard himself growl as he tightened his hold, then forced himself to slow down, to gentle his kiss and treat the woman like the long-awaited delicacy she was.

His tongue seamed her lips slowly, giving her time to comprehend what he asked, before she sighed into his mouth and opened for him. He sampled carefully, teasing and tasting the orange and clove flavor of her, then easing back and nibbling his way from her chin to the ear.

"Kiss me, Emmie," he breathed against her neck. "Don't think, just kiss me."

Another small sound of pleasure, and this time her mouth found his. Tentatively, sweetly, she tasted his lips with her tongue, and he had to force himself not to toss her on the bed and fall upon her like a beast.

"More," he urged, cradling the back of her head with his hand. Her tongue met his again, and he felt her shock when he plundered past her lips and went exploring.

Heat, want, arousal, pleasure, and need coursed through his veins as she capitulated utterly to his kiss. Emmie's hands were questing up and down his back, caressing, soothing, exploring so gently. She cuddled up against him like he was her favorite place to be, and the ache in his loins threatened to obliterate reason.

But it did not obliterate hearing.

"Emmie," he whispered. "Em. Sweetheart, wait." He drew back, stealing little parting kisses as she went still in his arms. "Voices."

In the corridor—beyond the *unlocked* door—Steen was murmuring to a footman.

"They are no doubt on the nursery floor, or even in the attics," Steen said. "His lordship is personally overseeing the repairs to the roof. I shall look in the kitchen, however, as he might have sought out Miss Farnum below stairs."

"Dear God," Emmie hissed. But when she would have pushed away, St. Just gently restrained her.

"Hush," he murmured. "They're gone. Just be still."

"We have been wicked," she moaned, dropping her forehead to his bare shoulder. "Wicked, wicked, wicked."

"We have not been wicked," he rumbled, pleased that she'd cling to him in her supposed remorse. "We have been foolish, perhaps, as the door is not locked. But a kiss is hardly wicked, Emmie." He kissed her temple to emphasize his point.

"A kiss can be wicked when we've no honorable intentions," Emmie replied stoutly even while she leaned more fully against him.

"It's still just a kiss."

"Well." She tried again to step back but got only far enough to meet his eyes. "I am sorry. I provoked you, and I should have made you stop. Now please let me go."

"You did nothing wrong, Emmie." He let her step back but kept hold of her hand. "And I will apologize for taking liberties but not for enjoying them." In his breeches, his cock was not apologizing for anything, but rather, stating some very definite demands.

"I cannot discuss this now," Emmie said, dropping his hand. "I just… I cannot."

He watched her march out of the room, spine stiff, cheeks suffused with hectic color. She'd left the tin on the bed, and he wondered if she realized she was going to smell like rosemary and lavender until she changed her dress. Locking the door behind her, he shucked out of his boots, unbuttoned the fall of his trousers, and stretched out on her bed, bringing himself to a leisurely, intense orgasm.

When he rose from her bed a few minutes later and put his clothing to rights, he was still musing on that one, very informative kiss. He'd learned that Miss Emmie Farnum was not indifferent to him nor indifferent to the pleasures he could share with her. He'd learned he had a thorough physical craving for Emmie Farnum, and though she was a decent woman, she was also independent and outside the usual strictures of society. He would not force her—of course he wouldn't—but he would invite and persuade and cajole until she told him his attentions were unwelcome.

And even if he never got her into his bed, the chase would be worth it, as she'd already proved to him his desire wasn't dead after all.

"What has you so pleased?" Douglas asked as the earl, once again decently covered, approached his own bedroom.

"I feel better." He smiled hugely at the understatement. "Come along." He hooked Douglas by the arm. "You will, too."

"Careful." Douglas extricated his arm. "That is one of my raking arms. Why do you suppose the term rake has the significance it does? I cannot recall ever being quite so sore in such inconvenient locations, short of illness and saddle sores."

"Shirt off," the earl ordered when they were behind Douglas's bedroom door. "And I have to agree with you. Saddle sores are about the worst discomfort imaginable, probably the only revenge horses are granted for all the ways we take advantage of them. Turn around."

Douglas complied, showing a back less burned than the earl's, but still pink.

"So what have you there?" he asked as the earl spread cool salve down the muscled length of Douglas's spine.

"I'm not sure what all is in it," St. Just said, taking care not to abuse burned skin, "but it smells of rosemary and lavender. I get a hint of mint and comfrey, maybe some arnica."

"I will get the recipe." Douglas sighed as the earl worked over his shoulders. "Don't forget my neck."

"Get your own scrawny neck," the earl growled, his fingers gliding over Douglas's nape. "I wouldn't bother with a neckcloth, were I you. Turn around and close your eyes. I'll do your shining countenance. Why in the hell wouldn't we know enough to wear hats?"

"We were too busy showing off for the lads, and it feels good to pretend we are eighteen and indestructible. Or it did feel good."

"You're supposed to let this stuff sink in before you put your shirt back on. And I've been meaning to ask you how much longer you can stay."

"At least another week. I would like for Rose and

her mother to have a little time to get reacquainted before I join them, but I do not want to wear out my welcome here."

"You could not do that if you tried," the earl scoffed, putting the lid back on the tin. "Winnie will be upset when you go, though."

"I think Miss Winnie is in a general state of upset," Douglas mused as St. Just appropriated a hairbrush. "She has lost a papa who didn't love her, and I think that in some ways is worse than losing one who does."

"How do you mean?" The earl shot a questioning glance at Douglas in the vanity mirror. "I should think he was no great loss."

Their discussion was interrupted by a tap on the door. Steen informed the earl he had callers, which provoked an undignified groan.

"Refreshments, Steen," the earl said, "and tell them their prey will be down directly."

"Alas, my countenance is hardly fit for polite society," Douglas noted solemnly. "Enjoy your guests." When St. Just tossed the hairbrush at him, Douglas had already nipped out the door.

Resenting the bother of finding a morning coat, St. Just steeled himself for the ordeal of the next hour. The formidable Lady Tosten, with whom he'd had a passing acquaintance in the south, had brought her own reinforcements, including her daughter, Elizabeth, a well-fed older woman named Mrs. Davenport, who was attired in garish pink, and that good lady's offspring, an equally garish pink little shoat by the name of Ophelia.

The tactic was clear, of course. Next to Ophelia's

stammering plumpness, Elizabeth looked even more serenely lovely.

St. Just had to dodge veiled and overt invitations, parry those artful pauses when he was supposed to extend an invitation, avoid fluttering lashes, and escape the near occasion of Elizabeth's bosom pressed against his arm. The dodging and parrying were exhausting and made all the worse because Douglas—damn his disloyal, married ass—neglected to appear at any point. Lady Tosten started angling for an invitation to luncheon in earnest, but that looming disaster was averted when Winnie came pelting around the corner, her smock hiked past her knees, her feet bare, her eyes dancing with mirth, and a carrot clutched in her fist.

"Oh!" She skidded to a stop. "Hullo, Rosecroft! I am hiding."

"Not very effectively," the earl remarked, "at least not from me." His eyes challenged her to be on her best behavior, and Winnie obediently waited for his cue. "Come here, Winnie, and make your curtsey to our guests." He extended his hand to her, expecting her to take off in the other direction, but instead she came docilely forward.

"Good morning, my ladies." She curtsied to each woman then turned her gaze to the earl.

"Well done, princess. You've been practicing. I'm impressed."

"Bronwyn Farnum!" Emmie bellowed as she, too, came pelting around the corner. Her bun was coming loose, she wore no bonnet, and—to the earl's delight—she was barefoot in the grass, as well. "You cheated, you!"

A stunned silence met that pronouncement while Emmie's cheeks flamed bright red. "I beg your pardon, my lord, my ladies. Winnie, perhaps you'd accompany me back to the stables?" She held out a hand, and at a nod from the earl, Winnie took the proffered hand.

"Miss Farnum." The earl turned a particularly gracious smile on her. "You are to be complimented on Winnie's manners. We'll excuse you, though, if Herodotus is pining for his carrots."

"My thanks." Emmie nodded stiffly and turned, leaving silence in her wake.

"Well, really." Lady Tosten was on her feet. "If that isn't a demonstration of like following like, really, my lord."

"Like following like?" the earl countered, his smile dying. "I don't comprehend."

"You are new here." Lady Tosten tut-tutted. "I will commend you for trying to take the child in hand, as she is young yet and might still learn her proper place. I will caution you, however, regarding the proximity you allow the child to Miss Farnum."

"Proximity?" The earl tasted the word and found it unpleasant. "As I understand it, Miss Farnum has no other living relations. Why shouldn't Winnie spend time with her?"

"Well, that's as may be, isn't it?" Lady Tosten exchanged a righteous nod with Mrs. Davenport, who set all three chins jiggling in agreement.

"So you are suggesting, Lady Tosten, that I should prevent Miss Farnum from spending time with her cousin?"

"Well, who's to see to it if you do not?" Lady

Tosten drew herself up. "Miss Farnum has a modest livelihood, my lord, and we do not begrudge her that as long as she keeps to her place, but it's no secret the Farnum women are no better than they should be, and if young Bronwyn isn't to follow in those same lamentable footsteps, she must be protected from pernicious influences."

"I see." The earl tried counting to ten; he tried counting to ten again, and all the while the damned woman blathered on about her willingness to advise him and good intentions and unfortunate realities. She was smiling at him indulgently, and he was strongly reminded of a time in Spain when he'd nearly fainted from heat exhaustion. All the sounds around him had blended into one undifferentiated roar, like the sound of a waterfall, making no sense but nearly driving him to his knees with the sheer, miserable volume of it.

"Hush, madam," he said, his words coming out much more loudly than he'd intended. "You dare to tell me how to care for a child when that child has run riot in your own backyard for the past two years? You've not lent her a pair of shoes, not spared her a sip of water, not permitted her to even learn the names of your sons and daughters, and then you think to tell me how that child should go on?"

He paced over to glare down at Lady Tosten. "Emmaline Farnum has shown Winnie the only thing approaching Christian charity since the day the child's mother died more than two years ago. Not you, not your pretty vicar, not the servants in this household, *no one but Emmaline Farnum* has given a thought to the child's health or safety in all that time. Winnie is an orphan, Lady Tosten, a bloody, damned orphan, and you begrudge her simple human kindness, yet you consider it your Christian duty to advise me to take from the child the one person she might still trust. For shame. You will excuse me if I do not heed this kind advice. Steen will see you out. Good day."

Having made his grand exit, St. Just stayed in his room for most of the afternoon, trying to write letters but experiencing aftershocks of temper that undermined his concentration. A soft tap on the door interrupted his latest effort to write to his brother, and so he crumpled up the paper and tossed it into the hearth.

"Enter."

Of all people, Emmaline Farnum poked her head around the door. "I don't mean to intrude."

"Come in," he said, getting to his feet, while some of his temper abated at just the sight of her. He'd kissed her just this morning. Kissed her thoroughly then pleasured himself on her bed thoroughly, before mucking up his day thoroughly.

"You are still in a temper," she observed, surveying the evidence of his failed attempts at correspondence. "I am sorry."

"What have you to be sorry for?" His back was burning, though he wore only a half-unbuttoned shirt; his muscles ached, and worst of all, he felt like a fool.

"You were defending me," she said, withdrawing the little silver tin from her pocket. "And you meant well."

"Was I yelling that loudly?" he asked, scrubbing a hand over his face.

"You were not," she replied, fleeting humor in her eyes. "At first. Winnie forgot her carrot, though, so I was much closer to the terrace than I might have been otherwise, and Lord Amery was approaching from the hallway, so he heard you, too. You meant well."

"Oh, famous. You will both see to it that on the tomb of my social ambitions, it is clearly engraved: He meant well."

"It isn't like you to pout." She frowned at him and glanced at the tin of salve. She arched an eyebrow, and he nodded, shrugging out of his shirt.

"It never used to be like me to rant at trivialities, either," he said, closing his eyes when her cool fingers went to work. "I was a steady fellow at university, quiet, bookish, and fond of horses."

"Something happened," Emmie commented, working the soothing cream over his back.

"Something, indeed. I do not sleep well. Until I got here, my appetite was indifferent. I drink my way through thunderstorms, and I cannot abide to be near harbors that use cannon for their signals. The gun I fired on Helmsley was the first one I'd aimed at a live target in more than two years, and my temper..."

She let her hand drift up to work gently over his nape.

"You and Winnie both," she said thoughtfully. "You've just described her, you know. She wanders at all hours and feels much safer out in a storm than trapped inside. She has tantrums like a younger child, and all of her strong feelings tend to express themselves as anger. She is only now regaining the habit of sitting at table, but for two years after her mother died, she would not sit down to eat."

"You describe an eccentric child," he said, closing his eyes as she shifted to treat his face.

"An eccentric child trying to cope with too much, and without an adult to take an interest in her. She had a nurse, at first, but Helmsley did not pay consistent wages, and so Winnie became... feral."

"And I am a feral earl, I suppose." He opened his eyes. "I'm surprised you trust me after the way I behaved this morning."

"I could have stopped you," she said, handing him the tin. His arms, back, neck, and shoulders felt better, but he understood her trust went only so far. She stepped aside and cocked her head, and he applied salve to his own chest.

"You have no outward scars," she remarked, taking a seat on his hassock. "At least not that I've seen."

"I suffered no wounds worth the name, though I think you imply I am not yet recovered from my years of soldiering."

"Do you think you are?"

"God, I hope not. I hope it is not my fate to rail at matrons for minor provocations, to leave my bed after two hours slumber and find memories rising up to trap me, seeming as real as the day I first experienced them."

"Your memories haunt you."

"I wouldn't say haunt." He frowned, putting the tin down and slumping back into the desk chair. "They are just too real, too powerful when they arise. Like the dreams you don't initially realize are dreams."

"I'm sorry," she said, her expression as bleak as he

felt. "You talk about those children in Spain, robbed of a real childhood, but things have been taken from you, as well."

He nodded, his throat abruptly constricting to the point where speech was too risky.

Seeming oblivious to his dilemma, Emmie went on. "I wanted to thank you for what you said to Lady Tosten, but also to let you know I don't entirely disagree with her."

"What do you mean?" He was immediately on guard, ready to reengage his anger to defeat her arguments.

She smiled. "At ease, Colonel. I do not want to say I warned you." Her gaze ranged around the room.

"No, that is Douglas's forte."

"I did tell you I am not received in this little slice of Eden, and association with me will not benefit Winnie beyond a certain point."

"Were I to take you from Winnie now, the child would be inconsolable. She would likely be wetting her drawers and sheets regularly, pitching tantrums at the table, and sleeping in the hay barn every chance she got. I have not even Douglas's limited experience with parenting, Emmie, but I understand that for now, Winnie needs you."

And I need you. While part of him conducted this very adult, necessary conversation with Emmaline Farnum, another part of him, part soldier, part orphan earl, part healthy man, wanted to haul her over to the bed and cover her body with his own. He wanted to bury his face against her shoulder and bury his cock in her soft, wet heat. Wanted to hear again those sweet, yearning sounds she made when aroused, wanted to feel her hands questing on his back for ways to be closer to him.

Those feelings, he told himself, were like many of his emotions, disproportionate to their cause. He'd shared a lovely kiss with Emmie, but that was all. And she wasn't asking him to repeat the moment.

Emmie was regarding him curiously, and St. Just had to hope what he felt did not show on his face. She broke what was becoming an awkward and charged silence.

"Perhaps it is not time for Winnie to start developing other associations, but sooner or later, it will be in her best interests to do so. When that time comes, I will understand and do what I can to help her."

"She will never stop needing you, Emmie. She can develop all the associations in the world, and she will still know you loved her when nobody else did. Children don't forget."

"And I will not forget you spoke up for me today." She smiled at him, a sweet, pleased benediction of a smile, one that lit his flagging spirits with warmth.

"I am your good knight," he replied, smiling back and coming to his feet.

"Will you be down for dinner tonight? Winnie is a little concerned for you, but we can send up a tray, if you like."

"I'll be down," he decided, completely at variance with his earlier plans. "Send up Douglas, and I'll treat his back for him before we change." He walked her to the door, feeling an ease that had eluded him all afternoon.

"You should have seen Mrs. Davenport," he said,

thinking back. "Put me in mind of a goose, flapping and carrying on, not knowing whether to gloat or commiserate with her familiar. I had the distinct impression Ophelia was trying not to snicker."

"Naughty man. I will see you at dinner." She rose up on her toes and kissed his cheek, then patted his sunburned shoulder very gently and departed.

Now why, the earl wondered, was that one little peck on the cheek warming his insides just as effectively as all his panting and pawing had done earlier? He was still leaning against the door, half clad and musing, when Douglas found him a quarter hour later.

"I come seeking relief," Douglas said, pulling his shirt from his waistband. "You smell as if you've just been dosed, sparing me the burden." He presented his back, which was, if anything, more pink than it had been hours earlier.

"How are we to sleep tonight?" St. Just asked as he worked salve over Douglas's shoulders. "I still ache, my skin stings, my lips feel chapped, and I'm bone tired."

Douglas sighed as the earl got to his nape. "I suspect we could order up tepid baths, maybe open up a bottle of whiskey, lace it with a tot of laudanum. God above, that feels good."

"Douglas?" St. Just leaned in, resting his forehead on the back of Douglas's neck.

"Devlin?" Douglas waited, though St. Just realized his friend had already given him the entire afternoon to brood.

"I fucked up today."

"Well." Douglas held his ground. If he was appalled by St. Just's display, he wasn't showing it in word or deed. Steady nerves, Amery had. The steadiest. "Did you, now?"

St. Just nodded against his friend's back. "I tore into old Biddy Saint Tosten like she was a recruit who had just wasted ammunition, shooting at steeple bells. I am ashamed, as I keep expecting my temper to be less ungovernable…"

"But"—Douglas reached behind him and drew one of St. Just's arms around his waist—"you keep having lapses, and you keep wondering if maybe you didn't shoot Helmsley as a function of just such a lapse. If maybe you have crossed that line, from soldier to killer."

St. Just nodded again, feeling at once awkward as hell to be all but holding on to another man and yet relieved as hell, too. Douglas laid his hand over St. Just's, and the relief obliterated the awkwardness.

"Every time it snows," Douglas said, tipping his head back to rest it against St. Just's shoulder, "I am out of sorts. The morning my mother died, we had one of those fairy tale snows that dusts everything in white, pretty as a picture. Both of my brothers died on snowy days. I've come to dread snow, though snow had nothing to do with any of their deaths. I know it isn't rational. You know your brother's wife is safe, and you know Helmsley wanted her anything but safe. You also know you would not have put the burden of killing that vermin on your brother."

"Bloody hell." St. Just sighed and stepped back. "That is part of it. I would do anything for Gayle or Val. I would die for them."

"And you would kill for them," Douglas said, regarding him gravely. "By far the harder choice, particularly for a man who has done more than his share of killing."

"You know, it's odd." St. Just went to his window and stared out across the drive to the pastures. "Nobody talks about the killing. The night before a battle, you might talk about what it's like to die. You write those maudlin if-I-die letters; you make all kinds of promises to comrades. You don't talk about the actual killing, the taking of one life after another after another. Shooting a man on purpose, with intent to put a period to his entire existence. In the hospital, after Waterloo, I overheard some Frenchmen talking about the same thing, and a few of the Dutch fellows allowed as how it was the same with them. We pray to the same God, using the same prayers, asking for the same things. It makes no sense, but we don't talk about it.

"And what would you say?" he went on then fell silent.

"You would say," Douglas said quietly from right beside him, "that it hurts like blazes. Seeing the light die in another's eyes, the confusion and pain and bewilderment, knowing you did that. It hurts beyond anything."

St. Just nodded silently, and Douglas left him there alone, bare to the waist, staring unseeing across the lovely green hills of Yorkshire.

Seven

EMMIE TOOK TO AVOIDING THE EARL, AND IN FAIRNESS to her, he understood exactly why. No young lady appreciated a man who tore a strip off his neighbors when first they ventured to call on him. He'd behaved badly, and no matter Lady Tosten had deserved every word of his tirade, he'd still bungled the encounter.

Lady Tosten, however, was *not* avoiding him. Three days later she was back, Elizabeth in tow and no Davenports in sight. On that occasion, Douglas, perhaps thinking the earl required closer supervision, bestirred himself to join the group. The unfortunate result was that Lady Tosten could maneuver so the earl was forced into Elizabeth's company as they strolled the cutting gardens.

For St. Just, it was a form of torture.

"You are doing much to bring Rosecroft back to its former beauty, my lord." Elizabeth peeked over at him from under her bonnet. "Tell me, do you believe you might revive the commercial aspect of the property, as well?"

"I know little about raising and selling flowers,"

he dodged, though he'd been considering just this project. "The work you see out here is the result of my houseguest's enthusiasm for gardening, as well as Winnie's efforts with Miss Farnum."

"So you, yourself, do not garden." Miss Tosten nodded, approving no doubt, as her prospective husband must not be in trade. "But I understand you are fond of horses?"

Fond of them? He'd supported himself very well buying, selling, and training them, thank you very much. He owed his life to horses many times over, and his passion for them eclipsed mere genteel fondness.

"I am," he replied, vowing he'd not disgrace himself with unruly speech again.

"As am I." She nodded again, gaining momentum. "They are so pretty and useful."

"That they are," he allowed, thinking of the emaciated, scarred, weary animals he'd seen littering countless battlefields. "But what are your other interests, Miss Tosten?" He most assuredly did not add "or may I call you Elizabeth?" because he could already see her beginning to plot in earnest: *The earl is interested in my accomplishments, Mama!*

"I play the pianoforte a little, of course." She wrapped a second hand around his arm as they walked along. "I sing and have modest talent with watercolors. I have not yet been to Paris, but Mama says we shall go next spring before the Season for some fittings and to polish my French."

"But what of the seasons other than spring, Miss Tosten? How do you fill the hours then?"

"One corresponds, of course." She blinked and

frowned as if in thought. "And we pay calls, and Mama is very active in local charities. I strive to learn from her example. Just this week, she motivated the Ladies Charitable Guild to investigate the state of widows and *orphans* here in the parish. Mama is a most charitable lady, and I hope to follow in her footsteps."

"I wish you every success," the earl said, his sarcasm apparently lost on her. *Oh, Mama*—he mentally winced—*the earl was most enthusiastic about the Orphan's Fund. How clever of you!*

Miss Tosten would never come to him with a new recipe that needed perfecting. She would never tear across the gardens barefoot in pursuit of a laughing child. She would never make soft, yearning sounds when he kissed her.

"Rosecroft." Douglas sauntered up behind them, Lady Tosten hanging on his arm. "I was just explaining to your guest we will not be able to attend their assembly, as I am going south in the next week or so, and you might well accompany me."

"Just so." The earl could have kissed Douglas on both cheeks. "My niece, Rose, is Lord Amery's step-daughter, and I have yet to make her acquaintance. I might have time to jaunt south and still be back here before harvest."

"Oh, never say it." Lady Tosten waved a hand. "Your niece has her entire life to make your acquaintance, but we have only the one summer assembly, your lordship. You must both stay."

"In our family," the earl said, gently disengaging Miss Tosten's arm from his, "we do not take one another for granted. As Rose is only recently out of mourning for her own father, she needs her uncles, and I'm thinking she might enjoy making Winnie's acquaintance, as they are already corresponding."

He watched as Lady Tosten registered that Winnie would be introduced to the Duke and Duchess of Moreland and all their progeny. "For the present, ladies, I must beg you to excuse us. There was a deal of correspondence delivered with the morning post, and it does not answer itself."

Lady Tosten almost hid it, but he saw her disappointment that again, no luncheon invitation would be forthcoming.

He'd no sooner dispensed with the Tostens, though, when Hadrian Bothwell presented himself, having arrived again on foot. Douglas excused himself, muttering something about drains and fall calves, so the earl rang for refreshments and wondered how anybody got anything done when the damned knocker was up.

⁂

"So will you really come south with me?" Douglas asked the earl over dinner. "Or was that merely an evasive tactic?"

Emmie glanced up at him sharply, as did Winnie.

"I don't know." The earl frowned at his soup. "It's tempting, but I don't want to ask one of my geldings for that effort again so soon… and I would miss my Winnie." Winnie's face creased into a bashful smile, but she said nothing. "Though I would be gone only for a few weeks, I suppose. Could you spare me, Win?"

"Would you come back?"

"I would come back. I give you my word I'd come back, and before winter, too."

"You'd go to see Rose?" Winnie asked, brow knit. "I suppose that would be all right. She is your niece."

"And you are my Winnie," the earl reminded her, but beside Winnie, Emmie was blinking hard at her soup.

"Emmie?" The earl turned his gaze on her. "Will it suit for me to make a short trip south?"

"Your roof and your stone walls are well under way," she said, "and harvest is still some weeks off. I'm sure Rosecroft could manage without you for a few weeks."

But what about you, the earl wanted to ask. He honestly could not tell if she was angry with him for contemplating this journey, or relieved or indifferent or... what?

"I will think about it," the earl said, his eyes on Emmie. She'd been keeping her distance from him all week, and he'd been content to let her. They were together at meals, and he frequently crossed paths with Winnie during the day, and hence, with her cousin. What he had not sought—had not felt welcome to seek—was privacy with Emmie.

≪❦≫

After the earl's disconcerting announcement at dinner, Emmie successfully eluded him for the rest of the evening. She should have known her efforts were doomed. He breached all protocol that evening and knocked on her bedroom door once the house was quiet.

"My lord?" She opened the door halfway but did not invite him in.

"I'd like a word with you, if you've the time?"

"In the library?"

"This won't take long," he said, holding his ground. She took the hint and stepped back, closing the door behind him. When he turned to face her, Emmie saw his green eyes go wide at the sight of her hair loose around her shoulders. Down and unbound. Not braided, bunned, or otherwise confined.

"You were brushing your hair," he guessed. "Which means you were almost ready for bed. I apologize for intruding." He wandered to her vanity and picked up a brush inlaid with ivory.

"It was a gift from the old earl," she said, watching him fingering her belongings. He ran his thumbnail down the teeth of her comb and picked up a blue ribbon coiled in a tray of hairpins.

"I have been considering how best to apologize to you," he said, winding the ribbon around his finger, "but I'm not sure exactly what label to put on my transgression."

Call it a kiss, Emmie silently rejoined.

"And was an apology the purpose of this conversation?" she asked, not knowing where in the room to put herself. She wasn't about to sit on the bed, and not on the fainting couch by the cold hearth either. She also didn't want to sit at her vanity, not with him standing there, acquainting his big, tanned hands with her belongings.

"I'm not just here to apologize." He smiled a slow, lazy smile at her. Not one of his company smiles, not a smile he'd give to Winnie or Lord Amery either. "Come sit, Emmie." He patted the low back of the chair at her vanity. "You are uneasy, wondering when I'll say something uncouth or alienate another neighbor. I regret that." He patted the back of the chair again, and on dragging feet, Emmie crossed the room.

She seated herself and expected the earl to take the end of the fainting couch or to slouch against the mantel. He caught her completely off guard by standing behind her and drawing her hair over her shoulders.

"I miss doing this for my sisters," he said, running the brush down the length of her hair, "and even for Her Grace when I was very young."

"She raised you?" Emmie asked, knowing she should grab the brush from him.

"From the age of five on. You have utterly glorious hair. Winnie will be the envy of her peers if she ends up with hair like this." He drew a fat coil up to his nose and inhaled, then let it drop and resumed his brushing.

"You should not be doing this," Emmie said, but even that weak admonition was an effort. "I should not be letting you do this."

"I interrupted you. It's only fair I should perform the task I disturbed. Besides, I wanted to talk to you about this trip Douglas has proposed."

Emmie rolled her eyes. "The one he proposed at the dinner table. In front of Winnie. What was he thinking?"

"He was thinking"—the earl kept up a slow, steady sweep of the brush—"to alert you to the possibility and to give you a chance to comment on it. But you did not."

"I said something." Emmie frowned, trying to recall what. Her common sense told her she needed breathing room—right this moment she needed breathing room, and in the days and weeks to come. She'd been trying to keep her distance from him, to avoid the near occasion of sin, but she couldn't keep him from her thoughts if he was always underfoot.

"You said nothing that told me what you think of the idea," he remonstrated. "One braid or two?"

"One. You should do as you please," she said, trying to rouse her brain to focus on the conversation.

"I hadn't planned on traveling south again until spring, perhaps when Gayle and Anna's child has arrived." He fell silent when the brush found a knot in the heavy abundance of her hair.

"So why go now?" Emmie asked when she ought to be telling him to go and stay away until spring.

"I'm not sure." He eased the brush through the knot. "I miss my family, for one thing. I didn't think I would. I spent much of the spring in Westhaven's household, and I saw a fair amount of Her Grace and my father then, too."

"But not your sisters, and you have yet to meet Rose, and your father is recovering from a heart seizure."

"He is. Easily, if my brothers' missives can be trusted. But what of Winnie? She is my family now, too, and I won't go if you think it would upset her too much. She's had a great deal of upheaval in her life, and I would not add to it."

"Winnie has given you her blessing." Emmie steeled herself against a lassitude that was making it difficult to keep her eyes open. "And Winnie is not a creature who ignores her own preferences. Just for God's sake do not fail to return, or I won't answer for the consequences."

"Will you miss me, Emmie Farnum?" He paused in his brushing, and Emmie felt his hands settle on her shoulders. She wanted to bolt to her feet and wrap her arms around him, to tell him not to go. She wanted to bolt to her feet and order him from her room, to tell him to go and not come back.

She sat in her chair, stock still, and watched in the mirror as he hunkered behind her chair and pushed her hair to the side, exposing the side of her neck.

"I told myself," he murmured, his thumb caressing the spot just below her ear, "I could behave if I had to track you to your lair tonight. I told myself that lie, and I believed it."

He leaned in slowly and pressed his open mouth to the juncture of her shoulder and her neck. His breath fanned over her skin, and Emmie had to close her eyes against the sight of him in her mirror. He rose, but only to let his hands drift down her arms and back up.

"You aren't stopping me, Emmie," he whispered.

"I will," she said, hoping it was true. But his long fingers were busy with the ties at her throat, and she felt her wrapper fall open as he bit her earlobe. Soon, she thought, soon I will stop him, but not just…

A large, warm hand settled gently over one breast, and Emmie could not prevent a little whimper of pleasure. Through the sheer fabric of her nightgown, she could feel the heat of him. His thumb eased across her nipple, coaxing it to firmness, and Emmie felt what little resolve she could claim evaporating.

"Rosecroft…" she murmured.

"Devlin, or St. Just, or my love, but not the bloody damned title." He shifted so he was kneeling before her and threaded his hand through her hair at her nape.

Another kiss, Emmie thought, her heart kicking into a gallop. *Just this once more, and then I'll be good.*

He made it a feast, that one kiss, by grazing his nose all over her jaw, her cheeks, her brow. Everywhere, he inhaled her scent and teased her with his own. She tried to capture his mouth, but he evaded such headlong behavior. His hand remained on her breast, cupping, teasing, and learning the shape and heft of her.

"St. Just," Emmie panted, "*Devlin*, please just kiss me."

He growled, a sound that held amusement and satisfaction, but he didn't capitulate to her demands until he'd undone the ties to her nightgown. Not until he fused his mouth to hers did he ease the material apart, though, and then he let his hand drop to her lap, leaving Emmie to focus on the way he plundered her mouth, stole her wits, and sent her best intentions and common sense begging down the lane.

Emmie opened for him immediately, her hands stealing around his shoulders, and those sexy little sounds starting up as soon as he touched his tongue to hers.

She wants it, he thought as his own lust spiked upward. *She wants me.*

And God knew he wanted her. His groin was throbbing with want, screaming with it, and demanding he make up for years of neglect in the next instant.

Emmie's hands were adding to the din, trailing up and down his arms then working at the buttons of his waistcoat. When she had those undone, she began to pull the hem of his shirt from his waistband.

"Emmie." He tried to catch her hands. "Emmie, love. Slow down." To get her attention, he broke the kiss, resting his forehead on her collarbone. "Easy now. Just… easy." She was breathing as hard as he was, gulping air, her hands coming to rest on his shoulders.

He lifted his head and peered around the room, then scooped her up and rose in one motion. "Bed," he whispered to her, kissing her nose before he lowered her onto the mattress. While Emmie blinked in consternation, he pulled off his shirt and waistcoat, then sat on the bed to tug off his boots.

"You stay right there," he muttered before rising and locking the door.

"I can't do this," she blurted out, rising up on her elbows. "I cannot… lie with you." He stopped, midstride, and frowned at her.

"Is it your courses? Because that needn't…"

Emmie shook her head. "No, it isn't… *that*." She blushed and turned her face away.

"I will not get a bastard on you, Emmie." He took the few steps needed to bring him to the bed and sat at her hip, gazing down at her. "You should know that at least."

"Are you God," Emmie said in quiet misery, "to prevent conception at will?"

Her sternum was open to his view, but the froth of her night clothes hid her breasts. She was breathing hard, he could see, with arousal, but also…

"Emmie." He reached out and brushed a lock of her hair back. "Let me pleasure you. You need it, I need it, and no one will be the wiser. I can ease your ache, and you can ease mine. It needn't be more complicated than that."

He trailed the back of his hand against the silky skin of her chest, moving her garments aside, baring a full breast to the candlelight. She closed her eyes, which he took for capitulation of a sort, so he leaned down and settled his mouth over her exposed nipple. He drew gently while his hand smoothed down over her ribs, over her belly, then back up.

Emmie's hands cradled the back of his head then went still, giving him the sense she was absorbing these shocking new pleasures. He knew he'd crossed the line from persuasion to seduction, for she'd said she would not lie with him. Could not. And he could not promise her if they joined, no child would result.

So he'd settle for half measures but make them such unforgettable half measures for her that she'd have no recriminations. He eased himself full-length onto the bed beside her and let his weight rest against her hip. Even that simple contact brought him some relief as Emmie arched into him, her refusals and remonstrations forgotten.

He pushed up and settled more of his weight against her. Her eyes flew open, and he met her panicked gaze, trailing a hand over her neck and sternum.

"I will not join with you tonight," he said, holding her gaze, "but neither will I let either one of us go unsatisfied."

Her eyes clouded with confusion even as he

lowered his head to kiss her. Slowly, tentatively, he felt Emmie's hands slide over his naked shoulders to join at his nape.

"That's it," he murmured, "we'll take it easy." His voice was a low rumble. He intended to reassure more than seduce and had no clue if he'd succeeded. He wanted his kiss, his voice, and his hand as it slowly explored her exposed breasts all to convey that there were eternities available for this pleasuring he offered her.

"Emmie," he murmured against her mouth, "spread your legs for me, love."

She startled when his hand settled on her mons. His fingers moved in lazy little circles across her pubic bone then back again, even while his tongue circled around hers. Then he shifted tactics, to comb his fingers through her curls, a slow caress intended to soothe as it aroused.

"Open," he reminded her, smiling against her mouth. "Please."

Tentatively, she let her knees ease apart two inches, but it was enough for his purposes. "That's my lady." He smiled again and began to move his hips, rocking his erection against her thigh. His hand moved in the same rhythm, but, oh the sweet places he touched…

Cautiously, he dipped a finger down the damp length of her sex. She flexed her hips to rub herself against his hand, then repeated the movement when he held his hand against her more firmly.

"Slowly," he cautioned, shifting his weight to give his hand greater range of motion.

"Not slowly," Emmie muttered in response. "Touch me, St. Just. You have to touch me."

She comprehended that much, he saw, but exactly how experienced she had was hard to tell. She was experienced *enough*, he decided, finding the bud of her pleasure and circling on it gently.

"St. Just…" Her fingers closed around his wrist, not restraining him, just experiencing the movement of his hand from that perspective, as well. "What are you…? Ah, God…" She lay open to him on her back, her knees now spread as his touch consumed all of her concentration. He increased the tempo of his caresses and felt her arousal kick up, as well. Her hips were rocking steadily, her breathing accelerating, and her grip on his wrist had grown tight.

"Easy." He leaned down and swiped his tongue across her nipple. "Let it come to you."

"I can't…" Emmie opened her eyes and met his gaze for one fleeting, bewildered moment. He knew then that at least this part of sex—her pleasure—was new for her. He lowered his head again and took her nipple in his mouth, drawing on it in a slow, relentless rhythm.

"St. Just…" She began to buck against his hand. "Devlin? *Devlin…!*"

He sank two fingers shallowly into her sheath, just enough that he could delight in the spasms clamping down in a hard, ecstatic rhythm. With his thumb, he brought a firmer pressure to bear on the apex of her sex, riding out the bucking, rolling undulations of her hips. His mouth drew on her nipple, easing the pressure only when he felt her pleasure begin to ebb.

"My lands," Emmie panted softly. "Oh, my lands, my lands…"

He smiled down at her and brushed her hair back with one hand.

"A triple 'my lands,'" he said, smiling. "I am content."

He wasn't, of course. He was hard as a pikestaff and throbbing for the very same pleasure he'd just given her, but seeing the wonder in Emmie's eyes, he *was* content. He could wait the few minutes it would take her to gather her wits.

She rolled up and wrapped her arms around him in a sudden, fierce hug.

"My lands," she said again before easing down to her back.

"You are so beautiful, Emmie Farnum." He brushed her hair back a second time. "So dazzlingly, glowingly beautiful in your passion. You are beautiful in your kitchen, too." He kissed her nose and cuddled her to him. Emmie surprised him by hooking her leg over his hips and settling against him with a sigh. Experimentally, he flexed his hips against her, but she only cuddled in more tightly.

His breeches would have to go.

"Give me a minute, love." He rolled away and shucked breeches and smalls in one movement, then rolled back to her. "How shall we go about this?"

She blinked at him, as if trying to decipher a rapid spate of some foreign language.

"Why don't I just take matters in hand, so to speak," he suggested, his hand dropping to caress the length of his erection, "while you assist?" He reached for her hand and brought it to his erection, then wrapped his own grip outside of hers. "Hold me, Emmie," he urged, "hold me this tight." He firmed his grip to show her what he meant and then turned his head to search for her lips.

"Hold me and kiss me," he said, his mouth open and greedy over hers.

❧

Barbarian, Emmie thought in the single word impressions her brain was passing off as thoughts. It tumbled through her mind with *kiss*, *more*, *Devlin*, *please*, *hot*, *shouldn't*, and *yes*.

His hips were undulating in a slow, powerful rhythm, his hand was fisted tightly around hers on his cock; when he groaned deeply, pulled her hand away, and held her snugly to him, his cock trapped between their bodies. He continued to move against her for another half-dozen hard thrusts, then he went still.

"My lands," he murmured into her ear. "My lands, my ever-loving most unbelievable lands."

The dampness on her belly told her he'd found his pleasure; the humor in his voice told her he was happy with the experience in ways beyond the purely physical. He shifted onto his back, reached for her hand, and kissed her knuckles.

"You have no idea, Emmie Farnum." He sighed and turned her hand over to kiss her wrist. "Not the first, least idea of the pleasure you've brought me."

He was, as she'd surmised, a generous lover. Generous beyond all telling with the pleasure he bestowed, generous with his words, and generous with his affection. Any one of those would have utterly slain her best intentions. Put them together with a pair of green eyes, broad shoulders, and a good heart...

Oh, what had she done?

"Let me clean us up," he said, drawing a finger down her nose. "Then I'm going to hold you."

She nodded, feeling tears threaten. He moved to the washbasin and wrung out a cloth, using it on his genitals with more briskness than Emmie would have thought reasonable. His member, so impressively turgid just moments before, had subsided to less intimidating proportions, though she still found it fascinating.

He smiled his barbarian's smile. "Keep looking at me like that, Emmie love, and I will be bothering you again in a trice." She blushed, looking at his feet instead, but even those struck her as masculine and *naked*.

"Lie back," he ordered, and Emmie complied while he wiped his seed from her hip and stomach. "Sex is so wonderfully messy," he said as he tidied her up. "There's no dignity to it. One wonders how the Archbishop of Canterbury goes about it, or say, the Bishop of London. You're quiet."

He wrapped his arms around Emmie and curled her up against his chest. "That is the most lovely experience of not lying with somebody I have ever had." He kissed her nose and then her mouth, lingering over it.

"Talk to me, Emmie." He rolled to his back and wrestled her to straddle him. "Tell me what's going on here." He tapped her temple.

"You didn't hear the echo?" she said, feeling his genitals, cool, damp, and soft against her sex. "There is nothing in there at the moment. Nothing but a long, undignified sigh of contentment."

"Your expression is not one of contentment, Emmie." His thumb stroked across her forehead. "I would say, rather, you are having the proverbial second thoughts." His hands on her shoulders urged her down so her chest was against his. "I am not inclined to allow it."

"You are not at your most rational." She sighed as his arms came around her. "I will not attempt a discussion of the many reasons why this is foolishness until at least one of us has some clothing on."

"Wise of you." His exuberant smile became a trifle hesitant. "Are you shy, Emmie, because a woman's pleasure has never befallen you before?"

She tilted her head up to assess his eyes, but they were giving away nothing. How much could a man tell from the kind of encounter they'd had?

She laid her cheek against his chest to escape that searching green-eyed gaze. "Or I am shy because I am naked in bed with the man who employs me, a fellow I've known of for about a month, give or take."

"But a decent fellow," the earl replied, his hand stroking over her hair. "I would not hurt you, Emmie."

"You are all that is considerate," she said, with a terse lack of warmth—but she tightened her hold on him nonetheless.

"We are going to talk about this, Emmie." His fingers found her nape and began to massage in slow, easy circles. "There are aspects of the situation you don't understand."

"I understand," she said without shifting to meet his eyes. "We are not married, and you seek certain liberties I intended to share with only a husband, or

the very near equivalent. You have brought me pleasure—unbelievable pleasure—but being with you like
this is not wise, and we both know it."

"You are letting the Lady Tostens of the world
dictate to you," he replied, frustration evident.

"The Lady Tostens of the world run the world, my
lord, for those of us who must make our own way."
She kept her tone patient, not the least accusatory.

"You will *not* stoop to angering me with formal
address, Emmie, not when I could be inside you in
the next two minutes." He arched up against her,
demonstrating graphically that while they'd talked, her
proximity had begun to stir his arousal again.

She rose up on her elbows to meet his eyes.

"You are not a rapist, and I am not a cock-tease nor
a whore." She moved to shift away from him, but he
caught her by the arms and shook his head slightly. His
hold was careful, and the look in his eyes was guarded.

"Please do not take away from me the good that
happened here with you," he said, matching her level
tone. "I can understand your virtue is precious to you,
and you are… upset, but I did not come here seeking
this outcome either, Emmie."

He held her gaze, a hint of pleading behind his
sternness, and she nodded then subsided onto his
chest. He had a point: She could have insisted on
meeting him in the library, could have grabbed him by
the ear and tossed him into the corridor.

In no way had he forced her; she couldn't be angry
at him.

"I am upset with myself," she said, closing her
eyes. She felt him nod then felt his hands sifting

through her hair again. His touch was slow, gentle, and comforting, even as it reminded her she must not—once this encounter was behind them—permit him to touch her in that same manner ever again.

"We will talk." He kissed the top of her hair. "For now, just let me hold you."

A fast, triple tap on her door had them both freezing.

"Miss Emmie?" Winnie's voice, followed by an attempt to lift the latch. "Oh, Miss Emmie, please wake up."

"She's wet the sheets or had a nightmare," Emmie said, dropping her forehead to his sternum for just an instant then swinging off him. "I'll take her back to her room." She scrambled into her nightgown and wrapper. "You be gone when I get back. She might want to sleep in here on the trundle."

"Emmie!" He hissed her name, grabbing her wrist as she paused by the bed to shove her feet into her slippers. She glanced over at him, and he bounded to his feet. In the next instant, his mouth was on hers, warm, plush, wicked, and sweet; then it was gone. He grabbed his clothing, blew out the candle, and slipped to the wall to the right of the door so when Emmie opened the door, he'd be hidden from view.

"I'm coming, Winnie," Emmie called softly, sparing him one look intended to convey longing, exasperation, and regret. "Just give me a minute."

Behind Emmie's door, the earl heard her voice trailing off, reassuring, teasing, making light of the situation. He eyed her bed in the moonlight streaming in her window and gave serious thought to simply dozing off right there. He had the sense she wasn't going to be reasonable about what had just happened, and the longer he let her stew and fret, the more unreasonable she'd be.

∾

"Do you think Rosecroft will get me a pony when he visits his family?" Winnie asked. She was bright-eyed and bouncing around the attic with restless energy, having gone right back to sleep the previous night as soon as Emmie had cleaned her up and ensconced her on a day bed.

In contrast to Winnie, Emmie had slept badly. She was torn between recalling the abundant, decadent… wonderful pleasures she'd shared with St. Just, and castigating herself for the whole business. It was one thing to pine for the attentions of a man she knew she couldn't have; it was yet another level of torment altogether to be shown just exactly what she'd be missing.

"Hello, my dears." The earl appeared in the entrance to the low-ceilinged attic, having to duck his head to pass through the door. "Find any treasures?"

"We did." Winnie skipped over to him and took his hand. "We found Aunt Anna's doll and Aunt Morgan's toy horse. There is a christening gown, too, and best of all, we found my papa's toy soldiers."

"No child raised on this sceptered isle should be without toy soldiers."

"See?" Winnie pulled him along. "I've set up a great battle, with the fellows in blue being the Grand Armee, and the fellows in red and so forth being Wellington's men. We even found some cannon and horsemen, but they're the wrong colors."

"You are having quite a war here." The earl hunkered amid Winnie's arrangement of men, cannon, and horses, and frowned. "So who's going to win?"

"Old Wellie's troops, of course," Winnie chided him, completely missing the care with which the adults were not looking at each other. "See, these fellows over here can gallop round this way, and that will leave the cannon up on the chair…"

"You're going to have trouble shooting your artillery straight down, but you are correct to use the rise for better advantage."

"Oh." Winnie sat back, surveying her troops. "Is that what real generals do?"

"At Waterloo"—the earl began shifting pieces around—"Wellington got word the French were approaching, so he arranged his lines along a ridge, like so. That put the French down here." He moved more pieces. "And the reinforcements, back here. That would be Blucher, for the Dutch were up on the ridge under Wellington."

"The reinforcements are too far away," Winnie said. "Why can't we move them up here?"

Quietly, Emmie watched as the earl moved cannon, horse, and infantry for both armies, explaining orders, strategies, and incidents to Winnie as he did. His face became oddly animated, excited but not happy… Just more and more tense.

"Well, why won't the bloody French just get on with it?" Winnie asked, sending some blue horsemen charging up the side of a trunk.

"Language, Winnie," Emmie chided quietly.

Winnie fell silent as the earl rose, his expression now carefully blank.

"If you'll excuse…" He turned and left without another word, his gait stiff but swift. Winnie frowned and gave Emmie a puzzled look.

"Was it because I said bloody French?" she asked, bewildered. "Everybody calls them that, or bloody Frogs. And Wellington won."

"He did. I think the earl recalls it as more than a little game of toy soldiers, Winnie. Let's leave him some privacy, shall we?"

"I'll put the soldiers away," Winnie said, puzzlement in her tone, "but then can we go bake something for dessert?"

❧

Why won't the bloody French just get on with it? Why won't the bloody French just get *on* with it? *Why won't the bloody French just get on with it…?*

The words circled in his head, present and past blending in one pounding drumbeat of fear, anxiety, and impending death. *Why won't the bloody French just get on with it?* Up and down the lines, the men had wondered the same thing. The cannons had gone silent, and the waiting had stretched for hours.

Smells came back to him, of mud, summer mud thick from the previous night's heavy rain then baked in the June heat. Damp woolen uniforms and the sweat of scared men, men who knew they'd already survived more battles than fate allowed.

Sounds beat against his sanity, the sound of restless horses, feet tramping in the mud, bridles and harness jingling with incongruous cheer across the still morning. The sound of men praying, muttering, swearing... *Why won't the bloody French just get on with it?*

"Shall I saddle up Wulf, my lord?"

His mind snagged on the thought that Wulf hadn't been at Waterloo. St. Just followed the voice with his gaze and found Stevens looking at him expectantly. Stevens, his groom... at Rosecroft... in Yorkshire.

"You all right, then?" Stevens asked, clearly uncomfortable.

St. Just shook his head and walked away, around to the back of the stables and then along the stone wall running down the hill from it. He took off his shirt, and with his bare hands, began to wrestle with the solid Yorkshire rocks, restoring them to order one backbreaking, sweating minute, by backbreaking, sweating minute.

From her bedroom, Emmie watched out the windows, seeing the earl wrestling with his stone wall. He'd be sunburned again, and he wasn't wearing gloves either. She could send Lord Amery down with a pair, but something in the earl's desperate focus suggested even that intrusion wouldn't be welcome. On and on he toiled, bringing a neat, solid form to what had been cascading into chaos. Emmie must have stood there for an hour, and still she was left wondering: If she'd allowed him to stay in her bed last night, if she'd trusted him with her deepest failings and fears, would he be out in the broiling sun, blistering his hands and straining his back trying to rebuild a stupid stone wall?

Eight

Almost a week after walking out of the attic and St. Just was still jumping at loud noises, tossing half the night, and eyeing the brandy decanter like a long-lost friend.

Which it was not, he reminded himself sternly. Banishing the thought of a drink at midmorning, he took himself off to the kitchens, there to accost Emmie Farnum and have the discussion they needed to have before his departure with Douglas.

He found his quarry rolling out sticky buns, the kitchen redolent with the smells of cinnamon, yeast, honey, and vanilla. He leaned in the doorway and treated himself to the sight of her elbow-deep in flour, her hair in its tidy bun, a plain blue day dress under her floury apron. He wrestled with the impulse to sneak up behind her, wrap his arms around her waist, and kiss the nape of her neck.

At his sigh of self-denial, Emmie's brows flew up.

"My lands! I didn't see you lurking there. If you've come to snitch, there's a tray cooling on the counter beside the sink." He sidled over to the sink, snagged a bun, and then went to the pantry to pour himself a glass of cold milk.

"What else are you making?" he asked between bites. She had flour on her cheek again, and it fascinated him. "These are good, by the way."

"I will finish up this batch," Emmie said, rolling up the dough and reaching for a sharp knife, "and then I have some pies to make. I'll do more cheese bread, and if there's time…" He'd come to stand beside her, right beside her, close enough to catch the subtle floral scent of her beneath the kitchen fragrances.

"Was there something you wanted?" she asked, arranging the cut buns in a greased pan.

He let off a bark of mirthless laughter but took another bite of sticky bun and watched as she moved away from him to put the pan in the oven.

"It is my imagination, Emmie, or has your business picked up?" he asked, eyeing the remaining sticky buns.

"No more," she scolded. "They'll ruin your luncheon. And yes, I am doing a greater volume of business. But you didn't come here to grill me on how my baking is going."

"I did not," he agreed, sitting down on the worktable with his milk. "I came here to discuss this trip with you."

"I am all ears." Emmie started measuring out butter, sugar, flour, and eggs for her next recipe.

"Emmie." He reached over and put a hand on her arm. "I know you are busy, but might you spare me a few minutes of your time? I don't want to talk to your sticky buns; I want to talk to you."

"Very well." Emmie untied her apron then grabbed

a mug of cider. "Let's go out on the terrace. I've been inside all morning, and some sunshine would be appreciated."

He let her precede him to the adjoining terrace, thinking the smell of horse was probably more bearable if they were out of doors. He also, God help him, watched the twitch and sway of Emmie's skirts and found himself again thinking of kissing her nape.

Emmie picked out a shady bench and settled herself. "What was it you wanted to say?"

St. Just frowned and, uninvited, assumed a place directly beside her. He was thinking of stealing kisses while she was... convening the town meeting.

"It occurred to me," he began, "Winnie is settling in here nicely, and at one time, I planned to find her a permanent governess."

"And when you do, I will take myself to the cottage as Winnie adjusts to her improved station in life."

"I don't like that idea." The earl frowned at his hands. "I'd bet Winnie positively hates it."

"She is becoming less resistant. This was your plan, my lord."

He glanced over at her sharply, scowling his displeasure at her tone and her retreat into my-lording him. "Are you running for cover, Emmie, because I shared pleasure with you?" he asked softly, staring straight ahead.

"I will be making a graceful retreat from Bronwyn's life," Emmie said, the edges of her words trimmed to a razor sharpness, "because it is in her best interests that I do so. And to be honest..."

He turned to regard her steadily.

"I am tiring," she said, her posture and her tone

wilting, and he knew that wasn't what she'd intended to tell him. "Looking after Winnie, keeping up with the orders, taking up the duties I promised Cook I would handle... You need a housekeeper, sir, and a few more maids and footmen wouldn't go amiss either."

"I can see to all that when I return," he said, regarding her with a frown. "I would like your word you will not depart this residence until I do come back."

"And when will that be?"

"By the end of September," the earl replied, admitting to himself he'd not set a date before this discussion. "I'm told winter sets in after Michaelmas, and ever since coming home from sunny Spain, I've hated English winters."

"What else did you hate?" Emmie asked, sipping her cider.

"Everything. The heat, the dust, the mud, the whining recruits, the arrogant stupidity of the junior officers, the bad rations, the boredom, the endless drilling, the insane orders, the killing, and the killing, and the killing..."

"You've had a setback," Emmie said, slipping her hand around his. "I should not have made you dwell on this."

"A setback." He sighed, savoring the feel of her hand in his. "One of many. Each time, I think maybe the gains I've made will be mine to keep. Each time, my horse is shot out from under me again."

"I don't believe that. Douglas says you are not the same man who came home from Waterloo."

"Maybe not." He lifted their hands and brought her knuckles to his lips. "I'm certainly not as hung over."

"You were drunk?" Emmie blinked and stared at her hand in his.

"For months. My baby brother, Valentine, was sent to fetch me home. I'd forgotten he was no longer a fourteen-year-old stripling, and though he had to beat me nigh insensible to see it done, he did get me back to Morelands."

Emmie cringed. "Your brother beat you?"

"Soundly. He's a piano virtuoso, and somehow I'd gotten to thinking of him as the soft one in the family. He's not soft, and those fists of his were lightning fast. He dropped me in short order, though I was fighting like a demon." And ranting at the top of his lungs and—merciful God—crying like a motherless child.

"I'm glad he brought you home."

"Oh, I was, too, eventually." And he was still glad Val had never mentioned that pathetic scene to a soul, either.

"You aren't telling me everything, are you?" Emmie's blue eyes were full of concern and faintly curious.

"I am not." He looked at their joined hands. "It is not a pretty tale, and you are such a pretty lady. Will you miss me, Emmie?" He'd shifted the topic adroitly, maybe even intending to fluster her with his compliment.

"Some day," she said gravely, "when you are ready, I want to hear the rest of it, Devlin St. Just. I don't care how miserable a tale, nor tragic. It needs telling."

"Or forgetting. And you've dodged my question."

"I will miss you," Emmie replied, trying to slip her fingers from his, but he held her hand in a firm, gentle grip.

Those words, four simple words, eased a tightness in his chest. His setback, as Emmie had diplomatically termed it, had shaken him badly. Whereas a week ago he would have been content to steal what pleasures he could with Emmie, now he was a more cautious man. Emmie deserved the attentions of a man who would not frighten her nor embarrass her with his nightmares, his temper, his bad memories, and his "setbacks."

But if she'd have him...

"I will miss you, too, Emmie Farnum," he said, leaning over to kiss her cheek. "I've thought about asking you and Winnie to come with us, but I agree with you the child needs no more upheaval. Then, too, we'll make better time without Winnie underfoot, and I flatter myself you will protect my interests in my absence."

"To the extent I can, though as to that, a female who is no relation to you has little consequence."

"I've left a power of attorney with Bothwell." He was reluctant to discuss his departure any further, wanting instead to talk of kisses and comforts and their shared concern for Winnie. "If there's any matter of significance, you may rely on Bothwell to stand in my stead. He'll be over here regularly to work the horses, and he seems to regard you highly."

"He regards my cheese breads highly. Though he is a good man, and I will alert him to anything of significance."

"He told me he offered for you. Were you tempted?"

Emmie gave an unladylike snort. "Of course I was tempted. Hadrian is an attractive man, inside and out, but he was asking out of loneliness and pity—maybe—and the knowledge that if a vicar is to indulge in carnal pleasures, it can be only with a wife or with a bothersome degree of discretion."

"So you declined because it wasn't a love match?" He had to smile at that thought.

"Not just that." Emmie wasn't smiling. "Hadrian is his brother's heir, and the viscount does not enjoy good health. He looks to Hadrian to secure the succession."

"You are not the stuff a viscountess is made of?" the earl hazarded. "I absolutely do not buy that, Emmie, and I've met a sight more viscountesses than you have." But he was watching her closely, and he comprehended why she'd turned Bothwell down.

The seat of the viscountcy was in Cumbria, while Winnie was bound to have remained in Yorkshire.

"Emmie." He slipped an arm around her shoulders. "You are not that child's guardian angel."

"I'm her family," was all she said, letting her head rest on his shoulder.

"When I return, Emmie, you and I are going to come to an understanding. You must know your place in Winnie's life is assured."

"No." Emmie raised her face and shook her head. "I must know Winnie's place in this life is assured, and I will be content with that."

"I will talk you around. For now it is enough we are united in the cause of Winnie's welfare. I know she and Rosecroft will be safe in your care, and I trust your word you will be here when I return. But be warned, Emmie, there is more we will discuss."

"Be warned yourself." Emmie smiled at him, her expression probably more wistful than she'd intended.

"I have asked you for that story, St. Just, the one that explains how a much-commended officer ends up beaten insensate and hung over on a packet home. We will discuss that, too." He didn't argue with her; he just gave her an answering smile and escorted her as slowly as he could back to the house.

The next day was spent in preparations for the journey. With luck, they'd reach Morelands within the week and be spared having to travel the next Sunday, or at least part of it. Douglas was dragooned into accompanying St. Just into York, where a sturdy saddle horse by the name of Beau was purchased for the earl.

The next priority was some provision for Winnie in St. Just's absence, which was quickly dealt with. When he came out of the solicitor's office, St. Just made a few other purchases then found Douglas waiting for him with the horses at the nearest green.

"To Rosecroft." The earl swung up and nudged Wulf into a trot. It wasn't quite home, but it was as much home as he had found anywhere since leaving for university sixteen years ago. That truth emerged only as a function of the fact that on the morrow, he'd be leaving Rosecroft.

And Winnie.

And Emmie.

✑

Somewhere in the house, a clock struck midnight, and the sound brought Emmie's attention to the drone of rain pattering against the windows. The night had grown almost brisk, and the cooler air had left her restless.

The cooler air, the earl's departure on the morrow, the entire mess her life had become since his arrival were all keeping her from sleep. She had to be up by five at the latest to get the day's baking done, and she'd already tried reading to distract her mind into slumber. Drastic measures were called for, and so she tied her hair back with a ribbon, located her slippers, and headed for the decanter in the library.

The room was dark other than the feeble light of Emmie's candle, but it was enough for her to find the decanter and a glass. She wasn't sure how much was required to sooth frazzled nerves, but she'd managed the amount the earl had served her, so she doubled that and took a cautious sip.

It still warmed, burning then soothing, as it trickled down her throat. She sighed and took another small sip.

"Have we reduced you to tippling, Emmie?" St. Just's voice rose from the sofa, where he'd been reclining in the dark. He loomed up from the shadows, barefoot, shirt open at the neck, and cuffs turned back.

"We have." She kept her gaze on the tumbler in her hand, lest she be caught staring at the earl in breathtakingly attractive dishabille. "I have to be up early, and I could not sleep. The brandy helped before."

"But what could possibly keep you awake?" the earl mused, taking her glass from her and stealing a sip. "Surely your conscience cannot trouble you?"

"Nobody's conscience should ever rest entirely."

"Not even in times of war?" he asked softly, glancing at her loose hair and state of undress.

"In battle, probably," Emmie allowed, noting his perusal.

"Probably?"

She met his gaze. "St. Just, what troubles you?"

"The night is not long enough even to start on that, Emmie," he said, eyeing her drink as if he'd like to consume it whole. "Suffice it to say I am plagued by unhappy and unflattering memories."

"We all have those."

"We do?" He reached out and lifted a skein of her hair, letting it trail over his fingers. "Have you ever wanted to kill someone, Emmie Farnum?"

"I have," she said, swallowing as his fingers brushed her arm. "You saw to the matter for me."

"Helmsley." The earl looked intrigued. "When did you want to kill him?" He took her by the hand and led her to the sofa, across the room from the light of Emmie's candle.

"When didn't I?" Emmie sat beside him and stared into the darkness. "It isn't something I think about, you know? As a very young man, he was merely spoiled, though I couldn't see it at the time. He became a menace, a thoroughgoing scoundrel who grew more reprehensible with each passing year, but none of that would have mattered, except for Winnie."

"He left her more or less alone." St. Just's hand trailed her hair over her shoulder, a repeated, rhythmic caress that seemed to be soothing him as it relaxed her.

"He did, but he would occasionally recall he had a daughter and summon Winnie to parade about for his friends."

"I wasn't aware he had friends."

"Not many," Emmie said, looping her linked hands

over her drawn-up knees, "and none of any honor. There was one in particular, Baron Stull. He was a huge, fat monster, and whenever he requested it, Helmsley would summon Winnie to sit on the man's lap. It was depraved."

"Before he departed this life, Helmsley implicated Stull in all manner of schemes, including arson and attempted kidnapping," St. Just said. "Stull has not the support in the Lords to escape his fate, and every so often, they like to convict one of their own as an example. But likely the thing that galls you most is that you could not intervene."

"Oh, but I did," Emmie said, smiling bitterly. "I taught Winnie to hide and I bribed the servants to warn her when Stull was about and I taught her how to hurt a man should he bother her. She knows how to get into the cottage even when it's locked up tight, and she knows every way to get out of this house. I told her she wasn't helpless, but she had to be very careful."

"So you gave her options," St. Just said, his thumb making slow circles on her nape.

"I did, and in that regard, even the bad memories are worth respecting."

"How can a bad memory ever be worth keeping?" St. Just's hand went still. "I would give a body part, Emmie, to forget some of things I've done and seen, the things I've heard."

"No you would not," Emmie chided. "Those bad memories, times you were angry or frightened or beyond the call of conscience, they are still memories of times you survived. You let those go, and survival loses some of its meaning, as well. You're alive, St. Just, but only because you made it through those worst times."

All of him went still at her words, and in the silence, the clock chimed the half hour.

"Say that again," he ordered softly.

"You lose the worst memories," Emmie said slowly, "and you lose memories of survival; forget them, and survival loses some of its meaning."

He repeated the words to himself silently while Emmie watched his lips moving. The rain spattered against the window in a wind-driven sheet, and he dropped his forehead to her shoulder.

"Sleep with me tonight," he said, "or let me sleep with you."

"You know we cannot."

"Just sleep, Emmie. I will not bother you."

In the dark, she could not read his expression, but she did know he was ripe for another setback. He wasn't sleeping in his bed, it was after midnight, and his memories were tormenting him.

"I will scream the house down if you misbehave, and I will not let you seduce me." It was a terrible idea—almost as terrible as the thought of not seeing him for weeks, not hearing him banter with Lord Amery, not watching as he slowly coaxed Winnie into a semblance of civilized behavior. It was a terrible idea, for she could not think of refusing him.

"Tonight, Emmie love, I could not seduce my own right hand. I've already tried." She shot him a puzzled look but kept her questions to herself.

"Take me upstairs, Emmie." He rose and drew her

to her feet. "Please." She made no reply, just took his hand, picked up her candle, and led him to her bedroom. While she finished braiding her hair, he locked the door then undressed, washed, and climbed under her covers. When her fingers hesitated at the ties of her nightgown, he met her gaze.

"It's up to you. Sleep however you are comfortable."

She blew out the candle before taking off her clothes and climbing in beside him.

"You will sleep?" she asked, her voice hesitant in the darkness.

"Eventually," he replied, pushing her gently to her side, "and so will you." He trailed his fingers over her shoulder blades then down her spine. "Relax, Emmie. I've given my word I will behave, and I would not lie to you."

She sighed and gave herself up to the pleasure of having her back rubbed and then, only moments later, to the pleasure of slumber.

"Better," he murmured, content just to touch her. The smooth, fragrant expanse of her flesh under his hands soothed him, distracted him from the rain and the rain scents coming in the windows. Her breathing evened out, and the tension in her body eased. Slowly, so as not to disturb her, he curved his naked body around hers and slipped a hand around her waist.

She sighed again and snuggled back against his chest, then laced her fingers through his. He felt himself drifting into sleep, Emmie's hand in his, her warmth against his heart, her fragrance blotting out the memories that had denied him sleep.

Peace. Finally, finally, I have experienced that thing referred to as peace.

❧

"Emmie." St. Just stepped closer, ignoring Stevens, Douglas, and Winnie across the yard. "I do not want to leave you."

"But you will," she said simply, "and this journey will be good for you. Your family is anxious about you, too, and if you don't go now, traveling will not get any easier until spring."

"I know." He slapped riding gloves against his thigh. "I know all that, but I also know I will miss you and Winnie and… oh, hell."

He spun her by her shoulder and fastened his mouth to hers. It was not a chaste, parting kiss but a hot, carnal, daring, reminding kiss. He'd taken her off guard, and she was slow to respond, but when she did, it was to frame his jaw with her hand and circle her arm around his waist. She allowed him his moment, neither resisting nor encouraging, but when he broke the kiss, she stayed in his arms, resting her forehead on his chest.

"Naughty man."

"Something to remember me by," he murmured, pleased with himself. "Take care of Winnie, write, and I will see you in a few weeks."

"Take care of yourself, Devlin St. Just." She held his gaze solemnly. "Let your family love you."

Her comment puzzled him, sounding like something Douglas might say, but there was no time to parse her meaning. He signaled to Stevens, who brought over the sturdy gelding purchased days earlier in York.

"Miss Emmie?" Lord Amery brought Winnie to her and passed Winnie's hand into Emmie's. "Good-bye, my dear. Winnie has assured me she will look out for your welfare, but you must know, have you need of me or my resources, *at any time*, you have only to call upon me." He wrapped an arm around her shoulders, and for the space of a slow breath, brought her against his lean frame. "I'll look after him, Emmie, but you might consider letting him look after you, too."

She was so startled by that whispered suggestion it barely registered when Douglas pressed a soft kiss to her cheek then stepped back. Both men mounted up, and with a final wave, cantered down the drive. The only sounds left when their hoofbeats had faded were the splashing of the fountain and Winnie's foot scuffing in the dirt.

"I hate that they left," Winnie announced, "and he didn't even get me a pony." Emmie caught Stevens's eye at that remark and returned his smile.

"The earl will be back, Winnie, and Lord Amery will probably visit again, too. Besides, we have too much to do to be missing them for very long."

"Beg pardon, Miss?" Stevens interrupted when she would have taken Winnie by the hand and returned with her to the kitchens.

"Stevens?"

"His lordship left summat for Miss Winnie in the stables," Stevens said, his blue eyes twinkling with mischief, "but not a pony."

"Oh, Miss Emmie." Winnie swung Emmie's hand. "Can we go see? Please?"

"Let's do." Emmie nodded at Stevens, and Winnie was off like a shot.

"So, where is it?" Winnie asked, peering down the barn aisle moments later. "What can it be doing in the stable if it isn't a pony?"

"Up there." Stevens pointed to the hayloft. "I'll fetch it down." Stevens came down the ladder moments later, moving carefully with something tucked under one arm.

"Said his name's Scout." Stevens put a wiggling black ball of puppy fur on the ground and passed a twine rope into Winnie's hands. "Bought him in York. He said Lord Amery weren't keen on leaving a pony behind and nobody to teach Miss Winnie how to ride it yet."

"A puppy!" Winnie squealed. "Oh, a puppy! Is he mine? Can I keep him?"

"He's yours," Stevens replied, smiling broadly, "and from the way he's taking on, I doubt you could get rid of him."

"A dog," Emmie said, nonplussed. And now, *now*, she felt tears welling. That blasted, sweet, barbaric, impossible man... A dog was such a messy creature, drooling and shedding and worse and so lovable... And Winnie needed some companionship.

As Winnie scratched her puppy's tummy and scuffled with him in the dirt, Stevens offered Emmie an apologetic smile. Winnie was in transports, giggling at her puppy, when just a few minutes before, she'd been near tears. "It's very thoughtful of his lordship, but that thing is going to be enormous."

The puppy was quite young, but its paws were proof of Emmie's words.

"There's something else, too, Miss Emmie." Stevens had gone bashful now, and Emmie was intrigued. "Here." Stevens beckoned her to follow him out the back of the stables, to where a separate entrance led to a roomy foaling stall. "He said you needed summat other'n t'mule, and you're to limber her up, as Miss Winnie will be getting a pony soon."

A sturdy dapple-gray mare stood regarding Emmie from over a pile of hay. She turned a soft eye on Emmie and came over to the half door to greet her visitors.

"Oh, Stevens." Emmie's eyes teared up again. "She is so pretty... so pretty."

"He left ye a message." Stevens disappeared back into the barn and came out with a sealed envelope. "I can tack her up if ye like."

Emmie tore open the envelope with shaking fingers. How dare he be so thoughtful and generous and kind? Oh, how dare he... She couldn't keep the horse, of course; it would not be in the least proper, but dear Lord, the animal was lovely...

> My dear Miss Farnum,
>   Her name is Petunia, and she is yours. I have taken myself to points distant, so by the time I return, you will have fallen in love with her, and I will be spared your arguments and remonstrations. She is as trustworthy and reliable a lady as I have met outside your kitchen, and at five years of age, has plenty of service yet to give. Bothwell has been alerted you will be joining him on his rides,

*should it please you to do so. And if you are still
determined not to keep the horse, dear lady, then
consider her my attempt at consolation to you for
inflicting Scout on the household in my absence.*
                                      St. Just

He'd drawn a sketch in the corner of Scout, huge
paws splayed, tongue hanging, his expression bewildered, and broken crockery scattered in every direction. The little cartoon made Emmie smile through
her tears even as Winnie tugged Scout out behind the
stables to track Emmie down.

"Are you crying, Miss Emmie?" Winnie picked up
Emmie's hand. "You mustn't be sad, as we have Scout
now to protect us and keep us company."

"It isn't Scout, Winnie." Emmie waved a hand
toward the stall where Petunia was still hanging her head
over the door, placidly watching the passing scene.

"Oh." Winnie's eyes went round. "There's a new
horse, Scout." She picked up her puppy and brought
him over to the horse. The mare sniffed at the dog
delicately, then at the child, then picked up another
mouthful of hay.

"Her name's Petunia," Emmie said, finding her
handkerchief. "The earl brought her from York so I can
ride out with the vicar."

"She's very pretty," Winnie said, stroking the
velvety gray nose. "And not too big." The mare was
fairly good size, at least sixteen and a half hands, and
much too big for Winnie.

"Maybe once I get used to her, I can take you up
with me, Winnie. Would you like that?"

"Would I?" Winnie squealed, setting the dog down. "Did you hear that, Scout? Miss Emmie says we can go for a ride. Oh… We must write to the earl and thank him, Miss Emmie, and I must tell Rose I have a puppy, too. I can knight Scout, can't I?"

"Of course you may," Emmie said, reaching for Winnie's hand. "Though you must know knights would never deign to be seen in the castle kitchens, except perhaps in the dead of winter, when it's too cold to go charging about the kingdom."

"Did knights sleep in beds?"

"Scout can stay with Stevens above the carriage house when you have repaired to your princess tower for your beauty sleep."

"I'll ask Scout."

It turned out Scout was a loquacious fellow, and on topics puppies did not normally expound upon. He decided sums were to follow penmanship, that Rose would like his portrait posthaste, that raspberry cobbler would do for dessert.

"Apple tarts will make me miss Rosecroft," Winnie explained to her dog, who was learning to play fetch on the terrace behind the kitchens. Emmie smiled at the puppy's antics and sipped her cold, sugared meadow tea. She admitted to herself she missed St. Just already, missed his stride on the polished wood floors of the manor, missed his scent when he leaned in to steal a kiss, missed the sight of him on his horses…

And knew, in her bones, in her heart, that were he not gone from the manor, she'd be hard put to deny him her bed again. She'd never spent the night in the same bed with a man before, hadn't slept with another person since she was a very, very small child, in fact. Just as with kissing, he had the knack of it. She could still feel his hand, gentle, soothing, and slow on her back. There'd been nothing sexual in the caress at all, but he had been *tender* with her, reverent almost.

She'd fallen asleep feeling more relaxed, physically and mentally, than she could ever recall. With his warmth spooned around her, she hadn't felt confined, she'd felt safe, *cherished, protected, adored*.

Thanks to all the gods in all their heavens he'd gone traveling when he had. It would take her a whole month to find the resolve to leave this house and the man who dwelled here.

Much less the child he was coming to love, as well.

Nine

"I AM GLAD TO SEE YOU PUTTING HER THROUGH HER paces." Hadrian Bothwell smiled at Emmie from Caesar's back. "A week is long enough for a placid animal to settle in."

"Petunia is not placid; she is dignified, and I could hardly join you without a proper habit, could I?"

"S'pose not. So have we heard from Rosecroft?"

"Not yet." Emmie patted the mare's neck. "But it has only been a week or so. Winnie has written to him twice and to her friend Rose, as well."

"When do you think he'll take Winnie to meet his family?" Bothwell held his mount back so they could ride side by side. "Or hasn't he told them of Helmsley's indiscretion?"

"I'm sure he has," Emmie replied as mildly as she could. Helmsley's *indiscretion*, indeed. "He was considering taking her with him on this trip but wanted to be able to travel quickly."

"One can see where a child would thwart that aim." Bothwell glanced over as if he'd belatedly sensed his poor choice of words. "I think Miss Winnie must be running you ragged, as well, Emmaline Farnum. You look like you've come off a hard winter, my girl."

"I am just a little fatigued," Emmie said, feeling her irritation spike, though she considered Hadrian a friend. When he'd first come by her bakery, he'd always chatted for a few moments and appeared to take an interest in her welfare—a little more than the interest of a vicar or a neighbor. Then he'd run into her a few times in town, making purchases, and insisted on walking with her and carrying her packages. Emmie had considered it his public declaration of tolerance for one in her position; but then had come his proposal. It had been almost two years ago, and she was still a little perplexed by it.

Flattered, but perplexed.

"Emmie." Hadrian steered his horse toward a small clearing that sported a gazebo and some vestiges of flower beds overgrown with asters. "There's something I've been wanting to speak with you about, but the moment hasn't presented itself. If you have a few minutes, I'd like you to hear me out."

His blue eyes were looking dreadfully solemn, and his handsome features were serious. Emmie let him assist her to dismount but felt the first twinge of anxiety when he held her by the waist for a moment, searching her eyes before stepping back.

Had that been an embrace?

"Come." He took her gloved hand in his and led her to the gazebo, leaving the horses to crop grass. When she sat on the bench inside the little wooden structure, he surprised her further by sitting beside her and taking off his gloves, then hers.

"Hadrian?" She looked up at him expectantly. "You're not going to propose again, are you?"

"I am," he said. "Before you reject me out of hand—again—I want you to know a few things." He laced his fingers through hers, his hand cool and dry against her palm.

"Go on," she urged, curious but unable to escape a sense of dread, as well.

"I've received word from my brother that his prognosis is not… cheering," the vicar began. "We've known for some time his health was fading, but it isn't something that was acknowledged, until now."

"Hadrian, I'm sorry," Emmie said, meaning it. The man had lost his wife just a few years previously, and as far as she knew, his brother was his only surviving family.

"I am sorry, as well. Harold is a good man and a better viscount than I will ever be, but as the saying goes, these things are in God's hands."

"Not much comfort now, is it?" Emmie offered him a wan smile.

"Not much, though as a consequence of Harold's situation, I will be resigning from the living at St. Michael's by spring at the latest, if not by Christmas. I've always put Hal off when he wanted to get into details of the estate management and the investments. But he's told me I'm not to stall anymore, and he means it."

"So you will be leaving us," Emmie concluded, feeling a definite pang. Hadrian had been kind to her.

"I will be leaving. I want you to come with me."

She shook her head and tried gently to untangle

their fingers. "I cannot. You do me great honor, but you must understand—"

"Understand what, Emmie?" he shot back in low, intense tones. "Rosecroft will see to the child. I'll make him dower her and establish a trust if you like before we go. He'll do it, too, if he hasn't already. You'd be shut of these rural busybodies, and you would be my viscountess."

He was so earnest, so convinced of the rightness of his plan, Emmie felt her resolve crumbling. It was best to be firm—she knew that—but were it not for Winnie…

"Don't answer me now." He laid a finger to her lips. "I can see you are torn, but, Emmie, my brother has been a good manager, and my family prospers, at least financially. You would never have to haul your own coal again, never have to lime the privy yourself, never have to set foot in a kitchen if you didn't want to."

"I am aware of the burdens you would ease for me, Hadrian," she said quietly, rising and turning to look out over the fields of Rosecroft. He stepped up behind her, and she felt him rest his hands on her shoulders.

"And I can understand, Hadrian, why marriage to you might appeal to me, or to any young lady who knows you. But what does marriage to me have to recommend it? I am not young; you will need at least an heir. I am not received, and for all you know, I would not be the most accommodating partner regarding my marital duties. There is absolutely nothing about this bargain that makes sense to me from your perspective." She stood with her back to him, feeling his hands resting on her shoulders.

His hands dropped, and he shifted to sit on the railing facing her, his expression thoughtful.

"If there is anything that moves me to anger," he said, holding her gaze, "it's the way polite society can wound without a word. A cut direct is just that, a cut to the bone of a person's dignity and self-confidence, and you've let them cut you, Emmie."

"So you pity me?" she asked, lifting her gaze to the manor house in the distance.

"I have compassion for you, and I admire you, as well. I do not seek another wife like the first, Emmie. Rue was dear, but she was a child, expecting me to do everything but slice her meat for her. She suffered my attentions twice a month in the dark under the covers and then only because she knew we'd a duty to the title."

"You should *not* be telling me this." Emmie felt heat creep up her neck. "I don't want to know it, and your wife would not appreciate your sharing marital confidences."

"My *late* wife," he said in uncharacteristically clipped tones, "complained of me to her sisters, so do not bark at me regarding marital confidences, Emmie Farnum. Rue and I did fairly well, considering our circumstances, but never more than that."

"Hadrian, I am sorry," Emmie repeated, not knowing what else to say. "What makes you think we would ever do more than fairly well should we marry?"

"Ah, Emmie." He sighed. "Do you think I'm not a man because of a silly little collar? Do you think I can't see the fire and life in you? You are one of God's finest creations, and I want you for my own."

Her alarms went off in shrieking peals of dismay

as she realized the man was going to kiss her. He was fair about it, too, taking her gently by the shoulders and looking her square in the eye before bending his head to hers.

Emmie found him far more proficient at the whole business than any rural vicar had a right to be. He was tall, nearly as tall as St. Just, though not quite as muscular or broad, and he brought Emmie against his chest with a surprising strength.

"Let me kiss you, Emmie," he murmured, his thumb feathering over her cheekbone as he angled her head to meet his lips. He moved his mouth over hers softly, slowly coaxing and inviting, not demanding. His tongue, when he deftly brought it to her lips, tasted of lemon and sweetness, and Emmie thought she should have found the contact enticing, except that it wasn't—quite.

"Open for me," he coaxed, but Emmie wasn't willing to mislead him that far. The truth was, his kiss—skilled, tender, caring, and in every way well presented—left her indifferent. She stepped back but allowed him to keep her in a loose embrace.

"I'm sorry," he said, dropping his cheek to her hair. "But I'm not sorry, either. I desire you, Emmie, on many levels, and I could make marriage at least pleasant for you. Promise me you'll think about it."

"I will think about it," she said. "Were I to answer you today, Hadrian, I'd respectfully decline." He nodded but smiled, and Emmie realized all he'd heard was that she hadn't said no.

"I'll accept that for now." He planted a swift, smacking kiss on her lips then dropped his arms.

"Hadrian?" With a hand on his arm, Emmie stopped him from bounding down the steps. "I will not have you displaying your intentions again. While your attentions were in no way unpleasant, neither your reputation nor mine could withstand the gossip."

He nodded once then gave her a perfectly proper leg up and a perfectly proper escort back to the stables. When he turned to assist her off her horse, however, Emmie rode up to the ladies' mounting block and got herself down.

She passed her reins to Stevens, who gave her an odd look, but then made her excuses and took herself directly up to the house. She spent a long time in her room, ostensibly changing out of her riding habit but mostly trying to locate her scattered wits. When she concluded the exercise was futile, she forced herself to head back down to the kitchen.

"I got a letter, Miss Emmie!" Winnie came scampering up to her, Scout's toenails clicking at her heels along the floor. "Two letters, one from Rose and one from Rosecroft. May I open them?"

"Of course you may." Emmie bent to take the letters from Winnie. "Let's attend your correspondence in the library."

Winnie had taken to sitting in the earl's chairs, both in the library and at the dinner table. She was particularly careful to watch Stevens and the vicar every time they schooled a horse in the ring, and just last night, Emmie had gone upstairs to check on the child before retiring and known a moment's panic. Winnie was not in her bed, and in the past that might have signaled the beginning of hours of peregrinations about the estate.

Emmie had found her curled up under a spare blanket at the foot of the earl's bed.

"Let's repair to the sofa, shall we?" Emmie sat in the middle and patted the spot beside her. Winnie budged up and peered at the letters.

Rose's epistle was a potpourri of little-girl gossip, but she did point out that when Winnie's Aunt Anna had a child with St. Just's brother Gayle Windham, then both little girls would be cousins to the baby. From Rose's perspective, this must surely require a visit on Winnie's part to her southern relations.

"A visit?" Winnie said, resting her head against Emmie's arm. "I should dearly love to visit, but spring is far away. Scout won't want to wait so long."

"He'll understand if you explain it to him." And in all honesty, the dog had learned a number of commands easily—almost as easily as he inhaled great quantities of kitchen scraps. "Shall we see what your other letter says?"

"Please." Winnie scooted around, her enthusiasm eclipsing her ability to sit still.

> *My dear Misses Farnum,*
>
> *Our trip down here was uneventful. I can honestly report your friend Douglas was a good boy, though he would be less saddle sore if he got off and jogged beside his mount more often. I trust by now you have trained Scout to devour intruders, or at the very least, subdue the occasional slipper. His pedigree is dubious, but I was assured by his breeder he is the equivalent*

of many an old-time duke, his antecedents being champions on all sides.

My family is in good health, and Anna James Windham in particular sends along her greetings to you both. She is in expectation of a blessed event and has managed to distract my dear brother from his infernal correspondence long enough that he joins us here at Morelands for the next week or so.

My brother Valentine has warned me a gift is being forwarded from him to Rosecroft, a sort of housewarming present. When I consider the way my youngest brother was the butt of jokes and pranks growing up, I am loathe to open any gift from him. If it snarls or emits noxious odors, you must promise to return it unopened.

I commend Winnie on her prompt issuance of correspondence, but fear I cannot agree Scout should be learning how to pass a teacup. A beer mug, perhaps, but nothing delicate. In the alternative, Winnie, you might teach him to roll over, fetch, or bark on command. The Viscountess Amery has apparently taught these same skills to all the males in her domain, with the command to lie down being obeyed with particular alacrity. Anna seems to be making similar inroads with the future duke—oh, how the mighty have fallen.

I miss you both and trust this finds you in good health and good spirits. The enclosed provides a few glimpses of my visit thus far with the last little sketch being of Winnie's new friend, Rose.

> Devlin St. Just
> Rosecroft

"What does he mean about the mighty falling?"

"I suppose he means his brother was a very serious man," Emmie suggested, "until your Aunt Anna married him and made him more lighthearted."

"Rosecroft is not lighthearted. He should get married, too. I'm going to go teach Scout to lie down."

In Winnie's absence, Emmie lifted St. Just's letter to her nose and found to her profound pleasure the stationery bore a faint whiff of his fragrance.

She was reminded by contrast of the vicar's attentions.

Hadrian Bothwell smelled good, too, she admitted. With the sense of a person staring over a sheer precipice, Emmie feared she might marry the man after all. She could learn to tolerate him in bed; on the strength of one kiss, she was sure he'd acquit himself competently in that regard. She could learn to socialize with his neighbors and keep herself occupied while her husband took his seat or went off shooting in Scotland or did whatever it was cordial husbands did when their wives had provided them sons.

Children, she thought with a pang. That was the real draw. Children to love and call her own and raise each and every day under her loving eye.

Except—she stood up and began to pace—if they were boys, they might go off to public school as early as age six. That decision would be her husband's, just as every decision regarding the rearing of their children would be.

And what if she couldn't tolerate Hadrian's attentions? A short, fully clothed kiss was one thing, but what about the more intimate dealings? Somehow, she could not imagine *ever* begging the man to kiss her, not the way she'd begged St. Just. She could not imagine crying in Hadrian's arms nor handing him her hairbrush nor asking him for an opinion on a recipe.

Maybe—she sat back down—the situation required a good deal more thought.

⤳

St. Just came in from his morning ride to find Douglas in the Morelands stable yard, checking to make sure the traveling coach was properly packed.

"I am pleased." Douglas said, his gaze traveling over the horse's lathered coat. "You are off your backside, no longer content to twiddle your thumbs while your sisters throw their friends at you."

"I am off my backside." St. Just swung down. "Beau was sufficiently rested that he was good for a gallop today. We went by some of my childhood haunts and found them blessedly still the same for the most part. But, ye gods, childhood was a lifetime ago."

"Can you see someday touring Spain and France and thinking the same thing?" Douglas asked as a groom took Beau.

"Yes," the earl said, surprised at his own answer as Douglas fell in step beside him on the path to the manor. "I can, actually. Not for years, but someday."

"Then ride every day. It was part of what you enjoyed about being at Rosecroft."

"I'm bringing a few more of my youngsters north with me when I go back," St. Just said, finding a tea cart on the back terrace laden with ice water, lemonade, and bread and butter. "Shall we sit?"

Douglas nodded and settled into a chair.

"I'm also nipping into London tomorrow and jaunting down to my own stud farm for a day or two. I've sent along a note to Greymoor, requesting word of any worthy prospects, though he charges a pretty penny for anything leaving his farm."

"Have you written to Emmie?"

"I write to them both," St. Just replied, chugging some cold lemonade. "Emmie chided me to observe the proprieties, so I have not written to her, precisely."

"If you did write, just to her, what would you write?"

St. Just sat back, more relaxed than he'd been in days for having had a good gallop. "I would tell her I miss her, that I am scared of being around people all the time, but only marginally less scared when alone. I'm afraid of the next rainy night, *still*, and I miss Winnie more than I thought I would. Winnie is just... good. Innocent, you know? I would tell her I am not sleeping as well as I did in Yorkshire, but I am managing not to drink much, so far. I would tell her—"

"Yes?" Douglas cocked his head, no doubt surprised at the raw honesty of these sentiments.

"I would tell her I was better when I could smell fresh bread in every corner of my house and know she was busy in my kitchen. I would tell her there are no stone walls here for me to beat my head against, and I miss her."

"Emmie is a stone wall?" Douglas eyed his water, his expression perplexed.

"In a sense." St. Just grinned ruefully. "A good sense."

Douglas rose to his feet. "If I were you, I would start writing."

"I'm not passing along such drivel to such a sensible woman." St. Just rose, as well, and eyed Douglas a little uncertainly. "She'd think my wits had gone begging."

"It isn't your wits," Douglas said sternly. He pulled St. Just into his arms, not for a quick, self-conscious, furtive male hug, but for an embrace, full of affection and protectiveness. "It's your heart, you ass. Now listen to me." He put a hand on the back of St. Just's head, effectively preventing St. Just from doing aught but remaining pliant in his arms. "I love you, and I am proud of you. I am grateful for the years you spent defending me and mine, and I will keep you in my prayers each and every night. Write to me, or I will tattle to Her Grace, Rose, and Winnie."

"A veritable firing squad of guilt," the earl said, stepping back. He turned his back on Douglas and reached for a linen napkin on the tea cart. "Damn you, Amery."

Douglas stepped up behind him and offered him one last pat on the shoulder. "You'll be all right, Devlin. Just keep turning toward the light, no matter how weak, shifting, or uncertain. Write to me, and know you are always welcome in my house, under any circumstances, no matter what."

St. Just nodded but didn't turn as he heard Douglas's steps fade away.

❧

"Esther." The Duke of Moreland smiled as he found his wife in their private sitting room, already dressed for the day. "I thought you were going to sleep in?"

"I thought I was, too, but Rose leaves us today, and this makes me restless."

"Ah, but, my love." The duke tugged his wife of three decades down to sit beside him on the settee. "Rose had a smashing good time, didn't she?"

"She did." The duchess smiled at him. "She got you out and about but kept you at a reasonable pace. Every fellow recovering from a heart seizure should be assigned a little granddaughter to keep him in line."

"I am recovering," the duke said, eyeing his wife. "Not a hundred percent yet, but I'm coming along. Morelands is good for me."

"Morelands is lovely."

"I don't think Morelands is agreeing with St. Just."

"What makes you say that?" The duchess kept her tone noncommittal, though His Grace thought she'd come to the same conclusion he had.

"I was on my way out to the rose garden to see how the white roses are coming along, and I happened to be on the other side of the privet hedge when St. Just was bidding Amery good-bye."

"I think they've gotten on well."

"St. Just was crying in the man's arms, Esther." The duke shook his head. "Nothing havey-cavey about it, he's just... He's still upset, and Amery doesn't pull any punches, God knows."

"Devlin cannot tolerate boredom," the duchess said. "His demons plague him when he's idle, and I fear we excel at idleness here at Morelands."

"Mayhap." The duke patted her hand, as pretty and slim as any girl's. "I have never known what to do with that one, Esther. He's just... he insists on holding himself aloof, and all he's ever asked me is to buy him his colors and one decent horse. Ten years later, England is victorious, two sons are dead, and another probably wishes he were."

"You think it's that bad?"

"Maybe not now." The duke stroked her hand, searching her eyes. "Val and Westhaven report his drinking has moderated, and he's been in regular correspondence with them, his steward in Surrey, and his man of business. Maybe he and Amery just went a bit nancy on us—happens in the army, I'm told. And the women in Yorkshire all look like sheep after a certain age, anyway."

"Percival Windham"—the duchess retrieved her hand—"you repeat that nonsense in polite company, and I will hide every tin of chocolates from which you are cadging your treats."

"Just a thought," the duke groused. "Something's still amiss with the lad, and I'll be damned if I can fathom it. Why don't you talk to him?"

"I'm not his mother," the duchess, said, but she couldn't hide the pain flashing in her eyes as she repeated a refrain His Grace had heard from her often through the years. She'd loved the boy from the day he'd arrived at the age of five, bewildered, heartbroken to be cast from his mother's side, and determined not to be intimidated by ducal grandeur; but Esther would not interfere between Percy and his firstborn.

"You are the only damned thing he's ever had that resembles a mother," the duke shot back, pleased to see he had her attention. "And maybe Amery has the right of it: The boy wants mothering or some damned thing like it. Now, how can we finagle another visit from our little Rose before Christmas?"

The duchess listened to him spin and discard a half-dozen schemes and bribes before he arrived to the least interesting but most effective option of all.

"Do you suppose, Esther"—he tucked her hand back into his—"we should just ask?"

"I've decided Rose must stay with me," St. Just informed her stepfather, who waited at the bottom of the front steps for his horse to be brought around. "You have John; you don't need Rose, too." He scooped his niece up into a tight hug then set her down near the traveling coach.

"You'll not kidnap my daughter," Guinevere Allen, Viscountess Amery said, coming out of the house with John in her arms. "His Grace tried that, St. Just. I frown upon it, and Douglas gets positively irrational."

St. Just grinned. "I should like to witness that, but perhaps not inspire it."

Gwen leaned up and kissed his cheek. "St. Just, thank you for keeping Douglas out of trouble these weeks. It's a thankless task, I know, as he's so naturally prone to mischief. Husband, mount up. Their Graces said their farewells indoors, and the aunts will not be out of bed for hours yet."

Douglas assisted his wife and children into the coach and gave the driver leave to walk on, then waited for Sir Regis's girth to be tightened.

"You might consider marriage, you know," Douglas

said as the horse was led over. "It solved a world of difficulties for me, and I do not refer to the financial."

"Perhaps you just want to assign responsibility for worrying about me to someone else."

"I will worry about you for as long as I damned well please," Douglas muttered. "Behave yourself, and—"

"I know." St. Just wrapped him a hug. "You love me, you are proud of me, and you will keep me in your prayers."

"Right." Douglas nodded, holding on for a moment before stepping back. "Glad to see you were paying attention."

"Be off with you." St. Just patted Sir Regis's neck. "And my thanks for everything." Douglas saluted with his crop, swung aboard, and trotted off, soon disappearing into the plume of dust raised by the coach.

St. Just sat on the steps, watching the dust drift away on the morning breeze. If nothing else, the past six weeks had brought a friend into his life. A truly dear, worthy friend, a man he would have served with gladly. It wasn't like having a brother back, not Bart nor Victor, but it was a profound consolation nonetheless.

Valentine Windham appeared at the top of the steps, his sable hair tousled, his green eyes speculative. He sidled down the steps, hands in his pockets, his lean form moving with sleepy grace. He lowered himself to sit beside his brother and frowned.

"Damned quiet without the brat," Val said.

"Rose stole your heart, too, did she?"

"She's a lot like Victor. I don't know how that should be, but she's droll and quick and passionate, and he's gone, but then there's Rose. And sometimes, in a certain light, she has a look of him around her eyes."

"And in the chin, too, I think. You miss him."

"I miss him." Val glanced up at the blue summer sky. "He rallied in the summers, at least when it was dry. I think the coal dust aggravated him, and the damp."

"And the dying," St. Just said. "The going by degrees and days and minutes."

"Many times he said he envied Bart, a nice, quick, clean bullet. Alive and cussing one minute, gone to his reward the next. No quacks, no nurses, no long faces around the bed."

"I miss Bart, too," St. Just mused. "No chance to say good-bye, no time to say what needed to be said, no period of grace to bargain with God and find some balance with the whole thing."

"Damned lousy," Val said, sounding more desolate than peevish. He laid his head on his brother's shoulder. "Promise me you won't pull a stunt like either of them."

"I promise. You?"

"Swear to God. Word of a Windham."

They were silent a long moment, the late summer morning barely stirring around them.

"That's why you beat the stuffings out of me, isn't it?" St. Just glanced over at his baby brother. "You might kill me with your bare hands, but you weren't going to let another brother be taken from you."

"That, and I was only then beginning to realize Victor wasn't ill, he was *dying*, and he was fighting it hard not because he enjoyed being trapped in a miserable body, but because we trapped him with our grief. I told him to let go, but he wasn't about to listen to me."

"And I wasn't even there to comment."

"You were drunk, I was coming apart with grief, and that left, as always, Gayle to impersonate the adult in this family."

"And he seems to be enjoying the role more and more."

"Adulthood has its privileges," Val said, lifting his head. "But are you enjoying them?"

"I'm doing better, little brother. My bad days are not quite as bad, and my good days are coming closer together. What of you?"

"Westhaven's nuptials have put rather a crimp in my designs," Val said, scowling. "I liked having the two of you where I could keep an eye on you, but I'm not about to share a home with a pair of newlyweds on the nest."

"So come visit Yorkshire. I warn you an associate of Rose's lives with me, Helmsley's by-blow. She is a handful and good for me."

"Her Grace mentioned this." Val gave him a puzzled look. "Since when did you acquire the knack of raising children?"

"She has pretty much raised herself, and my arse is going to sleep on these stones." He rose, rubbed his posterior, then gave his brother a hand up.

"You have calluses." Val frowned at his brother's hand.

"I am a stonemason, of sorts, but we can ensconce your behind on a piano bench, never fear. No calluses for my baby brother."

"I have calluses on my lordly backside from sitting on piano benches, but as I just sent you a grand piano,

I suppose it makes sense I'd go see it properly tuned and set up."

"You'll come with me?" St. Just asked, feeling a warmth settle in his chest at the words. He'd invited his first houseguest, and it was somebody he'd loved since birth.

"I will. It will get me the hell away from His Eternally Matchmaking Grace and our infernal sisters and their infernal marriage-mad friends."

"We need to douse you with eau de bastard," St. Just said. "It cools the heels of all but the most determined."

"Oh?" Val arched an eyebrow as they started up the steps. "But doesn't a quick dip in eau de earl bring them all out of the woodwork again?"

"In Yorkshire?" St. Just scoffed. "You can handle that crowd as long you don't let them hear what you can do with a keyboard."

⁓

"Scout says he misses Rosecroft," Winnie informed Emmie over dinner.

"So why doesn't Scout write to his long lost earl?" Emmie asked, barely able to keep her eyes open.

"He did. In my last letter I drew a picture of Scout. Are you sad?"

It's just my menses, Emmie thought. It's just three weeks of being run ragged, of dodging difficult conversations with Hadrian Bothwell, and baking more bread and goodies than all of Yorkshire should have been able to consume.

"I am not sad, exactly," Emmie said, knowing it was

a lie. Her heart was breaking, and as busy as she tried to keep herself, sadness was her constant companion. The longer she stayed here, the more difficult it was going to be to leave.

"You miss the earl," Winnie said. "I do, too, but he promised, and it isn't Michaelmas yet."

"Not for another week or so. Eat some carrots, Win."

"I do not understand why horses like these so much." Winnie eyed her carrot then slipped her fork into her mouth. "But I don't like grass either."

"You've tried eating grass?" Emmie couldn't help but smile.

"I was hungry." Winnie shrugged. "And the cows and sheep and horses all grow quite stout on it. The flowers of clover aren't bad, but I was still hungry."

"Winnie." Emmie reached over and gave her a one-armed hug. "You are impossible."

"I am possible," Winnie retorted. "Will Rosecroft bring me home a pony?"

And so it went. Winnie's favorite conversational gambits became more and more narrowly focused on questions regarding the earl, and fantastic declarations regarding Scout's expertise, opinions, and decisions. At one point, Winnie asked if the earl might bring a pony for Scout, and Emmie simply got up and walked out of the room.

Hadrian Bothwell had become not just a frequent visitor to the stables but an occasional guest in Emmie's kitchen, as well. He ensconced himself on a kitchen stool and proceeded to help himself to Emmie's freshest products while swilling milk or tea or chocolate.

Emmie was occupying Hadrian's vacated stool
when Stevens brought in the post, among which she
found another letter from the earl. As the letter was
addressed to Miss Farnum, she took the liberty of
opening it.

> *My dear Miss Farnum,*
>
> *I hope it pleases you to be informed I will be
> returning no later than the 23rd of this month and
> I am bringing my youngest brother, Lord Valentine,
> for an indefinite stay. I've endured my visit at
> Morelands well enough, spent time with my siblings
> and Their Graces, and while Kent has its appeal,
> Yorkshire is more peaceful. Douglas says I ought also
> to tell you I am managing not to drain the cellars at
> each rainstorm, though sleep has proven elusive.*
>
> *There are no stone walls here, Emmie, for me
> to take out my frustrations on. I ride, but Beau
> is such a steady fellow, I am leaving him with
> Westhaven to replace an old campaigner by the
> name of Pericles. I will be bringing more young
> stock north, so alert Stevens we might be on the
> lookout for another groom.*
>
> *There is a great deal more I would tell you, but I
> will be home not long after you read this. I've done
> the pretty with my solicitors and my man of business
> in London, and refurbished my wardrobe, as well as
> picked up a few things for the household. Mostly,
> though I look forward to being home, to waking up to
> the scent of fresh bread and sweet rolls, to commenting
> on your experiments, and seeing what can be done
> with the gardens before cold weather sets in.*

The trip has been useful, Emmie, but it's homecoming I look forward to most.

Devlin St. Just
Rosecroft

She was in tears when Winnie came through the door, Scout at her heels.

"Miss Emmie? I saw Vicar leave, but why are you crying?"

"I'm just tired, Winnie." Emmie dredged up a watery smile and didn't even bother reminding Winnie that the dog was not allowed in the kitchen. "As soon as I'm done with the cinnamon rolls, I think I need a nap."

"I think you do, too," Winnie said, plucking one roll for herself, another for the dog. "You're always tired."

"Winnie Farnum." Emmie rose off the stool. "You did not wash your hands, you did not ask permission, nor did you help make these rolls. And yet you have given one away to that garbage scow you call a dog, who is not supposed to be in this kitchen."

"Scout forgot."

"Bronwyn." Emmie's tone became stern as she planted her fists on her hips. "Scout is the dog, and you are responsible for him. This is the second time he's been in here today, young lady."

"C'mon Scout." Winnie sighed hugely, snapped her fingers, and led her beast from the kitchen.

Emmie sank back down on the stool and willed her eyes to stay open until the last batch of rolls was ready to come out of the oven. If she simply ignored the need to prepare her ingredients and kitchen for tomorrow's baking, she could go straight up to bed and sleep for maybe ninety minutes before it was time to have dinner with Winnie. She met Cook on the stairs, explained her plan, and dragged herself up the steps.

❧

Rosecroft,

I am pleased to inform you both Caesar and Wulf continue to execute consistently clean flying changes of leg, though Ethelred has developed a tendency to be late behind. Stevens has suggested work in counter canter, but I am more inclined to avoid the problem and leave it to your superior skills to address upon your return.

I must warn you, as well, a Canine of mythical proportions has taken up residence in Miss Winnie's heart. This beast follows her everywhere, though Miss Emmie insists the animal spend its nights in the stable, which, given his size, is only appropriate. The earth shakes when he moves, and if I could get a saddle and bridle on him, I'd suggest you add him to your training program.

I have notified my bishop it is my intention to quit the district before the year is out. I do not exaggerate when I say that means a replacement at St. Michael's will likely appear by May Day, or thereabouts. My brother's health is not sound, and I am needed at his side.

It is particularly pleasant, when family matters are not sanguine, to have the pleasure of riding your geldings. Miss Farnum accompanies me on her most excellent mare, who endeavors to set a good example for the younger fellows. Perhaps, if I am considering choosing my future viscountess, I should look to such as Petunia for my example. I have asked Miss Farnum to bear that honor, and have every hope she will agree this time.

I am asked at least a dozen times each week what has become of you and when you will be at services again. I assure one and all (by which I mean Lady Tosten, who is well versed in churchyard dialects), you have been carried off by bandits to be sold into slavery on the Barbary Coast.

Seriously, one hopes your journey goes well and you will soon arrive safely back to home and hearth. Miss Winnie, at the least, longs for the sight of you.

> Hadrian Bothwell, Vicar
> St. Michael's of the Sword
> Rosecroft Village, Yorkshire

Ten

"So you'll leave us on the morrow and take Mozart with you?" the duke asked as he pushed a brandy decanter toward his firstborn.

"Val seems ready for a change, and there's plenty of peace and quiet in Yorkshire," St. Just replied, pouring himself half a finger of brandy and watching as His Grace cut a deck of playing cards.

"Not drinking much these days, are you?" His Grace observed. "You're my witness; I'm trying to behave, as well."

"On the advice of the physicians?"

"Who else?" The duke rolled his eyes. "And once Her Grace gets wind of something like that, I am a doomed man."

"I've never quite understood how she manages you," St. Just said, taking a small sip of very good brandy.

"Neither have I." His father smiled. "That's part of her genius. Val gets his music from her, Westhaven his brains, and you..."

"Yes?" St. Just arched an eyebrow, for what could

he possibly have inherited from a woman with whom he shared no blood?

"Your heart, lad." The duke tossed his brandy back in a single swallow. "Hell and the devil, that's good stuff."

"My heart?"

"You were a puny little thing when your mother left you here." The duke eyed his strapping son. "I am ashamed to say I did not take an adequate interest in your early years, which is part of what haunted me about Rose's situation."

"Would you care to explain that?"

"Let's walk, shall we? Elsewise I'll be pouring myself one more tot, and one more, and so forth, and Esther will be wroth." He hoisted himself to his feet and led the way to the back gardens, St. Just ambling at his side.

"You were saying you were negligent," St. Just prompted.

"I was." His Grace smiled thinly. "Just as Her Grace informed me we were to become parents, the title befell me, and your mother attempted to renew her acquaintance with me. I sent her packing at first, but she was savvy enough to contact Esther a few years later and threaten to put it about I'd walked away from my by-blow."

"So you were indeed negligent," St. Just said, bewildered his father would so blatantly admit such a thing.

"It wasn't until she contacted Esther that your mother bothered to let on you existed." The duke sighed heavily. "Just as Gwen Hollister neglected to inform Victor of his paternity."

"The circumstances were very different."

The duke waved a dismissive hand. "Keep your powder dry, for God's sake. We can all agree those circumstances were unfortunate all around. But in your case, I assumed your mother got pregnant on purpose then bided her time until I was invested. She approached me then waited until we had both heir and spare in hand before threatening us with you."

"What do you mean, threatening you?" St. Just asked, his stomach beginning to rebel against even the small amount of brandy he'd imbibed.

"She wanted a king's ransom to keep her mouth shut. Said she'd talk to the gossip rags, write her memoirs, drag my name through the mud, and so forth. I was younger than you are now, lad, and hadn't much bottom. It was Esther who understood Kathleen's real agenda."

"Which was?"

"Kathleen said we could either pay, or she'd leave you on the doorstep for all the world to see. Esther told her we'd take you gladly, and Kathleen handed you over. The only condition Esther put on the transaction was that the woman was to stay away from me. My duchess is no fool." The duke smiled dryly.

"So that's why I never saw my mother again?"

The duke cocked his head. "You never saw her because she didn't want to cost you what providence had tossed in your lap. Her Grace wrote to your mother every six months until your mother died when you were twelve. She sent likenesses and a lock of your hair. She took you to the park so your mother could sit in a closed carriage and see you from time to time, and when your mother passed on, Her Grace kept in touch with your Irish cousins. Her Grace accurately divined that Kathleen's plan had become to see you raised under your father's roof."

St. Just heard his father's voice, a tough, pragmatic bray that had been part of his life for more than a quarter century, but the words were barely registering over the pounding in his chest.

"I don't understand," he ground out. "Why wouldn't my mother want me to know she was seeing me? I was five when she left me. I knew very well whose child I was."

"Your mother," the duke said with uncharacteristic gentleness, "wanted you to prosper, St. Just. She wasn't a bad woman; she was a good woman, in fact, but she made hard choices, and in the end, did what was best for you. She wanted you to believe you were a son of this house and felt you'd not make that transition were she tugging your heartstrings in a different direction."

St. Just sat there in the growing darkness, hearing crickets chirp and cicadas sing. A soft breeze was wafting over the flowers, and his whole life was being turned inside out.

"She didn't just walk away," he concluded.

"She retreated to a careful distance," the duke said. "I have every confidence had she survived, she would have reestablished contact with you when your discretion could be trusted. In this regard, she was much more praiseworthy than Maggie's mother."

"How do you reconcile yourself to this?"

The duke shrugged. "I was young and never expecting to inherit. There was not a more useless creature on God's earth than myself as a young man. I behaved badly and have tried to right the wrongs I've done. Her Grace has had her hands full with me."

"We all have," St. Just muttered. "You know there were times when Bart and I were up to our knees in mud, living off cattail roots and whatever we could hunt, and he would turn to me and say, 'At least His Grace can't lecture us about duty now.'"

The duke looked chagrined but nodded. "I made the same mistakes with Bart my grandfather made with his sons, and my father made with me. Pathetic, but there it is. So promise me, St. Just, you and your brothers will do better, hmm? I will be watching from the right hand of the Father, drinking all the brandy I please, ranting at your brothers, and waiting for Her Grace. You may depend upon it. And see that you join me there in due course, or Her Grace will be unhappy. Wonder how God will deal with that?"

"You'd best not take up that position quite yet," St. Just warned. "Rose told me before she left she wants more than this one summer with you. You are a bruising rider, and you know the best stories. As grandpapas go, you are in every way a capital fellow."

"And you allowed her this fiction." The duke smiled his most charming smile. "Your sons will do the same for you one day, St. Just."

"Assuming I have sons."

"Her Grace has remarked that your years of command will give you an edge when you take up parenting," the duke said.

"Because I'm used to giving orders?"

"Because you're used to having your orders ignored. But as to that, *Rosecroft*, I wanted you to know I've had a word with those fellows at the College of Arms."

"Regarding?"

"Your earldom, my lad." The duke glanced over at him. "And yes, I am meddling, but I don't think you'll mind if the language of your patent simply allows for your oldest child of any description to inherit."

"Are you announcing a penchant for the St. Just line to produce bastards?" St. Just asked. "Shouldn't it be my firstborn, natural, legitimate son surviving at the time of my death?"

"Should." The duke's tone became a bit frosty. "Should is not always a useful word. Your brother Bart should have lived, so should my older brother and your brother Victor. I flattered myself you would see any of your progeny inherit rather than have the Crown get its hands on what you will no doubt make a profitable little estate."

"You're sure I'll make the earldom prosper?" St. Just asked, knowing the damage was done in terms of legal language.

"No doubt in my mind." The duke grinned. "You and your brothers have the knack, unlike my humble self. I wield a wealth of influence, but had Westhaven not taken up the financial reins, that's all I'd be wielding."

"And you've told him this?"

"I have. Boy about embarrassed himself. Asked if I was enjoying good health or if I'd done something to aggravate his mother. I could answer yes to both honestly."

"As you are always doing something to aggravate Her Grace," St. Just concluded with reluctant affection.

"Just so, lad. Just so. For example, I am now going to wheedle my eldest into sharing just one more half a tot with his dear old papa, hmm?"

⁓

To St. Just's great surprise, the duchess was up and waiting for him when he rose to depart before dawn the next morning. Breakfast had been a hurried business, with Val bleary-eyed across the teapot, muttering distractedly about scores and manuscripts. St. Just took himself down to the stables, where three more geldings were being readied for the trip north. Val would ride one, St. Just the other, and the third would carry a pack.

And there, on a dusty old tack trunk, sat Esther, Her Grace, Duchess of Moreland, in a night rail and wrapper, sturdy sabots on her dainty feet.

"Your Grace?" St. Just frowned down at her in surprise. "Does His Grace know you've taken to drifting about *en dishabille*?"

"He is snoring peacefully," she replied, rising, "but Percy told me you'd been laboring under some misconceptions, and this is the last we will see of you for some time."

"Shall we sit?" St. Just offered his arm and escorted her out to a stone bench flanked by flower beds. He loved this woman, but he'd be damned if he'd ever gotten the knack of deciphering her silences.

"St. Just, I am a mother," the duchess began, "and you will recall this when I tell you your mother loved you. My heart broke for her the day she left you here, and it broke for you, as well."

It's still breaking for you. She didn't say the words. They were evident to him in the earnestness of her expression.

"My little heart was none too pleased with the situation either," he murmured. "I just wish…"

"Yes?"

"I wish I'd known she still… maintained an interest," he said. "I feel petulant and stupid for it, but why wouldn't a mother want a child to know she loved him?"

"Hard to understand, isn't it? Imagine what it would have taken were Douglas to walk away from Rose."

"I don't understand." St. Just frowned. "He would never abandon that child. He committed hanging felonies to protect her, come to think of it."

"Consider your mother carried you under her heart for nine months," the duchess replied. "She delivered you into this world at risk to her own life, prostituted herself to keep a roof over your head, and raised you every day for five years. How on earth could she have survived giving you up?"

St. Just shrugged. "I figured I wasn't much fun to have underfoot. Small boys can be a big nuisance when a woman depends on her social life for her livelihood."

"For God's sake, Devlin." The duchess stood and glared at him. "Would you have tossed one of your younger sisters to the press gang because she wasn't much fun to have underfoot?"

"Of course not." He got to his feet, using the advantage of his height to glare back at her. "My sisters are my family."

"No woman tosses her own child aside for mere

convenience," Her Grace said, abruptly every inch the duchess despite being in nightclothes and wooden clogs. "You would not treat a horse that way; what makes you think Kathleen St. Just would treat her child thus?"

"It made sense." St. Just stalked off a few paces, and for the first time in his life, raised his voice—not to a shout, but to an emphasis—at the duchess. "I was five years old. I thought my mother left me because she didn't want me. I never saw her again, never got a letter, a Christmas present, or a glimpse of the damned woman. How was I supposed to know that added up to a heroic sacrifice? *She left me*, and in the care of a man who never spoke when he could yell, and never showed affection. She left me in the care of a woman I was told to address as Her Grace. I never knew your name until I was off at school, for God's sake. How is that love to a little boy?"

He stood there, glaring down at a woman who had shown him nothing but kindness, who was still trying to show him nothing but kindness.

"You wait right here," Esther said to him sternly, as if he were quite small, "and do not depart until I have returned. We've done you a disservice, St. Just, by assuming the past should stay buried, but you do us a disservice, as well, by thinking we'd toss you to the rag and bone man were you anything less than a perfect little soldier. Your brother was rash and vainglorious and suited to the soldier's life, but I should never have let your father buy you a commission. I have regretted it every day for more than ten years, young man, and I will not stand by, heaping up more regrets, while you torment yourself with a fiction that your mother willingly orphaned you."

She stomped off, putting St. Just in mind of the Greek goddesses of old. Her green eyes had spit fire, her words had cut like a lash, and she'd been magnificent.

"What on earth was that about?" Val asked, strolling down the path from the manor. "Her Grace just whipped by me as if His Grace was in very serious trouble."

"Not His Grace." St. Just shook his head. "Me. Am I a perfect little soldier, Val?"

Val looked him up and down. "A perfect, somewhat largish soldier."

St. Just winced. "Perfect?"

"You were never injured, and yet you fought in every major battle on the Peninsula, as well as at Waterloo," Val said. "You were mentioned regularly in the dispatches, decorated like a German Christmas tree, and any horse you touch now sells for a small fortune based in part on your reputation among your fellow officers. You were perfect enough we can now hang an earldom around your neck—and those aren't dispensed like candy. I gather, though, you've acquired a little bit of tarnish around the edges?"

"The patina of age," St. Just murmured. "Are you ready to depart?"

"I am. You're not?"

"I am under orders to wait for Her Grace's return. I find myself reluctant to disobey."

"One can understand this, as the woman reduces Percival Windham to *blancmange*. And here she comes, albeit looking a little more the thing."

"Valentine." Her Grace nodded at her youngest son. "Did you eat breakfast?"

"I did. St. Just is my witness."

"St. Just." Her Grace shoved a packet of letters at his chest. "These should have been given to you a lifetime ago, but the moment was never right. Read them."

He took the letters from her but did not even glance down at the papers in his hand. "They're from my mother?"

She nodded, holding his gaze. "The last one was written about a week before her death, when she knew she would not recover. I still cannot read it without losing my composure. Now the both of you get on your horses and go before I start to cry."

"Good-bye, Mother." Val wrapped his arms around her and suffered kisses to both of his cheeks. "I will practice every day, mostly, and I will use my tooth powder, and I will keep St. Just out of trouble, mostly, and I will write, sometimes. I love you. Don't tell my sisters where I've gone."

"You naughty, honest boy," his mother said. "Safe journey, and I love you."

St. Just watched this scene, one like many stored in his memory of his half brothers casually teasing their mother, assuming she'd be there to tease when next they got around to paying a call. It made him a little crazy to see the same thing yet again today, so he turned to go.

"Devlin St. Just!" The duchess's voice had the whiplash quality to it again, and Val grimaced at him in sympathy. Devlin turned and prepared for the usual lecture on his duty to look after his little brothers, but the duchess simply opened her arms to him. He went to her and cautiously leaned in for a hug.

"You are not a perfect soldier," she whispered, "but you are a perfect son, and I love you." Her embrace was fierce, and in his arms, she did not feel like an older woman. She felt like a mother trying to get through to her pigheaded offspring.

"Good-bye," he said, "I love you, too."

She stepped back, her smile radiant. "Look after each other." She shook her finger at them both. "I have my hands full with your father and your feather-brained sisters. I can't be fretting about grown men."

"Yes, Your Grace," they said in unison, exchanging a smile. She let them go. She was still beaming from the front steps when they trotted down the drive.

"Can I play it?" Winnie asked, running her hands over the closed lid of the gleaming grand piano. It had been delivered that morning by four large men and four monstrous draft horses.

"Best not," one of the men said. "If, God forbid, something busted on the way, Lord Val will want it righted first."

Winnie looked disappointed but nodded.

"And I'd be keeping yon beast a safe distance, too." The driver nodded at Scout. "Some of them like to nibble the linseed oil in the finishes, and half-gobbled piano legs will not set well with his lordship either."

"He sounds like a man of particulars," Emmie said.

The driver shrugged. "Easy fella to like, for Quality. Don't be disrespecting his pianos."

"Well, thank you for your efforts," Emmie said as Winnie huffed out of the room with Scout at her heels. "Perhaps you'd like to come around to the kitchen before you head back to York?"

The man smiled. "That'd go aright, and where do the horses go?"

"The horses?" Emmie blinked. "You mean for some hay and water?"

The man shook his head. "Nah. The horses is from the other brother."

"Lord Westhaven?" Emmie wracked her brain, but she was sure the stud farm was in St. Just's possession. "Why would he send along such a team of... Sturdy fellows."

"The two of 'em's mares raised to the plough. All four is steady as 'ell and like as strong. Man's got land, he needs a team."

"I see." The team would hardly fit in the stables, so thank God it was only coming autumn.

The rest of the day was taken up with provisioning the deliverymen for their journey south, having Stevens take the men into the village, and rearranging the stables so the larger horses could use the foaling stalls and the others the loose boxes.

And in the general disruption, Emmie realized she hadn't seen Winnie since before luncheon.

Not this again. Winnie's ramblings hadn't exactly stopped since Rosecroft had taken over, but Winnie had willingly adopted the habit of announcing her intended destination, and then—bless the child—sticking to her itinerary. But the sun was setting, the evening air was not quite warm, and nobody had seen Winnie for hours.

Emmie wracked her brain for clues, but all she could come up with was Winnie's comment over breakfast that the woods were prettiest in the fall.

The woods… noxious plants, snakes, rocks that twisted ankles, the pond, rabid animals Winnie would think needed help…

"Stevens," Emmie said, voice shaking, "can we saddle up the mare? I want to make a pass through the woods before it's full dark."

"I'll saddle up Caesar, too," Stevens said. Emmie glanced at him, but her imagination had already started filling in the unspoken words… in case somebody needs to go for help, in case we need the vicar, in case there's a body that has to be brought back to the manor.

"Are there Gypsies in the area, Stevens?" Emmie asked as she hefted a saddle onto Petunia.

"Not this late in the year. They head south, down to Devon and Cornwall when fall comes. We'll find her, Miss Emmie. If need be, we can have Mr. Wentworth's hounds come looking in the morning, but the child knows how to bide through the night on the property."

"She does, but she's only six years old, and anything from wild dogs to a bad fall can interfere with her best efforts to stay safe."

"Let's go, Miss Emmie." Stevens led both horses out then handed her the reins while he doubled back into the barn for a lantern. "If we don't find her, I'll alert Vicar, and he can gather a searching party."

"We have to find her." The thought of having to tell Hadrian she'd lost Winnie—again—was no comfort at all. She hardly wanted to face the man, much less have to provide him with an example of his ability to solve her problems or succeed where she failed.

Shut up and ride. As Petunia dutifully picked up the trot, Emmie had the sense the admonition had come not from herself but somehow, from St. Just. His life had likely depended on his ability to do the next sensible thing, and now Winnie's life might depend on Emmie's ability to manage similarly. She did as ordered, keeping her mouth shut and eyes on the ground for any sign of Winnie or her dog, glad as the evening light began to fade that Stevens was with her.

And then she couldn't keep her mouth shut, so she started hollering for the child. It was all but dark, and the moon not due to rise for at least two hours, when Emmie heard a faint bark in response to her ceaseless bellowing.

"That way." She nodded in the direction of one of the tracks through the woods. "Toward the pond."

"Careful!" Stevens admonished when she would have kicked the horse to a faster gait. "The leaves on wet ground make the going tricky. If she's there, we'll find her."

So Emmie kept to a shuffling trot, nearly fainting with relief when Scout barked happily to greet them as they broke into the clearing. Winnie was sitting on a rock, pitching pebbles into the water.

"Hullo, Miss Emmie." Winnie looked up, perfectly at ease. "Hullo, Stevens."

"Bronwyn Farnum." Emmie got off her horse and stomped over to the child. "What on earth are you doing out here in the woods after dark?"

"I used to come here a lot," Winnie said diffidently, "and I wasn't hungry at tea time. Did you know Scout can swim?"

Stevens cleared his throat and glanced at the darkening sky.

"Winnie," Emmie said, gathering her patience, "you are not to wander off, and you know this. We'll discuss the situation further when we have you safely at home."

"C'mon, Miss Winnie." Stevens held out a hand. He stood the child on a boulder, mounted, then hefted her up before him.

"Where's Scout?" Winnie looked around anxiously. Stevens let out a piercing whistle, and the dog bounded out of the undergrowth to dance at the horses' feet.

"Home, Stevens." Emmie nodded at the trail. "Please."

When they reached the manor, Steven dismounted, lifted Winnie to the ground, then gathered up the reins and snapped his fingers at the dog.

"But Scout hasn't had his supper yet," Winnie said, her tone indignant. "He needs to come get his scraps."

"Winnie," Emmie said through clenched teeth, "there are no dinner scraps tonight because Cook did not make us dinner. You were wandering, and I was searching for you. Scout has not had his dinner; neither have I nor Stevens nor these horses."

"You know I always come home," Winnie shot back. "You should have told Cook that Scout would be hungry when we came back."

"To the house." Emmie pointed, her tone nearly vicious. "You have been rude, inconsiderate, and mean, Winnie Farnum. I am disappointed in you, exhausted, and not in the mood for your disrespect. If you want your dog to be fed tonight, then *march*."

Winnie shot her a murderous glare then stalked off to the house, indignation in every line and sinew of her form.

"She's so little." Emmie shook her head as she watched Winnie go. "Even the church would say she hasn't reached the age of reason."

"She's reached an age when she can fall in the pond," Stevens replied laconically as he began to loosen girths. "Not a parent in the world wouldn't be upset with her."

With that sentiment ringing in her ears, Emmie made her own way back up to the house. Her steps were heavy and slow, anxiety no longer fueling her movements, her mood despairing, and her stamina— physical and emotional—gone. She went in the back door and found Winnie sitting at the counter, a plate of buttered bread before her.

Bread Emmie had wrapped up for delivery to a customer tomorrow.

"Winnie?" Winnie looked up at her indifferently and kept chewing like a squirrel. "Did you even wash your hands?"

"I was playing at the pond all afternoon, and my hands were wet a lot."

"Your hands"—Emmie grabbed her by one paw— "are muddy, and you've also been playing with Scout, Winnie. What is the rule?"

"Wash your hands after you play with the dog," Winnie replied, talking with her mouth full. "But

Scout was in the pond, so he wasn't dirty." The dog had been a rank, sloppy mess. Emmie sat and propped her chin on her fist.

"Win? What has gotten into you? You aren't a nasty little girl, and yet for the past few days, more than that really, you've been a complete, croaking toad."

A flicker of humor crossed Winnie's face at that epithet, but it soon vanished.

"You've been a toad," Winnie said. "You're always tired and always baking and always making me do lessons. I like Scout better than you."

"Scout is a good fellow, but I've always had to bake, and you've had lessons since you were little. What's the real problem, Win?" But Winnie had said all she intended to say, taking a long sip of her milk and setting the mug down on the table.

"May I be excused?"

"You may not. You will wash your hands and your plate and cup, wrap up a loaf from the bread box, not the customer shelves, then make up some stale bread, milk, and cheese rinds for Scout's dinner. While you do that, I will have a bath sent up to your room, and I will most assuredly not be reading to you tonight."

Winnie scowled. "Why not? I'm cleaning up my mess and feeding my dog."

"And you've kept your cousin up late when you just told me you know I'm tired."

Rather than get into an argument, Emmie went upstairs and got out Winnie's nightclothes and bath accessories. She changed out of her own clothes and made a quick use of the bathwater while it was piping hot, then got out in time to dry off before Winnie reappeared.

You are tired, she told herself as she dressed, *and out of sorts, and your day was thoroughly disrupted.* She found her room, took down her hair, gave it a few swats with the brush before fumbling it into a braid, then climbed onto her bed. The sheets felt cool and clean against her skin, and as she closed her eyes, she sent up one prayer for Winnie's safety and happiness, and one that the earl arrived safely and soon. She couldn't help but sense that somehow, Winnie's bad behavior was tied to the earl's continuing absence.

Her sleep should have been dreamless, so utterly tired had she allowed herself to become. But Emmie rose to awareness near midnight, not fully awake but no longer dreaming, unless the sense of the mattress dipping under a heavy weight was imagined.

The single thought *he's home* floated sweetly through her mind, then she was wrapped in warmth and allowed to drift back to sleep. When she came awake a few hours later, *he's home* echoed in her mind again, and she realized she hadn't been dreaming. *St. Just was in her bed* and had been for hours. In the way of minds not yet fully alert, she felt the sentiment two ways: He is safely arrived to his home, and more convincingly, he is my home.

"Easy," St. Just murmured, moving his hands over her. "I missed you so, Emmie. Just let me hold you."

He sounded half asleep, and his hands fell still. A great undignified relief swept through Emmie, and she realized she'd been half expecting each letter from him would be to let her know he'd be staying in London for the winter or for the next five years. Or he was sending for Winnie so she might be raised in proximity to her Aunt Anna; or he was sending along a proper London governess, and Emmie's help would no longer be needed.

But he was home. None of those outcomes were going to befall her just yet, and if they did, St. Just would at least let her have her say first.

And the relief went beyond that because, damn the man, she'd *missed* him.

She rolled, fitting her naked backside to his front. When his hand came slipping around her waist to anchor her against him, she slid her fingers through his and let sleep claim her again.

Beside her, St. Just listened until Emmie's breathing had returned to a regular, slow cadence. When he was convinced she'd returned to sleep, he let himself relax, as well, musing that he hadn't made a specific decision to climb into the bed and fall asleep.

He'd decided to greet her before finding his own bed, but she'd already been fast asleep, not even rousing when he knocked quietly on her door.

He'd decided to treat himself to the sight of her peaceful slumbers, but he'd done so sitting on the edge of her bed, where it had been all too easy to trace his fingers across her sleeping features.

He'd decided to just hold her for a bit, a liberty she'd granted him already and surely no intrusion as long as he didn't wake her.

He'd decided to shed his clothes, as he'd been traveling, and a quick wash was only courteous before he touched her further.

He'd decided to climb into bed naked, because his

clothes were not clean and the bed linens and lady in the bed were.

He'd decided to close his eyes, just to rest for a moment in the inexpressible comfort of having her in his arms again.

And in every decision, she'd been wonderfully, tacitly complicit. And now, with the worst of his exhaustion and worry eased, he was deciding to steal just a kiss, something Emmie had permitted and even enjoyed with him before.

Cautiously, he eased her to her back and brought his body carefully over hers. Balancing on forearms and knees, he crouched over her, breathing in her beguiling floral scent before touching his lips to hers. She murmured something in her sleep then subsided, so he repeated the gesture, brushing his lips across hers in a hint of a kiss.

"Devlin." Her arms wound around his neck, and she sighed contentedly.

"Emmie," he whispered back, letting their bodies barely touch. He was mildly aroused—Emmie's derriere had been pressed to his groin—but now a pulse began to beat in his vitals. He kissed her again, more lingeringly, and brushed stray wisps of hair back from her forehead. "Kiss me, Emmie," he whispered. "I've missed you."

She angled up and brushed her lips over his. "Missed you, too."

Instead of a stolen kiss, it became one long spree of larceny and arousal and growing loss of resolve. He had not gotten into bed with her to seduce her, but by *God*, she seemed bent on seducing him. As her mouth opened to plunder his, Emmie began to undulate against him—breasts, hips, legs, hips, breasts, in slow, seeking waves of pleasure.

"More," she murmured, bringing her legs around his flanks, crossing her ankles at the small of his back and pulling him down to her.

"Emmie, no." He resisted, but the feel of her smooth belly against the head of his cock was making thought a struggle. "Look at me." But she wasn't in the mood to be told what to do.

"St. Just." She arched against him again. "Devlin, *please*." When he still hesitated, she searched across the sheet and found his hand, then brought it to her breast. "*Please.*"

"Oh, Emmie." He buried his face against her shoulder and palmed her breast in a gentle, gliding caress that had her turning her face to his chest and arching against him again.

She fused her mouth to his, even as those little begging, sighing sounds began in her throat. Her hands traveled up and down his back—kneading, coaxing, and putting his best intentions to flight.

"Emmie, I don't want you to… Emmie." He drew back, and his movement allowed her to trail her fingers over his nipples. "For the love of God, woman…"

He gave up trying to reason, to argue, to make sure she knew what they were doing and what the ramifications were. Joining his body to hers had become an inevitable, unstoppable certainty, and God bless the woman, sooner suited her better than later.

"Emmie." He caught both her hands in his and levered up over her. "Hold still, love. Look at me."

Unable to touch him, caged by his strength, Emmie opened slumberous eyes and met his gaze.

"Let me do this next part." He released her hands and brushed her hair back from her forehead. "You can scream down the house, claw my back bloody, or burst out in song in five minutes, but for right now, you have to relax and let me give the orders."

She nodded once, a smile of pained sweetness creasing her lips.

"All right." He closed his eyes in relief and anticipation. Carefully, he probed at her sex with his cock, and immediately Emmie was rocking her hips up to him, trying to glove him in her tight heat.

Fall back and regroup, he ordered himself, as Emmie was having difficulties with his initial strategy.

"Take me in your hand, Emmie. Show me where you want me." When her fingers curled softly around him, he thought he might explode on the spot, but by watching the wonder and concentration in her eyes, he held off.

She took her jolly time, stroking along his length, exploring the velvety glans and the turgid length of him, but still he remained poised above her. When she cupped his stones with deft, curious fingers, he groaned in desperation, and she looked up at him with concern.

"When you're ready," he gritted out. And please God, let it be bloody damned *now*.

She had the presence of mind enough to stroke him along the damp crease of her sex, wetting him thoroughly, reassuring him she was ready. When she finally snugged his cock to the vaginal orifice itself, St. Just expelled a pent-up breath of rejoicing.

"Now," he said sternly, "you let me manage this."

If he could, he thought desperately. Emmie was hot and wet and sweet and moving in the smallest, most arousing undulations of her hips. He pushed against her gently and gained the first glorious increment of penetration, then paused. She was blessedly—wickedly—tight, and he was loathe to move more forcefully lest he hurt her. This provoked a more determined rocking from Emmie, so he understood that giving her time to adjust to him wasn't her plan.

"Let me take it easy," he whispered, hoping to distract her with kisses. He moved his mouth as languorously as he could on hers, and thank the gods, some of her urgency subsided. He pushed a little farther into her body and set up a slow rocking rhythm of his own. She moved easily in counterpoint to him, sighing her pleasure into his mouth.

By careful, relentless degrees, he joined their bodies, using his mouth and hands and voice to distract, soothe, and pleasure her. She was still tight, her body enveloping him in heat and desire, but she seemed content to let him set the pace and make the decisions, as long as he kept moving in her.

And he never wanted to stop. His own pleasure was gathering, but still he took his time, kept his thrusts deliberate, his kisses languid, until he felt fire rising from the woman in his arms.

"St. Just." She lunged up to bury her face against his throat. "I need…"

"I know." He increased his tempo minutely. "And you shall have, soon."

But of all the maneuvers to pull out of her arsenal,

Emmie latched her mouth onto his nipple and suckled. Her hands sank into his buttocks, pulling him down to her with more strength than he'd thought she possessed. Then she bit him just hard enough to send fire shooting to his groin.

"Oh, JesusandalltheSaints, *Emmie…*" Restraint evaporated, and his own passion ascended. He thrust harder, faster, and deeper, and knew he wasn't going to last much longer.

But then—glorious, generous, lovely woman—she was keening and arching up, digging her fingers into his flesh even as her sheath convulsed around him in pounding spasms. Into the maelstrom of her pleasure, he spent himself, his climax wracking him for long, silent moments while he surrendered to drenching, mindless joy.

He tried to raise himself off her even as aftershocks coursed through them both, but Emmie shook her head and held him to her.

"Not yet," she whispered, eyes closed. He laid his cheek against hers and agreed, as movement away from her was yet beyond him. *Two damned years*, he thought dazedly. Two damned years since he'd even been able to enjoy a woman's body, but he'd go through every day of it again if he could know this was waiting for him at the end.

Emmie was stroking the hair at his nape, her breathing still labored. He could feel himself softening and knew he'd soon slip from her body.

"Push me off you," he whispered. "I can't move, and we're about to get messy."

Nothing, not a giggle, a sigh, or a helpful little

shove. He pushed up to his elbows then used one hand to carefully extricate himself from her, shifting up to avoid the clean sheets. He maneuvered off the bed and navigated his way, largely by feel, to the wash water. He wrung out a flannel and made it back to the bed without barking his shins.

"Bend your knees, Emmie." With one hand, he found her, letting his fingers drift up her thigh to locate her damp sex.

"It's cool," he warned, but his touch was gentle, and he knew the washcloth was soothing because he heard her sigh in the dark.

"There's my girl." He tossed the rag to the hearth. "Now, cuddle up. Do you know, I think you put bruises on my arse, woman?" He stretched out on his side, right smack beside her. "You have slain me, Emmie Farnum." He sighed happily and felt cautiously for her in the dark. His hand found her hair, which he smoothed back in a tender caress. "I badly needed slaying, too, I can tell you." He bumped her cheek with his nose and pulled back abruptly.

"I would have said you were in need of slaying, as well," he said slowly, "but why the tears, Emmie, love?" There were women who cried in intimate circumstances, a trait he'd always found endearing, but they weren't Emmie, and her cheek wasn't damp. It was *wet*.

"Did I hurt you?" he asked, pulling her over his body. He positioned her to straddle him and wrapped an arm around her even while his hand continued to explore her face. He thought he'd been careful, but at the end, he'd been ardent—or too rough?

"Sweetheart." He found her cheek with his lips. "I am so heartily sorry."

"For *what*?" she expostulated, sitting up on him. "I am the one who needs to apologize. Oh, God, *help* me, I was hoping you wouldn't learn this of me, and I tried to tell you, but I couldn't... I just..." She was working herself up to a state. Even in the dark, her voice alone testified to rising hysteria.

"Emmie." He leaned up and gathered her in his arms. "*Emmie, hush.*"

But she couldn't hush; she was sobbing and hiccuping and gulping in his arms, leaving him helpless to do more than hold her, murmur meaningless reassurances, and then finally, lay her gently on her side, climb out of bed, and fish his handkerchief out of his pockets. All the while though, he sorted through their encounter and seized upon a credible source of Emmie's upset.

"You were not a virgin," he said evenly as he tucked the handkerchief into her hand and gathered her back over him.

"I was n-n-not," she said, seizing up again in misery. "And I h-h-hate to cry. But of course you know."

I do *now*, he thought with a small smile, though had he thought otherwise, he wouldn't have been so willing to bed her—he hoped.

"Cease your tears, Emmie love." He tucked her closer. "I am sorry for your sake you are so upset, and I hope your previous liaisons were not painful, but as for me, I am far more interested in your future than your past." A moment of silence went by, his hands tracing lazy patterns on her lovely back, and then she looked up at him.

"You cannot mean that."

"I can," he corrected her gently. "I know you were without anyone to protect you, and you were in service. One of my own sisters was damned near seduced by a footman, Emmie. It happens, and that's the end of it. Has your heart been broken?"

She nodded on a shuddery breath.

"Shall I trounce him for you? Flirt with his wife?"

"That won't be necessary," she said, her voice sounding a little less shaky. "But you must see I am an unwholesome influence on Bronwyn."

"You are a very wholesome influence on me," he retorted, "and Winnie loves you. How can that be unwholesome?"

"Because if she remains in my care, she will grow up to be just like me, my aunt, my mother... The Farnum women are no better than they should be. Everybody knows it, and now you know it, too."

Female logic was a contradiction in terms, his father would say—not in Her Grace's hearing.

St. Just cradled her jaw with one hand. "You think I would have my pleasure of you then leap out of bed, shocked to my bones because you had some experience *before* I seduced you?"

"You should."

"We can shelve this debate for later. I am not bothered by your circumstances if you are not bothered I've been swiving willing women since I came upon a toothsome dairy maid when I was fourteen."

"*Fourteen?*" Emmie tried to rear up, but he gently restrained her.

"I matured early," he said with smug simplicity,

"and she was probably three years my senior. Now calm down and let me assure you Winnie is not going to end up like your mother and aunt."

"Not if I can help it."

"She's not," the earl went on as if Emmie hadn't spoken, "because you are going to be my countess, and Winnie will have to find her own earl."

"Oh, St. Just." Emmie groaned. "You're demented if you think I'd marry you after this."

"Not demented." He kissed the top of her head. "Just determined, but I know for form's sake you will argue, so I won't propose this minute. I am a reasonable man, most of the time anyway, but also quite tired and utterly content, thanks to you. Just hush, Emmie Farnum, and let me hold you while you sleep."

She subsided into silence, but St. Just wasn't fooled. She was no doubt marshalling those arguments, getting ready to convince him that despite the preciousness of what they'd just shared, despite her being lovely and dear and destined to be his, they should not marry.

Silly woman.

She was home and peace and safety and light. She was what every weary soldier had ever vainly sought in the arms of a whore, a tavern brawl, or a tankard of ale. She was the laughter of children and the reason old men would smile in remembrance. She was his heart, his soul, his sanity, and having finally found her, he was never, ever going to let her go.

When he awoke, still replete and happy in the broad light of day, she was gone.

Eleven

"GOOD MORNING!" ST. JUST WRAPPED HIS ARMS around Emmie's waist and pressed his freshly shaved cheek to the side of her neck. "You smell good enough eat."

"My lord!" She batted at St. Just with a towel and wrestled herself out of his embrace. When she kept swatting at him, not in play but perhaps in panic, he stepped back and let his hands fall to his sides.

"What on earth do you think you're about?" she panted, spearing him with an incredulous look. "I will not be accosted in the broad light of day as if…"

He arched a dark eyebrow. "As if you're capable of driving me beyond reason between the sheets?"

She whirled, turning her back to him, and when he tried a tentative hand on her shoulder, she flinched.

"Emmie?… Sweetheart? Are you crying?"

"Don't call me that!"

"Can we discuss this outside?"

"No we cannot." She whipped back around. "I have to get the scones out of the oven by nine, and then start Winnie's lessons so I can have the next batch of bread

in before luncheon, and then work on the Weimers'
wedding cake this afternoon, and I haven't planned
anything for dessert, and your brother is here…"

She paused to take a deep breath, but as she spoke,
St. Just realized that though they'd made love last
night, her room had been dark, and he hadn't *seen* her
since setting foot on his property the day before.

"I'll do Winnie's lessons," he said, thinking as quickly
as he could. He'd felt a difference last night when
Emmie was naked in his arms, but his mind had been
clouded by lust, anticipation, and gratitude. By daylight,
he could see she'd lost at least a stone of weight, her
features were drawn, and her eyes were underscored by
shadows. Her hair, usually confined in a tidy bun at her
nape, was coming undone on one side, and her movements were brittle, as if her bones ached.

"I can't let you do Winnie's lesson. You don't
know what she's working on."

"She'll work on what I tell her to work on," he
said, reverting to the habits of command.

"St. Just." Emmie took a deep breath and let it out
slowly. "We have to discuss Winnie and her recent
behaviors."

"Will your scones burn if we do it now?" he asked,
relieved beyond measure to be embarking on something resembling a discussion.

"Oh… Yes." Emmie looked on the verge of tears.
He wanted more than anything to take her in his arms
and comfort her, but instinct cautioned him she'd only
be more upset.

"Even if I sit here and you tell me how to make
bread dough while we talk?"

That earned him a ghost of a smile. "I am not asking the Earl of Rosecroft to make bread."

"The earl used to be known around the campfires as a fine hand with the biscuit dough," he rejoined. "I am not a stranger to the process of preparing food, Emmie."

"Well, sit," she said, some of the tension leaving her. "I'll bake, and we'll talk."

"About Winnie?"

"Yes, about Winnie." Emmie's mouth compressed into a thin line. "She ran off yesterday morning. Stevens and I found her by the pond when it was all but pitch dark. She was not the least contrite, but rather chastised me for not having Cook set aside scraps for Scout's dinner."

"He was a puppy when I left. Somebody has been feeding him something."

"He's not a bad dog," Emmie said as she slid hot scones onto a wire rack. "But Winnie has become increasingly defiant, disobedient, rude, and unpleasant. I am loathe to admit it, but she has reminded me lately of her father."

"She was a little cool toward Val at breakfast. That is unusual, as Valentine is the most charming man in my family, save His Grace when he's wheedling."

Emmie dropped more batter onto the tray. "I am hoping she was just worried your absence would become protracted, and with you here, she will settle down."

"But?" The earl resisted the temptation to help himself to a hot scone.

"But Winnie has been through a great deal, and she will go through another transition when I leave."

"You are not leaving."

"I will not argue the matter with you when Winnie can walk into the kitchen at any minute."

"Fair enough, but you will listen to what I say, Emmie Farnum. You are too damned skinny, you aren't getting enough rest, your temper is short, and I don't care if your menses are going to start this afternoon, you have no call to be treating me like I'm your enemy."

"Do not," she hissed, "mention my bodily functions outside of a locked bedroom door."

St. Just ran a hand through his hair in exasperation. "I want to help, all right? All I'm saying is you seem frazzled, and if Winnie is part of the problem, I'll tackle that, but we need to find a way to talk that doesn't leave us at daggers drawn."

His tone was reasonable, almost pleading, and when he saw her shoulders relax, he knew he was making some progress—not much, but some.

"If you would keep Winnie occupied today, I'd appreciate it."

"Done. And when you are through here, please just take a nap, Em." He glanced around the kitchen. "Leave the mess. I've got staff, and they can clean up for once. Don't come down to dinner if you don't want to, either. Val understands—he plays his piano for hours most days, and if we see him at meals, it's a coincidence. Just…" He looked her up and down, trying to keep the worry from his expression. "Just get some rest," he finished with a tentative smile. "Please?"

She nodded, able to return a small smile of her own.

Taking his chances, St. Just stepped over to her,

brushed a kiss to her forehead, and took his leave. He was more alarmed that she merely bore the kiss silently rather than swat him again with her towel.

He took Winnie up on Caesar and purposely hacked through the woods, but Winnie sat before him, silent and sullen, only occasionally calling to Scout.

He left her up on the horse while he himself got down, putting her above him while he spoke. "You're in a taking about something, princess. When you want to let somebody in on it, talk to me. For now, are you ready to coach me over fences?"

"I am, but Caesar likes Vicar, so you might find him less willing to mind you."

"Everybody likes Vicar." *Hell, I even like Vicar.*

"I don't. He seems nice, but he's been kissing Miss Emmie, and that isn't nice at all."

What?

With admirable calm, St. Just merely tossed Winnie up onto the fence rail, resisting with saintly force of will the urge to turn the child into his spy.

"I rather enjoy kissing," he said, "certain làdies, that is." He planted a loud kiss on Winnie's cheek—"and some horses"—another one for Caesar's nose—"but not dogs, old lad." He blew a kiss to Scout, who looked—as he usually did—a little confused.

"All right, you." He plunked Winnie onto his shoulders as Stevens led the horse away forty-five minutes later. "Time for luncheon. What did you think of the rides today?"

"You ride better than Vicar," Winnie said with heartening loyalty, "but I don't think Wulf and Red are right-hoofed, you know? They like to go this way"—she twirled a finger counterclockwise—"better than the other way."

"My heavens," he exclaimed in genuine astonishment. "What a good eye you have. Have you told Vicar this?"

"I don't talk to him."

"I know. He kisses Miss Emmie." Much as it pained him to—bitterly, piercingly—he went on. "You know, Miss Emmie might like kissing him, Winnie, in which case it is none of our business." As Winnie was sitting on his shoulders, he could feel the tension and anger flowing back into her.

"It's nasty. My father was always kissing the maids, and that was nasty, too."

"Do you think it's nasty when I kiss my horses?" the earl asked, hefting her to the ground.

"No." Winnie shook her head. "Red and Caesar and Wulf don't think so either."

"What about when I kiss you?"

"You are always silly about it. That's fine."

Relieved and realizing there was more to discuss with Emmie, St. Just took the child into the house, supervised a thorough washing of the hands, then another washing of the hands as Scout required eviction after the first round.

They shared a convivial lunch with Val, who obligingly took Winnie by the hand and went off to hold a tea party with Scout and Mrs. Bear. St. Just repaired to his library, where he wrote his thank-you note to Their Graces for their hospitality, and then jotted off a similar note to Greymoor, in whose home he'd stayed for a couple nights in Surrey.

There was more of course—he eyed the remaining pile of unopened mail with distaste—but it would keep.

"Your brother is a demon for his technique," Emmie remarked when St. Just found her at the kitchen table. "Is he making up for missed time, or is he always so dedicated?"

"He's always dedicated. He was closest to our brother Victor and barely out of university when Bart died. In some ways, Val is my… lost brother."

"Your ages are the most different. Can I get you something?"

Well, he thought, she was in a better mood at least, and something to eat in Emmie's kitchen was never a bad idea. It gave him an excuse to linger, if nothing else.

"I will accept whatever you put before me, provided you made it."

"It seems all I do these days is bake." She was banging her crockery around, dumping ingredients into the large bowl, and stirring furiously.

"Val told me he got up to check on the piano, Emmie." The earl watched as she flitted around the kitchen. "At five in the morning, you were mixing bread dough."

"I usually am, and I had the wedding cake to start." She was also frowning mightily at her bowl.

"And Stevens tells me," the earl went on, "it now takes several hours to make your deliveries. And"—he rose and stood before her, frowning right back—"you used to have an assistant over at the cottage, and you told her she wouldn't be needed for as long as you're baking at Rosecroft."

"My lands!" Emmie threw up her hands. "I

suppose you also took it upon yourself to learn how I take my tea."

"You like it very hot, rich with cream, and sweet," he said, and somehow, though he hadn't intended it, the words had an erotic undertone, at least to his ears.

"Is there a point to all of this?" Emmie whipped something into the bowl with a wooden spoon.

"There is," he said, his frown turning to one of puzzlement. Why had she permitted him intimacies? Had she simply been too worn down to resist him? Too weary and lonely? Was the vicar leading her a dance?

He sat and scrubbed a hand over his face. "I am trying to make your life easier here."

"By poking into my business and accosting me while I work?" But then she stopped her furious whipping and set the bowl down. "Ye gods, I sound like Winnie. I'm sorry, I'm just... There is too much to do for us to be indulging in pointless conversation. I made a mistake with you last night, St. Just. I was tired and... lonely and I wanted..."

"Yes?" He kept his tone even, as if he were verifying expected dangerous orders for his next mission riding dispatch.

"I don't know what I wanted, but misbehaving with you is not the answer."

"What do you want, Emmie?" he asked in the same carefully steady tone.

"Now?" She sat with a thump. "I want... to sleep. But people will have weddings and this cake is supposed to be over at the assembly rooms tomorrow morning and even if you wanted to help, I doubt there was much call for decorating wedding cakes in the cavalry."

"Now there you would be surprised." He shifted to sit beside her. "The men were forever getting married, and their wives were forever running off or going home to mama or catching their fellows in the wrong tent, and so on. Compared to battles and drills, it was almost entertaining."

In the room above the kitchen, Val switched to a slow, lyrical etude, and for a few minutes, Emmie just sat beside him while they listened.

"He is very talented, isn't he?"

"Appallingly so," St. Just said, eyeing her hands where they rested in her lap. "And at everything he turns his hand to. He rides better than I do, paints better than Her Grace does, sings as well as Westhaven ever did, but hides it all behind his keyboards. Em?" St. Just's arm settled around her shoulders. "Do you regret what we did last night?"

When he thought of her eagerness, her ardor in the night, and then compared it with her behavior with him today...

She blew out a breath, and beneath his arm, he felt her shoulders drop. "I do not regret it the way you might think. I will always treasure the memory and..."

"And what?" His fingers began to circle on her nape, and he felt all manner of tension and anxiety flowing out of her.

"And that's all." She sighed, bowing her head. "I made a mistake with you. It isn't my first mistake, but I hope it will be my last. I can't survive another such mistake."

He was silent, not asking her why it was a mistake. He could guess that.

"I think I'm getting better," he said quietly. "I go for as much as a week between nightmares, and the last time it rained, I was able to stay away from the brandy. I haven't had to build a wall now for a few weeks, Emmie."

"Oh, St. Just." She rested her forehead on his shoulder. "It isn't you. You must not think it's you. You're lovely, perfect, dear... And you *are* getting better, I know you are, and I know some lady will be deliriously happy to be your countess one day."

He listened, trying to separate the part of him that craved her words—lovely, perfect, *dear*—from the part of him that heard only her rejection.

"Is there someone else?" he asked as neutrally as he could.

Emmie shook her head. "Again, not in the sense you mean. I am not in love with anybody else, and I don't plan to be. But I am leaving, St. Just. I have thought this through until my mind is made up. My leaving will be for the best as far as Winnie is concerned, and she comes first."

"I don't understand," he said on an exasperated sigh. "You love that child, and she loves you. She needs you, and if you marry me, she can have you not just as a cousin or governess or neighbor, but as a mother, for God's sake. You simply aren't making sense, Em, and if it puzzles me, it's likely going to drive Winnie to Bedlam."

He glanced over at her, and wasn't that just lovely, she was in tears now.

"Ah, Emmie." He pulled her against him in a one-armed hug. "I am sorry, sweetheart." She stayed in his embrace for three shuddery breaths then pulled back.

"You cannot call me that."

"When do you think you're leaving?" he said, dodging that one for now.

"Sooner is better than later." Emmie wiped at her tears with her hand, which had St. Just tucking her fingers around his handkerchief. "When can you have a governess here for Winnie?"

"I'm not sure." He spoke slowly, mentally tallying weeks. If he dragged his feet long enough, it would be winter, and Emmie would be bound to stay. "I've started the process for filling a number of positions, and we'll have to see who comes along. Winnie won't tolerate just anybody, and neither will I."

"But certainly by Christmas?" Emmie said. "It's more than two months away, and you are hardly parsimonious with your wages."

"Is that why you're accepting every order that comes along, Emmie?" He brushed a lock of her hair back over her ear. "You are saving against the day you leave here and your business might not be so brisk?"

"I am saving against the day I'm too old to work in the kitchens hour after hour, against the day I turn my ankle and miss a week's business, or the day when I have to replace Roddy."

"Petunia is trained to drive."

"I can't keep her." Emmie got up and went back to work with her bowl and spoon.

"Do you mean you cannot afford to keep her or you do not think it proper to keep her?"

"Both." She shot him an indecipherable look where he sat. "She is lovely, and the gesture was lovely."

Lovely. He felt an immediate, irrational distaste for the word, but their discussion had been productive on a number of levels. First, he comprehended he had at least until Christmas to change her mind. Second, he understood part of Emmie's bad mood and skittishness was due to sheer exhaustion, which he could address fairly easily. Third, Emmie had not expected him to react as he had to her lack of virginity. She had anticipated he would reject her for it or judge her, and it was a consequence she was willing—almost eager—to bear.

So he didn't have her trust—yet. And he did not have all the facts. Emmie was keeping secrets, at least, and if Winnie's disclosure regarding Bothwell was any indication, Winnie had a few things to get off her chest, as well.

Just like managing a group of junior officers. Always a mare's nest, always making simple problems difficult, and always needing to be hauled backward out of the thickets they should never have blundered into. Except, he mused as he regarded Emmie's drawn features, he hadn't been in love with his recruits, and males were infinitely less complicated than females.

Thank the gods Bonaparte had not been female, or the empire would already have encompassed Cathay.

⁓

"So where's your kitchen general?" Val asked as they settled in for a brandy in wing chairs before the hearth in the library. "She missed tea and dinner."

"She's asleep." St. Just had sent a tray up to her at teatime, then checked on her just an hour or so ago. The food was half gone, and the kitchen general was facedown on her bed, one foot still wearing its stocking. He'd wrestled her out of her clothes and tucked her in, all without her even opening both eyes.

"She's the prettiest kitchen general I can recall meeting," Val said, toeing off his boots. "And she looks at you like you are the world's largest chocolate cream cake."

"She does not." She might have once upon a dark night, but she was obviously retrenching from that happy aberration.

"She does too. When you're out there on your horses, she glances repeatedly out the window, then just stops and stares and sighs and shakes her head and starts glancing again. When she came into the music room looking for the child, she asked me what kind of music you like best."

"I like anything you play," St. Just said, running his finger around the rim of his snifter. "When I was in Spain, I used to occasionally catch someone at a piano when I took dispatches into the cities, and even more rarely, hear a snatch of something you might have worked on. It made me more homesick than any letter."

Val stared at him. "I had no idea. I'm sorry."

"It isn't something to be sorry for. A soldier needs to be homesick, or he forgets why he fights. Scents were even worse, as they've wonderful roses in Spain. They reminded me of Morelands in the summer, and Her Grace."

"Did you read those letters she gave you?"

"I'm working up my courage."

"Shall I read them for you?"

"Thank you." St. Just smiled slowly at the fierceness in Val's offer. "But no, I'll read them. It's just that things here at Rosecroft have gone widdershins in my absence. My womenfolk are not at peace."

"Your womenfolk being Emmie and Winnie?"

St. Just nodded and slouched against an arm of the chair. "There's a burr under Winnie's saddle. Emmie thinks my absence did not sit well with the child. I suspect it's Emmie's flirtation with the vicar that offends Winnie."

"Could be both," Val said, pursing his lips, "but I doubt the local vicar has made any significant progress in your absence. I've seen how Emmie regards you, and Winnie must see that, too."

"The child sees entirely too much." St. Just eyed his drink. "She was allowed to wander the estate, more or less, when her father was alive, and Emmie has curtailed that behavior since his death. Just yesterday, however, Winnie purposely ran off."

"Running away is usually an effort to draw attention, at least it was when we did it. Sophie and Evie ran off when you and Bart joined up, and spent the night crying in the tree house."

"And you run off to the piano bench. I run off to wrestle with rocks. I take your point, and Winnie has seen much upset in her short life."

"Are you sure Helmsley is her father?"

"Her mother said so, apparently." St. Just blew out a considering breath. "The earl acknowledged the child openly upon her mother's death."

"Who was her mother?"

"Emmie's Aunt Estelle." St. Just set his empty glass down. "She was not a particularly virtuous female, nor was Emmie's mother, though I gather they both were loyal to individual protectors and not available on street corners."

"Does Winnie have any siblings?" Val asked, refilling his own glass.

"None Emmie is aware of." St. Just watched as his brother sipped at the second drink. "Being a professional, I assume the woman knew how to prevent such things."

"And what was Winnie, then?" Val cocked his head. "Divine intervention? Or did the woman think to trap Helmsley into marriage? If she'd a brain in her head, she had to know that man was only going to marry money."

"And stupid money at that."

"Doesn't make sense, Dev. This aunt had some sort of pension from the old earl, didn't she? And a place to live. Such a woman had no motivation to set her cap for Helmsley, particularly not a woman ten years his senior, nor a woman trying to provide her niece a decent upbringing. I can't imagine she was hungry to waste her remaining years on Helmsley's bastard, either. You're telling me she had to be older than you are now when the baby came along—several years older. Doesn't add up to me."

"It is puzzling," St. Just said slowly, thinking through the questions Val had just raised. "And you're right: It doesn't add up."

❧

Emmie awoke the next morning, horrified to see the sun was already up. How on earth was she to get the cake to the church hall and still have her deliveries on the wagon by noon?

She had to admit, though, as she hastily put up her hair and donned a clean day dress, she had *slept*, and some of the leaden, creaky feeling in her body had abated as a result. She'd slept more than twelve hours, in fact, and knew she could have bested even that record had the drapes not been drawn open.

She washed and dressed quickly and had the insight that lately, she was so tired it was hard to work efficiently, creating a spiral of inefficiency and fatigue she'd been too exhausted to see. She shook her head over that and repaired to her kitchen.

"Good morning, Miss Emmie." Anna Mae Summers emerged from the pantry, all smiles. "I've set the bread to cool, and I'm almost ready to start on the hot crosses. The dough for the cinnamons is rising on the hearth."

Emmie smiled in return. "What on earth are you doing here, Anna Mae? I thought you were off to visit your sister while I'm here at the manor."

"I've been back more than a week." Anna Mae set to mixing up some icing. "I was dying of boredom when his lordship's footman came by yesterday afternoon. This kitchen is bigger than yours and better laid out."

"It's very nice, but how long can you stay?"

"I didn't come to call, Miss Emmie. I came to *work*. That wedding cake is going to look a treat, too. Enough to make me wish old Eldon Mortimer might take a girl to wife, you know?"

"The cake!" Emmie whirled, the morning's deadlines looming up once more.

"It'll be fine," Anna Mae assured her. "His lordship has the dogcart hitched to take you over, and the layers are all boxed in the pantry. I've put the repair icing in the jar, and you'll want a cloak, as it's not exactly warm out."

Emmie sat at the table and sent a bewildered look at Anna. She wanted to be indignant over matters running so smoothly without her, but her relief at not being behind was just too great. Then, too, she'd gotten more sleep in the past night than she had in the previous three put together.

"And, yes"—Anna Mae set the bowl of icing aside—"you have time for a nice cup of tea before you go. His lordship said he'd be in to fetch you when he had the beastie hitched."

His lordship… Emmie got up to pour herself some tea. His lordship had taken Winnie off her hands yesterday, retrieved Anna Mae, shown Anna Mae what orders needed to be filled, and was now preparing to escort Emmie and her cake to church. She owed the man a debt of gratitude, one particularly profound given the way she'd treated him yesterday.

And the way she'd treated him the night before. God above, she'd all but attacked him… As she sat sipping her tea—hot, with lots of cream and sugar—the object of her musings appeared in the back hallway.

"I see you woke up after all." He smiled at her, and Emmie knew with sudden certainty just who had tucked her in and opened her draperies. "Good morning."

"Good morning." Emmie offered a tentative smile. "My thanks for your efforts. I slept like a log, and the rest is much appreciated."

"You aren't going to castigate me for being high-handed?" He helped himself to a sip of her tea. "I thought you needed some reinforcements, and Anna Mae seems glad to be here." Anna Mae winked at him for that pronouncement, and Emmie held her peace as the earl fastened her cloak for her then escorted her out to the gig. Three white boxes sat on the seat, each holding a layer of wedding cake. Caesar stood placidly in the traces, though the air was almost nippy.

"Don't worry." The earl handed her up. "I've driven the fidgets out of him already, and the church is only a short drive. You look a little less exhausted though." He climbed up and settled himself beside her.

"Pretty morning," Emmie said after they'd tooled along for several minutes. "And I really do appreciate your taking a hand in matters. I was about at the end of my rope with Wee Winnie."

He smiled over at her. "You needed a nap, Emmie."

"I did. I feel like I could use another one just as long."

"Then take it. Anna Mae greeted me like I was Wellington himself, and she seems to have matters in hand."

"What about Winnie?" Emmie frowned even as she stifled a yawn.

"Winnie has me and Val and Mary Ellen, if need be," he reminded her as they pulled into the church-yard. "I get no end of satisfaction out of watching my little brother take tea with a stuffed bear and a dog.

When my sisters played house, Val *always* got to be the baby."

Emmie ushered him into the church hall, which doubled as the local assembly room. While she busied herself with setting up her cake, St. Just was sent to fetch the "repair icing" from the gig. He tarried long enough to release Caesar's checkrein, allowing the horse to crop the soft fall grass in the churchyard.

"But, Emmie"—Bothwell's cultured tones drifted through the back doors of the hall—"you know I've missed you."

Emmie's reply was murmured in low, unintelligible tones, causing St. Just to pause. The damned Kissing Vicar was about to strike again, but as a gentleman...

As a gentleman, hell... St. Just did not pull the door shut loudly behind him, which would have afforded Bothwell a moment to protect the lady's privacy. He charged into the hall, boots thumping on the wooden floor, jar of icing at the ready.

"Now, Emmie..." Bothwell *was* kissing her, one of those teasing little kisses to the cheek that somehow wandered down to the corner of her mouth in anticipation of landing next on her lips.

"Excuse me, Bothwell, didn't realize you were about."

"Rosecroft." Bothwell grinned at him, looking almost pleased to be caught at his flagrant flirting. "I'd heard you were back. My thanks for the use of your stables."

"And my thanks for keeping those juvenile hellions in shape. You need a horse, man, congregational politics be damned."

"Maybe someday." Bothwell's smile dimmed a little as his gaze turned to Emmie. "But for today, I've a wedding to perform."

And Bothwell had known, probably from experience, Emmie would be bringing her cake over. Absent a special license, the wedding would have to start in the next couple of hours, and St. Just suspected the vicar had been all but lying in wait for Emmie.

"Em?" He brought her the icing. "Shall I go offer up a few for my immortal soul, or will we be going shortly?"

"I won't be long," she said, brows knit as she positioned the second layer atop the little pedestals set on the first. "I just need to put the candied violets around the base when I've got the thing assembled, and maybe a few finishing touches."

"She'll be hours." The vicar smiled at her so indulgently that St. Just's fist ached to put a different expression on the man's face. "Come along, St. Just, and we can at least spend a few minutes in the sunshine." They ambled out into the crisp air, St. Just willing himself to hold his tongue. Silence made most men talkative, and the vicar was no exception.

"It galls me," Bothwell said, smile fading. "People around here will pay good coin for Emmie to make these gorgeous cakes—and they taste as good as they look, St. Just—but they won't invite the woman to their weddings and parties and picnics. She's never put a foot wrong, never flirted with anybody's husband, and even after what—twenty-five years of spotless behavior?—they still judge her."

"Your defense of her does you credit," St. Just said

with grudging honesty. "But Emmie does not curry their favor, and that, I believe, is what costs her admission."

"And you've put your finger on the real truth." Bothwell frowned, his gaze traveling over the tidy village green across from the church. "Enough of that, as there has been churchyard politics as long as there've been animal sacrifices to the pagan gods, but I think Emmie has just concluded touching up the cake, and the wedding doesn't even start for an hour," Bothwell said, turning toward the doorway to the hall.

"I'm ready to go." She smiled at St. Just. "Nice to see you, Vicar, and these"—she held out a package of buns—"are for you."

"My thanks." He took the package then bowed over her hand, pressing a lingering kiss to her bare knuckles.

St. Just silently ground his teeth at that shameless display and even let Bothwell hand Emmie up into the gig. As St. Just took the reins, the Kissing Vicar patted Emmie's hand where it rested in her lap.

Except it was more of a stroking pat, St. Just noted, a caress, the filthy bugger.

"You're quiet," Emmie remarked, lifting her face to the sun. The relief in her expression suggested she hadn't been interested in lingering in Bothwell's company.

"Is Bothwell pestering you, Emmie?"

She glanced over at him, a furtive, assessing glance that he unfortunately caught and comprehended too well: It isn't bothering if the lady welcomes it.

"He is a friend," she said, lapsing into silence when St. Just said nothing more.

He reached over with one hand and gently peeled Emmie's index finger from her teeth. "No biting your nails. Whatever it is, you have only to ask, and I will help."

"Is it possible to love someone and hate them at the same time?"

"It is. I love my father, in a complicated, resentful, admiring sort of way, but when he gets to tormenting my brothers, which he used to do brilliantly, I would rather Bonaparte himself had sired me than that scheming, selfish old man."

Emmie grimaced and looked like she wanted desperately to bite her nail. "That is quite an indictment, especially coming from you."

"He's a quite a character. I don't know how my mother..."

He fell silent: Her Grace was not his mother. Twenty-seven years after meeting her, St. Just was still making the same mistake he'd made when he was five years old.

"You never talk about your mother," Emmie said. "I've heard stories of each brother or sister, Her Grace, your papa, Rose, her family, and even the dogs and horses, but you never talk about the woman who brought you into this world. You forgot her, I suppose."

He drove along in silence until Caesar brought them back to the kitchen terrace. St. Just set the brake, climbed down, then came around to assist Emmie. He paused first, frowning up into her eyes. Then he settled his hands on her waist and lifted her to the ground.

In the normal course of such a courtesy, Emmie set her hands on his shoulders, and there they stayed as he continued his hold on her, even when it was clear she no longer needed his support.

"What?"

"I never forgot her, Em," he said, closing his eyes. "Never… but not for lack of trying."

She slipped her hands around his waist, hugged him for a brief, fierce instant, then retreated again to her kitchens and the endless work to be found therein.

Twelve

To Her Grace, Esther, Duchess of Moreland,

Thank you for your recent letter. I pray by the time you've received this, young Devlin is once again in robust health, tagging after his brothers and enjoying the pleasures of a country summer. I'm happy to report the farm here will prosper this year, but as harvest approaches, I find my thoughts turning to the day I parted from my little boy. As I am sure you recall, it was in mid-October, a bright, beautiful fall day, a day too pretty for as much as it pained me.

I am consoled, however, to hear Dev has taken to riding with his father and brothers, and he excels at this endeavor. Even as a babe in arms, he was taken with horses. I used to walk with him to the mews and hold him up so he could stroke the great velvety noses of the carriage horses. They seemed to sense his wonder with them, his heart for them.

Still, you must promise me, Your Grace, though it is rank arrogance to ask such a thing, that you will not encourage him to recklessness. Many a laughing boy has fallen to his death from the back of a horse…

St. Just stopped, unable to read further as he recalled all the laughing boys he'd seen fall to their deaths. Nearly a month he'd had these letters in his possession, and he could barely get through three paragraphs. Ever since Emmie's innocent comment about forgetting his mother, the letters had been burning a hole in his awareness. Like an addict who knows there's a pipe of opium inside a drawer, he'd held the letters in his hands countless times, letting hope and fear and loss and so much more reverberate through him.

His mother had worried for him, she had remembered him, she had kept him in her prayers, and never, ever stopped thinking of him. If only three paragraphs told him that much, how could he bear to go through seven years of letters? Because he knew he had to, somehow, he had to find the strength—the courage—to read every word.

"Are you all right?" Val cocked his head where he stood in the library doorway. "You are pale beneath your plebeian tan, and… You're not all right." He closed the door behind him and locked it. "Talk to me, Dev." He came over to the desk, no doubt seeing correspondence laid there and more in his brother's hands. "Is it bad news? Did the old bugger finally shuffle off this mortal coil?"

St. Just managed a swallow and a shake of his head.

"So then what is it?" Val asked softly. But St. Just was staring a hole in the window, and the letters in his hands were shaking with some elemental exertion of will he could not have named to save his life. Carefully, Val extracted the folded paper from St. Just's hands.

He'd see it was a woman's hand and that the paper was yellowed and frail with the passage of time.

While St. Just ordered himself to rise and move, to say something, to escape the grip of the emotions choking him, Val studied a letter at some length.

"You haven't seen these before," Val said, sidling closer and putting the letter far to the side. St. Just shook his head and began to blink, his throat working with the effort of expelling words.

"Oh, child." Val slid his hips along the desk and rested his hands on St. Just's shoulders. "I am so sorry."

"Val?" It was little more than whisper.

"I'm not going anywhere."

"I remember," St. Just got out as he wrapped his arms around Val's waist and held on. "I remember petting the horses... With her..."

They wept, as soldiers often do, in absolute soul-wrenching silence.

∽

They sneaked out through the kitchen like a pair of truants, Val grabbing a bottle to slip in with the sandwiches, and a book to keep the sun off his face. For most of a long, lazy afternoon, they read Kathleen's letters to each other, sometimes falling silent for long moments before resuming. When the stack was complete and reverently folded and put aside, they lay on their blanket watching clouds laze across a brilliant blue sky.

"Feel all better?" Val asked, taking a pull from the bottle and passing it to the brother on whose stomach his head was pillowed.

"I want my mother." St. Just's hand drifted over his brother's hair. "You'd be surprised, young Valentine, how many dying men call for their mothers. Not their priest, not their wives of twenty years, not their God, not their firstborn. They want their mothers."

"I had a kind of grudging admiration for old Boney before." Val laced his fingers on his stomach. "Thought he was a determined rascal, valiant little prick, and all that. But hearing you…" Val closed his eyes. "Loving you, I have to hate that little bastard with everything in me. Why didn't you come home, Dev?" The question echoed through the fears of an adolescent boy who'd seen two of his brothers ride off to war and only one come home.

"Riding dispatch, you think the orders you've stuck in your shirt are the ones that will turn the tide of some battle or see the enemy's magazine blown up. When you're on the battlefield, you charge in and disrupt the infantry lines, get under cannon range, and tear into their forces; then the real fighting can begin. You think you're necessary."

"You were necessary," Val said, accepting the bottle. "But you were necessary to us, too, Dev."

"You weren't going to die without me," St. Just countered, but his hand brushed over Val's temple again. "You were safe and sound back in merry old England, which was exactly where I needed you to be."

"I thought about joining up. Her Grace cried, and that was that. His Grace forbid it, and I caved. Some soldier I'd make. Her Grace said I lack the ability to defer to my betters."

"Because you have none, but you mustn't speak ill of Her Grace, or I will have to thash... thrash you."

"Here's to Her Grace." Val held up the bottle. "She loves you best, you know."

"Oh, shut up." St. Just chuckled, the mirth making his stomach bounce under Val's head. "You take this business of being the baby too seriously."

"You were a pathetic little orphan," Val went on. "Women are suckers for pathetic orphans. Trust me on this. Every time you slipped up and called her Mother or Mama, she nearly left the room in tears. But you slipped up less and less."

"Perfect little soldier," St. Just murmured. "This is why one needs nosy little brothers, who remark one's maturation more carefully than one does himself." He paused and sorted through his last profundity. "I'd forgotten about calling her Mother. I thought she left the room because she didn't want me to be embarrassed."

"Are you embarrassed now?" Val twisted his head to peer up at his brother's chin. "She loved you to distraction and still does. She was the one who jumped on this earldom when Westhaven mentioned it; then he got all excited, and Anna chimed in... you were doomed."

"It's not so bad, being doomed. Read the one about the trip to the park again."

Val fished through the letters, and with his brother absently petting his hair, he reread the second-to-last letter Kathleen had written. From his strategic location on St. Just's stomach, he knew his brother was weeping again, but it was a soft, untroubled kind of weeping—just an expression of honest sadness.

"Want to hear it again?" Val asked as he passed the bottle back up, then a clean handkerchief.

"We'll be late for tea."

"Bugger tea."

"Maybe just the last two paragraphs."

Val read the whole thing yet again, slowly. They didn't go in until it was dark, the drunk was wearing off, and the air growing cold again.

⤜⤏

The next day dawned cold and overcast, gray clouds hugging the tops of the distant hills. St. Just rode Red, Caesar, and Wulf before going in to breakfast, lest rain cheat one of the geldings of his exercise.

When St. Just came into the house, the familiar scents of yeast and cinnamon wrapped around him. Val's fingers were busy at the keyboard, and Scout sat panting outside the door of the music room.

Would it be so bad to be married to this? He hadn't formally proposed to Emmie, but she knew the offer had been made, just as he knew it had been rejected.

He'd finished his morning rides convinced Emmie was being stubborn for a *reason*. Emmie was a sensible woman, not prone to flights and fits. She cared for him—he'd wager Caesar on that—and she cared for Winnie—he'd bet his life on that. There had to be a reason she'd walk away from both of them, something beyond her insistence that she wasn't fit for polite society.

"You are lost in thought," Val said as he emerged from the music room with Winnie at his side. "Either that, or you are trying to communicate with the dog by divining his thoughts."

"My lord?" Steen emerged from the morning room. "You have visitors. The Tosten ladies are here to welcome you back from your journey."

Val arched an eyebrow. "Ladies?"

"Come on, Scout." Winnie stomped away without another word.

"Ladies." St. Just closed his eyes. "Lady Tosten, Miss Elizabeth. Had the pleasure last spring at one of Her Grace's at homes, and now I am their bosom beau." He turned a martyred expression on Steen. "I don't suppose there's any chance I'm not at home?"

"They saw you come up from the stables, my lord," Steen murmured sympathetically. "I'll bring them tea and explain you need to see to your toilette."

"Suppose I do at that." St. Just blew out a breath. "Val, you are honestly better off lying low. Once word of your presence gets out, the Vandal hordes will descend."

"Wouldn't think of it." Val grinned. "Winnie has deserted me, so I'll entertain your callers while you turn yourself out in proper attire. Take your time."

He didn't take his time, as the gleam in Val's eye hadn't been quite trustworthy, but he did manage to run the Tostens off in summary fashion when Val explained to the ladies, straight-faced, he never practiced his piano when there were guests in the house. Lady Tosten's disappointment at being denied an invitation to luncheon for the third time would have been comical but for being blatant.

"God Almighty." Val ran a hand through his hair. "That was work. Do they call often?"

"Once is too often," St. Just replied. "There's

nothing wrong with Elizabeth, and from what I saw at church, she's the belle of the valley, but somehow…"

"Don't do it." Val pointed a warning finger at St. Just's chest. "If you have to talk yourself into a woman, a man, an encounter, a deal, then don't do it."

"Words of wisdom from my baby brother?"

"She would flutter you senseless in a year," Val assured him, "and you might think, yes, well, but a fellow can get an heir in the dark, and then we'd just live our separate lives, send the boys off to Eton, and needs must and all that. Ask Sir Tosten how marital bliss appeals after twenty-five years with Elizabeth's mother. Ask him why Elizabeth is an only child. Ask him why he's around his wife and daughter for only a few weeks in the spring and perhaps over the holidays. Am I making my point?"

"You are," St. Just said as they headed for the kitchen, "but why so emphatically?"

"Good little soldiers"—Val poked that finger at his chest this time—"do stupid things because the general says so. Lady Tosten is a general—an enemy general. You leave her to me."

"Valentine… You are not to do anything rash."

"Protective of the sweet young thing?" Val retorted. "She isn't helpless, St. Just."

"Of course she isn't." St. Just sighed, wondering where the argument had started and why. "But we are gentlemen, need I remind you, and we do not trifle with ladies."

Val narrowed his gaze, pursed his lips, propped his fists on his hips, and started to say something, only to change his mind.

"You're right." His hands dropped to his sides. "We absolutely do not trifle with the women we respect."

The off-balance mood of the household continued for the rest of the day, with Winnie pitching a tantrum at the dinner table when Emmie asked St. Just about the governess candidates. Val watched the unfolding scene and suggested St. Just write to Her Grace about little girls who pitch public fits.

"You have a point." St. Just eyed his brother across the table. "It can't hurt." He shoved to his feet. "I'll just dash off a couple more notes then seek my bed. You will excuse me, Val, if I eschew the decanter?"

"Get your rest"—Val waved him off—"while I flirt with Emmie and winkle recipes from her." St. Just bowed to Emmie and departed, hoping Val would mind his manners while he was flirting and winkling.

St. Just came out of the library some time later and headed for the stairs. His first thought was to make directly for bed, but a light shone from Winnie's bedroom, and the child's outburst still troubled him. He tapped lightly then let himself in, finding Winnie sitting on the bed, a single candle burning while she labored at her lap desk.

"You'll lose your eyesight by the time you're old enough to dance, child." He ambled into the room and considered lighting more candles. "Did you light that one yourself, or did Mary Ellen leave it for you?"

"I asked her to leave it."

"But you told her it was because you were afraid of the dark"—St. Just lowered himself to the foot of her bed—"not because you wanted to stay up, writing royal warrants of execution for every adult in the house."

"What's a warrant of execution?"

"Win." He leaned his head back against the bedpost. "You'd better come clean soon, or you'll miss more than dessert the next time you're rude to Miss Emmie."

"I don't want a governess," Winnie said. "I don't need a governess. I can already do sums and read, and double and divide a recipe. I can write letters, and I know my prayers. I don't need a governess."

"*Weisst du, das Ich liebe dich?*" he asked, "*Ou je t'aime? O, yo te amo?*"

"What?"

"I just told you I love you in three different languages, Winnie Farnum, but because you're not done with your education, you could not comprehend my words. Emmie might be able to teach you a smattering of one of them."

"You can teach me the other two," Winnie shot back, "and I can understand English fine."

"My point is that Emmie loves you, and I love you, but there is more you need if you're to do well in this life. A governess is not being hired to punish you, but to help you."

"I don't want help," Winnie said through clenched teeth. St. Just was too tired to argue, too tired to chastise the child for her tone of voice, her disrespect, or her stubbornness.

"So what do you want?" St. Just asked quietly. Winnie looked away, reminding him poignantly of Emmie in the midst of difficult discussions. "What do you want, princess?" he asked again.

"I want…" Winnie's little shoulders heaved, and still St. Just waited. "I want Emmie to s-s-stay." She hurled herself across the mattress, sending her writing implements flying in her haste to throw herself into St. Just's arms. "Don't let her go away, *please*," Winnie wailed. "I'll be good, just… Make her stay. You have to make her stay."

He wrapped her in his arms and held her while she cried, producing a handkerchief when the storm seemed to be subsiding. All the while he held her, he thought of Her Grace raising ten children, ten little hearts that potentially broke over every lost stuffed bear, dead pony, and broken toy. Ten stubborn little chins, ten complicated little minds, each as dear and deserving as the last, and all with intense little worlds of their own.

Ye Gods. And what to say? Never lie to your men, St. Just admonished himself…

"I don't want her to go, either," St. Just murmured when Winnie's tears had quieted to sniffles. "But Emmie has her business to run, Win. She won't go far, though, just back to the cottage, and we can visit her there a lot." *Like hell.*

"She isn't going to the cottage," Winnie replied with desperate conviction. "She's going to marry Vicar and his brother will die and she'll be rich, but far, far away. Cumbria is like another country, farther away than Scotland or France or *anywhere*."

"Hush," St. Just soothed, fearing he was about to witness the youngest female crying jag of his experience. "Emmie hasn't said anything to me, Winnie, and I think she'd let me know if she were going somewhere."

She had, however, told him to find another governess by Christmas at the latest.

"She's going," Winnie said, heartsick misery in her tone. "I know it, but she'll listen to you if you tell her to stay."

"I can't tell her, Win." St. Just rose to turn back the bedcovers. "I can only ask."

"Then ask her," Winnie pleaded as she scooted between the sheets. "Please, you *have* to."

"I will ask her what her plans are, but that doesn't affect your needing and deserving a governess. Understand?" When Winnie's chin jutted, he dropped onto the bed and met her eyes. "We haven't hired anybody yet, we haven't even interviewed anybody yet, and we won't expect you to tolerate anybody who isn't acceptable to both Emmie and me, all right?"

"I don't want a governess," Winnie said, but her tone was whimpery, miserable, and hopeless.

"I understand that, and I only want you to have a governess you're going to like, Winnie. All I'm asking is that you give somebody a chance to help you learn, whether Emmie's here, back at the cottage, or married to the Vicar."

"I love Emmie," Winnie said, reaching for Mrs. Bear. "I love Emmie, and I don't want her to go, and I don't want her to marry Vicar."

"Neither do I, princess." St. Just blew out her candle. "Neither do I."

He waited by her bedside until her breathing signaled sleep, and realized that as gray and threatening as it had been all day, the rain had held off. The weather was no doubt contributing to the heaviness in his chest, the roiling in his gut, the sense of being unable to string two useful thoughts together.

Somehow, Winnie had come by her conviction Bothwell was going to snatch Emmie away, and the threat was driving the child nigh crazy.

Just what we need, he thought as he headed back down to the library, *another lunatic at Rosecroft*.

◆◆◆

Emmie wondered where St. Just had gotten off to. He wasn't taking his customary morning shift in the library, though she herself had seen him coming up from the stables after breakfast. After a ride, he always looked windblown, happy, and relaxed, unless one of the horses had been particularly fractious, but this morning there had been something... troubled about his posture. The riding hadn't set him to rights, and Emmie was coming to dread the next meal with Winnie.

"My apologies." St. Just appeared in the library doorway, his hair brushed, his riding attire apparently discarded for clean clothes. "Shall we begin? Halton has interviewed no less than twelve possibilities... What?"

Emmie was frowning at him in consternation.

"No 'Good morning, Emmie'? No 'Wonderful crepes at breakfast today'? No 'How did you sleep after Winnie's little dinnertime drama, Emmie'?"

He flicked an impersonal gaze over her as he closed the door behind him.

"Good morning, Emmie. I trust you slept as well as you could, given Winnie's unfortunate display of sentiment. Breakfast was as always *lovely*. Now shall we begin? I haven't all day to spend on locating your replacement."

"St. Just?" Her voice betrayed dismay and wariness. "What has gone amiss?"

"Not one thing, Miss Farnum," he replied, pausing before his desk. "May we be seated?"

"No, damn you." She marched over to him. "What in blazes has gotten into you?"

"I am not in the habit of explaining myself to women affianced to others, Miss Farnum. I don't know whether to thrash you for your deceit or strangle you for the hurt you do that innocent child."

"St. Just," she said, her voice quavering just a little, "are you having another setback?"

"No." He closed his eyes and clenched his fists. "I am *not* having another setback—yet. But if I do, you may hold yourself quite accountable, as you are clearly accountable for the setback Bronwyn has been treating the household to for weeks."

"Explain yourself," Emmie said, feeling gut-punched at his words.

He speared her with a glacial look then went to stand facing the window, the gray, bleak day complementing his demeanor.

"I went upstairs last night," he began in the same terse tone, "to check on Winnie. She was writing to Rose but put her correspondence aside to treat me to a six-year-old version of a female tantrum, Miss Farnum, because she has learned of your plans. I do not appreciate having to learn from a child that congratulations are in order, by the way. When she finally quieted, I came back down here, unable to sleep, and no, I was not going to raid the damned… I was not seeking a drink."

He paused, and Emmie waited. Congratulations for what? People congratulated women on conceiving, but...

"I thought I might quiet my mind by reviewing correspondence, and imagine my surprise when I found a note to me from dear Vicar Bothwell, delivered up from Morelands belatedly with some scores Her Grace forwarded to Val."

"And the significance of his note?" Emmie asked, but the dread congealing in her stomach didn't need his answer.

"Bothwell, to his credit..." St. Just paused and reined in the tempo and volume of his speech. "The vicar wrote quite cheerfully that he had asked you to marry him and anticipated being able to leave with you for the Landover estate not later than Christmas. I know not how, but Bronwyn knows of this proposal and your acceptance of it. She knows his brother is failing and where his estate is, and in her own way, just how far Cumbria is from the little girl who loves you."

"She knows?" Emmie said in horror. "Winnie knows?"

"Winnie knows." St. Just kept his back to her. "And now I know, too. When is the happy occasion?"

"What happy occasion?" Emmie asked, mind reeling. How could Winnie have learned of this?

"It is customary that when a man in need of heirs seeks a bride, for the bride upon acceptance of his suit to set a wedding date."

"I haven't accepted *anything*," Emmie said, dropping onto the sofa. "He asked, but I didn't give him an answer, and I told him if I did answer, it would be no..."

"Winnie perceives it differently," St. Just said. "If she does, your vicar does, too. I saw the man kissing you, Emmie." St. Just turned to eye her. "You might not be setting a date, but he is."

"He kissed my cheek," she said, touching her lips with her fingers. Her eyes met his then, and she had to look away.

"Was he the one who broke your heart?"

~&~

St. Just knew how to bellow loudly enough to shake the rafters, and he knew even better how to pitch his voice quietly for a more devastating effect.

"Emmie, did Bothwell break your heart?" He repeated the question even more softly, his tone lethal, though it was an unworthy question. A man ought to cede the field when he'd been bested, and right now, Bothwell had gotten a cordial stay of sentence, while St. Just's attempts to propose had been summarily batted aside.

But she made love with me, he reminded himself. That had to count for something with her, because it counted for the world with him. Incongruously, though he was furious with her, feeling betrayed and confused, just looking at her sent a spike of hot lust through him. *She made love with me...*

"He did not break my heart," Emmie said, "but he did propose—again—and he did steal a kiss, and somehow, Winnie must have seen this."

"She saw it, and she heard it. Not too discreet, your vicar."

"He is not my vicar," Emmie wailed.

"He thinks he is," St. Just rejoined. He eased his hips down to the windowsill, crossed his feet at the ankles, and shoved his hands in his pockets. "You have to tell him—and Winnie—what your intentions are, Emmie."

"I have to what?"

"Winnie is in torments, thinking you plan to move to Cumbria. I suspect a good deal of her misbehavior has been as a result of the fear that you, like her mother, father, her aunts, the old earl, and God knows who else, will abandon her. You owe her at least an acknowledgement of your plans, whatever they may be."

"I don't know what they are." Emmie could barely stand to meet his gaze. "I have not accepted Hadrian's proposal."

"Not yet," St. Just spat. "Well, let us all know when you do and, until then, I will do my best to keep either myself or Bronwyn from any avoidable *setbacks*." He shoved away from the window and stalked out of the room, slamming the door behind him. Emmie stared at that door, then out at the bleak Yorkshire day, and felt such an ache in her chest that her heart had to be physically breaking.

Lord Val found her in the kitchen when he wandered down from his bed just before noon.

"Good morning, Emmie." He smiled a rumpled, cheerful smile at her then frowned. "I see it is not a good morning. Did your soufflé fall?"

"Lord Valentine," Emmie said, "how would you take it if I went out to the woodshed, picked up the ax, and started laying about with it on your lovely piano?"

"Like you hated me. Does somebody hate you, Emmie?"

"St. Just." Emmie nodded as she beat the hell out of a bowl of egg whites. "Or he will, if he hasn't gotten around to it yet."

"He's not a hateful person. Why would he be provoked to such an emotion with you?"

"Because I have to leave," Emmie said, pausing in her beating, then resuming with diminished fury. "I cannot stay here and be Winnie's governess. I cannot marry him, for he'd hate me then, too, and God help me, someday Winnie will hate me, as well. Even Hadrian will be entitled to hate me, and you, too, I suppose."

"Seems a deuced lot of hating going on for such a sweet woman. Don't suppose you'd tell a fellow why?"

Emmie shook her head, and the eggs whites took the brunt of her frustration.

"And you won't confide in St. Just, either, will you?" She just shook her head again and closed her eyes, heartbreak and unshed tears radiating through her. Val put an arm around her waist and pulled her against his side.

"Pies," Emmie said, turning her face into his neck. "I have to put this meringue on the pies."

Val patted her shoulder, gave her a little squeeze, then took his tea and left her in solitude.

Up on the servants' stairs, St. Just leaned against the wall, trying to sort through the conversation—if he could call it that—he'd just overheard. Emmie was miserable; that much was beyond doubt and even brought him a little, nasty pleasure. She was destroying a helpless child, after all, and then, too…

She wasn't destroying him, not like she was Winnie, but she was devastating him nonetheless. And for what? To bake bread in Cumbria for her vicar, for God's sake?

Why would he hate her for marrying him? Was she barren, perhaps, and she could not provide him an heir? Why would Winnie hate her if this business of marrying the vicar didn't accomplish that task?

St. Just finished his letter to his brother and closed his eyes, trying to hear the pattering rain as just that, merely a typical late autumn evening's weather in bucolic Yorkshire. Memories nagged at him, tried to drag him back in time, but he resisted, turning his mind instead to the day's rides and the soft, lilting melody drifting through the house from the music room.

Emmie had not told her vicar she would marry him, but as October drifted into November, St. Just knew she hadn't turned the man down, either. It had taken some time to see why the decision was difficult, though he'd initially considered that he held the trump card—Winnie.

Except there were low cards in his hand, as well, something he was finding it difficult to come to grips with.

In the army, his men had become loyal to him for three reasons. He did not have charm, luck, or diplomacy in sufficient quantity to inspire followers, but he was, first, foremost, and to the marrow of his bones, a horseman. In the cavalry, a man who truly admired and understood the equine, and the cavalry mount in particular, was respected. St. Just's unit was always a little better mounted, their tack in a little better shape, and their horses in better condition, primarily because St. Just saw to it. He commandeered the best fodder, requisitioned the best gear, and insisted on sound, sane animals, though it might cost him his personal coin to see to it.

The second attribute that won him the respect of his subordinates was a gentleman's quotient of simple common sense. Stupid orders, written for stupid reasons, were commonplace. St. Just would not disobey such an order, but he would time implementation of it to ensure the safety of his men. In rare cases, he might *interpret* an order at variance with its intended meaning, if necessary, again, to protect the lives of his men and their mounts.

But when battle was joined, St. Just's third strength as a commander of soldiers manifested itself. His men soon found those fighting in St. Just's vicinity were safer than their comrades elsewhere. Once the order to charge was given, St. Just fought with the strength, size, speed, and skill of the berserkers of old, leaving murder, mayhem, and maiming on all sides until the enemy was routed. His capacity for sheer, cold-blooded brutality appalled, even as it awed, particularly when, once victory was assured, his demeanor became again the calm, organized, slightly detached commanding officer.

And Emmie Farnum had no use for that latent capacity for brutality. She'd seen its echoes in his setbacks and his temper, in his drinking and insomnia, and St. Just knew in his bones she was smart enough to sense exactly what she'd be marrying were she to throw in with him.

Barbarians might be interesting to bed, but no sane woman let one take her to wife. Nonetheless, having reasoned to this inevitable, uncomfortable conclusion, St. Just was still unable to fathom why, on the strength of one intimate interlude, he could not convince himself to stop wanting her to do just that.

Thirteen

"I CAME IN HERE WHEN I SHOULD BE SEEKING MY BED," Emmie seethed at St. Just. "I thought to review your infernal list of prospective governesses, and I find *this*." She waved a beribboned document at him, holding it between thumb and forefinger as if it dripped something malodorous. "I was not attempting to snoop, but good God, St. Just, you leave it in plain sight where anyone might see it."

He crossed his arms, grabbed for some civility, and tried to keep his voice even.

"It's merely an order of court, which, when signed, will give me the right to act as Winnie's guardian and adopt her at a later time." He was dead tired, and to make matters worse, it had been pouring rain for two days, meaning he hadn't been able to ride at more than a cautious trot up and down the lanes. He felt ready to explode with unresolved tension and to collapse with the weight of back-to-back bad nights.

"You want to *adopt* her?" Emmie's question bordered on the hysterical, and even through his irritation and exhaustion, St. Just felt a spike of alarm.

"At some point in the future," he said slowly, "if Winnie will allow it."

"If *Winnie* will allow it!?" Emmie glared at him through suspiciously shiny eyes. "I am her family! I am the only family she's known, besides her dratted father, for at least the past two years, and I am the only family who has given her welfare a single thought in all that time. Yes, her aunt will be a duchess, but her aunt has been racketing about these two years, leaving Winnie to face a man Anna herself would not confront. And you think *you* should adopt her?"

For the first time in days, St. Just allowed himself to both look at and *see* Emmie Farnum. He'd tried to avoid her; he'd communicated through Val, Winnie, notes, and silence, so difficult had it become to be in the same room with her. She was everything he'd ever wanted and every dream he'd never see come true.

But the passage of time was being no kinder to her than it was to him.

Her eyes were shadowed, her features were honed and drawn, her pleasing feminine curves were fading beneath clothing gone loose and ill-fitting. And now she was finally looking at *him*, her eyes full of heartbreak and bewilderment.

"Emmie?" He dared not say more but risked putting a tentative hand on her shoulder. She closed her eyes and stiffened momentarily as if he were hurting her; then she was sobbing in his arms, trying to push words past her misery and failing.

"Oh, Emmie, hush." He walked her over to the sofa, keeping an arm around her waist. "Just hush… It'll be all right, it will, but please don't take on so. Please…"

She bundled into his chest, keeping her arms locked around his neck, her breath hitching and catching around her futile attempts to gather her arguments and her wits.

"Let me hold you," he murmured when she quieted momentarily. "I'll wait all night if you like, Emmie. Take your time, and we will talk, but just give yourself a minute. Let me hold you…"

His hand moved over her back then settled at her nape, where his fingers made slow, easy circles. To give her something to focus on, and to give her *anything*, he offered her the sound of his voice. On and on he pattered, apologizing for upsetting her, telling her how each gelding was doing, how badly the rain was interfering with his training schedule, *anything*, to pull her back from the panic and hopelessness he'd seen in her eyes.

He didn't know how long they sat on the sofa, how long he'd held her, how long she'd cried and cried, but eventually, she let out that huge telltale sigh, signaling the end of the storm.

"I'm all right now," she said, her voice still husky with tears. She tried to pull away from him, but he held her gently, a hand cradled along her jaw, caressing the bones and textures of her face.

"You are not all right," he said, *any more than I am*. "You are going to turn into a ghost, Emmie. What good will you be to Winnie then?"

"Winnie will get used to my absence," she said in the tones of one informed of a date with a firing squad. "I apologize for all this… drama. I was just caught unawares."

"Which is in part my fault." His hands traced her features, though even as the tactile pleasure of her skin beneath his fingers filled his heart, so too did the knowledge that she was tolerating him in a weak moment... nothing more. "I have not wanted to raise the issue with you."

"Nor have I been willing to broach it with you," Emmie said, tucking her face against his collarbone. "Of course you should adopt Winnie, if you're willing to take on that burden. I would like to be able to visit her someday."

"So you've decided to move to Cumbria, then?" He turned his face to inhale the fragrance of her hair, wondering how a man could breathe through so much heartache, much less speak intelligibly.

"It isn't Cumbria," Emmie said, tears welling again. "I just need to know Winnie has taken root here, and she cannot do that if she thinks I am an option for her."

"I do not," St. Just said in low, intense tones, "and I never will, agree with your decision in this matter, but neither can I convince you to reconsider it."

"Just hold me," Emmie whispered. "Please, for the love of God, just hold me."

"Let me build up the fire," he suggested a few minutes later. He hoped simple activity and even a few feet of distance might allow rational thought to find him again. He eased away from her, added several heavy logs to the blaze on the hearth, and turned to face her where she sat on the sofa.

"St. Just?" She'd pulled her feet up and propped her chin on her knees.

He hunkered to meet her gaze at eye level. "Emmie?"

She drew in a deep, shuddery breath and let it out before meeting his eyes. "Lock the door."

❦

Don't do it, his common sense screamed. *You'll regret it, she'll hate you for it, this is stupid, stupid, stupid... Think, man!*

"Why?" he asked. Not why lock the door—he didn't even pretend to himself regarding that answer—but why allow such intimacies now? She smiled in response, a heartbreakingly tender, wistful smile.

"I am being selfish, St. Just." She turned that smile on the crackling hearth. "I need you. I know it isn't wise, not for either of us, but I am so..." He sat back on the raised hearth and mentally filled in the silence: Lonely, frightened, bewildered, *cold*...

"What of Bothwell, Emmie?" he pressed, his voice grave. "I will not trespass where there's a betrothal. He doesn't deserve that from either of us."

"I have not given him an answer. There is no betrothal."

Yet. The word hung between them, and St. Just felt a spike of wry self-pity. She wanted a little fling, perhaps, some comfort over her decision to abandon the child, some pleasure before she must accept the saint over the barbarian. She wanted the oblivion of passion and knew she could, at least, count on him for that.

"You are sure?" he asked, tossing one last meager bone to his conscience. "I would not become one of those fellows who used you ill, Emmie. Not for anything."

"I will use you ill," she said, that same sad smile

flickering across her tired countenance. "If you will allow it."

"And if you get a child?" he asked, closing his eyes against the part of him that would sell his soul to ignore the question.

"It's not likely right now." And for no reason he could fathom, this seemed to make her even more sad.

"You must not answer Bothwell until you know," St. Just said, but he realized Emmie would have promised to dance naked through York at that moment, so desperate was she for the oblivion he could provide.

"I will wait." She met his gaze. "And if I've conceived, I will refuse Bothwell."

His best, most noble, and unselfish motivations, his self-discipline, his very reason went sailing right up the flue, but still—even having handed him a means of thwarting the vicar—Emmie held his gaze. She had not said she'd marry St. Just, either, and they both knew it.

He rose on a sigh, feeling both buoyant that she should turn to him and desolate that he was truly going to lose her. "I have not the strength nor the virtue to deny myself what you offer."

Emmie closed her eyes and nodded, but he could almost hear her thinking: *Thank God*... He stood, gazing down at her. How to begin this unlooked-for feast of pleasure and heartache? How to give her the abandon she sought in such exquisite, overflowing measure she might even doubt her determination to leave?

Naked, he thought, the image of Emmie gilded by firelight igniting in his imagination.

"Come." He tugged her to her feet. "You deserve

a bed, and no one is about at this hour." She silently complied and let him lead her through the darkened house, his arm about her waist, her head on his shoulder as if she could barely find the strength to move.

"Last chance to change your mind," St. Just murmured as they neared his bedroom door. She shook her head and followed him into his room.

He locked the door behind them and saw his room through her eyes: It looked almost unlived in. A fire had been lit, but the covers were not turned down to warm the bed, the candles were not lit, the wash water had not been moved to the hearth for warming. Though the rest of the house was showing the benefits of additional maids and footmen, his own quarters were not.

"You wash first," Emmie suggested. "I'll see to my hair and the bed."

He nodded and began to strip out of his clothes, as casually as if they'd done this for a thousand nights. Emmie turned down the bed, found his hairbrush, and sat on the end of his raised canopy bed to take down her hair. St. Just stayed near the warmth of the hearth, systematically removing his clothes. Naked as he came into the world, he turned to the side and propped a foot on the low brick hearth.

"That water has to be cold. Wouldn't you like some hot from the kitchen?"

"It will serve," he said, starting on his face, neck, and arms. He paused to pour a measure into the pot kept on the swing in the hearth and shifted it over the fire. "We can warm some up for you." He turned his attention to his chest, his arms, his torso, each part methodically attended to before he shrugged into his dressing gown in exact repetition of his nightly routine. He did not get into clean sheets unless he'd washed.

"Care to borrow?" he said, smiling slightly as he held out his toothbrush. She nodded, accepting the loan. When she came out from behind the privacy screen, St. Just was holding his hairbrush.

"I'm more than willing to finish your hair for you. I think you were about ready to start on the second side?" She been on stroke number eighty-seven, but he didn't feel a need to reveal just how closely he'd been watching her.

And she had been watching him, her gaze grave and her perusal silent and thorough. She didn't answer him immediately but reached out and fingered his dressing gown—not his skin.

"Second thoughts?" he asked, trapping her fingers in his own.

"Not that." She brought his hand to her lips and kissed his knuckles. "Will you be my lady's maid?"

Good, he thought on a rush of relief and gratitude. He wanted hours and hours with her, he wanted every depth and manner of intimacy he could cadge from her, and being her lady's maid suited him perfectly.

"Turn around, my lady." He smiled down at her. "Though I cannot promise my services will be rendered with any particular speed."

"We are in no hurry," she said, giving him her back. "None at all." He started at her nape, letting her feel his fingers on the hooks holding her dress closed. But, ah, then it wasn't his fingers at all, but his mouth. For each hook undone, he brushed a kiss to her skin, down the length of her spine, one soft, sweet imprint of his lips at a time. He ended up kneeling behind her, his cheek pillowed on the soft swell of her derriere.

He rose, her dress hanging open down her back, and stood so the warm press of his erection would be starkly obvious against her lower spine.

"I want you," he whispered, setting his lips against the turn of her neck. "I always will."

She closed her eyes and let her head fall back against him as he slid one shoulder of her dress down her arm. She shivered, but his response was to brush the other shoulder of her gown down to trap her arms at the elbows. He held her, one arm around her waist, pinning her back against him while his free hand went plundering.

He inhaled deeply then exhaled slowly as he slid both hands up to turn her by the shoulders. He held her gaze while his hands went to the ties of her chemise, and when she would have raised her hands to hurry the task, he trapped them in his, kissed each palm in turn, then set her hands at her sides.

"Let me," he murmured. His progress was slow, and all the while he looked at her. Looked at each inch of flesh he was exposing, watched the rise and fall of her breathing, noted the flush spreading across her features. Still, he would not hasten his hands. When she stood naked in the pool of her dress and chemise, he stepped back, and as if he were escorting her onto the dance floor, lifted her hand so she could step free.

Kiss me, her eyes silently begged. *Kiss me, and for God's sake let me touch you.*

He scooped her up and laid her on the bed in one

fluid motion, then stood beside the bed, gazing down at her.

"I want the night, Emmie. Not an hour, not the next little while. I want this night with you." She nodded but said nothing as he laid his dressing gown across the foot of the bed and stretched out on his side near her but not touching.

"It's trite"—he smiled faintly as his gaze traveled over her—"but you are so beautiful, Emmie Farnum. I could almost spend this time getting drunk on just the look of you here in my bed."

"And you," she said, reaching over to trail her fingers along his jaw. "I love looking at you, and not just naked in your bed. I love to watch you ride, to see you with Winnie, to watch you bantering with your brother. I've spied on you when you build your stone walls and work with your horses. You're beautiful to me."

He closed his eyes, his smile becoming a wistful quirk of his mouth. She raised herself up to press her lips to his.

"I am dying for the taste of you," she murmured, settling back. "The feel of you, the scent of you."

"Ah, Emmie." He curled down to bury his face against her neck. He'd planned to take eternities just stroking and caressing and touching her all over, so her contours and hollows would all be his to recall. He saw then he wasn't going to be able to hold to that course. She wasn't going to allow it.

He shifted his body over hers and heard her sigh of pleasure.

"Better," she murmured, swirling her tongue against his shoulder. "A little better."

He held still while she tasted him, closed his eyes and focused on the soft eddy of her tongue against his flesh. She moved on to his neck, his throat, the underside of his chin, silently asking him for his mouth. Asking, not begging.

"Soon," he whispered, "soon, my love." He cruised his lips over her forehead and eyebrows, inhaling the fragrance of her hair, letting her have just enough of his weight so his erection throbbed against her mons.

He captured her mouth, teasing her lips with his own, tasting, pausing, and savoring, then giving her a little more. She opened for him immediately, pleasing him with the feel of her hands sweeping over his back, pulling him into her body. Her legs wrapped around his hips, hugging him so she could rock up into him in a slow, insistent rhythm.

"St. Just." She drew back enough to evade his kiss. "Not slow, please. Not this time."

"Not slow," he assured her, "but not rushed, either. Trust me, Emmie. You'll have your pleasures." He drew a hand down her side. "I promise."

She curled up to seek his kiss again and let one hand smooth over his chest, finding a nipple and feathering her fingertips over it. He tensed then bent his head to kiss her, this time giving her his tongue. She seized on that concession and built the kiss hotter and deeper.

"Managing," he murmured, his voice redolent with affection. "Managing, demanding, passionate, beautiful, and… delicious." He bent his head, escaping her kiss, and took her nipple in his mouth, feeling her instantly go still then arch up to him.

"St. Just... *Devlin*." Her voice held wonder and such sweet longing, he felt a plundering, physical joy. "Devlin, you have to... oh, *please*." She rolled her hips against him again, trying to take him inside of her. He ignored her pleading and switched to the second breast.

"Emmie." He released her breast and raised his face to meet her eyes. "Emmie, look at me." Her great blue eyes opened then focused on him. When they would have fluttered shut so she could chase him with her hips, he feathered his fingers over her forehead. "Love, *look at me*."

Slowly, he brushed the head of his cock over her mons, once, twice, and Emmie met his gaze. He brushed lower, giving her the freedom to raise her hips to meet his caress. Oh, he'd wanted to put his hands on her, his mouth on her. He wanted to tease and taste and torment, but this would do just as well—better, as his own self-restraint was taxing him sorely.

"There," she breathed as he fit himself to the opening of her body. "Oh, *yes*."

He paused, memorizing the dreamy pleasure in her eyes, the languorous heat of her gaze. This much of him, he thought, she truly did hold dear.

"More, St. Just," she urged as she almost had him where he could not tease and evade as effectively. "Now."

He hitched his hips, settling all of his weight more closely around her, then eased just the tip of his erection into her damp heat. Still she met his gaze, reaching up and cradling his jaw with her hand, relaxing her body under his.

St. Just felt her focus shift, from her need and her pleasure to *their* needs and *their* pleasures. He sighed his relief and began to move his hips, advancing in slow, sure thrusts as Emmie's hands drifted over his back. Without warning, her grip became urgent, and she pressed her face tightly against his neck.

"Devlin…"

"Don't fight it," he whispered, his pace still smooth and relaxed even as she spasmed around him. "Let it happen, love. Let me give you this."

She clutched him to her as her body seized with pleasure, and still he kept his cadence almost soothing. The effect of his easy rocking thrusts was to drive her deeper into her pleasure more surely than if he'd tensed and thrust hard in response to her body's pleading.

"St. Just…" She panted against his shoulder. "I can't…" Her hands settled on his buttocks, asking him for a moment of stillness, and so he paused, kissing her gently. He nuzzled at her neck, then her jaw, then levered up to regard her.

"I'm all right." She smiled up at him. "Or as nearly all right as I can be when you love me witless."

"I do, you know." He tried to keep the sadness from his voice, from his eyes, from his smile. "Love you." He dipped his head to kiss her again, covering her mouth just as she inhaled on a gasp.

"You must not say such things."

"I mustn't keep it unsaid, but I won't belabor the point." He kissed her again but knew he'd blundered— she certainly hadn't returned the sentiment, now had she? But she deserved the words, and it had been a relief to say them, even if only the once. It had been sheer relief to acknowledge he loved somebody, *that he could love somebody* other than the people he'd known since birth. She would always have his gratitude for that, if nothing else.

And he wanted to tell her that, too, but the time for words was quickly passing. Emmie again found his nipples, first with her fingertips, then with her mouth.

"Emmie," he rumbled, "go easy." She gentled her touch obligingly but did not desist.

"It's your turn," she murmured against his chest.

"Our turn," he corrected her through gritted teeth. She was maneuvering her heavy artillery into place, experimenting with her inner muscles, closing her body around him every time he moved to withdraw and thrust again. She caught his rhythm, turned the slow, relentless push and drag of his thrusts against him by adding her own push and drag to the dance.

"Don't fight it," she whispered, a thread of humor in her voice. "We need it."

"I don't want to hurt you," he growled, his movement becoming more urgent.

She laughed at that and held him closer. "You couldn't," she murmured. "Let go, Devlin. I'll catch you."

Let go... Something he hadn't done in any way, shape, or form for *years*. He hadn't let go of his temper, his physical conditioning, his grief, his loneliness, his terrible weariness of spirit. Hadn't permitted himself uncontrolled laughter, a mean drunk, a howl of rage or indignation. Hadn't... *Let go.*

Something in him broke free. He gathered Emmie closer, anchored one hand under her tailbone, shifted the angle of his penetration, and hilted himself inside her. His movements became not faster but more intense, more focused. He settled his free hand over her breast and closed his fingers around her nipple.

Emmie tightened her hold on him, and St. Just knew he was moving beyond reason. He would not hear her words, but he would hear her body. She strained to meet him, thrust for thrust, arched her breast into his hand, buried her fingers in his hair and held him to her with all her strength. He found her mouth with his, even as inarticulate sounds of need and arousal welled in her throat, and still he drove her on.

"Ah, God, Emmie love," he murmured fiercely, and then, "Sweet Christ…"

She exploded beneath him, keening her pleasure into his kiss, writhing with mindless abandon in counterpoint to his thrusts. He chased her into a long, grinding wrestling match with satisfaction more pure, intense, and shattering than anything he'd known. And still, when they were reduced to shuddering in reaction and fighting for each breath, they held each other tightly.

"Ye gods, Em," he whispered in disbelief, trying to raise himself even two inches off her boneless form. "I can't ever…"

She placed two fingers over his lips without opening her eyes. "Hush, love." With her hand on the back of his head, she urged him to lay his cheek against hers. "I just need a minute."

He, on the other hand, thought he might need a lifetime to recover from what had just transpired. For a long moment in her arms, his awareness had expanded beyond his own body to encompass hers, her pleasure, her desire in addition to his own, and even beyond that. He had been formless and weightless and yet more real than he could ever recall being.

He struggled to his elbows, giving them both room to take deeper breaths, but kept his cheek next to hers. He waited, mind drifting, letting his erection subside, so when he disentangled from her, she would not be uncomfortable.

"You'll be sore," he whispered, contrite and concerned. "I'm sorry."

"I will not be sore," Emmie murmured without opening her eyes. "Though I might be moving a little slowly tomorrow."

"Emmie, I am sorry. I never imagined I was capable of such a loss of self-restraint." He tried to shift off her, but she caught him in a surprisingly strong grip.

"Don't you dare be sorry," she said, eyes finally open and glittering in the dim light. "You did not lose your self-restraint, Devlin St. Just. For just a few moments, you let go of the dead weight on your heart and your spirit. Maybe all that sorrow and regret won't hold you so tightly after this."

He buried his face against her neck, not knowing what to say. She was right: For a few moments, he'd felt alive and whole and glad to be that way. But those moments were over, she was still leaving him, and sorrow was crowding close once more.

St. Just extricated himself carefully from her body and lifted himself off the bed. Emmie watched while he used some of the warmed water to wring out a flannel cloth then wash off his genitals. He rinsed out the cloth again and brought it to the bed.

"Let me." He sat at her hip and waited while she raised and spread her knees. "You are swollen," he remarked, brushing the backs of two fingers over her engorged flesh. Even that light caress caused her to flinch, and he smiled wolfishly at her response. "Swollen and beautiful." But he covered her gently with the warm cloth and held it against her sensitive skin until he felt her ease.

"Thank you," she said when he draped the cloth on the edge of the basin. "Would you like me to return to my room now?"

"I do not ever want you to go back to your room or your cottage or your vicar, Emmie Farnum. I thought you agreed to give us this night." She nodded, and he saw she was shy and uncertain rather than looking for a way to leave him so soon.

"So." He put one knee on the bed. "You'll hold me now?"

"Haven't I been holding you?" Emmie looked hesitant but flipped the covers up so he could join her under the blankets.

"There's holding"—he eased down beside her— "and there's holding." He pillowed his head on the slope of her breast and brought one arm and a leg across her body. "Tell me if I'm too heavy for you."

Emmie slipped her arms around him, resting her cheek on the tangled mess she'd made of his hair. "You're not too heavy."

❧

And that seemed to be all he wanted, just to cuddle up in her arms and share a warm, comfortable silence.

Once she realized she wasn't going to be evicted nor expected to make coherent conversation, Emmie let herself enjoy of the privilege of such a trusting embrace. How much more quickly might he have healed if he'd had a place of such pleasure and trust and caring to come to each night?

"What?" he asked, flicking his tongue over her nipple. "You had a thought, and it made your body frown."

"It did not." She brushed her fingers over the end of his nose in the gentlest parody of a reprimand. He'd been right, of course. The idea that she wasn't going to share more such embraces with him, ever, made her frown mightily. He deserved this, he'd earned it, and she wanted to give it to him. Worse, she had a sneaking suspicion that once she left, he wouldn't admit to such a need ever again, with anybody else.

He'd soldier on, riding his horses only to sell them, raising another man's child, making a routine that wasn't a life, two hundred miles from the people who loved him.

"Don't cry, Em." He leaned up and brushed a kiss to her cheek. "Whatever it is, we still have tonight." She nodded, but in his words was the tacit admission tonight was all they had, and to her surprise, she was able to start to talk about what came next. Needed to, in fact.

"Winnie will want Gany and Io," she said when he'd turned her on her side to rub her back. And they tiptoed through more that needed to be said.

"Have you any miniatures of your aunt or yourself that Winnie can keep?" That *he* could keep for Winnie.

"There's a portrait up in the playroom of Winnie's father on a pony," Emmie recalled. "She might like it in her room."

"Was Winnie's mother or father musical? Will you write to her?"

"Will you encourage her to write to me? Will you at least let me know how she goes on if she's too upset to write to me?" And she did not ask: *will you let me know how you go on?*

Then conversation would drift off to the meaningless intimacies of lovers.

"Is this a bruise?" He traced a finger over a slight discoloration on her shoulder.

"Winnie's birthday is at the end of February, and she will be seven."

"The age of reason," St. Just murmured. "And when is your birthday?"

But as those painful questions and thoughts slipped out between other less painful exchanges, it became apparent to St. Just that Emmie was not truly thinking through the upcoming separation. She would not—or more likely, could not—organize the practicalities while she suffered under the weight of the emotions.

He'd been so angry with Emmie and so confused by her insistence on leaving, he had not measured her heartache against his or Winnie's. Holding her, listening to her dance around a wound too painful for her to even clearly admit to herself, he realized, of the three of them, Emmie was the most unlikely to recover from her decision to leave.

The least he could do was manage the transition for her. His years in the army prepared him to do that, much as elderly relations understood the practicalities of organizing a funeral.

But first he would complete the gift of this one night, he thought, spooning his body around hers. He entered her gently and let her drift easily from one peak to the next before withdrawing and rolling her to her back. Throughout the night, he let her alternate between dozing in his arms and being treasured with his loving. He used his mouth, his hands, his cock, his every resource to give her pleasure upon pleasure.

This should have been our wedding night, he thought as he gazed at her in sleep. A clock chimed three times downstairs, and Emmie's eyes fluttered open.

"Go back to sleep." He kissed her forehead. "You are forbidden to set foot in the kitchen this day. It's your turn to have a cold."

Lying on her side facing him, she met his gaze and reached out to stroke a finger down the side of his cheek. "Devlin?"

"Here."

"I need to go," she said, swallowing, "from Rosecroft and Winnie. I can't seem to make myself do it."

He wanted to close his eyes so she wouldn't see the pain in them.

"I'll interview the top three candidates for governess, Em. Let's plan on moving you back to the cottage at the end of next week, and I'll have your choice of the three start the week after that."

Her eyes filled with tears, but she just nodded and crawled into his arms to cry herself to sleep. When she was truly beyond awareness, he lifted her into his arms and put her in her own bed. Because the sheets were cold and her fire burned down, he climbed in with her, warming her with his body until she was again deep in slumber.

And how tempting it was, to be discovered in her bed, to take away the option she most wanted to exercise and give himself the one he wanted for himself. That, he sternly admonished himself, would not be the way a man showed he cared for a woman in difficulties, though; so he pressed one last kiss to her forehead, built up her fire, and returned to his own bed.

There to toss and turn until the sun came up two hours later.

Fourteen

THE DAYS DRAGGED AFTER THE NIGHT ST. JUST HAD
spent with Emmie. When it was fair, no matter how
cold, he spent long hours with his horses and riding
out on his estate. He conferred with Emmie in the late
afternoons over the details of moving her baking back
to the cottage, but when he asked her what would
become of her business when she moved to Cumbria,
she gave him a blank look.

"Anna Mae can do it, I suppose." She blinked,
looking puzzled. "I can lease her the cottage or give
it to her."

"You don't want the cottage held in trust for Winnie?"
St. Just suggested, sitting beside her on the sofa.

"Oh. I suppose I could do that, couldn't I?"

St. Just resisted the urge to wrap her in his arms. She
didn't look as tired and pale and wan as she had—he
was insisting she sleep more—but she looked even more
lost. "Have you spoken with Bothwell about this?"

"He is off at Ripon. There's some gathering of the
clergy of the West Riding, and he won't be back for
at least a week."

"I see." For a woman on the verge of a very estimable match, Emmie did not seem to care that the vicar had left the area. "And how did you learn of his plans?"

"Anna Mae told me," Emmie replied, missing entirely the consternation on St. Just's face. He'd considered Bothwell was not calling at Rosecroft in a display of tact, and had not concerned himself with how the man was communicating with his intended.

Tried not to concern himself, anyway. It appeared there was no communication, at least not lately, and there were no plans to transition Emmie's thriving business.

"Emmie, have you thought about a trousseau?" he asked gently. "Where you'd like to be married? When?"

"No."

Just that, one word.

"Are you pregnant?" he asked, bewildered. How could a woman be so set on a plan and be doing so little to implement it?

"I don't know yet," she said in a small, miserable voice.

Well, that must be it. She was on tenterhooks waiting to see if their night of passion had ruined all her plans.

"You'll know soon?" he asked, hesitantly patting her hand only to see her glance down at his fingers with dismay.

"A day or two. If I'm not, I will tell you."

"We wait, then," he said, rising but frowning down at her. "If there is a child, the banns should be cried immediately."

"I doubt Bothwell will want a wife pregnant with

another's child," Emmie said, rising, as well. "He does have a title to consider."

"*Emmaline Farnum, for God's sake*. If you carry my child, you will marry *me* and no other. How could you think I'd let my child be a cuckoo in Bothwell's nest?"

"I'm sorry." She glanced down, not meeting his gaze. "I didn't think that… I just…"

"It's all right," he said, bringing her hand to his lips. "When we know what our situation is, we'll go from there. Get some sleep."

She left the room without meeting his eyes.

Could she do that, Emmie wondered as she stumbled off to her room? If she carried St. Just's child, could she condemn him to a lifetime of marriage to a woman who would never make a creditable countess? A woman no longer pure of body or heart? She'd have to tell him the truth first, but in his mind, the only truth would be that his child not be born to bastardy.

God Almighty, she thought as she prepared for bed, how could she have been this shortsighted, this selfish, this *simpleminded*, to take advantage of St. Just's generous and lusty nature without any thought to the consequences for them both?

And for Winnie.

She drifted off to sleep, wondering how much worse things could get before the weight on her heart began to lift.

In the morning, she found she was not expecting a child, and for all the contradictions and complications it implied, the weight on her heart doubled.

≪∂≫

"Wee Winnie." St. Just hoisted the child onto his lap where he sat at his desk in the library. "There was something I wanted to ask you concerning a discussion you had with Lord Val."

Winnie's brow knit. "If he told me a secret, I won't tell you." She scooted around, settling with her head pillowed on his chest.

"I won't ask you to tell secrets. This had to do with asking if you wanted to move to Cumbria with Emmie."

"I don't," Winnie said with perfect equanimity.

"Why not?" St. Just inquired in the same pleasant tones.

"It's complicated," Winnie said warningly, "but it goes like this: If I am here, then Emmie might come home if she's unhappy in Cumbria. If I am there, then Emmie will stay in Cumbria and try to make me happy there. Besides, Emmie went away before."

"What do you mean?" St. Just asked, smoothing a hand over Winnie's blond curls. When had the child's hair gotten so long? It was almost to her shoulders, almost long enough to pull into two pigtails if not quite braids.

"My mama told me Emmie lived with us when I was very little, but then Emmie went away to Scotland. When she came back again to care for the old earl, she lived in her own house. Emmie went away to school before I was born, too."

"You didn't expect her to stay here, then?"

"I hoped she would. But you won't go away."

"I already have," he countered. "I went away to Morelands."

"That was just a visit, to see your mama and papa and to meet Rose. That wasn't going *away* away. You live here now, and you'll stay."

"Why will I stay when Emmie, who was raised here, will not?"

"She's a girl," Winnie said patiently. "She will marry Vicar and go away. You are not a girl, and besides, you were in the army for a long time."

"What has that to do with anything?" St. Just asked, prepared for any answer. There was no telling where a child's mind turned and doubled back. He'd learned that much already.

"You don't run away," Winnie said, meeting his eyes. "Soldiers are brave, and they stand and fight. You fought and fought and fought, longer than I have been alive, Lord Val says, because you didn't stop fighting until old Boney was done for, did you?"

"I did not stop until we won." St. Just smiled. He'd still fought after Waterloo, until he had to be dragged off to the stables like an old warhorse—lame, scarred, and dazed, unable to comprehend the cessation of violence.

"So I will stay with you," Winnie said, the logic settled in her little-girl mind, "and I hope Emmie is miserable with her silly old vicar and that she wants to come home lots."

"We might need another plan, Win. Like Miss Emmie is happy as a hog in slop with her vicar, and you can go visit her for weeks and weeks every summer. It's very fashionable to see the Lake District in the warmer months."

"I am not the one running away just so I can have

a title and wear jewels," Winnie said with chilling evenness. "Let her come visit me, and if Scout and I feel like it, we'll invite her to tea."

"I'm not too happy about her leaving, either," he admitted, "but when I joined the army, Her Grace cried and cried and cried, and still I went. People don't always do what you want them to."

Winnie rolled her eyes then closed them and snuggled into his chest. She'd dropped off to sleep a few minutes later when Emmie tapped on the door and joined him in the library.

"Have you said anything to her yet?" Emmie asked, glancing anxiously at Winnie.

"Nothing specific," he said, keeping his seat in deference to his burden. "She knows you plan to leave the area."

Emmie just nodded, but she was glancing around the room anxiously, not meeting his eyes.

"Em?" He did get to his feet then and deposited Winnie on the sofa, draping an afghan over her sleeping form. Emmie met his gaze and began to blink, then threw herself at him.

"There's no baby," she murmured in a miserable whisper. His arms closed around her, not sure if she was relieved, unhappy, or just upset on general principles.

"Thank you for telling me." He stroked her back, then her nape, while she cried in silence. "This will make your situation easier, though, I hope?"

She nodded but soaked his cravat with a fresh flood of tears. He pushed his handkerchief into her hand and waited her out, the sleeping child momentarily forgotten.

"Emmie?" He had hoped... He had so desperately, selfishly hoped... And now he was tempted, tempted to join her in her bed again, for he'd every confidence, as flustered and unsure as she'd been of late, he could seduce her into accepting further intimacies from him.

She gave a genteel sniffle then tried to step back, but he permitted her to retreat only far enough that he could see her eyes.

"You will be all right?" he asked, keeping his voice very quiet.

"I will. I just need to put this move behind me. You're sure the governess will be here next Monday?"

"I've already sent her the first month's salary. You don't want to meet the woman?"

"We'll meet," Emmie said, leaning in for one more moment in his arms. "I'm sure we'll meet at some point."

"And Bothwell will be back next week, as well," he said, knowing he should set her from him.

"I suppose," Emmie muttered, burying her face against him. He gave up and cuddled her close until he felt Emmie's lips against his skin.

"Emmie," he chided, "you need to behave..." But she cut him off by settling her lips over his, and for just an instant, a blessed, fleeting instant, he tasted her in return.

"We agreed," he reminded her, cradling her head against his chest. "You have to help me on this, Em. I'm not made of steel."

"Parts of you might be," Emmie muttered, nudging him with her hips.

"Damn it, Em." He retreated one step, his hands on her upper arms. "No fair. Against the rules of engagement, and shame on you." But he dropped his forehead to hers and amended his judgment. "Shame on us both."

"I'm sorry. I just… I'm just upset."

He said nothing, silently acknowledging the truth of her statements… nothing more. He was more than upset himself, thank you very much, and a particular steely part of him was ready to commit high treason in his breeches.

"I'll see you at breakfast," he said, putting his hands in his pockets to mask the effect of her proximity. When she was safely gone, he peeked out into the corridor, and without grabbing a coat, went directly down to the stables. It was cold as hell, thank God, and certain treasonous body parts lost their steely quality in the face of the elements.

Neither St. Just nor Emmie bothered to look back as they'd left the library, or they might have seen innocent, puzzled blue eyes turn calculating and determined as they peered over the back of the sofa.

"It needed only this," St. Just growled. Emmie was leaving in two days time, the house felt like somebody was laid out in the parlor awaiting burial, the roads were a mixture of slush and mud, and now company was coming to call.

"Never fear." Val clapped a hand on his shoulder. "You have reinforcements, St. Just." The grin on his face received no answering smile from his brother, who was truly incapable of seeing humor in anything.

Val deloped for his piano precisely at the half hour, allowing St. Just to start verbally herding his guests toward the door, though Elizabeth flung up a last-minute resistance as he did.

"I understand Miss Farnum will be removing to her cottage soon, my lord. You must be relieved to have Rosecroft resuming normal operations." Elizabeth gave him a perfectly guileless, perfectly nasty smile over a teacup that had to be empty for as often as she'd brought it to her lips.

"In fact"—he smiled right back—"I will miss her sorely, as well as the wonderful goods she makes and the wonderful scents filling my house as a result of her industry. I admire a woman who can put in a hard day's work and have something delicious on the table to show for it."

"One does admire honest labor in the working class," Lady Tosten put in.

"It isn't just her industry," St. Just went on, feeling mean and knowing he should just shut up. "Emmie has been the soul of kindness to Miss Bronwyn during the worst of her bereavement, and even helped me locate a suitable governess for the child, as well as suitable candidates for the other staff positions we've had to fill here. Winnie and I will both be frequent guests at the cottage, I am sure, and not just on baking days."

Emmie, forgive me. It wasn't well done of him to use Emmie for a decoy, but the Tostens were hardly being subtle in their campaign, and time spent with them was purely time wasted.

"Your gratitude to the woman does you credit,"

Lady Tosten allowed, finally coming to her feet as Steen appeared with their cloaks. "Come along, Elizabeth, we must still pay a call on that nice Mr. Neely and his girls, as their cousin Jeffrey has come to visit them. St. Just, a pleasure."

"Ladies." He bowed, closing the door behind them, leaving Steen to see them out. When he heard the front door slam, he stuck his head in the music room, where Val was hammering away at finger exercises. "They're gone, you can come out now."

Val burst into a thundering version of the "Hallelujah Chorus," winking at his brother from behind the keyboard.

St. Just slumped against the wall of the music room. "If I haven't told you lately, little brother, I do adore your playing."

"And my dear self, too, of course," Val said, bringing the volume of his playing down and beginning to improvise on Handel's theme. "So why do you put up with them? Why not just growl and throw your food bowl and appear with tea stains on your half-unbuttoned shirt?"

"Is that how it's done?" St. Just opened his eyes to smile at Val. "I'm not sure how that will fit in with the plan to marry me to the girl. Might put her off a bit, don't you think?"

"Her?" Val shook his head. "Not possible, not with that reptile of a mother. Elizabeth, I'm sure, would marry you if you were drooling and cross-eyed, just to get free of her dear mama."

"Give me a week," St. Just muttered, "and I'll have the cross-eyed and drooling part down."

"Time for a trip to York?" Val hazarded as he crossed the left hand over the right.

"You interested?" St. Just cocked his head.

"I am not," Val said, bringing his little concert to a close. "I have spent many, many happy hours cozying up to a certain Broadwood in a brothel, but the few times I was persuaded to go upstairs, it didn't feel right. You will just have to go into York on reconnaissance and let me know what you find."

St. Just turned toward his brother then, closing the door before he saw that Emmie stood just beyond, her expression dumbstruck. She made her way back to the kitchen before St. Just came upon her.

"Be grateful, Emmie," he said ten minutes later while pouring himself a proper cup of tea and fixing it precisely to his liking. "Be glad, even, that you are not accepted by likes of those Tosten women."

"Winnie doesn't seem to care for them," Emmie said, her voice remarkably steady for a woman who has just heard her lover—her *former* lover—casually announce both a possible betrothal and an intention to visit the brothels.

"Winnie's instincts are sound," St. Just said, sipping his tea, "but she needs to refine their expression. I'm going to meet with my solicitor tomorrow. Is there anything you need in York?"

"I thought Mr. Halton normally came here."

"I can use the exercise and so can Caesar."

"I'll think about it," Emmie said, keeping her attention on the piecrust she was rolling out.

"Are you making apple tarts?" St. Just came over to pinch off a bite of dough. "You are. You dear lady."

He put an arm around her shoulders and pressed a kiss to her temple. "Bothwell is not good enough for you nor for my apple tart recipe." He dropped his arm and stepped back. "Best make extras, though, as Val and I might both want seconds."

He sauntered out. A little snitch of dough, a casual squeeze and a kiss, and off he goes, Emmie thought, her mind in turmoil. Rationally, she knew he had every right and even an obligation to marry, just as Hadrian Bothwell did. Rationally, she knew he was a passionate man and one she must not dally with further. Rationally, she understood the young men of the aristocracy were tomcats—with mistresses, sweethearts, and wives rotating through their beds depending on the time of day. Rationally, she should…

Oh, hell, she hated him *and loved him* and hated Elizabeth Tosten and hated herself most of all. That she loved St. Just came as something of a relief. It exonerated her for sharing intimacies with him on some level and made her a bona fide, unredeemable fool on another. He was a good man, no doubt about that, and worthy of loving, but thank God she hadn't made any declarations, as his sentiments were apparently more superficial than hers.

She would not tell him. They were in enough confusion and distress without any more great dramas—and feelings were tricky. She'd thought she was in love once before, long ago. Then, too, the situation had been difficult, and then, too, Emmie had found herself dreaming dreams much loftier than her lover's had been.

So she went to bed that night, sternly admonishing herself to put her dealings with St. Just in a neat little memory box, where, in a very short time, they could stay for the rest of her days.

◈

St. Just turned his horse toward the muddy track leading from York, relishing the time alone. He needed to think, and think clearly, because he had a strong premonition Emmie was making the mistake of three lifetimes—his, hers, and most significantly, Winnie's.

It took longer than he'd planned to transact his business, as the solicitor was knowledgeable and answered his questions in detail before St. Just made his final decisions. The trip home was spent brooding over the wisdom of his choices, and a cold, sleety rain started when he was about an hour from Rosecroft. Caesar slogged on, and just as every part of St. Just's body felt numb with cold, he gained his own property. Stevens took the horse, and St. Just let himself into the back of the house, the odors of cinnamon, clove, and baking apple assailing him. The back hallway was warm though dark. He could hear Val playing the piano and Emmie humming along in the kitchen as he shed his boots and sopping outer garments.

Emmie, he thought, closing his eyes and digging down for strength. If he wasn't careful, what he'd done would show on his face, in his eyes, and in the words he did and did not say.

"You're home." Emmie stopped her puttering, a luminous, beaming smile on her face, a pan of apple tarts steaming on the counter before her.

"I am home"—he returned her smile—"though soaked and chilled to the bone."

"I thought I heard the door slam." Val appeared at Emmie's elbow. "It looks like a half-drowned friend of Scout's has come to call. Come along, Devlin." Val tugged at his wet sleeve. "Emmie had the bathwater heated in anticipation of your arrival. We'll get you thawed and changed in time for dinner, and then you can regale us with your exploits."

"Behold," Val announced when they returned forty-five minutes later, "the improved version of the Earl of Rosecroft. Scrubbed, tidied, and attired for supper. He need only be fed, and we'll find him quite civilized." Emmie smiled at them both, and Winnie looked up from the worktable where she was making an ink drawing.

"I made you a picture," she said, motioning St. Just over. "This is you."

She'd drawn Caesar and a wet, shivering, bedraggled rider, one whose hat drooped, whose boots sagged, and whose teeth chattered.

"We must send this to Her Grace," St. Just said, "but you have to send along something cheerier, too, Win. Mamas tend to worry about their chicks."

"I thought she wasn't your mama," Winnie countered, frowning at her drawing.

"She is, and she isn't." St. Just tousled Winnie's blond curls—so like Emmie's—and blew a rude noise against the child's neck. "But mostly she is."

"When will you go see her again?"

"I just did see her in September. It's hardly December."

"She's your mother," Winnie said, taking the drawing back. "Every now and then, even big children should be with their mothers."

In the pantry, something loud hit the tile floor and shattered. Val and his brother exchanged a look, but Emmie's voice assured them it had just been the lid to the pan of apple tarts, and no real harm had been done.

"That's fortunate," St. Just said, going to the pantry and taking the pan from Emmie's hands. "Watch your step, though, as there's crockery everywhere."

"I'm sorry." Emmie stood in the middle of the broken crockery, her cheeks flushed, looking anywhere but at him. "It was my own pan, though, so you won't need to replace anything of Rosecroft's."

"Em." He sighed and set the tarts aside. "I don't give a tin whistle for the damned lid." He lifted her by the elbows and hauled her against his chest to swing her out of the pantry. "We've a scullery maid, don't we?"

"Joan."

"Well, fetch her in there. I am ravenous, and I will not be deprived of your company while I sup tonight."

"You didn't stay in York," Emmie said, searching his eyes.

"There is very little do in York on a miserable afternoon that could compare with the pleasure of my own home, your company, and a serving of hot apple tarts." She blinked then offered him a radiant smile and sailed ahead of him to the dining parlor.

"Winnie," St. Just barked, "wash your paws, and don't just get them wet. Val, it's your turn to say grace, and somebody get that damned dog out of here."

Scout slunk out, Winnie washed her paws, Val went on at hilarious length about being appreciative of a brother who wasn't so old he forgot his apple tart recipe nor how to stay clean nor find his way home.

Except at the last part, about St. Just finding his way home, Val speared his brother with a meaningful look even while St. Just was regarding Emmie with the same degree of intensity.

And in the midst of an otherwise boisterous and congenial meal, Winnie surreptitiously buttered rolls and tucked them into the pocket of her pinafore, ready to tell anybody who asked that they were for the banished dog, upon whom she'd recently conferred an honorary barony. If asked, she'd say the buttered rolls were a gesture to soothe his hurt baronial feelings.

Fifteen

"SHE HAS YET TO ACCEPT MY SUIT, YOU KNOW," Hadrian Bothwell informed his caller. He'd been surprised beyond telling to find Lord Rosecroft on the doorstep of the vicarage at the challenging hour of eight in the morning.

The earl nodded tersely. "I am aware of that, but with this document executed, I have no doubt you will be successful in your efforts to win the lady's hand."

Bothwell frowned and considered the earl, who was still standing in the entrance hall of the house. Something was not adding up, and it was too deucedly early for arriving at sums anyway.

"Come in." Bothwell gestured toward his study. "I'll fetch us some tea, and you can explain yourself while my brain wakes up. I got in quite late last night, and the weather turned foul well before I saw home."

St. Just hesitated; but with a sigh that sounded resigned, he followed Bothwell into a tidy, comfortable room boasting a cheery blaze in the hearth, two overstuffed wing chairs pulled up to the fire, and a desk angled to take advantage of the light from a bay window.

"I do some of my best thinking here with my feet up on the hearth and my chin on my chest."

"And your eyes closed to allow better concentration, no doubt," St. Just added. "How hard is it, really, to be a vicar?"

"Depends on the parish, I suppose, and the vicar. For me, it's getting harder and harder." He tugged a bell pull twice. "The memories here are not... easy, and I know my brother needs me. Then, too, when I arrived four years ago, I flattered myself my more worldly outlook might assist my flock in broadening their views, but in that regard, I am a miserable failure."

A rotund older woman came to deposit a plain tea service before the vicar. Once she departed, Bothwell lifted the lid of the white porcelain teapot to peer at the contents. "I like it quite strong. You?"

"At this hour, strong will do nicely. Was your replacement identified at this meeting in Ripon?"

"My replacement?" Bothwell gave a short, unhappy bark of laughter. "Trying to get rid of me, Rosecroft?" He kept his tone teasing, but the question was genuine, too.

"I am not." St. Just sighed and sat back. "This brings us back to the reason I have intruded on your privacy at such an ungodly hour."

"Your order of court." Bothwell passed his guest a strong cup of tea and poured a second cup for himself.

"The order of court, yes. If Miss Emmie has custody of Winnie, then I believe your chances of making her your viscountess will be improved." They discussed the matter for a few more moments, or traded elliptical comments in the manner of men treading lightly over unsafe ground.

"So you're moving Miss Emmie back to the cottage today?" Bothwell inquired as St. Just rose to leave. "Do you need any assistance?"

"We do not, thank you. We've been moving pots and pans and racks and crockery bowls and all manner of kitchen equipment for most of the week. Emmie did not bring all of her personal effects to Rosecroft, so moving the lady herself will be fairly simple."

"Perhaps I'll call on her after services." Bothwell nodded and grinned, mind made up and in happy contemplation of his meeting with Emmie. "Have to whip up a sermon on the evils of disappointing one's vicar, don't you think?"

"It would be pointless, wouldn't it?"

"Why is that?"

"Emmie has never been persuaded by her vicar to attend services," St. Just said as he headed for the door. "Your wisdom would be wasted on the pious believers."

Bothwell frowned, not sure if he'd been teased, insulted, or reprimanded, but he remained silent until he heard the front door closing softly. The two cups of tea had helped, but yesterday had been a monumentally stupid day to travel. Still, one more day among his sanctimonious, overwhelmingly *married* brethren, and he would have started muttering every profanity he recalled from university and public school put together.

Hadrian Bothwell lowered his tired frame into his favorite of the two wing chairs, poured himself a third cup of tea, and propped his feet on the hearth.

He downed the tea in a few swallows and set his mind to thinking about the three little lambs of his flock—a lamb, a ewe, and a ram, technically—who resided at Rosecroft. He considered his obligations to each of them, as pastor (though that was stretching it a bit), friend (stretching it more than a bit), suitor, and potential stepfather. The duties and considerations tangled up, crossed, and tangled up some more, until Bothwell's chin came to rest on his chest, and slumber claimed him.

St. Just glanced up at the clock in his library and scowled. He'd spent the last hour reading his mother's letters, something that had become like a regular devotion. He frequently tucked one or two of them in a pocket and took them out at odd times of the day, reading over and over what he'd already memorized. On this day, it was particularly comforting and yet also poignant to have his mother's words in hand. He folded up the last three letters, tucked them into an inside pocket, and mentally tried to prepare himself for what he faced.

His next task was to take Emmie back to the cottage and see her settled there. He'd return to Rosecroft for dinner and face a very unhappy Winnie, and possibly a less than sympathetic Val. By this time tomorrow, he would likely have heard Emmie had accepted Bothwell's suit, and there was not one damned thing he could do about any of it. Better she marry the vicar than disappear to parts entirely unknown in her quest to see Winnie well settled at Rosecroft.

"Have you said good-bye to Winnie?" St. Just asked when Emmie came bustling into the front hallway.

"Winnie is not very pleased with me," Emmie said. "I think she's purposely hiding, and if you don't mind, I'd just as soon have the leave-taking over with."

"You checked in her room?" It wasn't like Winnie to avoid a confrontation, but he wasn't keen to search the entire house only to spend another hour drying tears and losing arguments.

"I did," Emmie said, her expression miserable, "and the stables. I assume she's hiding in the music room with Val, who will no doubt be better company than I."

"As you wish." St. Just picked up the one ancient used-to-be-black valise that held the last of Emmie's personal effects, and offered her his arm, then handed her up into the gig. It had held off raining, snowing, sleeting, or whatever ugliness the sky portended, but the clouds were lowering threateningly.

"Appropriate weather for the occasion, don't you think?" St. Just remarked as he secured the valise behind the seat.

Emmie glanced at the sky and grimaced. "I suppose." She kept her eyes forward as St. Just climbed up beside her and took the reins.

"You can still change your mind, you know," St. Just said softly. Emmie glanced at him, as if to decipher whether the offer was about going back to the cottage, marrying Bothwell, or rejecting St. Just, but she just shook her head.

He clucked to the horse, and they made the short, unhappy journey in silence. Emmie waited until he came around to hand her down, and if she hesitated a moment before putting her hands on his shoulders, then hesitated even longer before stepping away from him, St. Just declined to comment.

"So you're here," he said, when he'd set Emmie's valise down in her front hallway. "Let me get your fires going, at least."

"I was…" Emmie looked around as if she hadn't seen the house before and rubbed her arms. "I was going to get the teapot on. Will you have a cup?"

"Emmie…" He regarded her with a frown, not sure what the kind thing to do was. At his hesitation, she looked ready to beg, so he capitulated. "One cup, but if we're going to that bother, let me put Caesar in a stall and see Roddy is settled in while I'm at it."

"One cup." Over which, she looked inordinately relieved.

While she bustled in the big kitchen, St. Just put the horse into a stall with hay and water, scratched the mule's furry forehead, and lit fires in the downstairs parlor and up in Emmie's bedroom. He'd never seen the room before and found it pretty, feminine, and welcoming. Emmie's bed was huge and so adorned with pillows and shams and skirts and lace it looked like a giant bonbon.

Closing the door behind him and wishing he'd not seen that bed after all, St. Just came down the back steps to the kitchen.

"You've been home only a few minutes, and something already smells good."

"I tossed a little cinnamon in the steamer. Your tea?" She handed him a mug, not a teacup, and gestured to the bench near the hearth. "The kitchen fire was lit this morning, so this room is probably the only one truly warm."

She sat on the bench, leaning back against the wall, and he settled silently beside her. They sipped tea—the universal antidote—and listened to the fire, to the clock ticking, to the end of what might have been.

"You'll be all right?" St. Just asked, setting his empty mug aside.

"I will." She spoke around the fingernail she was nibbling. He rose, thinking to get the hell out of the kitchen so the poor woman could cry in peace and perhaps leave him to do the same.

"St. Just." Emmie lurched to her feet and wrapped her arms around his waist. Much more slowly, almost reluctantly, his arms came around her. He wanted to offer words of comfort, but his throat was constricted with misery; so he just held her, closed his eyes, and inhaled the sweetness and fragrance of her for the last time.

"Hold me," Emmie whispered desperately. "I shouldn't ask it, and you've every right…"

"Hush," he murmured, his hand circling on her back. "I'll hold you. It's all right."

She cried silently, much worse than any of her previous, noisier outbursts, and all he could do was hold her. There was no comfort to offer, not to her, not to him. No soothing white lies, no polite fictions to murmur. There was simply sorrow to be borne. When she was quiet in his arms, St. Just walked with her back to the bench and again sat beside her.

"I can't help but think, Emmie"—he held her hand between both of his—"if a path is this difficult, perhaps it's the wrong course."

"Nonsense." Emmie wiped her cheeks with his handkerchief. "This can't be any more difficult than much of what you and every other soldier has faced. It's just…"

He waited, wondering if now, now that her decision was becoming a reality, she would finally talk to him.

"I'll miss her."

Three true words, but they bespoke a lifetime of sacrifice and heartache.

"She'll miss you," St. Just replied, "as will I. I'll send Stevens over tomorrow to see if there's anything you've forgotten, anything you need."

Emmie nodded but closed her eyes for an instant, and he knew she was absorbing his warning: He would not be coming around like an orphaned puppy, making excuses to take tea in her kitchen and further torment them both. He owed her more than that, and he quite frankly could not have borne the knowledge he was lusting after her even after she'd committed herself to Bothwell.

"Farewell, then, Emmie Farnum." He raised his hand and cradled her cheek. "Be happy."

"You," she said, turning her face into his palm, "you be happy, too, St. Just. You deserve to be happy, and… thank you. For everything."

Those were good words to part on, or as good as any. He grabbed his cloak from a peg and prepared to go out the back door to hitch up his gig—and get on with his stupid, miserable life—when a loud banging came from the front hallway.

"Are you expecting callers?" he asked. Darkness

had fallen in the short time they'd tarried, making it unlikely anybody was out socializing.

"Of course not," Emmie said, grabbing his hand and pulling him with her to the front door. Val stood on her porch, bundled up against the cold but breathing heavily.

"Valentine?" St. Just raised a puzzled eyebrow.

"Come in." Emmie drew him into the house by his wrist, but it was still several moments before Val could catch his breath.

"Can't find Winnie," he said between panting breaths. "I thought she was up in her room, avoiding you." He nodded at Emmie. "Once you'd left, I went to look for her. Didn't want her to... be alone."

"Take your time," St. Just said, mentally cursing the child for her dramatics. "She's probably visiting Scout in the stables, or in Emmie's room, where nobody will think to look for her."

"No!" Val said, frustration ricocheting in that one syllable. "I had Steen organize the staff; we searched the entire house, Dev, even the attics. We searched the carriage house, the stables, the cellars, everywhere. There's no sign of Winnie or Scout."

"Oh, God." Emmie's arms wrapped around her middle, and she abruptly looked small, lost, and on the verge of collapse.

"Come into the kitchen," St. Just told his brother. He slipped an arm around Emmie's waist and kept her anchored against his side. "We'll sort this out, Emmie. She can't have gone far on foot, and she had sense enough to take the dog. He'll at least leave a trail and make plenty of noise."

"But it's so cold," Emmie whispered. "Cold and miserable, and she's so stubborn. She won't realize how dangerous it is to take a chill. My aunt *died* after taking a chill."

"Hush," St. Just said, putting both arms around her waist. He stood with his chin on her crown, letting her absorb what warmth and strength and calm he had to offer, even as he continued to learn what he could from Val.

"When was Winnie last seen?"

"At about nine of the clock. You had just gotten back from your ride, and she went into the music room to practice, according to Steen."

"That was this morning," Emmie said, tone aghast. "And all this time, I was trying to pretend she was just being difficult."

"She's being difficult, all right," St. Just muttered.

"There's more," Val said, glancing meaningfully at Emmie, who was still bundled against St. Just's chest.

"Spit it out," St. Just said. "We've no time to waste."

"Stevens says there's a set of tracks heading down that path you broke along the stone wall behind the stables. Not Winnie's, but Scout's. In the lee of the wall, there's still some snow, and that's how he first noticed the pattern. Scout went that way recently. The mud is soft after yesterday's weather, and Stevens knows the dog's sign."

"So Winnie has headed into the woods," St. Just concluded. "She'll be out of any wind, but the temperature will drop sharply now that it's dark."

"Oh, dear God…" Emmie's face, pale to begin with, became ashen. "She ran away to the pond once before, and it's beginning to freeze. I saw it just two days ago on one of my trips over here from Rosecroft. If she thought it was solid enough to play on, she could have fallen in."

St. Just stepped out of Emmie's embrace to retrieve his cloak. "Val, you go back to Rosecroft, because Winnie might have found her way home. Take the gig, and take Emmie with you. If Winnie does turn up, it's Emmie she'll want to see."

"I'm not going to sit in your kitchen sipping tea," Emmie said, chin rising belligerently. "Not while you stumble around in those woods until you're lost, too."

"I know where the pond is, Emmie," St. Just said as calmly as he could. He pulled a lantern off the wall and checked to see it had oil.

"You don't know those woods as well as I do," Emmie shot back. "And there's no moon, and, Devlin, I can't just do nothing. This is my fault…"

"It is not your fault," St. Just replied more sharply than he'd intended. He lit a taper from the stove and used it to light the lantern. "The child has wandered before, Emmie, but as God is my witness, she will not wander again. Please go with Val."

"I will not," Emmie replied, crossing her arms and reminding St. Just strongly of the little girl they were so worried about.

"Very well," he conceded, unwilling to waste more time arguing, particularly when Emmie was right. "Val, get you back to Rosecroft, on foot if you'd rather not spend time hitching up Caesar. Emmie, have you a firearm?"

"I have an old horse pistol. Why?"

"So I can signal if we find her. Val, two shots, spaced well apart. Keep somebody posted outside so they can acknowledge with the same sign. You'll find the key to my gun cabinet in the bottom drawer of my desk."

"Two shots," Val said, "spaced well apart. You've got a good half-dozen horses that can be saddled, and men set to searching. Shall I get that under way?"

St. Just shook his head. "Not yet. With the leaf carpet still thick in the woods, tracking her will be difficult enough without a half-dozen horses tromping all sign underfoot. Let's see what Emmie and I find first, but one shot will mean organize the search party. Acknowledge that with return fire, as well."

"Got it," Val said, leaning in to kiss Emmie. "We'll find her, Em. The entire house is praying for her safety, and she does have the dog."

"Right. Sir Scout. Thank God for that."

"Baron Scout," St. Just corrected her, pulling her toward the back hall with one hand, lantern in the other. "But after this, I'll give the damned dog my bloody earldom if he can keep that child safe. Bundle up. It's colder than hell out, and I suspect it could start snowing at any moment."

"Not snow," Emmie murmured, donning the second of two cloaks, gloves, and a scarf that covered her ears as well as her mouth.

"We'll find her," St. Just said as they struck out across the backyard, "and when we do, we'll take turns hugging her and spanking her."

Emmie said nothing, though they both knew if Winnie drowned, she'd require laying out, not spanking.

"We'll find her," St. Just said again. "You pray, we'll keep walking, and she'll turn up, Em."

St. Just moved cautiously, for the ground was littered with wet rocks now sporting a coat of ice and wet leaves, ready to trip the unwary. Soon enough, they were staring at the patch of blackness that was the pond, once a place of such sunny pleasures, full of memories for both of them, now more ominous than a graveyard.

"She's not here," Emmie said miserably, "unless she's in there." She nodded toward the fathomless darkness of the water.

❧

Winnie's teeth were chattering, her fingers and toes were numb, and she'd long since eaten the stale rolls and butter she'd pilfered for her and Scout. Scout's usual cheerfully bewildered expression had turned to Winnie gently reproachful, and Herodotus looked downright disdainful as he munched his hay in complete indifference to his guests.

"You almost gave us away," Winnie huffed at the mule. It had been a near thing when Rosecroft had come bustling into the little stable. Winnie had barely pulled Scout out the back door before the earl had led Caesar to the spare stall. Caesar had known there was somebody behind the barn, but it was Herodotus who'd craned his runty neck over the door and practically pointed the way Winnie and Scout had gone.

"At least you kept quiet." Winnie patted Scout, who was wonderfully warm though not the most pleasingly fragrant source of heat. "But, Scout, what are we going to *do*? I ran away as long as I've run away since forever, and Miss Emmie still left Rosecroft."

The good baron reserved comment, but his ears pricked up, alerting Winnie to voices coming across the backyard. She put a cautionary hand over Scout's nose—his cold, slimy, wet nose—and strained her ears to hear.

"We'll find her," St. Just growled, but the rest of his words were swallowed by the cold, dark night as they headed into the woods.

"Well, good," Winnie whispered to her dog. "They should be looking for me. Maybe we'll move to Surrey and live with Rose and Lord Amery. He would talk some sense into Miss Emmie, and maybe even Rosecroft."

But for now, it was too cold to think of launching that great adventure. Winnie was hungry, cold, thirsty, and she had to pee something fierce but was loathe to expose enough of herself to the cold air to get that job done.

"Come on, Scout." She crept out of the stables. "They won't think to look right where they've just left, and by morning, the whole parish will know what a nodcock Miss Emmie is. Vicar won't marry her if she insists on staying with us, and that's exactly what she should do if she doesn't want to spend more nights stomping around with Rosecroft in the woods."

Brave words, but they did not seem to impress the fragrant baron. Winnie let them into the house through the back door, stealing into the warm kitchen with a real sense of relief. It had been getting too cold out—much too cold.

"Come on, Scout." Winnie motioned to the dog. "There's a fire in the parlor, too." She rummaged in the kitchen, which had been well provisioned in anticipation of Emmie's return, and buttered more rolls, fresh ones this time. Scout chomped his out of existence in two bites, but Winnie had to wash hers down with cold milk.

Within minutes, Winnie was fast asleep, her faithful hound steaming contentedly before the hearth, her dreams sweet.

❧

"She was here." St. Just knelt in the leaves and bracken and mud, and held the lantern close to the ground. He carefully, step-by-step, examined the entire perimeter of the pond then rose. "She might have fallen in from that rock." He pointed at the place Emmie had knelt to wash her hair months ago. "But other than that, there's no place on the bank that looks like she might have slipped in. The tracks head off in that direction." He gestured toward Emmie's yard. "But I lose the trail in the leaves."

"So what next?" Emmie stared at the water as if she expected answers from it.

"We fire one shot off that horse pistol," St. Just said, taking her hand and tugging her in the direction of the cottage. "If you have some food, I could use something in the way of tucker, but it looks like it will be a long, cold night."

When they reached the cozy warmth of the kitchen, Emmie tried to unfasten the ties of her cloaks, but when he saw her hands were too clumsy with cold, St.

Just pushed her fingers aside and did it himself, leaving the cloaks draped around her shoulders. He then pulled off her gloves and chafed her hands between his.

"How can you possibly be so warm?" Emmie asked, submitting to his tending without protest.

"Sheer size is part of it. I'm like those draft horses, with enough meat and muscle the cold doesn't slow me down as badly, at least for a time. Tell me where that pistol of yours is, and I'll get Val busy with the search team."

"In the parlor," Emmie said, withdrawing her hands. "In the shelves beside the fireplace."

"Have you the equipment to clean it?"

"It should be in the same case."

"I'll fetch it. How about finding us something to eat—anything simple will do."

He took the lantern from where he'd left it lit by the back door and made his way to the parlor. He examined the shelves from the highest, which was at about his eye level, to the middle, where he found the pistol in its wooden case. He hadn't been in Emmie's house enough to know if something was out of place, but in the dimness of the firelit parlor, something didn't *smell* right. Emmie's environs had always smelled clean and usually better than clean.

But tonight, in the parlor, there was a hint of something musty and unpleasant. He turned slowly, and the lantern light caught the reflection of a pair of shining green eyes several inches above the floor in front of the sofa. His first thought was that some rabid animal had found its way into the warmth, or perhaps he was about the meet the famous Gany, but then the beast attached to the eyes lumbered to its feet and came over to lick his hand.

Relief surged through St. Just as he held the lantern higher and spied the sleeping child on the sofa.

"Good boy." He patted the dog soundly but spoke quietly. "Very, very good boy." Scout, status confirmed, ambled back to the spot he'd already warmed by the sofa and resumed his nap.

St. Just turned on silent feet and took the pistol toward the kitchen.

"Emmie." He took from her hand a knife she was using to cut bread into slices, put the knife down on the counter, and led her to the darkened parlor. "Winnie's home safe."

Emmie's hand went to her mouth, and only St. Just's fingers around her wrist stopped her from flying to the couch and hugging the breath out of the prodigal child. Instead, she let St. Just take her back to the kitchen, where she fetched up against his chest.

"Thank God," she whispered. "Oh, thank God, thank God."

"Shall I be about cleaning that pistol?"

"Yes." She stepped back and waved a hand. "Go ahead, and just… go ahead."

While he tended to the gun, Emmie stood in the doorway of the parlor, gazing at Winnie where she snored gently on the couch. Dimly, Emmie heard one shot fired, a pause, and a second shot, then a faint echo of the pattern. St. Just must have walked off a ways with the gun, she reasoned, as his shots were not as loud as they might have been closer to the house.

Such a considerate man, she thought, realizing she

hadn't found a reason to label him barbarian in many weeks. What on earth had she been thinking? He was a good man, not always an easy man, but good.

She would miss him—for the rest of her life.

Emmie tore her eyes from the sight of Winnie curled on the couch and returned to the kitchen.

"If you're still hungry," she said, "I can feed you dinner."

"No need for that," St. Just said, making no move to take off his damp clothing or boots.

"Shall I waken Winnie?" Emmie asked, trying to mask her disappointment.

"Waken her why?" St. Just seemed genuinely bewildered.

"So she can go home with you to Rosecroft," Emmie said as levelly as she could. Why was he making this harder?

"Emmie…" His confusion turned to incredulity. "You cannot ignore that Winnie was willing to risk her life to keep you from going. She needs to be with you."

He'd kept his voice down, and Emmie knew what an effort that was because she herself wanted to shout.

"Surely you realize," Emmie countered, "that child cannot be made to suffer even one more change, St. Just. Rosecroft is her home, you are her guardian, and you have already assured me you will put every resource available to you at Winnie's disposal."

He ran a hand through his hair then pressed the heels of both hands to his eye sockets. "I suppose you'd better put on the teakettle."

"And you'd best take off your wet things," Emmie said, still keeping her voice quiet. "We can hang them to dry while you have your tea." St. Just let Emmie help him out of his overcoat, then unbuttoned his waistcoat, as well, and handed both to her. Emmie moved silently to the parlor and spread the overcoat over the back of a wing chair, and the waistcoat over the arms. Paper crackled in some inner, known-only-to-gentlemen pocket of the waistcoat, so Emmie fished through the material, then drew the documents out and put them on the opposite chair, lest the general damp destroy the writing.

When she returned to the kitchen, it was to find St. Just laying out a pan of cheese toast, completing the task Emmie had started when Winnie had been discovered. They brought the tea tray and cheese toast to the table and took chairs facing each other.

"What is it you would tell me?" Emmie said, wanting to get it over with but not wanting him to ever go.

Nor Winnie. Of course she didn't want Winnie to go.

"You cannot leave that child with me, Emmaline Farnum," he said in a low voice.

"Nonsense." Emmie took a fortifying sip of tea. "Winnie has a better chance of growing up on the straight and narrow and being accepted by decent society in your care than in anybody else's. We've been over this, Devlin."

"You don't know what sort of man you would inflict on that child," he said, holding his cup between his two hands. "You think you know, Emmie, but you don't."

"Tell me. If you think you've some terribly

objectionable quality, St. Just, and that you must unburden yourself of it to me, then I will listen. I doubt I will change my mind though."

"You asked me once to tell you about Waterloo," he said, swallowing and closing his eyes as he got the name of the town past his lips.

"I did," Emmie replied, the first frisson of unease creeping up her spine. He'd seen and done terrible things; that much she knew. Things soldiers were expected to manage in times of war, but something about the dread in his eyes told her this was worse—at least to him.

"You know I've killed many men," he said. "I've killed men so young as to be more properly called boys; but because they wore enemy uniforms, that is excused."

"I don't just excuse it"—Emmie set her tea aside, wanting to take his hands—"I applaud you for it. I am grateful to you for what you did, though I regret the toll it has taken on you."

"I've killed two women, as well," he said, watching her eyes. "Executed them as spies for the French. They were not in uniform, Emmie, and I actually pulled the…"

He stopped and dropped his gaze while Emmie reached across the table and put her hand on his wrist.

"They were the enemy," she said gently. "All the more heinous because they were women, and much more difficult for you to execute. It was *war*, Devlin, and they knew the costs."

He nodded again but carefully withdrew his hand from her grip.

"I will tell you about Waterloo," he said in a soft,

resigned voice. "You have a right—a need—to know what Winnie will face if you leave her with me."

Emmie waited, listening to the fire blaze in the hearth.

"Bonaparte's army wasn't the most disciplined; they hadn't the best equipment nor the best horses. They were not the most professional, but by God, they were brave. When Bonaparte escaped from Elba, he moved them the length of France and on toward Brussels, when all had hoped he would stop at the border. Wellington had time to range his lines along a ridge outside Waterloo, and there he waited for the emperor to advance farther across the border."

His voice had become distant, his gaze focused inward, but in his eyes, Emmie saw looming horror.

"You've noticed I am… unnerved by thunder." His gaze flickered up to hers.

"I have, though it seems to be getting better."

"It isn't just thunder, Emmie. It's rain, thunder, the buzzing of flies, the smell of mud, the sound of a Spanish guitar, the sound of horses galloping en masse… For the first few months after Val dragged me home, I wanted only silence or the sound of his playing. He sensed I needed almost every other sound drowned out… But I digress."

He took a slow, deep breath and let it out before continuing.

"It rained the night before battle. Not just a little summer shower, but ugly, cold torrents that made deploying along that ridge a nightmare. I will never forget the smells if I live to be one hundred. The mud, the wet uniforms and soggy tack, the fear… The next morning, the heat came on and made the day even more unbearable, and the artillery, of course, went to work. But then, just when we thought we'd go mad from the damned cannon, the guns fell silent, and that was much worse. We waited, expecting the French to charge any moment, because our reinforcements drew closer as the day wore on."

Emmie watched as his memories fought to overwhelm him and recalled the scene with Winnie's soldiers: Why don't the bloody French just get on with it? *Oh, God…*

"Eventually, they came on, and the ground was still a boggy, horse-laming mess, but the French had to charge up that hill, over and over again, and each time they tried, there were more bodies, more maimed and dying horses running loose, struggling to get up, more comrades fallen who could not move to safety."

He fell silent for a long moment, though Emmie feared all that narrative was just setting the stage. She gripped his hand again, and this time he allowed it.

"When the fighting was over, there were fifty thousand dead and wounded soldiers, and almost half that again in dead or mortally wounded horses. I led a detail of men onto the battlefield to recover what gear and tack we could. The scavengers were already at work, rifling the pockets of men not even dead. The medics went through ahead of us, but my unit was to collect what arms and tack and ammunition was… salvage… salvageable."

"Some of my party were wounded, but they knew to admit to serious injuries was to be cashiered out, so we slipped and struggled and cursed our way from one fallen horse to another, but Emmie…" He gazed past her with eyes that saw into hell. "They weren't all dead. Some of them had been wounded two days prior, some just a few hours before, and they weren't…"

Emmie squeezed his hand and held on tight, and though she wished he wouldn't, she willed him the strength to resume his story.

"Every man in that detail gave me his weapons and ammunition, and when we found an animal still suffering, I shot it." He swallowed, eyes fixed on his terrible memory. "This was a violation of orders, but not one man protested the use of ammunition for such a purpose. When we ran out of shot, we used our knives until I lost count…"

He was gripping her hand with punishing strength, but Emmie held her silence. He needed to tell this tale, or he'd be haunted by it for the rest of his life. That much she knew from carrying her own secrets and burdens for too long. She could do this much for him and be privileged to have his confidences, no matter how bleak and hellish.

"There was a mare," he said, his voice dropping to an ominously dispassionate softness. "An elegant little black mare who'd made it as far as a copse of trees. Horses will do that—ask any seasoned officer, and he'll tell you of a horse that suffered a mortal injury but carried the rider to safety before succumbing. Her side had sustained damage from a bayonet; there was blood… everywhere, but still she struggled to get up. She was badly weakened, but she kept up that pathetic tossing of the head, and flailing, all without making a sound. Her rider was nowhere about, and I hoped for her sake he'd survived. She knew, Emmie…"

He stopped speaking again, and Emmie saw his cheeks were wet though there was no hint of tears in his voice.

"She knew I was there to end her suffering and stopped struggling long enough so I could cut her throat and wait with her until she was dead. I said the usual, stupid, useless prayer, and moved on with my unit. We hadn't gone far, though, when a party of scavengers worked their way back to those trees. I don't know why I even paid attention, but they were so jolly, thanking the emperor for filling so many stew pots, and so on… I should not have looked, should not have let myself look, but when I did… They were butchering the little mare where she fell. She was dead… I knew she was dead… But I thought, what if I hadn't gotten there a few minutes earlier… and I lost… I disgraced my command."

Emmie gripped both his hands in hers and bowed her head. Tears began to course down her own cheeks.

"I moved too quickly for my men to stop me," St. Just went on, bitterness creeping into his tone. "I had several knives on me, as the men had offered me theirs when the guns were useless, and I hurled them, one, two, three, at the fat, jolly man making such a party over that mare's corpse. I wish I'd had better aim."

"You didn't hit him?" Emmie asked, relieved for him but furious anyway.

"He slipped," St. Just said simply. "He slipped at the last moment on the bloody, *bloody* mud. The mare's spilled blood saved him, quite literally."

"I am more troubled by his survival than your lapse

of protocol," Emmie said fiercely. Did he think she would find him unfit to raise Winnie over *this*?

"The man came up yelling, threatening to have me court-martialed for trying to feed his family; and had an old gunnery sergeant not threatened to relieve me of command, I would have been facing murder charges."

"But you listened to your sergeant," Emmie said, noting St. Just's knuckles were still white.

"I did, and to his punishing right cross. I was all but dragged off the field, though all of the men present refused to discuss the incident with my commander."

"So what became of you?" Emmie asked, rubbing her thumb over the back of his hand.

"The general on whose desk this mess landed knew me from Spain and gave me two choices: I could sell my commission and go home a hero, or I could try to fight the charges, but there were witnesses to condemn me for throwing not just one but three knives at civilians… to protect what? The honor of a dead horse? That would embarrass not just my command but also my family and even the memory of my brother. I sold out and started drinking, but I did something for myself first."

"What did you do, Devlin?" Emmie was using both thumbs on his hands, trying to communicate her acceptance and sympathy and approval for *whatever* he'd done.

"I buried the horse," he said, dipping his chin so Emmie could not see his face. "I just had to, and when the general found that out, he told me I'd be a fool not to go home, as my career was over whether or not there was a court-martial, but Emmie…"

"I'm here," she said around the lump in her throat.

"I sometimes think burying that mare was the only decent thing I did in my entire military career. That all of it was just so much brutality and mayhem and…"

Emmie moved around the table in one swift lunge and wrapped her arms around his shoulders. She pressed his head to her chest and held on tight until she felt his arms steal around her waist, embracing her with the same desperation. His grip was that of a drowning man—a dying man—and she would not let him go.

She held him until her back ached and her balance began to weave, then held him some more. She held him as heat and tears and awful fits of tension seized him then eased, only to seize him again. He shuddered and clung and held on, until finally, he pulled her down into his lap and held her yet more.

Emmie's heart broke for him, for the hurt and self-doubt and sheer, miserable loneliness his service to the crown had cost him. It had cost him while he served, and it cost him every day since.

"You've paid enough," she said, her voice husky with her own tears. "Devlin St. Just, you were right to throw those knives and you were right to bury that mare and you were right to come home. You were right and you are not crazy and damn them all. Just damn them to bloody hell."

"Emmie, no," he said when she'd finished her rant. "I was not right. I was not even rational, I was needlessly, murderously violent over nothing. I am barely sane, a killer, and when the damned rain starts, all I can think to do is drink. You cannot forgive me such things; you cannot entrust Bronwyn to such as a one as I. You shouldn't trust me with your mule, for God's sake."

"Hush." Emmie put a hand over his mouth. "Just hush. You had a bad moment; you've had others. You are human, St. Just. The things you've endured have threatened that humanity, but yet you do care for Winnie, you are kind to her, you dote on your horses and are much loved by your family. Do not bury yourself with that poor horse. Do not."

"Emmie," he said, his tone tired but implacable. "I've killed more men than I can count. I was respected for that, for my brutality in hand-to-hand fighting. I was determined to do what it took to prevail in every battle, and even if we retreated or outright got trounced, I took out as many of the enemy as I could—permanently."

"And did you enjoy killing others?" Emmie asked, pulling back to study his eyes.

"Of course not."

"Not even a little?" she pressed. "Not the respect it gained you, not the sense of victory?"

"No," he said harshly. "The worse I became, the more my men wanted to stay near me in the fighting, and then I felt I had to fight to protect them, too."

"Devlin." Emmie waited until he met her eyes. "I thought when I met you and listened to you snapping out orders and pronouncements even while you appropriated the manners of a gentleman, that I was dealing with a bone fide barbarian."

"I am…" he began, nodding, but Emmie cut him off.

"You are not a barbarian," she said firmly. "I know you are not because I've known the tenderness you're capable of."

"Soldiers do their share of…"

"Would you hush!" Emmie felt tears rising again. "You are not a barbarian. I know this because you have loved me, not swived me, you damned man. And the part of you that killed and maimed and threw knives at civilians, is the part of you that wants desperately to *live*. Saints do not survive this world," Emmie said, her tone gentling. "Saints sit on clouds and play harps, but humans, good, kind, decent humans can't help but seek to live; they fight to live, St. Just. They don't just throw a punch or two, maybe fire a few rounds at the enemy and take their chances. What you've done to survive tells me you are not a barbarian at all but very, very human. Nothing more, and by God, Devlin St. Just, nothing less."

She dropped her forehead to his, and having said her piece, fell silent.

She rose from his lap some moments later and gathered up their teacups. He watched as she blew out the lantern then paused by the back door.

"It's snowing," she said quietly, "really snowing."

"I'd better get moving," he said, rising to his feet slowly, as if he were ninety-three years old. "But I thank you for listening. Now you will see why Winnie must stay with you."

"I see no such thing," Emmie said. "I see you've talked yourself into believing monstrous untruths of yourself. You called it murder or killing. I call it protecting, Devlin. You scoff at the patriotic call to arms, but it was a call to protect those like Winnie who could not protect themselves. She will be safe and protected and cherished in your care."

"Emmie." He closed his eyes, suffering etched on his features. "I am a bastard, a killer. I cannot vouch for my composure the next time it rains. I couldn't even sp-p-p—" He stopped abruptly, looking as if some horrible blasphemy had come hooting out of his mouth without his volition. "I could not even speak clearly," he went on with great care, "until I was an adult. I am not elegant, I have no refinements, I prefer animals to people for the most part, and I will probably never be able to enjoy a summer rain. You cannot leave that child with me."

"I am tired of arguing," Emmie said, "but I am loathe to let you out in this storm. Will you stay with me?"

"No." He shook his head swiftly. "I cannot *stay* with you. I cannot suffer again to know such pleasure, Emmie, only to have you cast it back in my face come morning. I want to, Jesus *God*, do I want to, but I cannot. Call it the part of me that wants to survive, call it pure meanness, or call it an unwillingness to have you accept another's proposal while the scent of me yet lingers on you… I'm sorry." He stopped, looking bleakly around the room. "That was vulgar and unkind, not worthy of either of us."

"All right," Emmie said, seeing only that he hurt as badly as she did. "If you cannot make love to me, all right, and I suppose I have to agree with you. It would be ill advised." It would hurt like hell, in fact, but if she was going to hurt like hell anyway… She saw by his face, however, he was already hurting worse than that.

"The couch is spoken for," Emmie said more quietly, "and the weather is too bad for you to take the gig back tonight."

"I'll ride your mule bareback," St. Just growled, starting for the parlor where his wet outer clothing had been spread to dry.

"He isn't broken to ride," Emmie said with the same intensity. "I'll behave, St. Just. I'll sleep with you as you've slept with me previously, without transgressing or putting the *scent* of you on me, but please, just don't…" She stopped and took a breath. "I can stay down in the parlor with Winnie. Devlin. Just please, please, don't go out there tonight all alone."

St. Just turned his back to her and tried to locate his reason. It wasn't that far to the manor, the snow wasn't that deep, he wasn't that tired… Except he was, utterly, absolutely weary. He'd told no one, not even Val, the story of how he'd left the military. His brothers were too perceptive to ask, and his father had probably heard the tale through the ducal gossip vine, which spread information more quickly than galloping horses. No doubt His Grace was ashamed of him and willing to let the matter drop.

But Emmie had not been ashamed of him, and that… compassion meant the world to him. It meant hope and peace and kindness and a world worth living in. She had been *proud of him*, and *she had understood*.

"I will stay," he said, "but don't expect me to hold you the night through, Emmie. I am not that strong, particularly not… I am just not."

"Very well." Her voice, her eyes, everything about her was steady. "Then I will hold you."

Sixteen

When they moved up to her room, St. Just brushed out Emmie's hair for her and braided it in a single plait. She helped him finish undressing and let him assist her out of her clothes. As he built up the fire, she used the wash water then climbed on the bed to watch as he made his ablutions. When he lay on his back beside her—not touching her if it killed him—Emmie reached for his hand under the covers. He closed his fingers around hers and sighed.

It was going to be a long damned night in any event.

"Winnie has a trust, you know," he said, apropos of nothing.

"A trust? You've created this for her already?"

"I did not," St. Just said, taking some comfort in the prosaic topic. "The old earl set it up as part of his estate—she was his only grandchild, after all, but as Helmsley was the trustee, more effort was spent trying to plunder the estate assets than manage them."

"Is the trust bankrupted?"

"It is not," St. Just said, not even aware his thumb was brushing over the inside of Emmie's wrist.

"You have some funds for her," Emmie said, "that is good to know."

"Emmie, I applaud your stubbornness, and I know life has not allowed you to be otherwise, but you also need to know I am not Winnie's guardian."

"I saw that order," Emmie countered, turning on her side to regard him by firelight. "It named you as guardian, and I understand now why you had it drafted."

"Drafted," St. Just agreed, "but not signed. When I was in York yesterday, I had a different order signed, one naming you as her guardian."

"You are one to talk about stubbornness." Emmie closed her eyes and closed her fingers more tightly around his.

"Well, there's more," he said, turning to his side, as well, "and you might want to march me naked right outside and off to Rosecroft when you hear it."

"Interesting picture. What have you done?"

"I visited Bothwell this morning," he told her, holding her gaze and speaking very deliberately. "I did not mention the trust, which I regard as your exclusive province, but I did inform him of the guardianship."

"And why did you take it upon yourself to have this discussion with our vicar?"

Your vicar, St. Just mentally corrected her.

"Because it was his affidavit that allowed me to petition for the order on your behalf," St. Just said. He reached out with his free hand and drew a single finger along the firm line of Emmie's jaw. How he loved the determination in that jaw and the texture of her skin and the way her eyes held his even when difficult things were to be faced.

"How would Hadrian have anything to do with Winnie?" Emmie asked in puzzlement.

"He visited your aunt while she was sick," St. Just reminded her. "I expect he heard her confessions such as they were, and he certainly heard her dying wishes as regards the child. She wanted Winnie with you. Bothwell has no objection, by the way."

"I know what she wanted, and I respect she thought that would be best for all concerned."

"We are not going to argue this again, are we?"

"We are not." Emmie reached across the space between them and set her hand on St. Just's nape. "We've said what we need to say and done what we each thought was best for all, and your orders can be undone if need be. But it will all wait until morning. Come here, Devlin, and let me hold you."

He shifted on the mattress and tucked his face against her shoulder, not even thinking of protesting. He loved her, and he had chosen to stay with her tonight, a dishonorable, painful, and just plain stupid decision, but he was damned if he'd regret it yet. He let a hand drift across the soft warmth of her stomach and hiked a knee across her thighs.

"Tell me if I'm too heavy," he murmured, closing his eyes.

"You're not," she assured him, turning her face to kiss his temple. "You're warm and you smell good and you feel just right."

He nodded, echoing the sentiment in silence before falling into a dreamless and profoundly restful sleep. Emmie felt his body ease and his mind let go of the tumult of the day, while she tried to hold sleep at bay. She could not afford to consider at this point that St. Just might have the right of it. She could not afford to admit how good it had felt to come upstairs with him tonight, knowing Winnie slumbered on in safety below them. She could not afford to reflect on how much patience they had with each other when they argued now, how carefully they handled their differences.

So she succumbed to sleep in the end, and her dreams were not particularly sweet.

When she awoke in the morning, he was already stirring, propped on his elbow and regarding her with a severe expression.

"You're awake." She reached over and brushed his hair back from his forehead and made no protest when he captured her fingers and kissed them. There would be no more cuddling, but no artificial, silently recriminating propriety either.

"I am feasting on your morning beauty," he replied, "but the natives are restless below, and a certain young lady on your couch needs a very stern talking to."

"And a certain gentleman who did not get much dinner needs to break his fast," Emmie agreed, "and a certain baron needs to heed nature's call."

"He's already outside," St. Just said, his smile not reaching his eyes. "I looked out the window, and nature's call is attended to."

"Fortunate. I do not want to leave this bed, Devlin."

"Nor I." The smile did reach his eyes, but it was so, so sad.

"Just hold me," she said, closing her eyes lest he see the desperate plea in them. He settled his naked weight over her one last time, his body caging hers in warmth and tenderness as his cheek rested against hers.

"Just for a bit," he agreed softly, but she clung tightly, and she couldn't help wishing and wishing... She eased her hold, and he shifted off her and out of the bed. He was a soldier, after all, a man who had done the impossible and suffered the unbearable on so many other occasions.

He tossed her a dressing gown. "How do we do this?"

"This?" Emmie sat on the bed and flipped her braid outside the wrapper.

"There is a child down there." St. Just stepped behind the privacy screen, but in the way of men, did not need to stop talking. "One who misses nothing and is not easily swayed when she gets an idea in her head. Bothwell would accept her at Landover."

"You have mentioned this," Emmie said, finding her hairbrush and undoing her braid.

"And I am in the presence of another female not easily swayed," he said while appropriating her tooth-brush and powder.

"How about if I go down first and start on break-fast," Emmie suggested, "and you come down, having spent the night in a guest room?"

"I suppose that will serve," he agreed, drawing on his clothes. "Emmie." He leveled a look at her when she was still peeking at him several minutes later. "Get dressed, please."

She rose and handed him the hairbrush then went to her wardrobe and found a comfortable old day dress of sturdy blue velvet. The fabric had faded to a soft shade, one exactly matching the gray blue of her eyes. The garment also fit loosely enough that with some twisting and maneuvering, she could do up the hooks herself.

As she would be for the rest of her blighted, stupid life.

❧

"Let me." St. Just brushed Emmie's hands aside and did up the most difficult hooks in the center of her back. "You must promise me to sit on your backside and actually eat some of what you bake, Emmie Farnum. You are too skinny."

"As the colder weather starts, I usually drop weight. The baking picks up when people are indoors more."

He stepped back, having heroically resisted the urge to kiss her nape. There was nothing sexual in the impulse at all, just a longing to touch his lips to that spot on her body and taste her sweetness and inhale her fragrance as one would inhale the aroma of a gorgeous bouquet of roses.

"I'll lace your boots," he heard himself say. He'd never laced a lady's footwear before in his life, but he wanted any excuse to touch her. She allowed it, to his relief.

"Pretty feet." St. Just frowned as he slipped thick socks over her toes. He'd neglected to kiss these feet, a permanent oversight he tossed on the growing pile of his regrets. He'd neglected Emmie's back rub last night when they'd succumbed to the need to hold each other; he'd never sung a duet with her; he'd never brought her flowers; he'd never told her…

He straightened but remained on his knees before

her. She stayed sitting, meeting his gaze as if she'd been reading his thoughts.

"I would have gone mad by the third thunderstorm, were it not for you," he said. "You and Win. At home in Surrey, I'd learned how to manage, but up here, with everything unfamiliar—"

"You would have learned to manage here, too," Emmie interrupted him, her hand settling on the back of his neck. "You would have been fine; you will be fine. I am as stubborn on this point as any other, you see, and it is rude to argue with a lady, particularly when she is right."

He nodded, swallowed, and made another try.

"I was dying, Emmie. I was managing, as you say, but at a great cost. Every time I got through a thunderstorm, a setback, a bad day, I grew closer to the time when I no longer wanted to make the effort, so…" He leaned in and kissed her mouth with infinite tenderness. "Thank you. I will always be in your debt."

She shook her head but didn't let go of his neck. "Thank you," she said, "I was not managing very well either, and you've been so kind and patient…"

He rose and drew her to her feet.

"I'm not feeling very kind or patient now, Em." He stepped back. "Don't keep Bothwell waiting for months. The man's brother is dying, and Winnie and I can't take any more lingering farewells. All right." He ran a hand through his hair. "Charge?" He made it a polite question, lifting his eyebrow with gallows humor before opening the door and bowing her through. Emmie swept past him, head held high, but he waited at the top of the steps until he heard voices in the kitchen.

He sat down on the top step for a few minutes, gathering his courage and savoring memories now as painful as they were sweet. He gave the room a last visual inventory, as he would look over a campsite left at the start of a campaign, then went down the stairs into the kitchen.

"Good morning, Miss Emmie." He saw Winnie sitting at the table. "Miss Farnum."

Winnie met his gaze. "I'm in trouble, aren't I?"

"More trouble than you can possibly imagine, young lady, but good morning anyway. Seems we've had some snow. Is there tea, Emmie?"

"On the hob," Emmie said, moving around as if they shared this kitchen in the ordinary course. "And I'm heating up some scones and butter, but I'll be happy to make an omelet, as well."

"Both sound good," he replied, pouring himself a mug of tea. "So, Winnie Farnum, have you anything to say for yourself?"

"I'm sorry?"

"For what?" St. Just asked as he fixed his tea.

"For making everybody worry," Winnie said, staring at her empty mug, "and for keeping Scout out so long when it was cold."

"That's a good start." St. Just slid onto to the bench beside the child. "You've finished your tea, I see. Would you like some more?" Winnie nodded, not objecting to his proximity but rather relaxing against him with a little sigh. "Take mine." He kept his seat and slid the mug over to her. Winnie peeked up at him and took a sip. "Helps with just about everything, a good cup of tea does." He fell silent and Winnie held her peace beside him. "The trouble is," St. Just said, lips pursed in thought, "you frightened everybody who cares about you, Win. Val came pounding over here in the cold and dark, Emmie and I were poking around that pond, hoping you hadn't fallen in and drowned. We cried."

"You cried, too?" Winnie said, her misery plain on her face.

"Like my heart would never mend," St. Just assured her. He let her stew with that thought, took a sip of the tea, and passed it back to her. "We thought you were dead, Win," he went on. "Cold and wet and frozen at the bottom of that pond. I will never see it as such a pretty place again. I will see the water, black and icy, and our dear Emmie, trying not to cry while she near freezes to death herself. Not well done of you, my girl."

Emmie stood at the sink, her back to them and suspiciously rigid.

"I wanted to run away," Winnie finally said, "so Emmie will know how I'll feel when she runs away to Cumbria." She wiggled down the bench and pelted off into the parlor, the door swinging several times back and forth in the ensuing silence.

"Oh, Devlin." Emmie turned, her arms wrapped around her middle, but St. Just did not cross the kitchen to comfort her. He instead met her gaze for a long moment.

"And you know what, Em?" he said, turning his tea mug by the handle. "Winnie and I are going to feel like that—bewildered and hurting and scared—for much more than a few hours or a few days. She'll carry some of that feeling with her for the rest of her life. She'll do the same stupid things you did because your papa ran off, and the same stupid things I did because my mother passed me off to Their Graces. Think about that while I fill up your wood boxes."

His tone had been perfectly, utterly civil, musing even, but Emmie felt like Winnie had slapped her soundly and St. Just had followed up with a swift kick to the ribs.

Like my heart would never mend, St. Just had said. Emmie watched through her back window, listening to the steady, solid *wump!* of the splitting ax cleaving seasoned logs, underscored by Winnie's soft weeping from the parlor. She went to the child and put her arms around her.

"I'm sorry, Win," Emmie said, meaning it like she'd never meant it before. "I'm sorry I'm running away." Winnie nodded, wrapped her arms around Emmie's neck, and cried harder.

Hadrian Bothwell loved a pretty snowfall. Here there was real beauty, and lots of it. He'd cadged a useful idea for the sermon from one of his confreres the previous week; in fact, he'd come home with a whole recipe box of homilies and traded off some his more popular efforts in exchange.

Which meant yesterday had been available for much-needed rest and even more-needed thought. He was to resolve his situation with Emmie Farnum today, and Rosecroft's visit yesterday morning had plagued him unmercifully. He'd gone to bed falling back on that old chestnut of faith, that the way would be made clear if he just showed patience and attentiveness.

Here it was, though, Sunday morning, bright and

early, and the way was no more clear than it had been a day ago.

So he took his rested self out on a morning constitutional, his most trusted means of organizing a sermon for presentation and one of his favorite pastimes. He got an early start because he had been such a sloth the day before, but also because he loved a fresh snowfall, and this one was perfect. There was probably six inches of soft, powdery snow blanketing the entire landscape. The sky was a brilliant blue, the rising sun casting everything in sharp, bright relief, and no one was about yet. It was a perfect morning for a walk in the woods. God was in His heaven, and all was right with the world.

❧

"Eat something, Winnie," Emmie pleaded. "You hardly had anything yesterday, and you'll need energy if you're to be out in this cold."

"Scout kept me warm yesterday. I'm just not very hungry."

Emmie's gaze met St. Just's, but he gave a slight shake of his head and reached for Winnie's plate of eggs. The child wasn't being manipulative, she was simply honestly upset.

"I'll eat these, then," St. Just said, "as they are very good, and even the Duke of Scout does not deserve something quite this tasty."

Winnie frowned. "The Duke of Scout?"

"Every hour you were gone," St. Just said between bites, "every hour he stayed with you and protected you and kept you warm, his title was elevated. He ought to be some kind of deity, but one doesn't want to disrespect our regent."

Winnie smiled faintly at this nonsense. "I could call him Your Grace, just like Rose's grandpapa."

"Like Rose's grandpapa, indeed." St. Just arched an eyebrow. "But if you're not going to eat breakfast, Win, you need to finish getting dressed and bundle up. It looks warmer outside than it is, with all that bright sunshine."

Emmie came over and cleared Winnie's tea mug.

"You have some old clothes up in your bedroom, Winnie. Wear at least two sets of leggings and a sweater, if you can find one." Winnie disappeared up the steps, Scout trotting along at her heels, oblivious to his newly acquired consequence.

"I'd better bundle up, as well." St. Just rose and brought his empty plates to the sink. "Are my clothes still in the parlor?"

"I'll get them," Emmie said. "Have another cup of tea."

He did, for no reason other than to comply with her order. She brought his waistcoat and cloak to him, both warm and stiff from being near the fire for so long.

"I also found these in your pocket," Emmie said, passing him some folded papers. "I took them out so the damp wouldn't get to them. They seem all right." St. Just paused as he was buttoning up his waistcoat and recognized three of his mother's letters.

"Thank you," he said, taking the letters. "Those are of sentimental importance to me, and I would have missed them." He should make copies of the entire lot for safekeeping—something to occupy him while he was missing Emmie.

"I'll see what's keeping Winnie," Emmie said as she watched him closing the fastenings of his heavy cape.

He frowned at her retreating back and looked at the letters where they sat on her wooden table. Something was stirring in the back of his mind, just as it used to stir when he was about to figure out how to dodge murderously stupid orders from a pompous general. The best solutions often came to him that way, emerging whole from below his awareness rather than approaching by steady steps of reason and calculation.

His gaze switched to the letters, which sat right in the shaft of a bright winter sunbeam. The letters...

"Oh, ye gods..." he murmured, but not ye gods, ye *mothers*. His mother, Kathleen, and his mother, Her Grace, had given him one last round of very heavy artillery indeed, and he was going to fire it broadside at Emmie's heart, even as she thought he was making his final retreat. He resisted the urge to trot up the stairs to see what was keeping the ladies and sat down to read the letters instead.

Both ladies were fairly composed when they gained the kitchen, but Emmie looked unnerved to see both St. Just and Winnie dressed to leave.

"Where's His Highness, Win?" St. Just asked.

"Scout!" Winnie hailed the dog from the far reaches of the house. "He's here," she said unnecessarily when Scout was panting at her side.

"So he is. Why don't you let him out to romp for a minute while I go find something to use for a bridle on Caesar? I'll meet you in the stables."

"C'mon, Scout." Winnie snapped her fingers and headed for the door.

"Let her go," St. Just murmured in a low voice. "This is not the last time you'll see her, and she's trying to stay composed as it is." Emmie glanced at him sharply, for he'd allowed something almost fierce in his tone, but she didn't argue. "No need to come to the stables, Em," he said, moving toward the back door. "I'll ride us over on Caesar and send Stevens for the gig when the roads are more passable. Thank you." He paused and smiled down at her, "for everything."

She accepted his hug but did not move to kiss him.

"Those letters you found?" he said as he stepped back. "I don't want to risk them falling in the snow, as they are precious. I'd like to leave them here for the present."

"Of course." Emmie murmured, her eyes huge and conveying some nameless desperation. The barking of the dog and happy shrieks of his owner only underscored the heartache of the moment.

"But I have a favor to ask, Emmie Farnum."

"Anything. Anything at all."

"Read those letters. There are only three, and you can send them back with Stevens later, but read them before your vicar comes a-courting, please?"

She blinked, and he could tell he'd surprised her. She'd no doubt been expecting him to ask that she write to Winnie, or possibly to him, that she not give away his apple tart recipe, but not… this.

"I promise," she said, walking to the back door with him.

"Don't come out here," he warned as he gained the

porch. "It's damned cold, and you were out in nasty weather yester—"

But she was plastered against him anyway, hugging him as if her heart would break, as if it had broken and would never, ever mend.

"Good-bye, Emmie," St. Just said, giving her one last answering squeeze then stepping back. "Read the letters. You promised."

She nodded and wiped a tear from her cheek.

"Inside with you now," he said gently. "Winnie will see you crying and then I'll start crying and Scout will howl and Winnie will know we're daft." She smiled at him brokenly, whirled, and fled back to the warmth of the house.

Scout came bounding up the porch steps, obviously pleased with the snow, while Winnie trudged along more slowly.

"Emmie was crying again, wasn't she?" Winnie said in a tired old voice.

"She was, a little." They crossed the yard in silence, Scout snuffling in the snow after some scent or other.

"Rosecroft?" Winnie called over her shoulder as she fed a carrot to Herodotus in his back stall.

"Yes?" He sorted through the gear in Emmie's stable and found a serviceable old bridle as well as some grooming equipment.

"Yesterday, did you cry so hard your stomach hurt?" Winnie asked as she broke off part of the carrot for the mule then took a bite for herself.

"I did," he said, watching her pet the mule. "I cried like a motherless child."

"It's stupid," Winnie said, giving the mule one last

pat on his shoulder, "getting that upset when it doesn't change anything. I'm not doing it again."

"Me neither, until next time."

"What does that mean?" Winnie frowned and fed the last bite of carrot to Caesar where he stood in the cross ties.

"It means, if something were to happen to you today, Winnie Farnum, I would probably cry that hard again, or at least hurt that much. If something happened to His Highness, you would be just as upset. You can't tell your heart what to do or how to feel. If you love somebody, then you can hurt for them."

"So you love Miss Emmie?"

"I most assuredly do, and I love you, too."

Winnie was silent for a long moment, stroking Caesar's muscular shoulder. "Are we going to visit Rose in the spring?"

"We well might. Your new cousin is due to be born then, and Rose will cut me completely if I do not introduce the two of you posthaste."

"Do you think Scout would like to live in Surrey?"

"He might. Why?" St. Just straightened and reached for the bridle.

"Rose might want a dog. He'd be happier with her."

❧

There was something chilling in the way Winnie casually considered giving away her beloved pet, and Hadrian Bothwell's own stomach was getting a little unsettled at what he'd overheard. After ambling through the woods, he thought he'd stop by and pay his respects to Emmie's mule, a creature he considered a wise, thoughtful sort of animal, one who might bring a little wisdom to weighty matters on a vicar's mind.

But as he slipped from the woods, Bothwell had seen Emmie and Rosecroft come out onto her back porch. She was barely dressed, but he was obviously ready to travel.

What was the man doing in Emmie's kitchen at this indecent hour? Bothwell stored that question away, determined to believe there was an innocent explanation. The earl could not have spent the night under the same roof as Emmie, not when there were only a few inches of snow on the ground and he lived the very next property over. Still, the uneasy feeling escalated to an ache when Bothwell noticed there was not one human track marring Emmie's entire yard beyond her wood box. Unless the earl had flown onto the roof and come down the chimney, he'd arrived yesterday evening before the snow started.

But then, God help him, Hadrian had seen Emmie's face as she'd hugged St. Just good-bye. It was only that—a hug, no torrid kiss or prolonged embrace, but her face…

St. Just had spent the night, that much was obvious, but he wouldn't be spending any more; that was the first thing Bothwell had concluded from Emmie's expression. The next thing anybody with eyes could have seen was that Emmie loved the man, and in the protective posture of his body around hers, St. Just cared for her, as well.

This was not good news, reminding Bothwell strongly he'd prayed for guidance, and as usual, when he allowed himself specific requests of The Almighty, the answer was not necessarily what he'd expected.

So he'd retreated behind the stables, only to hear Winnie's piping soprano coming across the yard, talking about everybody crying so hard their stomachs hurt, and St. Just's calm answers, his matter-of-fact declarations that he loved Emmie and Winnie, just like that.

There was a soul-deep conviction in the man's words. A solid, *knowing* quality when he spoke of loving, as if he knew his love was permanent, a part of him for all time. Bothwell was honest enough to admit he hadn't loved his own wife that way, God help him, though he might be able to say he loved his brother in such a fashion.

And as he slipped away between the trees, he kept hearing St. Just's self-deprecating comparison: "I cried like a motherless child."

Well. A motherless child, indeed.

That was guidance, if ever guidance there was. If there'd been doubt in his mind before about the wisdom of keeping the Farnum ladies under the same roof, there was only certainty now.

❧

St. Just vaulted onto Caesar's furry back and extended a hand down to Winnie. She grabbed onto his wrist and was soon perched behind the horse's withers, her gloved hands grabbing fistfuls of mane. They rode home through the sharp, sunny daybreak in silence, walking Caesar right into the stable yard before Stevens even knew they'd returned.

"Morning, your lordship." Stevens handed Winnie down. "Morning, Miss-Winnie-Where-Did-You-Go?"

"To Miss Emmie's. And Scout came with me, and he's back, too. He's a duke now."

"Your Grace." Stevens bowed, clearly pleased to see the prodigals returned. "It just wasn't the same without himself there stirring around in the carriage house all night."

"I'm sure Scout missed you, too," St. Just said, deadpan. "If you'll see to Caesar, I'd appreciate it, and if you could find some time this afternoon to fetch the gig home from Miss Farnum's, as well as some correspondence I left there, that would be appreciated, too."

"Aye." Stevens tousled Winnie's hair, and led Caesar away.

"He didn't tell me it's the Sabbath," St. Just murmured, wondering if he was in need of more than a shave. "Come along, Winnie, and we'll probably find a second breakfast, if you're more interested in your victuals now."

Winnie grabbed his hand. "Only a little."

"We must encourage you to drink chocolate in the morning, I suppose." St. Just gave up trying to match his steps to hers and swung her up to his hip. "You certainly don't weigh very much, Bronwyn Farnum."

"But I'm good at climbing trees," Winnie said on a forlorn smile as they approached the back terraces.

"That you are, but I am able to divine your thoughts," he went on as he stomped his boots at the back door. "I know what you're thinking."

"What am I thinking?" Winnie closed her eyes and squinched up her face.

"That we're going inside this house, but Emmie isn't here, and that makes you feel sad."

Winnie nodded, and in an instant, all her courage seemed to desert her. She turned her cold face against St. Just's neck and kept it there while he walked into the back hallway.

"What ho!" Val emerged from the kitchen. "It's the snow monster from Rosecroft village, with two heads and bright red ears on both of them." He stepped closer and put down his mug of tea. "What's wrong, princess? Not feeling so cheerful?"

Winnie shook her head without looking at him, keeping her nose against St. Just's neck.

"We're sad," St. Just said, "because Emmie isn't here."

"Ah." Val nodded, his eyes conveying a world of understanding. "Win, you have to let Uncle Val teach you some of his sad-day songs." He stepped closer, maybe intending to take the child from his brother's arms, but as he reached out to encircle Winnie, his arms, whether by design or inadvertence, embraced his brother, as well.

"We're all sad," Val murmured, hugging them both, "but we're happy, too."

"Why are we happy?" Winnie was sufficiently affronted at that pronouncement that she glared at him.

"Because." He did lift Winnie away from St. Just and maneuvered her onto his own back, "my Princess Winnie is home safe and sound and she brought my big brother home, as well, and—best of all—she brought Scout back, too. I was really worried about Scout," Val went on as he flounced her into the kitchen, "but I knew he had you to protect him."

"I'm smart and very strong for my size, and Scout is warm."

"Warmth can be an endearing quality in a fellow otherwise lacking in impressive attributes," Val allowed. He sat Winnie on the table and began to take off her outer garments.

"What are attributes?"

"Paws."

"But he does have impressive paws," Winnie argued, holding out a foot for Val to take off her boots.

"My brother is misleading you," St. Just said as he ambled into the kitchen. "He does this frequently with young ladies. Attributes are qualities, Win, strong or weak points, like smelling good or being smart."

"Scout smells good to other dogs, and he's smart for a dog, too."

"Brilliant," Val agreed, removing the second boot. "Now go upstairs and get your slippers, then take yourself off to the music room. I've kept a fire going in there, and the piano is waiting for you to make up all the time you missed practicing yesterday."

"I'm going." Winnie hopped down off the table, hugged Val impulsively around the waist, and tore off.

"Thank you," St. Just said. "From the bottom of my heart, thank you."

"Not feeling so good, princess?" Val asked again, grinning sympathetically. He slung an arm around St. Just's shoulders and squeezed hard. "Are you ready to swear off women? Move back to Surrey? Take holy orders?"

"Please do not mention the church," St. Just said, sidling out of his brother's grip. "Nor the exponents thereof."

"So what was Winnie's reason for running off?" Val asked, pouring a mug of tea, adding cream and sugar, and putting it in his brother's hand.

"She wanted to make Emmie feel as scared and anxious and upset as Winnie will feel when Emmie runs off to Cumbria without her."

Val gave a low whistle. "There's a genius to her logic, and diabolical determination."

"Diabolical determination," St. Just said, but there was a hint of pride in just those two words. "Just like any soldier when dedicated to a worthy cause."

"Music is a worthy cause," Val pronounced, turning on his heel and leaving.

"So," St. Just muttered to the empty kitchen, "is true love."

∽

Through her parlor window, Emmie watched Caesar plodding up the lane. Winnie and St. Just were obviously enjoying a ride in the fresh morning air as the horse took them home. When the horse's broad rump had disappeared past the hedgerow, Emmie realized she was still staring at the horse's tracks in the snow.

She wondered, as she poured herself a cup of tea, if this was how a soldier's wife felt when she saw him off to war. Except she wasn't anybody's wife...

Her gaze fell on the letters St. Just had left behind, the ones he'd asked her to read, the ones he'd said were of sentimental importance to him. Carefully, she put the teacup down and reached for them, wanting any connection to him she could derive from any source, no matter how inanimate or obscure.

Seventeen

FOR HADRIAN BOTHWELL, THE MORNING WAS INTER-
minable. The congregation was very pleased to see
him, of course, as he'd played truant the previous
Sunday by nipping off to Ripon. Intuitively, he sensed
word of his impending departure was out, having been
passed along on the rural church grapevine with a
speed that put the Royal Mail to shame.

And he was doomed to smile and make small talk
for at least another thirty minutes, when all he wanted
to do was grab some luncheon and then complete his
interview with Emmie Farnum. The task had taken on
an urgency since he'd returned from Ripon, and she
would no doubt appreciate having matters resolved,
as well.

While standing up in his kitchen, he ate a cold
sandwich, it being the Sabbath and his housekeeper
off the premises. Usually, he treasured the solitude of
his Sunday afternoons, but today the ticking of the
grandfather clock in the hallway was aggravating.

A function, he concluded, of the upsets suffered on
his morning constitutional.

He had to get himself to Cumbria... the sooner the better. He hiked along the snowy lane leading to Emmie's house, and his mood lightened. Three of her chimneys attested to fires within, and in the bright sunshine and new snow, her property looked clean, tidy, and welcoming.

Would that Emmie was welcoming, too, he thought as he rapped on the door. He had to rap again some minutes later before his quarry presented herself, and though she offered him a smile and waved him into the house, he sensed immediately she was preoccupied.

"Good day, Emmie." He smiled as she took his hat, gloves, and scarf. "I missed you at services, of course."

"While I did not miss trying to convince myself that bustling around in this cold was anything but arduous. Would you object to tea in the kitchen? It's warmer than the parlor and closer to the teakettle."

"I would not object." They both knew he shouldn't be there alone with her, but when a man and woman discussed marriage, even the most proper society allowed them privacy to do so.

She led him to the kitchen and took the kettle off the hob to pour a fresh pot.

"I understand you had some excitement with Miss Bronwyn yesterday," Bothwell said, leaning against the wooden mantle over the kitchen hearth.

"How did word get out so fast?" Emmie asked, not turning but assembling a tea tray.

"Stevens had a celebratory pint when Lord Val announced she'd been found," Bothwell replied, thinking even in the kitchen—maybe especially in her kitchen—Emmie Farnum was graceful and attractive. She would be a comforting wife—quiet, competent, affectionate…

"You'll be baking here again tomorrow?" he asked, waiting for Emmie to seat herself first.

"I will." She moved a sheaf of papers aside and sat. "Do sit down, Hadrian. You needn't stand on ceremony with me."

"I like that about you," he said, sliding onto the opposite bench. "I like a lot of things about you, in fact."

"And I like you, as well," Emmie said, but her tone and her smile were both sad, not gleeful nor gloating as they might have been if she were in contemplation of marrying a man she adored. His spirits sank again as he accepted his tea from his hostess. When their fingers brushed, she gave no hint she'd even felt the contact.

"Your hands are cold, Emmie, but your kitchen is cozy."

"My feet are cold, too," Emmie said, her smile becoming apologetic as well as sad. "Read this." She shuffled through the papers and handed him what appeared to be a missive written in a lady's hand.

To Her Grace, Esther, Duchess of Moreland,

The physician has taken on the forced cheer of one who fears my ordeal will soon be over, but I do not share his doubts or his anxieties. I know I will soon be gone from this world and facing my Maker. I know, as well, He will be compassionate with me, for I have seen in you, dear lady, the kindness and generosity of spirit available this more flawed side of heaven, so I cannot fear what lies in my future.

I do, however, suffer greatly over what lies in my past. I have sinned, of course, and for that I can and have sought forgiveness. I have also, though, made grave mistakes, and knowing I have little time to make reparation for those errors, I humbly implore you to do me yet one more kindness—me and the young fellow whom you have taken in and loved as you do your own sons.

Seven years ago, when Devlin was five, I chose to accept your gracious offer to take him into the ducal household. I told myself this was best for him, and see now, as I am prepared to give up this life, how prescient that decision was. Devlin has the benefit of knowing his paternal siblings and of knowing you and His Grace, as well. The boy is acquiring the beginnings of a gentleman's education, a gentleman's speech, a gentleman's manner and deportment. He will go on well in this life, by the lights that most people would measure.

But I am not most people. I am his mother, the only family he had for the first years of his life, and I have watched carefully from my closed carriage on those instances you have brought him to the park for me to see. He is growing quite tall and obviously fit and sound of limb, but even from a distance, I see in his eyes the reflection of my worst, most painful error.

Devlin is not so much sibling to his younger brothers as he is their bodyguard. He does not laugh with the spontaneity of an adolescent boy; he watches carefully to see what is expected of him and how he might leap to do it before he is bid. He does not speak with the carefree self-expression he had as a young child; he stammers and struggles and more often than not, simply remains silent lest his efforts embarrass him, or worse, his ducal family.

In his young eyes, I see the self-doubt I put there the day I took myself from his life. I see the distrust of all that appears good and worthy and permanent. I see the hurt and confusion of a small child who will blame himself for the loss of a loving mother, no matter how outwardly competent and successful he appears to become as a man.

I was mortally, terribly wrong to allow him to be parted from me as I did. Though I thank God nightly for your generosity and kindness, I also pray nightly that somehow my son will know my living and dying regret was that I made the wrong choice for him those years ago. I had options, Your Grace; I could have taken the allowance you offered; I could have asked for a few more years with my son; I could have allowed you to find me a decent fellow who would accept a settlement, a tarnished if repentant wife, and a dear stepson. You urged those options on me and showed your greater understanding as a mother in the process.

But I thought I knew best, and may God help my little boy, for I was wrong. At the time, I thought the sincerity of my love for Devlin would justify the consequences were my choice in error. To a small child, however, love is not love that steals away into the night, never to be seen again. I know this now, when it is too late, so I ask only that someday when the time is right, you convey these

sentiments to him, as well as my unending love and
pride in him and all he does.

With gratitude,
Kathleen St. Just

Bothwell sat for long minutes, staring sightlessly at the document on the table before him. Emmie silently passed him the remaining papers, and he read on. One letter was an effusive thanks from Kathleen for the privilege of seeing her five-year-old son play in the park, and a minute description of a small boy's every adorable antic.

"She writes well," Bothwell remarked, "but even in her happier lines, there is heartache." Emmie merely nodded and passed him the third epistle, probably the first one the woman had written to St. Just's stepmother. Kathleen detailed the child's preferences, fears, pastimes, accomplishments, favorite articles of clothing, sleeping habits, dietary habits, and disclosed that he still sucked his thumb when he was very tired or upset.

"She knew her son," Bothwell said, putting the letter aside.

"But she did not know best for him," Emmie replied, staring at her cold tea. "Just being his mother did not make her infallible."

Bothwell patted her hand. "I have the privilege of working for the only infallible parent known to man."

Emmie didn't even smile at that.

Bothwell withdrew his hand. "Emmie, you know I would accept Winnie into our household. Her steppapa would not be a duke but a lowly, rusticating viscount's heir, though I would do my best by the child and by you. I have to agree with this lady." He gestured to the letters. "Where there is no compelling reason to the contrary, little children should be with their mothers, particularly if she's the only parent to hand."

Emmie nodded but said nothing, letting the silence stretch.

"Emmie." Bothwell moved around the table, sat beside her, and took her hand in his—her very cold hand. "I need to hear you tell me, my dear. You can turn a fellow down, but you have to actually go about it with some words. You know the speech; you delivered it nicely last time: Hadrian, you do me great honor… You recall the one?"

"All right," she said, taking a deep breath. To Hadrian, it felt as if she'd been so intensely preoccupied with her internal landscape that the process of speech had to be actively recalled before she could rely on it. "No, Hadrian, or no thank you. I can't seem to muster my former eloquence, but I am grateful. You mean well, and you do me honor, but I cannot be your viscountess."

"Well, that suffices." He offered her a wan smile. "But, Emmie? What will you do now?"

For that smile, for not dropping her hand and making a hasty, awkward departure, Emmie found she did love Hadrian Bothwell just a little. He *was* doing her an honor, both by proposing again and by remaining seated at her side when she'd rejected him.

"Thank you." She kissed his cheek and sat back,

their hands still joined. "I don't know what to do, Hadrian. I have perpetrated falsehoods and betrayed trust and been stupid."

"As bad as all that? Haven't you also loved and loved and loved?"

"No." Emmie shook her head. "Love trusts."

"Winnie trusts you," Hadrian insisted, but Emmie did not meet his gaze, and the man was perceptive enough to hear what wasn't being said.

"Ah." He did drop her hand then, patting it a little to soften the gesture. "Well, then, Emmie, if love trusts, then you must show some trust now and give St. Just a chance to repair this damage you feel you've done. He is a good man."

"I know," Emmie said, rising and gathering up the tea things. Bothwell did not rise, which was fortunate, as Emmie needed to be up and moving, and she needed to move away from him and away from her recent admissions. "He is a very good man, but he will not forgive this."

"He does not strike me as the judgmental, righteous sort, Emmie."

"You are being blessedly honest, Hadrian."

"Blessedly, indeed." His tone was dry as dust, suggesting there was a man inside the collar he wore, not just a church functionary.

"I owe him an accounting, but I also believe Winnie is attached to him, too, and no matter what option I choose, Winnie will now suffer."

"You don't know what your options are," Bothwell said gently. "I will not renew my proposal, as even lowly vicars are permitted some pride, but if you need help, Emmie, I am more than willing to provide it."

"Thank you," she said, resuming her seat beside him but determined to starve in the gutters of York in wintertime rather than ask for help.

"Let me put it a different way," Bothwell said, taking her hand again. "If you do not allow me to assist you and Miss Winnie should the need arise, I will be hurt, angry, and disappointed—more disappointed, even, than in your refusal to marry me."

"I understand. I will accept help from you for Winnie's sake, but St. Just says Win has a trust of some sort, and I am the trustee."

"You are also the child's guardian," Bothwell said, letting her hand go. "You need to talk to St. Just, Emmie. He notices things and is probably more tolerant than you think."

"Does he know he has such an ally in you?" Emmie asked while she walked him to the front door.

The vicar smiled sardonically. "I rather think he does, but he plays fair, Emmie, and he will with you, too."

She helped him into his heavy coat and brushed her hands down over his shoulders, smoothing the fabric as she would Winnie's cloak. He whipped his scarf around his neck and accepted his hat and gloves from her, but put them down on the sideboard and frowned down at her.

"I will not expect you at services," he said, "but then, I look forward to the day when I don't expect me at services either."

"You've done well here, though. People trust you."

"They trust me, but they don't know me. I like to

curse, Emmie, and ride too fast and play cards. I like chocolate and cats and naughty women, though not the trade they ply, and I loathe getting up early on Sundays to spout kindly platitudes all morning, and I would dearly love—"

"What would you love?" Emmie asked, curious. Naughty women?

"I would dearly love a good tavern brawl," he said. "There. You see, you are not the only one perpetrating falsehoods, but at least you have not talked yourself into being somebody you don't even recognize, much less want to spend time with."

"Do viscounts engage in tavern brawls?"

"It is one of the stated privileges of the rank."

"Then you will be happy with that title," Emmie concluded, glad to be able to genuinely smile about something.

"Eventually." He looked perplexed. "I hope."

"I hope so, too," Emmie said, leaning up to brush a kiss to his lips. When she would have stepped back, his hands settled on her hips, and for just the barest procession of heartbeats, he deepened the kiss, turning it into a tasting of her, a farewell to intimacies that might have been.

Just when Emmie would have protested, he stepped back, and now his smile was a thing of beauty and mischief.

"Don't begrudge me that, not when the walk home was going to be cold enough without your rejection." He kissed her cheek with vicarly perfunctoriness. "And don't stew too long, Emmie. St. Just needs to know what you'll do about the child."

Emmie nodded, too stunned by his kiss to find words. He let himself out and went swinging through the yard with every semblance of a happy man—a barbarian vicar. Who would have thought of such a thing?

❦

It took a week for Emmie to get over her cold, get up her nerve, and figure out what to bake. In the end, it was simple: Apple tarts, of course. Devlin's recipe with a few of her enhancements. She waited most of the day, hoping the hand of God would descend from the pressing overcast and pluck her troubles from her shoulders, but that Hand was as contrarily invisible as ever, so she donned two cloaks, put on her sturdiest walking boots, and headed off through the woods, apple tarts still warm in their basket.

The closer she got to Rosecroft, the more the sky seemed to press down on the wintery landscape. There were still patches of snow clinging to the hedgerows and fence lines from the last little storm, and there was a pervasive grayness that suited her mood. Her discussion with St. Just would be difficult, but what she wanted—to be with Winnie—was no more than what he'd urged on her from the outset. And as for being with *him*, well, nothing much had changed. She was still a baseborn baker from nowhere, he was still the firstborn of a duke, titled in his own right, a decorated war hero, and far above her touch.

Then, too, she had lied to him. There was that detail.

She gained the back door, stomped her boots, and scraped the mud off them as best she could, then raised her fist to knock. She lowered it slowly, her heart having begun to pound.

"Emmie Farnum," she spoke to herself sternly, "you are being ridiculous. St. Just is not a barbarian."

Except, in a way, he still was. She watched a half-dozen lazy snow flurries drift down from the pewter sky and was still trying to locate her resolve, when the door opened, and the barbarian himself stood there, frowning.

"Are you coming in?" he asked, stepping back. "Or is it sufficient to chat with yourself on my back steps in the bitter air?"

The sight of him, just the tall, frowning, slightly untidy sight of him standing there, cuffs turned back, no neckcloth, an ink stain on the heel of one hand... When Emmie only stared, he plucked the basket from her hand and took her by the wrist into the warmth of the house.

"I'll put these in the kitchen." He lifted the basket slightly, sniffing.

"I can't stay long," Emmie said to his retreating back, but he moved on as if she hadn't spoken. Like an imbecile, she stood there for another moment then realized she had two cloaks to unfasten. He was filling a teapot when Emmie stood in the kitchen doorway, feeling uncertain but determined.

"How's Winnie?" She asked, chin tipping up minutely. He was not required to tell her, of course, but then, legally, she was still Winnie's guardian—she hoped.

"Winnie is managing," St. Just said, putting the kettle on the stove. "Let me put us together a tea tray, and we can discuss that, if you've the time?"

All right, Emmie thought, in the kitchen, then.

"Shall we investigate these tarts?" he asked, his voice even. "Or did you intend them for dessert tonight?"

"Why don't we split one?" Emmie suggested, slightly mollified. "I'll get the plates." At least he wasn't going to refuse her baking.

They assembled their fare and sat on opposite benches at the table.

"Winnie is managing?"

"She is." St. Just was frowning again. "I don't wish to give offense, Emmie, but shall you pour, or shall I?"

"You pour," Emmie said, schooling herself to patience. "You like your tea just so, and I am not as likely to get it right."

He did the honors and passed her hers. "I never had any complaints when you fixed me tea, Emmie." She let him savor the first sip of his tea then prepared to grill him again on Winnie's situation. He spiked her guns, however, by tossing a question at her while she was still stirring her tea.

"So how are *you*, Emmie?" he asked, regarding her through hooded eyes. "You look pale and not particularly hearty."

"I've had a cold," Emmie said, seeing no harm in the truth, "and I was tired. I'm doing better now. And you?" She realized the question was genuine. She was concerned for him and wanted him to be well and happy. He didn't look particularly hearty himself, but weary and a little rumpled.

"Like Winnie." He didn't quite smile. "I am managing."

"I wanted to talk to you about Winnie," Emmie said, setting her teacup down a little too loudly.

"What did you want to say?" he asked, staring at his tea.

"I miss her. I really, really miss her."

"She misses you, as well."

"If the offer to assume the rearing of her is still open," Emmie said, heart abruptly pounding, "then I would like to discuss it further."

"It is still open, on certain terms."

"What are your terms?"

"Shall we negotiate over an apple tart?"

"I won't taste it," Emmie said in a low, miserable voice.

"I beg your pardon?" He took a knife and cleanly divided a warm, steaming tart.

"I hope they taste good," Emmie improvised, but St. Just kept his focus on the task of shifting one half of the tart to each of two plates, adding a fork to each, and passing one plate to Emmie.

"Emmie." He sat back, his expression suggesting he'd heard her perfectly well, "don't be anxious." He glanced around the kitchen as if he might spy just the right words sitting on the spice rack or the hearth. In the end, his words were simple and devastating. "I would not keep you from your daughter."

She could not catalog the emotions prompted by his weary disclosure, did not even try, but both grief and relief figured among them. "How long have you known?"

"I still can't say I know," St. Just said, studying her. "I drew some pointed conclusions when I began to learn more about your aunt. Neither she nor Helmsley look like Winnie, but you do. You were here, and then you weren't, which might allow for a pregnancy to be covered up, but I don't have the details. For some reason, your aunt wanted you to have the raising of the child, not the late earl—that was odd, too. Mostly, Emmie, I recognized in you the same desperation I'd sensed in my own mother when she tossed me into the ducal miscellany at the age of five."

"She didn't toss you anywhere!" Emmie retorted in horror. "Didn't you read her letters?"

"I can recite each of her letters to you word for word," St. Just said evenly, "though they didn't come into my possession until I traveled south this fall. I wish I'd had them earlier."

Emmie raised her gaze to his and saw only a kind of tired acceptance, or relief maybe, to have the truth out between them.

Without her choosing to open her mouth and speak, words began to flow from her, her own relief colored by the sadness that comes from having to admit a lie.

"I was sixteen when I really met Helmsley. Oh, he'd been about the property before, but I was home from school for only a few weeks here, a few weeks there. That summer, he took an interest in me, probably because he knew it would aggravate the old earl to do so. My aunt saw what was happening and before Helmsley could do any real harm, whisked me back to Scotland for the rest of the summer to stay with friends."

She paused, glanced around the table, then met St. Just's eyes again. His gaze held no discernible emotion except for a kind of sad acceptance, but his hand slid across the table and squeezed her fingers before retreating to his teacup.

Fortified by that surprising gesture, Emmie went on.

"The next summer, I was a year more determined to thwart my elders, a year more foolish and stubborn. Helmsley was a year more lost to propriety, and I allowed myself to become entangled with him. He was going to marry me, of course, as soon as I was of age, and we were going to banish the earl to a dower property and live like king and queen of Rosecroft. I was a selfish, stupid young girl, with no sense of my station nor of the many kindnesses my aunt, the earl, and his countess had done me, and Helmsley was a selfish, unprincipled man."

"Were you... willing?" St. Just asked quietly.

"I was willing to do what it took to prove my aunt was wrong, to prove I was worldly enough to make my own decisions. Helmsley wasn't entirely inconsiderate, but he had not dealt with many virgins, I don't think."

"I am sorry," St. Just said. Just that, and Emmie felt tears welling. She swallowed them down, finding that having the ear of a compassionate listener, she did want to relate her story. She'd thought it had died for all time with her aunt's passing, but now, years later, it was time to speak these words aloud.

"I was sorry, too," she said. "After the first time, I began to have doubts, to avoid him, to become disenchanted and look for a way out. It had all been a game to him, of course. The pursuit far more interesting than the capture. And he'd wanted to thumb his nose at our elders. I was a means to that end. When it was time to go back for my final year of school, I confessed to my aunt I was glad to be leaving and why. She asked me some very pointed questions and delayed my departure for another week while she conferred with the old earl."

Emmie paused again, the details of that very difficult year rising up from their resting places in her imagination. She'd been so endlessly *upset* that year. With Helmsley, herself, her body, her future…

"I was sent back to friends in Scotland," Emmie said very quietly. "I had no idea what my aunt planned, but in those months, she must have contracted a liaison with Helmsley, at least enough so he wouldn't doubt she could bear him a child. After the holidays, it was put about she was journeying to Scotland for my final semester at school. Winnie was born in early February, but she was small. When my aunt and I came back from Scotland that summer, we kept Winnie away from prying eyes, and Helmsley would not have known if he were looking at a newborn or a six-months babe anyway. He never questioned my aunt's story that Winnie was the bastard he'd gotten on her, and I was seldom home after that. I had six months with my child…"

She looked away then, the pain of that long-ago parting threatening to break her heart again.

"You can have the rest of your life with her," St. Just said gently.

"What if she won't have me?" Emmie asked softly. "What if she can't understand? She's six years old, St. Just. I've let her think she's had no mother for half her years on earth, and I was ready to turn my back on her completely."

His fingers closed over hers, and this time he didn't simply pat her hand and let go. "You were trying to do the best you could in difficult circumstances. You wanted what was best for Winnie, and she will eventually understand that. It will work out. I know it will."

"I can only hope so, and I can only continue to try my best."

"Winnie is reasonably tolerant of her new governess." St. Just sat back and let her hand go. "If you want to leave the child with us, she is loved and safe here and can go to Cumbria when you've settled in with Bothwell."

"I beg your pardon?" Emmie blinked and straightened her spine.

"Bothwell's brother is not well," St. Just replied, "and I thought you might want to give Winnie a few more months here, as she's settling in fairly well. Then, too…"

"Yes?"

"I will miss her," he said, looking uncomfortable.

"You will?"

"She watches me ride and has a surprisingly good eye. She has taught that dog of hers to do practically everything a dog can do, except perhaps how not to stink. Her letters to Rose are delightful and let me know exactly what mischief she's up to. Val dotes on her and says she's a musical prodigy—she's very, very smart, you know, for her age—and I… what?"

"You are attached to her," Emmie said softly, a warmth uncurling in her chest.

"Of *course* I am attached to her. Anybody would be. I just can't imagine not bringing her south to meet her new cousin in the spring, never hearing her giggle with Rose over little girl secrets, never seeing her drag Douglas up into the trees again—"

"Oh, Devlin, I am so sorry. She should have those things, too, but I am not going to Cumbria."

"Bothwell is keeping this backward little living?" St. Just frowned. "I took the man for a saint not a martyr."

"I don't know what he's doing, and beyond wishing him well, I don't particularly care."

"You're marrying Bothwell," St. Just said, his frown becoming a thunderous scowl. "Aren't you?"

He was having trouble discerning the meaning of Emmie's words, so fascinated was he by simply drinking in the sight of her, the sound of her voice, the scent of her. She was here in his kitchen, she was confiding in him, and she was admitting her error where Winnie was concerned.

He should be content with that, but he had to ask her one question *for himself*: "You're marrying Bothwell, aren't you?"

She would not meet his eyes, and in his chest, Devlin's heart began a slow, painful tattoo.

Then she looked up, the most hesitant of smiles on her lips.

"I am not marrying him. I have figured out he knew Winnie was my child."

"He might have." St. Just had come to the same conclusion, but he was having trouble wrapping his mind around Emmie's decision not to accept Bothwell. "I surmise your aunt told him when she became so ill."

"Perhaps. Hadrian proposed a couple years ago, in part to fortify me against Helmsley. Helmsley knew I was powerless and poor and so didn't interfere with my attempts to befriend Winnie. It could not have hurt, though, that I was well thought of by the heir to a viscountcy."

"I would not put such thinking beyond Bothwell." St. Just nodded, willing to be generous, seeing as Emmie had rejected the man and his title twice. Bothwell, *whom she was not marrying*, was a decent, perceptive man.

"I was hardly going to drag Hadrian into Helmsley's sphere, though." Emmie grimaced. "Helmsley had a way of turning all he touched to dross and disappointment."

"He's gone, Emmie."

"Thanks to you." She hunched forward, and he saw a shudder pass through her. "You have no idea… Of all the men I could have chosen to be father to my child, he was about the worst imaginable."

"Not the worst." His heart broke to think she'd place this burden on her conscience, as well. "There are men selling their young daughters on London street corners, Emmie. Men drinking away the little funds available to feed their children. Men beating their children for crying at the cold or the hunger or the pain of the last beating. You bedded down with a miserable specimen, but as far as Winnie is concerned, he was merely uninterested, not the devil."

"I suppose." She didn't sound convinced. "Winnie is what matters."

"She is." St. Just nodded, but in the part of his mind that processed tactical information even as he faced an opponent in battle, it was still sinking in that Emmie had turned Bothwell down—twice—and wasn't engaged to anybody.

So now what? A lifetime of tea and apple tarts while they discussed the child? Would she allow that? If so, he could campaign again to win her affections...

Except she didn't want him, as much as she might from time to time let herself enjoy his affections. No woman would want to lash her life to that of a man who jumped at thunderstorms, woke sweating with nightmares he couldn't speak of, spent more time with horses than people, and cared nothing for society—nothing *whatsoever*.

"So what do we do?" Emmie asked, her gaze dodging his. "Winnie is growing comfortable here, but I am her mother and her guardian—aren't I?"

"You are, and you control her funds."

"But this has become her home," Emmie pointed out. "You, Lord Val, the animals. She's lived here for the past few years, but you've made it a home for her."

"You should also know I tried to talk her into going to Cumbria with you and Bothwell. She wasn't keen on it."

"Did she give a reason?" Emmie asked, squaring her shoulders.

"She said I was a soldier, and I would not run away, and if she were with you in Cumbria, you would try your damnedest to make Cumbria work, even if you were unhappy there. She had some notion a married woman and a viscountess could just scamper home to my kitchen if she were unhappy."

"Why would she think that?"

"Because"—St. Just did smile, a crooked, hopeless,

self-mocking twist of his lips—"I would have welcomed you with open arms."

Silence.

Ah, well, he thought. He was just being honest, and ridiculous, but his dignity wasn't too high a price to pay if it meant Emmie understood what his feelings were. If they were going to have to deal with each other, Emmie couldn't be teasing him nor flirting nor dallying.

His heart couldn't take any more of that.

"I beg your pardon?" Emmie asked slowly. "You would have offered me refuge here if Bothwell and I found we did not suit?"

"I would have offered you refuge," St. Just said, but he wasn't willing to hide behind that fig leaf. "I would have offered you my adulterous bed, my coin, my home, my anything, Emmie. I know that now."

Another silence, which left him thinking perhaps his heedless abandonment of dignity had gone quite far enough, because Emmie looked more confused than thrilled with his proclamations.

"I don't understand, St. Just. I have lied to you and to my daughter. I was under your roof under false pretenses. I have taken advantage of your kindness, and I nearly succeeded in foisting my daughter off on you under the guise of my mendacity. Why would you want to have anything more to do with me?"

"Do you recall my telling you once upon a time that I love you?" St. Just asked, rising, and leaning against the counter, hands in his pockets.

"I do." She stared at her hands. "It was not under circumstances where such declarations are made with a cool head."

"We're in the kitchen now, Emmie," he said very clearly. "It is late in the afternoon, a pot of tea on the table, and I am of passably sound mind, and sound, if somewhat tired, body. I am also fully clothed, albeit to my regret, as are you: I love you."

That was not an exercise in sacrificing dignity, he realized. It was an exercise in truth and honesty and regaining dignity. Perhaps for them both. As romantic declarations went, however, it was singularly unimpressive.

"I see." Emmie got up, chafing her arms as if cold, though the kitchen was the coziest room in the house.

"You don't believe me," he said flatly. "You cannot believe me, more like."

"I am…" Emmie met his eyes fleetingly. "I do not trust myself very far these days, St. Just. You mustn't think I am attributing my own capacity for untruth to you."

"I know how your mind works," he said, advancing on her. "You think it a pity I believe myself to be in love with you, but you can't help but notice that in some regards, we'd suit, and it would allow us both to have Winnie in our lives. That's not good enough, Emmie Farnum."

❦

He was speaking very sternly, and for all the tumult inside her, Emmie could hardly focus on the sense of his words. He loved her. *He loved her, and he was rejecting her.*

"It's not good enough?" she asked, folding her arms over her waist.

"Not nearly," he said, shifting to loom over her. "I

know what I am. I left the better part of my sanity on battlefields all over France and Spain. I am a bastard, regardless of whose bastard, and I will fare best if I maintain a mundane little existence here in the most isolated reaches of society, where I can stink of horses and spend most of my day outdoors. I have setbacks, as you call them. I never know when a sound or a word or a memory will rise up and shoot me out of my saddle. Sometimes I drink too much, and often I want to drink too much. But I am human, Emmie. I will not shackle myself to a woman who feels only pity and gratitude and affectionate tolerance for me. I won't."

"So what do you want of me?" Emmie asked, bewildered.

He gave a bitter snort of laughter.

"A fairy tale. I wanted a goddamned fairy tale, where you love me and we have Winnie here with us and more children, and they tear all over the property on their ponies and the table is noisy with laughter and teasing and the house always smells wonderful because you are my wife and the genie in our kitchen. On the bad nights, you are there for me to love and to love me, and the bad nights gradually don't come so often. I want—"

"What?" Emmie asked, her throat constricting with pain. "Devlin, what?"

"Just that," he said tiredly. "I want that small, mundane, bucolic existence. A wife, children, love, and a shared life here at Rosecroft. That is my idea of what makes peace meaningful. It can't be built on pity or convenience or simple affection, Em. Not with me. I'll run you off in less than two years, but we'll have a child by then, so you'll stay, and next thing, we'll have separate bedrooms, and the brandy decanter will seldom stay full for long. I won't live that way, and I won't let it happen to you or our children either."

Another silence, while Emmie's mind scrambled for what to say.

"But I do love you."

"Of course you do." He raised his gaze to the ceiling, a man reaching for the last of his patience, and Emmie felt a consuming fear that if she didn't convince him of this *now*, then the brandy decanters were *never* going to be full, and he wouldn't have even one single child to love and to give meaning to the peace he'd fought so hard to secure. "You love that I can keep a roof over your head and that I am attached to your child. Not enough, Em, but thanks for the gesture." He turned to go, his eyes registering surprise when she stopped him.

"No," she said, gathering the front of his shirt in her fist. She shook it to emphasize her point and glared up at him.

"No," she said again. "You will not make such sweeping declarations then stomp off without giving me even a minute to recover. You will stay here in this kitchen and hear me out, Devlin St. Just. You will." He nodded carefully, and she let his shirt go then smoothed it down with an incongruous little pat of her hand.

"Thank you," she said, returning his nod. What to say? What on earth to say to make him believe her?

"I love you," she said slowly, her hand returning to stroke down his chest again, "because you wrestle with stone walls when you'd rather drink yourself mindless.

I love you because you take my recipes seriously and you gave me your apple tart recipe, asking nothing in return. I love you because it matters to you when I cry and when Winnie is scared and difficult and lost. I love you because you pray for dead horses and you bought that awful, stinky dog so Winnie wouldn't be so lonely. You went to see Rose and you forgave your mother and you've fought and fought and fought…"

She leaned in against him, her arms around his waist, while his remained at his sides.

"You fought for Winnie," she went on, voice breaking. "You fought my stupid, wrongheaded schemes for Winnie, so Winnie wouldn't suffer what you did, so I wouldn't die of a broken heart as your m-mother did. I love you because you fought so hard… I surrender, Devlin St. Just. I love you, and I surrender for all time."

She wept against him, not even registering when his arms slowly crept around her nor when his chin rested against her temple.

"You surrender?" he murmured quietly, his hands rubbing slow circles on her back. "Unconditionally?"

"Not unconditionally," Emmie replied through her tears. "I demand you take me prisoner."

"It will be my pleasure," St. Just replied. "But, Em? I surrender, too."

And thus, for the first time in history, did all sides win the war, even as they were also captured—foot, horse, heart, and cannon—by their opponents for all time.

Acknowledgments

Thanks go to my editor, Deb Werksman, who spotted what needed polishing and made the rest of this story shine brighter as a result, and to the crew at Sourcebooks, Inc., who take straw and spin it into gold—Cat, Susie, Skye, my very skilled copy editor, the art, marketing and bookmaking departments, Danielle, and others who are the unsung heroes of the book you're holding in your hands. A very particular thanks goes to author Robin Kaye, who—despite her own maniac schedule (three teenagers, enough said)—read the manuscript when I was in a dither and prevented me from doing Something Stupid to the ending when my courage was wavering (again).

And thanks to my readers. The pleasure you take in my books is small compared to how much it means to me that you enjoy them.

About the Author

Grace Burrowes's debut novel, *The Heir* was named one of *Publishers Weekly* Top Five Romances for 2010, and the sequel, *The Soldier* was named a *Publishers Weekly* Top Ten Romances for Spring 2011. When the final book in The Duke's Obsession trilogy, *The Virtuoso*, has been polished, Grace will be hard at work on the stories of the five Windham sisters, starting with *Lady Sophie's Christmas Wish*, to be released late in 2011.

Grace is a practicing attorney specializing in child welfare law. She lives and works in rural Maryland. She loves to hear from her readers and can be reached through her website at graceburrowes.com, her email at graceburrowes@yahoo.com, or through her fan page on Facebook.

READ ON FOR A SNEAK PREVIEW OF
GRACE BURROWES'S

THE *Virtuoso*

COMING NOVEMBER 2011
FROM SOURCEBOOKS CASABLANCA

One

"MY BEST ADVICE IS TO GIVE UP PLAYING THE PIANO."

Lord Valentine Windham neither moved nor changed his expression when he heard his friend—a skilled and experienced physician—pronounce sentence. Being the youngest of five boys and named Valentine—for God's sake!—had given him fast reflexes, abundant muscle, and an enviable poker face. Being called the baby boy any time he'd shown the least tender sentiment had fired his will to the strength of iron and given him the ability to withstand almost any blow without flinching.

But this… This was diabolical, this demand David made of him. To give up the one mistress Val loved, the one place he was happy and competent. To give up the home he'd forged for his soul despite his ducal father's ridicule, his mother's anxiety, and his siblings' inability to understand what music had become to him.

He closed his eyes and drew breath into his lungs by act of will. "For how long am I to give up my art?"

Silence, until Val opened his eyes and glanced down to where his left hand, angry and swollen, lay uselessly on his thigh. Beside him, David appeared to be making a polite pretense of surveying the surrounding paddocks and fields.

"Possibly for the rest of your life. It might heal but only if you rest it until you're ready to scream with frustration, Val. Not just days, not just weeks, and by then you will have lost some of the dexterity you hone so keenly now. If you try too hard or too soon to regain it, you'll make the hand worse than ever."

"Months?" One month was forever when a man wanted only to do the single thing denied him.

"At least. And as long as I'm cheering you up, you need to watch for the condition to arise in the other hand. If you catch it early it might admit of less extensive treatment."

"Both hands?" Val closed his eyes again and hunched in on himself where he sat on a low stone wall bordering David's pretty, tidy and not so little patch of Kent.

"It's possible both hands will be affected. Your left hand is more likely in worse condition because of the untreated fracture you suffered as a small boy. It's also possible you're right handed and so the right hand is stronger out of habit."

Val roused himself to gather as many facts from David as he could. "Is the left weak, then?"

"Not weak, so much." David, Viscount Fairly, pursed his lips where he sat beside Val on the wall. "It seems to me you have something like gout or rheumatism in your hand. It's inflamed, swollen, and painful, without apparent cause. The test will be if you do rest it and see improvement. That is not the signal to resume spending all hours on the piano bench again, Valentine."

"It's the signal to what? All I do is spend hours on the piano bench, and occasionally escort my sisters about Town."

"It's the signal you're dealing with a simple inflammation from over use, old son." David slid a hand to Val's nape and shook him gently. "Many people lead happy, productive lives without gluing their arses to the piano bench for twenty hours a day. Kiss some pretty girls, sniff a few roses, go see the Lakes."

Val shoved off the wall, using only his right hand for balance. "I know you mean well but I don't *want* to do anything but play the piano."

"I know what you want." David hopped down to fall in step beside Val. "What you want has gotten you a hand that can't hold a tea cup and while that's not fair, and it's not right, it's also not yet permanent."

"I'm whining." Val stopped and gazed toward the manor house where David's viscountess Letty was no doubt tucking in their infant daughter for the evening. "I should be thanking you for bothering with me."

"I am flattered to be of service. And you are not to let some idiot surgeon talk you into bleeding it."

"You're sure?"

"I am absolutely sure of that. No bleeding, no blisters, no surgery, and no peculiar nostrums. You tend it as you would any other inflammation."

"Which would mean?" Val forced himself to ask. But what would it matter, really? He might get the use of his hand back in a year, but how much conditioning and skill would he have lost by then? He loved his mistress, his muse, but she was jealous and unforgiving as hell.

"Rest," David said sternly as they approached the house. "Cold soaks, willow bark tea by the bucket, and at all costs avoid the laudanum. If you can find a position where the hand is comfortable, you might consider sleeping with it splinted like that. Massage, if you can stand it."

"As if I had some tired old man's ailment. You're sure about the laudanum? It's the only thing that lets me keep playing."

"Laudanum lets you continue to aggravate it," David shot back. "It masks the pain, it cures nothing, and it can become addictive."

A beat of silence went by.

Val nodded once, as much of an admission as he would make.